Sonata

THE NOCTURNE SYMPHONY

Sonata

4 Horsemen
Publications, Inc.

LYRA R. SAENZ

4 Horsemen
Publications, Inc.

4 Horsemen Publications, Inc.
1497 Main St. Suite 169
Dunedin, FL 34698
4horsemenpublications.com
info@4horsemenpublications.com

Typeset by Niki Tantillo
Edited by Jen Paquette
Triskele design by Sea Cat Art - Instagram @sea.cat.art

Library of Congress Control Number: 2022931311

Paperback ISBN-13: 978-1-64450-389-8
Hardcover ISBN-13: 978-1-64450-744-5
Audiobook ISBN-13: 978-1-64450-387-4
Ebook ISBN-13: 978-1-64450-388-1

DEDICATION

To the cat who sits on my lap for the sole purpose of letting me know how much she disapproves of my constant attention to an inanimate device.

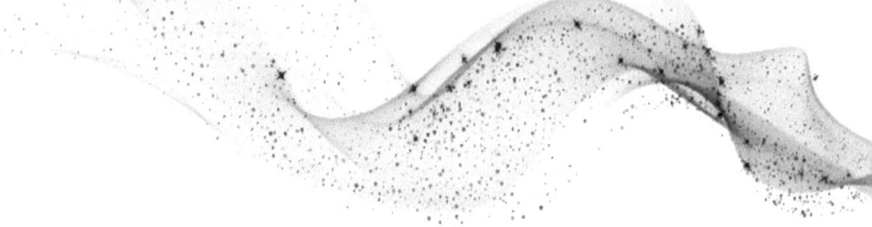

TABLE OF CONTENTS

The Wastes

Aighneas

New

London

Orisumi

Se K

Ebele

Deri

atidomus
City
Shinka
Temple
Lorelei
City
Tokiseishu
Aureus
New
Chernobyl
Murasaki no Umi
The Tai Tai
tierra

Prologue
THE LOVERS (REVERSED)

WREN

8th Day in the Month of Falling 1877 **A.P.** – 3:00AM

SOMETHING WAKES WREN AT GLOOMTIDE, Kai's arm thrown over her waist—the same old witching hour wakefulness. A nightly happening ever since her magic awoke, she's long grown accustomed to the sleeplessness.

Despite the darkness, she can see Kai's face clear as day, a little perk of being a creature of the night even if the gentle browns of his hair and the lavender tones of his skin wash out in the murky wash of nightshade. Her hand gently traces from his brow over the slumbering tech nodes at his temple, and they flicker in response. Her fingertips glide to the ridge of his cheekbone, past the smooth plain of his cheek, and across the edge of his jaw to his where a line of prickly stubble grows, inciting a quiet snuffle from the sleeping technomancer.

As her lover settles back, Wren sighs. What might it be like to have this every night, to wake up to this every morning? Between her legs, she can still feel the evidence of their tryst, damp with just a touch of soreness for spice. She purrs, rubbing her knees together and feeling the residual heat of their intimacy.

Kai's breath fans over her fingertips as she outlines the bridge of his lips, into the divot of his cupid's bow, and through the slight scruff of facial hair grown out in the night. He nuzzles into her palm, and Wren shifts to replace her fingertips with her lips but winces as the cuts on her forearm throb.

When she shifts to examine her arm, a horrible sticky sensation travels across her skin. The bandage is soaked, stained a blackened crimson.

She scrambles out of bed, stumbling into the bathroom. The three cuts on her arm drip rivulets of blood like veins taking root outside her skin and staining the countertop. She yanks on the cold-water faucet and shoves her arm under the water. Swirls of red spiral down the drain.

Unceasing, the bleeding does not slow, and her vision blurs, edges darkening despite the brightness of the mirror lights.

¡Mierde! How long has she been bleeding?

A sound above the sink draws her attention: a long, croaking rasp rattling out of smoke-soaked lungs. She looks up, and out of the mirror, burning hands reach for her throat, a woman's face scorched and twisted in rage.

"Betrayer!"

Wren chokes on her own scream as charred fingers wind around her throat.

The witch wakes from her nightmare, the very real cuts on her arm still bleeding though at a much more sedate pace than in her night terror. She draws herself out of the embrace of her lover, goes to solve this new mystery—a burning woman calling to her in her dreams—but the hour following her wake-up call is a waking nightmare all on its own.

While some children in Deriva have nightmares of *El Cucuy*, Wren has never been afraid of such fantasies. Sleep-generated ghosts and whimsies true nightmares do not make. The bogeyman, the vampyric visitor, the howl of a wolf in the night, the old hag who kidnaps and devours children: nothing so mundane could ever truly frighten Wren. She's spoken to too many spirits, befriended too many monsters, chased off too many demons. No. People scare Wren. Conversations and expectations, responsibilities laid on her shoulders, and the judgements of strangers... these are what fuel Wren's most primal fears.

And for Wren, being chased from Kaito's arms is worse than any haunting or night terror she could face.

Chased from the first safe place she's found since before her first death for the simple crime of being who she is, for the name she bears, for the glowing markings on her skin, a part of her wishes she'd never come back in the first place. At least in Death's embrace, she knew she wouldn't be chased out.

But... then again.

She was ripped from that safe haven, too.

To quote the famous play, Hamlet:

"There are more things in heaven and Earth, Horatio, than can be dreamt of in your philosophy."

But Shakespeare had it wrong. Even in a reality as seemingly unlimited by magic and technology as ours, the waking world will always be limited when compared to boundless depths of the imagination, for nothing can stand against its cruelty, its malice, or its unending capacity to dream.

The last words of Holly Bishop
Hexen Philosopher, 1279 A.P.

1

THE ACE OF CUPS

4 Hours Later – 8th Day in the Month of Falling
1877 – 7:32AM

KAITO MIYAZAKI TILTS THE VISOR OF HIS helmet up, the sun glinting off the glass as Õr transitions from the orangey-red hues of dawn into the radiant white of true morning. According to the digital clock on his comm, he is scheduled to deliver a mission debrief to his brother in less than thirty minutes. It is a mission debriefing he will not be attending.

Hikaru can entertain himself through the morning.

By the time anyone realizes he will not be showing up, he'll be miles from Yuki Ga Furu, possibly even beyond Tokiseishu's city limits if traffic is good. Either way, there is no chance he will be tracked down. He's left nothing to chance, the Jade Wing locked down to all but Renki's investigation, Wren's abandoned belongings tucked into his belt, and his swords strapped to his back.

Once again, he finds himself looking for Wren. His witch, his lover who has by some miracle been returned to the living world. Wren escaped death and, by the tides of fate, found her way back into his arms only to be banished from his view, driven into hiding once more for what and who she is. Her right to stay at his side taken from her by his own blood.

It is an offense he won't soon forget.

Fifteen Years Ago – 2nd Day in The Month of Songs 1862 – 7 **Months After the Fall of Deriva**

In the wake of learning Wren's fate, Kaito mourns.

Mano, Wren's bloodstained prosthetic, wrapped up and delivered to the Alliance compound like a consolation prize, haunts Kaito's dreams. The macabre remnant of a beloved companion seared across his eyelids like a waking nightmare.

When there are no missions to be led, the second prince of Murasaki no Yama pours his grief into his music, playing an unending concert of lamentations to an audience of none. The piano keys resonate unheard in the quietest parts of the night when all but the dead sleep.

He wears the traditional grays and lavenders of his people's mourning colors and garbs himself in the plain fabrics appropriate for funerary rites. Not the ideal choice of wardrobe for battle but appropriate for the tumult of emotions that threaten to wash him away. Mirai, Fumiko, and Hikaru can only support him, quiet sentries at his side as Kaito wrestles with his grief.

Wren was more than his lover, after all. Wren was... Well, Wren was Wren.

So, the technomancer takes on mission after mission after mission, flinging himself into his duties. His augmentations buzz, hungry to tear down enemy barriers and tech, and where Wren's voice no longer can, his blades sing, thirsty for blood. The months pass in a blur of battle and chaos. The mocking proclamation of

Wren's death acts as fuel for Kaito's rage, a resounding reminder of what he is fighting for in this civil war.

Civil war—technomancer against technomancer/Seraphim and their nuclear might against the rest of the League—the great rift across the continent grows more and more harrowing the longer it progresses. So long they've fought against hexen, they never thought what kind of destruction could ensue if they ever turned their technologies against each other. Only seven months since this war began, and already its impact proves catastrophic.

Losses on all sides. Whole cities irradiated, bombings on civilians, forests and mountains destroyed, whole parts of the ocean poisoned, the rains turn to acid, and the sun blisters through the clouds even though the summer months are yet to come, and as much as the Alliance tries to put an end to the conflict, Seraphim manages to regain the upper hand every time they press their advantage.

In the midst of a recent battle along Ebele's border, several Murasakan and Sekhmetian operatives were overcome when their neural enhancements were detonated inside their own heads. The incident turned the tide of the battle in Seraphim's favor, necessitating a retreat from the Alliance.

Kaito enters virtual reality to find the source of the problem—a coded minefield laid within Ebele's servers. Each mine guarded by at least one virtually trapped soul—human spirits pulled from their rest to inhabit the synthetic space between life and death, the cyberscape. Trapped in the mainframe and unable to move on, they become datafiends.

Even with a retinue of highly trained Murasakan adepts and technomancers, it's hours of mind-numbing work, coding and decoding, eradicating the specters one by one before deactivating the mines. Combat in the virtual realm may not involve physical muscles, but the human psyche is a powerful force; the body experiences what the mind experiences. Virtual injuries become very real afflictions as nerve endings die and internal organs fail. Transhumans who die in cyberscape die in real life; their systems shut down, never to be rebooted.

SONATA

Kaito battles on his own against a group of datafiends. The mainframe ghouls gnash their teeth at him, hungry to suck down his vital essence. Tsukuyomi and Amatsu sing together as they slash through virtual sinew and skeleton. Each fiend goes down with a bloodcurdling scream, the coded mines they guard dealt with via a deactivation command integration. He works for so long, reaches so far out, he finds himself outside the parameters of the day's scope. Beyond even the parameters of the designated field.

Isolated. Alone. And therefore, open to attack.

As he makes the decision to turn back, a strange fog wraps around him. It shudders with movement, pulses like a heartbeat, expanding and contracting, breathing, living. The wisps curl and uncurl, tugging at his skin, hair, and clothes. A dull, green light passes before his vision with a hiss. Growling in his ear and the glimpse of something unnaturally dark in his periphery. Something nudges his shoulder, and he pivots to catch sight of it. Whatever it is, it vanishes, and when he turns back around, the cyberscape before him is gone.

The holographic rise and fall of a grid-lined landscape shifts, replaced with sand, seaweed, and the rolling roar of the ocean. The steady wash of waves mimics perfectly the reality of the Pacificum's coastal waters. The sensory coding for salt and sun and summer alights on his synapses, creating the illusion of scent.

Another glance around, and he recognizes the floating villa of Cresta de Corail, the home of Deriva's royal family. Its bright sea blue banners and coiling architecture rise up in sweeping folds just beyond the island florals, sand dunes, and sunbaked docks where he stands.

He takes a step forward, and the world shudders, staticky and unstable. When the scape refocuses, a woman wearing a bathing suit, sarong, and sunglasses, stands barefoot in the dark sand at the edge of the tide some 20 meters away. Her blonde hair, an ashy platinum shining almost white in the sunlight, fans out in the wind from under a firmly gripped sunning hat practically squished to her head to protect the pale, milky white skin of her face.

THE ACE OF CUPS

She calls out for someone in the surf, hands cupping her mouth, but her voice is muted to Kaito's ear.

A moment later, a little girl, no older than five, runs out of the surf. Raven-colored locks of hair whip around her head in wet, carefree tangles, the wild curls reflecting blue in the sunlight. Her skin is a warm, sun-kissed olive, her little blue dress soaked through as she runs barefoot to leap into the woman's arms. The woman, who, despite the difference in their features, must surely be her mother, spins the child in the air before cuddling her against her chest, dotingly fussing at the girl's hair and clothing. The little girl squirms in protest, only settling when her mother pulls off her sun hat and playfully presses it down onto her head with an affectionate tousle.

This time when the child sings with laughter, he hears her joyful cries, a melody reminiscent of seashells on a wind chime. The little girl pulls the hat off and places it back on her mother's head as the woman sets her back on her feet, and the child takes off, racing along the shoreline, her mother chasing after her—they have the same blue-green eyes.

The projected pair pass Kaito, still laughing, only to disappear, dissolving into the mainframe's border. As they fade, he notices for the first time the other spectator watching the scene. This girl—No, this woman, an older mirror image of the laughing girl, sits farther from the shore among the salt grasses gently swaying in the breeze, her sea-green eyes glazed over as though hypnotized. Wren Nocturne, the woman for whom he wears the colors of bereavement.

"Wren?"

No reaction. Just a hollow stare.

He approaches, wary of a trap, wary this might be a sick game custom-programmed to torment him, but there are no other objects in his periphery.

A quick scan confirms she is not a mainframe ghost or datafiend. This woman is not a data memory or a program. If she was, she would register to his sensors as having no lifeforce. She would be lined with coding and empty on the inside. This is not the case. Quite the opposite, she is brimming with energy. Enough lifeforce courses through her form to accommodate two energy signatures. However, while the energy is surplus, the essence of it is dulled like smoke, an indication she is not here of her own volition, a prisoner in her own mind.

But why would they put her in a memory-scape?

The reality they stand in shifts. The ocean recedes and the beach blows away to reveal the coding beneath the illusion before the numbers shift, altering the module, and when they reorganize, he finds himself standing in Shinka's shooting range, watching himself confront a laughing, rule-breaking version of Wren, a scene taken from barely more than a year ago.

It's odd seeing himself as she sees him, haughty and abrasive in his enforcement of temple rules. The computer-generated versions of themselves fight, a perfect replay of their first less-than-amiable dance. His data-generated clone takes an elbow to the gut while hers has her feet swept from under her.

When he looks around, he finds the older Wren sitting on the dock watching the two sensory phantoms flit around each other. The same hypnotized gaze and fluttering lifeforce reminiscent of an injured bird, caged and dying in isolation.

It's color, too, concerns him. The texture of it sets his teeth on edge.

In the past, his lover's lifeforce always blazed pure, bright gold, as warm and as blinding as her smile, but now, the color is a fluorescent green, and as glittering as it is, there is a wrongness about it he cannot shake. It is dark around the edges like mold, iridescent like a poisonous mushroom, and viscous in the way blood clings to skin.

With unease, he approaches.

Kneeling before her, he reaches his hands up, grips either side of her head, and upon meeting no resistance, pushes saibāki into her consciousness, finding and sifting through the familiar coding of his lost lover to bring her back to herself. Minutes pass while he searches for the locks and bolts he needs to release inside her virtual personage, and she remains comatose. Tearing down the restraints and hallucinogenic technologies keeping her trapped in this virtual memory, he finds coding he doesn't recognize, coding which should never be read on the interface of a technomancer.

Before he can analyze them, the last trapdoor falls away, and she jerks back from him violently.

The shadows of their past selves freeze right before they hit the water. The reflections stutter forward then stop, stutter then stop, stutter then stop as though buffering through a bad connection before dispersing entirely.

"Wren, can you hear me?"

She shakes her head from side to side, looking around, at first in confusion, then sorrow, then horror. When she finds his face, she looks him directly in the eye, eyes dilated. She does not look comforted to see him. If anything, she draws further into herself, frightened as though he were another potential phantom here to torture her.

"Kai? Are you real?"

"I'm real."

"That's what you always say..."

"Wren, it's me. Feel for my signature."

He takes her hand and pushes his own violet lifeforce in to mingle with hers. There is a moment when the green pools of her energy dance away from his own purple power, retreating first, fighting back second, and then, finally, entangling with his own like vines around a windowpane.

Endorphins flood his system as her signature curls around his, a languishing limb wrapping around a lover's body. It's weak, pale in comparison to the last time they did this, but just as intimate and so much more significant in the shadow of everything that's happened. Her expression opens, and her eyes glitter.

"It is you." A tear escapes her lashes. "Where are we? What are you doing here?"

He brushes the teardrop away with his thumb.

"This is the cyberscape. You…" She's alive! His hands find hers and hold on tight. "You've been missing for months. How long have they been keeping you here?"

"I don't know."

"Everyone thinks you are dead."

"I'm not. At least, I don't think I am."

"Where are you? Tell me so I can find you."

"I don't know. I don't know where I am. I don't know what is happening to us."

Her hands rest on her stomach, and a forlorn look glimmers in her eye.

"Us?"

"I didn't get the chance to tell you."

"Tell me what?"

"I—!"

She shakes her head, tears springing into her eyes afresh. When she makes no indication to continue, he raises his hands to her head again, this time with every intention of tracing back her virtual synapse to her vital body. A firewall blocks him, powerful enough to shock him back. He starts to press her meridians further, but a sound to the left pulls his attention. A new creature settles on the edge of his periphery.

It can't be.

Kai draws Tsukuyomi from her sheath and brandishes the blade toward a panther-like creature. The catlike, translucent visage is familiar, identical to the beast he and Wren found during the Lorelei case. The very same beast summoned onto this plane by the witch Summer Helsdottir. The one Wren freed from the summoner's sway instead of killing.

It hisses at him, circling round. He rotates with it, on guard, waiting for it to pounce, keeping Wren securely behind him. A hand, light and hesitant, closes on his bicep.

"It's alright, *mon rivage*."

The beast chirrs at him, its hackles rising. Wren reaches her left hand forward, flesh in this virtual realm rather than mechanical. The creature displaces into mist and fog. The same fog which engulfed him earlier enshrouds them.

Did this monster bring him here?

The fog circles before settling on the palm of her hand and disappearing into her flesh. He watches transfixed as the new energy integrates itself into her system.

"She brought you to me."

The words are hollow as they drop off her tongue, metallic and devoid of emotion. The shooting range and dock are gone, replaced with the linear landscape of unmanipulated cyberscape. Her lifeforce has brightened somewhat. The neon of the green intensifies to a viridian as though the presence of the netherbeast is giving her strength.

"She comes and goes, on and off. It's always a little better when she's here."

"What is a displacer beast doing in cyberscape?"

"I don't know, but I think she's the reason we're still alive."

"We" again? Who is she talking about?

A fit of coughing wrecks her form. She covers her mouth, and when her hand comes away, blood burns red in her palm. She crumples in his arms, her hands clenching at her abdomen, and terror strikes him as blood begins to seep through her clothing. Something is happening to her physical body.

She flickers, screaming in agony.

He grasps her head again. The firewalls wage war against his servers, the blistering agony nearly crippling, but he persists, Wren's pain-filled sobs all the motivation he needs to press forward, push harder, keep fighting. His heart pounds, racing against time, and then, at last, the firewall crumbles under his assault. In microseconds, he has her location traced backward to the VR headset she's hooked up to. In the next moment, she disappears, slipping right through his fingertips.

He snaps out of cyberscape with a pained groan. His head spins, and he pukes into the nearest wastebasket. Dei, Deus's smaller moon, is setting, dawn approaching. He's been in cyberscape hours longer than he should have been.

He wastes not a moment.

The technomancer follows the origin of the trace, and where he expected to find a dungeon or prison, he finds instead the charred remnants of a hospital or rather, he discovers as his people search the place from top to bottom, a slaughterhouse. Bodies of soldiers, doctors, and medical personnel, all wearing Seraphim badges, all of them dead either from the building collapsing on them, the fire melting their skin, or their heads being crushed in by some unknown force.

There are magical arrays etched into the floor, chaos magic stains the walls, and evidence of medical and surgical cruelty everywhere. More disturbing is the large pit behind the building filled with corpses. Corpses of women, many with their stomachs ripped open. Corpses of infants, warped by heinous experimentation.

A butcher and chop shop.

Any records of the kinds of experiments taking place were either lost in the fire or taken with the Seraphim employees who managed to escape the flames. There is a wide variety of stolen tech left behind as well. Most of it charred, but the higher quality materials survive relatively unscathed. Their tracers identify tech from every major nation: mechanical limbs, headpieces, neural receptors, muscle enhancers, endo and exoskeletons. Each piece surgically removed and held for examination by the runners of the facility.

There are also the bodies of several technomancers stored separately from the pit of corpses in a chilled morgue, their tech removed, their forms extracted of any and all data possibly wrung from them. Alliance doctors would discover this afterward, after the bodies had been exhumed and autopsied and finally put to rest.

But Wren is not among the dead.

Kai stands amidst the debris of the facility while the adepts under him search out and find as much as they can gather. Xipilli Moctezumo, Arturo Lionheart, and Chike Nagi, the three technomancers who took point with him on this raid, approach him.

Xipilli, Wren's older half-brother, is a walking inferno. Fury and frustration roll off the newly crowned Vulcan in very apparent waves. His dark eyes burn with killing intent.

"Whatever misfortune fell on this place, they had it coming," sneers Xipilli.

"All of the bodies in the pit have been identified as civilian, both organics and augmented," says Arturo. "They were keeping the adept bodies as cadavers for parts. We are working to identify everyone now. Some of these adepts have been MIA since before the war."

Chike clicks his tongue and says, "Seraphim brandishes their religious zeal like a shield, but then we find them responsible for this."

"Whatever they were trying to accomplish here, we are fortunate they failed."

Art's statement does not sit well with Kai. There is a falsehood there.

"Did they fail, though?" asks Kaito.

Xipilli scoffs.

"Do you see the state of this place? Even if they did manage something, their results clearly blew up in their faces."

Kai doesn't answer.

"How did you know this place existed, Kaito–kun? You did not explain yourself very well before we departed from Ebele."

He looks from Xipilli to Chike to Arturo, but he does not answer as a Derivan adept runs up to Xipilli. "Vulcan! We've found something."

"What is it?"

The adept bows low, holding out a sealed plastic bag holding a small microchip as well as a tangle of bloody wiring and mechanical parts.

"This was recovered from one of the laboratories."

"And why are you showing it to me instead of placing it with the others?"

"We've identified these as having belonged to Lady Wren, Your Majesty."

"My sister! She was here?"

"It would seem so, Your Majesty."

"Check everything again. If my sister was here, if she is alive, I want every trace of her found, now!"

"Yes, my liege!"

The Derivan adept runs away as quickly as she can with the orders on her tongue.

"Xipilli," cautions Chike. "We have no way of knowing if Wren was here yesterday or six months ago. There may not be anything left to find."

"My sister was here, Chike. I don't care how long ago. The knowledge is enough."

But Kaito knows. Kai knows for certain she was here only hours before their arrival. This just confirms it.

While they speak, Kai makes his own rounds about the facility. There are charred summoning circles and the burned remains of what indeed was once a VR system. The headset is covered in blood. Wires dangle from a metal table, the metal browning from the blood essentially baked into it. It is here he picks up a trail despite the damage of the fire, following it to a separate room in the hospital. This room is different from the others; in some ways it reminds him of a NICU, especially considering the broken remnants of an incubator crushed underneath the fallen ceiling. The trail ends here in a spot on the floor, eerily pristine and untouched by the fire. At the center of it is where the blood trail ends. Blood which, he confirms later, belongs to Wren.

None of his findings on this day would prepare him for the reunion that would take place a year later on a rainy, war-torn isle. Wren Nocturne, his lover who was a prodigy of technomancy, would return to the frontlines with the most forbidden of magics, commanding an army of corpses and wielding a soul-eating blade in the center of a bloodstained battlefield.

Wren—a witch hellbent on revenge.

The Autumnal Equinox typically falls between the 10th and 13th days in the Month of Falling. Determining the start of the fall season, people throughout the continent host various harvest festivals on this day as the plows rev to life to collect the first fruits of hard labors. It is a time to celebrate balance, equilibrium, and weigh in on the highs and lows of the year thus far before the daylight hours wane into the darkest nights of the year.

This year, the Autumn Equinox falls on the 12th and should be a most auspicious day for celebrations of health, love, and family.

Excerpt from *The Old Ways Farmers' Almanac*
Spice and Wolf Publishing - Author Anonymous

2
FOUR OF WANDS

S OMETIMES WREN MISSES HER MOTHER.
Every mother is a goddess in the eyes of a daughter, but Wren's mother really truly was the closest a mortal could get the ethereal. In the eyes of many, Wren's mother was a living embodiment of beauty and divinity, the incarnation of the goddess for which she received her namesake. Freya Nocturne had been resplendent not only in her beauty but also in her stories and songs, in her poise and mannerisms, in her wisdom and kindness.

Wren remembers long summer days with her mother in Deriva, the island country where she was born. The floating isles with their gleaming cliffsides and white sand beaches. People loved to visit the white sands of her home. Popular honeymoon and vacation destinations, the beaches of Deriva were known for their beautiful views, romantic sunsets, boundless health benefits, and their superior photographic appeal. You could travel all of Deus and never find a place as easy to capture with a lens as the sandy, porcelain beaches of Deriva, unmatched for how the sand glitters like stars in the moonlight and shines like mirrors in the sunlight.

But the beach by Cresta de Corail, her childhood home, the palatial villa of Deriva's Vulcan and his family, has black sand. Photographs of the villa rarely feature the inky black dunes, the cameras ignoring the seashore entirely.

Most of the photographers who came and went from the villa when Wren was little were more interested in the swooping architecture of the home Deriva's Vulcan. Half of the villa is built on the water, suspended by a foundation of carefully designed piers and masterfully executed carpentry. The walls and beams are crusted with pearl, coral, and sea-glass, intricate artwork designed to give homage to the Pacificum. A mystical sight to behold, really. Who wouldn't want to capture its beauty?

But the beach... The beach was, and probably still is, a thinly veiled stain to most people. Harsh for its coloration and a reminder of the angry eruptions which once carved Deriva from the sea, the black sands are considered unphotogenic and ornery, as temperamental as the volcanic activity to which they attribute their color.

Atzi and Xipilli used to hate walking on the beach during the summer, the sand burned so hot, but Wren always enjoyed skipping barefoot along the shoreline, dancing through the burning sand until her toes squished into the damp sand where the waves washed during high tide. When she was really little, she would beg her mother to take her down to the shore so she could splash in the water and build sandcastles. She doesn't remember a time her mother said no.

Freya's skin was the palest of porcelains, sensitive to the sun and easily burned, but whenever Wren asked, her mother would dress herself in light linens and don a well-loved wide-brimmed hat—the thing made Freya look more like a farmer's wife than the second wife of the Vulcan of Deriva, but it was her favorite—and she would take her beloved savage of a daughter to the shore to frolic and play in the shallows. Wren would roll in the sand and splash in the ocean until the sun started setting and her mother called her back. Then came the moonrise dances. Freya would coax Wren into a dance along the beach until mother and daughter lost themselves in their songs and circles or Wren's father came to collect them.

But even Tlanextli, for all his serious façade, could be swayed into ten more minutes on the beach by his wife's sparkling green eyes and his youngest child's glittering laughter. Freya even once got him to let them bury him in the sand. Imagine, the highest ranked man in Deriva, a fearsome technomancer and monarch, buried up to his neck in black sand carved in the image of a fairy tale mermaid. Seashell bra and everything. He used to laugh and wrinkle his nose, always sunburned despite the deep toffee of his skin tone, at Wren, demanding recompense in the form of hugs and kisses.

A love tax, her mother called it, and she always said Wren's father was a greedy man. At least for hugs and kisses.

The witch sighs.

Who is she kidding? A lot of the time she misses her mother.

Wren eases the lightcycle off the speedway. She needs to stop to recharge the battery, and food would probably be a good idea even if she isn't really hungry. She hasn't eaten anything since she left Snowfall, too listless to stomach the idea of eating.

Sometimes she wonders if her mother had had more time with her, would she have been stronger? Perhaps, if Freya had been given more time to instill her knowledge in her daughter herself, Wren wouldn't have struggled so much with her identity. Perhaps if she hadn't had to learn her mother's lessons from the pages of a worn journal, she would've been better prepared for a slew of things. For meeting her soulmate and feeling love's first flutters in her heart only to have it all ripped away with the slaughtering of her family. To have her body broken, to have her very being torn to barely recognizable pieces, to come out the other side a witch whose life was no longer her own.

Fruitless follies.

Nothing could have prepared Wren for those things, but at least, if Freya had lived, she would have had her mother's arms to curl into. Had Freya survived, she would have torn the whole world down to find her lost daughter much like Demeter when Persephone was taken from her, but before the pair could be united once more, Persephone found her own strength and became the Queen of the Dead. Hmm... What an interesting comparison. While Wren didn't return to the frontlines as the Queen of the Dead, she did return with dominion over them. But Wren's heart would never have had room for Hades. It was already spoken for by then. Besides, her technomancer is far superior to any Death God and equally steadfast.

I have mourned you for twelve years...

No, Kaito Miyazaki is more than steadfast. He kept her memory safe in his heart without any promise she would ever return. Yet, return she did.

A day's travel from Tokiseishu, the ache in her chest has dulled even if the glide of Kai's skin against hers still lingers, the evidence of his touch still burned into her skin. It shouldn't be so hard, moving on alone. She's done it before; she can do it again. And Kaito's brother made it very clear. Eyes would not be turned blindly again to an illicit affair between a "whore" witch and a prince among technomancers.

It's better this way, she thinks as she parks the cycle in the darkened alley between two skyscrapers. If there is one thing Wren never wanted, it's for Kaito to forsake his family, and Wren has too much unfinished business to let him. He's the crown prince of Murasaki no Yama, for crying out loud. It would be stupid for him to tarnish his reputation by associating with her any further. It's bad enough she helped him wipe a curse off his family's land just days ago. If any of the other League nations discovered Murasaki willingly consorted with a witch, let alone the Songstress of Lorelei herself... The risk is too high, and Hikaru knew well enough to throw her out of the palace before Kaito could get wind of her next movements lest he do something foolish like help her deal with her own unfinished business.

She'll have to remember to applaud the emperor when she's less angry. At least, she knows Kaito won't be dragged down if Wren's whole operation blows up in her face, and who is she kidding? It most definitely will. It doesn't matter how perfect the forged IDs in her pocket are; something will expose her. It's as inevitable as the eventual burning out of Deus's sun. Granted, she doesn't think she has over a billion years, but the sentiment is there.

The cuts on her arm twang as she takes her helmet off. The bandage needs changing again, bloodstained and dirty as it is.

There's a large fairground across the street from where she parked, and it is bustling with activity. Bright fiery orange and red banners, neon electric torches glowing along the walkways, children playing with light-up hula hoops and poi sticks. A DJ jams to the thrumming bass pulsing from his speakers. Vendors line the walkways selling food and goods while people dance and cheer to the music.

She wipes the sweat from her brow, shivering a bit in the breeze of the coming dusk and tugging her cloak tighter around her body. To the human eye, and to most supernatural eyes, Wren looks like an older teenage girl with long, sunshine blonde hair, mahogany skin, and dark, hooded eyes. Nothing like her actual self, carefully hidden under the magical glamour of a girl who sacrificed her life to return Wren hers.

"Welcome to the Xīndì, milady." A gentle-looking old woman with no visible augmentations greets her at the entrance to the park. She is dressed in a mix of bright colors and wooden decorations. A large hat sits on her head, and the wooden carvings around her neck clatter as she moves. "The day's celebrations have just begun."

"Celebrations for what?"

"Summer's End, of course. It is time to trade the physical for the ephemeral. To sell monotony for passion and innocence for knowledge. Here is the last stop before the dark, cold winter of reality destroys whimsy. So, we celebrate while we can before it all gets swept away."

"So, a festival?"

"Can you think of a better place for someone to trade their soul?"

Wren nearly snorts. It's all cryptic mumbo jumbo. Pretty and unusual words thought up by normals to describe a hexen practice. This woman wouldn't know the first thing about selling her soul to satisfy a want, or worse, in exchange for something she needs. Wren herself never quite understood what a soul-debt meant until she found herself back among the living, yanked from the veil in a discombobulating spiral of pain and agony.

Who'd a thunk a would-be coven of sanatorium patients would manage to bring back anyone from the dead, let alone a witch burned to death in her own self-inflicted madness?

Katrina, LuQin, Atalia, Sarah, Emilio, Hoshi, Amani, and Nadia. It is Atalia whose face she currently wears: a spell affixed over her whole body to hide her blue-black hair, aquamarine eyes, and pale wheat skin. It's terribly macabre, using the glamour of a dead girl as a disguise. The illusion masks not just her real visage but also the most damning of identifying markers on her body: her witch's indicia—the triskelion on her brow and the wild script that dances viridian across her skin whenever she weaves magic.

Wren hums as she walks, a silly little ditty Freya sang to her every Mabon when she was a child. One that never rhymed or made much sense other than it was about the fall.

Daisies wilting on the Summer's edge
Dandelions floating on the winds of change

Pumpkins singing in the pumpkin patch
Plump little apples sliced and baked in spice

Harvest moons alight in orange light
Have a dance before the first snow bed

Call it whatever you'd like: Summer's End, Mabon, the Autumn Equinox, Alban Elfed, etc. The wheel of the year turns in celebration of the first harvest and a means to say thank you to the universe for what has been given. Unfortunately, its meaning has long been warped outside hexen circles. So much so, the feast of gratitude is more of an excuse for people to glutton themselves on rich cuisine and lavish gifts. A festival of fools. Luxury to distract from disparity. Even the cyborgs laugh at the "traditions" despite taking part themselves. They keep the economy running, and if this small village is any indication, plenty of people are willing to travel to take part in such festivities.

Countless stalls line the thoroughfare.

"Get your hand sculpted in wax!"

"Fine gems for a fine lady, madame!"

"Candles! Hand-made candles!"

"Apples, pears, and peaches. Freshly picked! Come and taste the ambrosia of the gods!"

Merchants sell their wares, farmers sell fruits and vegetables, and artisans sell their crafts: handmade jewelry, beautiful portraits and paintings. There's even a glassblowing booth. Long toiled over labors wrapped in neat boxes and fine tissue paper for the waiting buyer.

Small stages stand erected throughout featuring musicians and dancers. She leaves credits for the performers as she passes. *Selling their souls, indeed. How poetic!*

To put time and dedication into something, to baby it and watch it grow in the soil of your sweat and tears, only to sell it for something as cheap and common as money. The various artworks cry under her hand, mourning the loss of their makers and distraught by the prospect of being sold as common goods. So much of their creators poured into them just to be passed to the next person.

The people don't notice though. Why would they? Too giddy on food, drink, and goods for empathy—Oh! Listen to her! Feeling sorry for inanimate objects now? The curse of being an empath!

There are more of the usual types of booths she would expect to find in a marketplace, street food sellers and spirit fountains, no absinthe though. She's forced to settle for a cheap wine to drink with the chicken chuan'r she bought from one of the food booths which, in all honesty, doesn't pair too badly.

There are other, more suspect, activities for festival goers to take part in. Though if Murasaki no Yama really has declared itself a haven for hexen, these kinds of things probably shouldn't surprise her.

Tarot card readers, palmistry practitioners, and other so-called psychics sit scattered around the park, hawking their skills to the adventurous and superstitious. They aren't witches. Not really. They bear no visible indicia, and any magic they might be selling is purely theoretical, which is another kind of witchcraft but inherently different from true clairvoyance. She would hate to judge them charlatans without knowing any of them, but ... she's always found something distasteful about taking money from the lonely, the hopeful, and the innocent.

On the more human+ side of illicit, a few DIY-inventors haggle with buyers over obviously modified tech: comm units with a larger broadcasting range, a kitchen gadget which doubles as a wireless router, and a telescope capable of seeing through walls—she won't venture to guess what sort of diabolical misuse it might inspire. It's amazing there are no adepts or security drones scoping the place. The local division would have a field day with the number of potential misdemeanors hidden under the counters of some of these stalls.

She chews and drinks and strolls her way along the path. A few children pass by with sparklers in hand. A juggler entertains a family standing together—a father, mother, and their young daughter. The little girl giggles as the magician produces a rainbow-colored daisy and tucks it into her hair. Wren's smile grows somber, and she hurries along the path.

Toward the central hub of the park is a lovely garden and several elegantly decorated tents erected in a small cluster. A picnic area, it would seem, with finely embroidered blankets laid out on the grass. To the unknowing onlooker, it would look like a lovely spot for a family outing, and it is, but not for the reasons most parents would think. The painted flags decorating the perimeter tell a story far more nuanced than any run-of-the-mill picnic spot.

This courtyard is a place for beauty, delight, and earthly pleasures.

Each banner bears a six-petal amaryllis in bloom, webbed and enfolded in a circle. A few of the flags have embellished the image with spiraling decorations and florals. Additionally, wooden lanterns decorated in silk streamers and living flowers dot the set up. Upon true nightfall, those lanterns will sparkle with the glow of fireflies.

These are the marks of a travelling sparkle of Fireflies, men and women specially trained to be the League's most sought-after companions, and if Wren's memory serves her right, this sparkle is from L'amour Lux, Deus' most respected guild of Fireflies.

Whelp! Time to test out her shiny new ID.

She tosses her waste into a nearby disposal/recycling bin and makes her way toward the tents. Male and female Fireflies, six in total as far as she can see, are scattered throughout the courtyard. Several already entertain their habitue.' A beautiful ebony-skinned gentleman dances a classical Sekhmetian dance for a small group of patrons, his various jewels and bangles jingling and sparkling in the warm sunlight. Another pair of women plays a duet of a dizi and guqin for an enchanted crowd.

Magic weaves gently in the air.

Not witchcraft, though many Fireflies, like Wren's mother, are often rumored to indulge in witchcraft, even if their status protects them from persecution. Nor is it technomancy, though there are quite a few Fireflies scattered around with implants and augmentations. (The dizi player definitely has a rebreather enhancement judging by the steady ease with which she handles the flute. She hasn't taken a breath since Wren started listening. And Fireflies may not be the only ones to opt for beauty enhancements, but it was a privilege many of them felt a necessity for their livelihoods.) No, it's gentler, this magic, woven in the fine patterns of their clothing and the oils perfuming the air. It's in the lotions rubbed into their skin and in the heated thrum of exhilaration.

Love magic is its own branch of the arcane, and since it isn't seen as a threat to the League, the practice of it is overlooked. While it is not possible to use it in combat, its weaving honey-slow and intimately sticky, its potency is not to trifle with. Calming tempers, inspiring lust, increasing fertility and virility, encouraging a flower to bloom or water to heat—Wren has even seen it used to heal physical, mental, and emotional injury. Whether to calm a panicking friend or arouse a lover, sexual magic is a masterful way to bring to the surface a person's innermost truths and potentials.

The woman who greets Wren at the center canopy wears a sheer veil over the lower part of her face, her robes as elegant as any Wren has seen on the royal family of Murasaki though not of the same cultural origin, a daxiushan if she remembers the name of the garment correctly with long flowing sleeves and elegantly draped fabrics in fine silks and soft lace.

"Blessed waking."

The traditional Firefly greeting, given regardless of the time of day. Wren pulls Atalia's identification card from her pocket, presents it to the grande dame, and gives the traditional response:

"And may your daydreams dance before you."

The woman quirks a finely manicured eyebrow at Wren before looking at the ID.

"Miss Vaishi. Just passing through or were you planning on engaging in the festivities this evening? You aren't exactly dressed for entertainment."

"Just passing through, madame. Though, I was wondering if you would give me the privilege of browsing your callboard before I continue my travels."

"Our communique is always available to registered Fireflies of the guild. Come, child. Enter."

Wren bows her thanks as she steps into the carpeted floor of the tent. The communique is on the far side of the pavilion, a portable charging station for a small monitor, and she pads her way there after removing her shoes. There are two Fireflies lounging against a mountain of pillows on the opposite side of the space. They laugh and share a bottle of sake, spilling the tea, as it were, on their recent customers.

The callboard's screen is already powered up, and streaming is a varied list of potential clientele and events for Fireflies to attend. Most of the events are for aristocrats and noble houses. No better way to heighten the rank of your party than by having a few Fireflies present.

Wren runs a search on the hub. What she has access to here will pale in comparison to what she had been working with through Kai's network, the Miyazaki clan resources far greater than any Firefly server, but it will do. Besides, she isn't so much looking for information as a means by which to garner information. With L'amour Lux's systems, Wren can see in live time when a call is answered, various usernames popping in and out as responses are published and requests made, and after a bit of filtering, she is not disappointed.

"Pharoah Jamar Sahra to host conference in preparation for upcoming Technomancer Trials at The Shard, the World Trade Center of Sekhmeti," reads the inquiry. "L'amour Lux certified Fireflies are invited to attend in service to the greatest names on the technomancer council. Registered attendees include Vulcan Xipilli Moctezumo, Art Lionheart, President Ackram, Emperor Hikaru Miyazaki, and the Primarch himself, Donarick J. Thames alongside his wife, Chiamaka Nagi—Orisha of Ebele."

Staring at Chiamaka's name and picture, the weeping cut on her arm throbs.

Chiamaka, a mundane human and League aristocrat, using witch's magic. Chiamaka killing a boy, barely made a man, in cold blood. Chiamaka spinning a curse on Shinka's sacred grounds and on the Miyazaki family.

Her nightmare:

Chiamaka's burning face in the mirror.

"Betrayer!"

A vision had at the height of passion:

29

Golden banners, desert heat, and blood in the sand...

Her vision. The one she had in Kaito's arms as he brought her to peak. Kaito's body hard and pulsing over and in her, warm and comforting. His smell, his taste, his touch, his devotion—a prelude to a promised future played through the glide of his fingers over her body. Their passion had been a high note coaxed from the Songstress's lips in ecstasy for the newly rekindled flame for the only person in the world, man or woman, she could ever truly see.

Wren swallows down the need to cry and grips her forearm in favor of feeling the physical pain over the emotional.

Happy endings are for princesses and heroines, not Wren Nocturne. Not for witches, not for monsters left sleeping in the dark, woken up and brought back from the dead with a mission for vengeance. She has three people left to kill, and if her visions are anything to go by, Chiamaka is her next target, but...

The woman's scorched face, angry and smoldering in the bathroom mirror, like Bloody Mary but far more real than any children's game, appeared to her in the silence of a gloomtide nightmare and screamed her rage.

Betrayer!

The descriptive has been used for her in the past, but something in the way the nightmare spectre flung the word at her didn't feel like an accusation.

Wren makes a note in her comm, submits her credentials to the event, and logs off. She knows where she's going, into a pit of vipers, but she'll need a different outfit to present herself in once she gets there. Perhaps one suitable for her next death?

Honestly, though, getting shot by a bullet sounds way better than having your soul ripped to shreds. Bullets are survivable. Soul purges are not.

Tap, tap, tap...

Wren looks up from the monitor. Long, spidery fingers drum a slow rhythm into the case of the communique, but they are not living fingers. Translucent and charred, cracked nails click, click, click against the metal. Wren follows the line of an arm up to find dead black eyes staring down at her from a face half-melted from her skull. Wren swallows, mouth dry as a faceless ghost fumes down at her, head tilted, unseeing and all-seeing at once.

And the apparition is literally fuming, threads of spiritual smoke wafting off her in waves. The burning woman crouches, a swirl of rage and volatility, like a contorted animal on top of the communique, looking at her through bloodied, half-melted eyes. Bloodlust rolls off the woman's spirit, the brute of it hammered into Wren's mind with a 12-ton mallet and sharp as iron on her tongue. This spirit wants revenge, and she wants it badly, and Wren can't exactly do anything about it right now because she is in a very, (Repeat!) very public place.

The ghost's mouth opens, smoke swelling from her throat. The burning visage screams at her, her fury silent as the grave she's shunned, and she lunges for the witch. Wren reels back, falling on her ass, the fuming ghost scratching for her face.

Flames burn her hands, crossed to shield her face, and those phantom claws yank on Wren's hair, the strands burning in her phantom grip.

The ghost yanks on her empathy like a power cable, siphoning in enough bloodlust and rage to short-circuiting her synapses. Wren bites her tongue to keep from screaming and through gritted teeth spits out a spell:

"Verschwinde!"

Her command banishes the spirit's touch from her body, and she disappears, shoving her smoldering resentment into Wren before vanishing into the ether and leaving Wren gasping for air on her back.

What the hell?

Her head pounds, marbles banging around in her skull in the aftermath of the psychic assault. Goddess above! When was the last time something attacked her psychically? She doesn't remember, and she quite frankly doesn't want to.

"Atalia?!"

As long as I can make them laugh, it doesn't matter how; I'll be alright. If I succeed in that, the human beings probably won't mind it too much if I remain outside their lives. The one thing I must avoid is becoming offensive in their eyes: I shall be nothing, the wind, the sky.

Excerpt from *No Longer Human*, an Old-World Text
Osamu Dazai, 1948 A.D.

3

QUEEN OF CUPS

I T TAKES WREN A MOMENT TO REGISTER 'HER' name being called, and she whirls around like a child caught with their hand in the cookie jar.

"Umm... yes?"

"Are you alright, dear? What are you doing on the floor?"

Behind her is a tall, will-o-wisp of a woman. Her skin is a luscious shade of coffee and her head crowned in an intricate knotting of dreaded locks struck through with gray. She has a sweet demeanor and an even sweeter emotional texture. Kind, adoring, happy. Nothing really alarming. Except under those emotions is the odd texture of unexpected surprise, and below that—and this is what makes Wren's palms break out in a sweat—recognition.

Wren scrambles to pick herself up off the floor. Checking herself over, she sees her hands are not burned to a crisp. She has no new injuries other than a lovely bruise on her ass, and oh, thank the stars, none of her hair was actually scorched away by the ghost. It may not look like her hair right now—Atalia's hair a sunny blond shade in contrast to Wren's blue-black locks—but it is Wren's hair.

Glamours don't create mass. She can't make herself taller or shorter or wider or thinner, and in the same way she can't make her hair longer or shorter. Were someone to come up and chop off the ends, they would be chopping off her real hair, and she's never been a fan of short haircuts, at least, not since her big brother spat a piece of gum into her hair. She'd been all of six at the time and was forced to cut half of it off by the mess made of her head. Wren didn't speak to Xipilli for a whole week, not until he begged her forgiveness with her favorite stolen snacks from the kitchens, and after she finished the peace offering, she made sure to give him a good wallop in retaliation.

But anyway... Back to the present and the stranger in front of her who knows 'her face.'

"I'm fine. Just a bit of a stumble is all. You know how it is. No grace outside of a performance, right?"

The woman chuckles, stepping closer.

"True enough. Ah! Look at you," she exclaims, taking 'Atalia's' hands in hers. "Why I never thought I would see one of my students here of all places. As a fully graduated Firefly at that!"

"I didn't think I would see you here either, *mon saga*," she says, bowing her head.

"Oh, Atalia, no need for that old title. Just Mishka. I always told you as much."

Oh, right... How could she forget?

Merde!

"Oh, of course! Mishka. Sorry, my memory is terrible these days, keeping track of names and places. It's a miracle I found my way here without making a wrong turn."

Mishka smiles.

"You always were absent-minded."

Well, that's a relief.

"And you're a Firefly now!" continues Mishka. "I didn't know you finished your training. When did you go back to court?"

"Oh, I, uh... I finished in Murasaki. Tokiseishu has a brilliant program."

Queen Of Cups

Tokiseishu, the capital city of Murasaki no Yama where Snowfall (*Yuki ga Furu*) Palace is nestled. Kaito took her there after an unfortunate encounter with a kenku left her unconscious not long after her resurrection. She'd been wearing Atalia's face then, too, not that the ruse had fooled him.

"I actually just came from the city. Looking for work, you know."

"I always did think you were a natural Firefly. Though I'm surprised to hear another program accepted you. The traditional protocol is once a chrysalis is dismissed from one program, they are ineligible to apply for another."

"It is, yes, but his excellency asked them to make an exception for me. Emperor Hikaru is a most admirable monarch, and they were gracious enough to overlook my history."

She says this with as convincing a smile as she can, and Mishka's eyes dance kindly.

"I never supported Chiamaka's decision to dismiss you. The whole circumstance was... well, I won't go into it here. I'm sure it's the last thing you want to talk about."

But Wren's interest piques.

Is she talking about Atalia's rape? Could she possibly know the culprit? The information might lead her to one of the people the asylum inmates wanted her to exact revenge against. But how can she ask without giving herself away as not being Atalia? Before Wren can figure out the answer, Mishka changes the topic.

"You're registering for the technomancer conference?"

Mishka looks around Wren's arm to see what she has pulled up on the holoscreen. Wren glances back to see her registration has gone through.

"Uh, yeah," she answers, pulling her ID card from the slot and tucking it back into her bodice. "Thought it would be a good opportunity to get a few new patrons."

"You realize Chiamaka is going to be there, right?"

Oh, does she realize Chiamaka is going to be there! That's kind of the point. Blasted vision-tainted nightmares! Waking her and pulling her from Kai's arms! She would've much rather curled right back into his side, closed her eyes, and forgotten all about the damned cuts on her arm.

But no! Several someones decided to sell their souls to summon an evil entity back to the living world to exact vengeance on their behalf, and Wren just so happens to be said "evil" entity. (Really, she tortured a man to death one time and got herself labeled a vengeful demoness for her troubles. Everybody's a critic!) Now, couple the whole situation with the nameless, faceless, apparently, ruthless ghost hounding steps, and here she is! Barreling head-first into technomancer territory to find out just what the hell is going on around here.

Wren looks at Mishka with a smile. The pavilion's walls flap lazily as the wind blows outside.

"Oh, I highly doubt her majesty remembers me at all."

Chiamaka isn't of any consequence to her. The only question is, does Wren's vision mean for her to set the woman on fire herself, or is this something that will come to pass without or without her help? This whole clairvoyance thing is new, strange, and unusual, and she dearly hopes it won't be sticking around after this curse is rectified.

Mishka looks at her strangely. Wren is clearly missing some important piece of information because Mishka's expression goes from incredulous to downright pained. Three guesses why...

"So, what brings you here?" asks Wren, changing the subject as quickly as possible.

"Oh, I came to meet with the grande dame. While I don't teach at a formal school anymore, I have classes for youngsters interested in learning about their sexuality. Teenage pregnancies have decreased since I started offering the lessons, so the locals have received it well."

Wren's eyebrows rise.

"Giving back to your community by unclouding the mysteries of the human body." Imagine that! A generation of sexually empowered teenagers. Such a force could conquer the world. "I'm sure madame will be happy to hear it."

Mishka looks sheepish.

"Yes, well, as of late something has gone awry with my pupils."

"What do you mean 'awry'?"

"Since last week, five of my students have suffered attacks in the night without explanation, four girls and one boy, all of them teenagers, and I haven't any idea what caused them."

Wren tilts her head sideways. "Attacks?"

"Seizures and night terrors coupled with suffocation. They've all needed to be hospitalized afterward."

"Do your students have anything in common other than being under your tutelage?"

"I've cross referenced as many things as I could, and I still don't have any answers. None of them led the same lifestyle. They don't even attend the same schools, and the two who do walk in completely different social circles. Their only commonality is they're all my students, their families regulars at my tea shop."

"No one other than your students have been attacked?"

"No one. Not even those who frequent the shop. Only my young charges. I put a request in for the League to investigate, and they were kind enough to respond quickly, but the technomancer they sent didn't find anything."

"Who did they send?"

"Umm... Sir Lionheart... I think his first name is Arturo."

Lionheart graduated with Wren and Kaito during the 247th technomancer trials. Wren didn't work with him very much when she was a technomancer herself, but the few times she did, she remembers him being thorough, even if his hero-complex was a little grating. At least, it had been before she died. People change in twelve years after all.

"And he didn't find anything?"

Mishka's eyes light up.

"He spoke with all of the victims and investigated the town from top to bottom. He even went into the sewers to see if anything was hiding out in the muck, but he didn't find anything. Unfortunately, the Primarch summoned him away before he could finalize his investigation."

"The council took him off the case?"

Mishka nods.

A technomancer removed from an active case? Preposterous! The League Wren grew up in would never summon a technomancer away from an open case. Of course, the League Wren grew up in didn't have a Primarch at the center of it with the power to command every registered technomancer in Deus. There was no would-be king capable of flinging his weight around as he pleases for everyone to pander to like milk servants.

"Yes, he couldn't share the details with me, but something more urgent came up, and since no one has died yet, well... Our case got put on the back burner. He was regretful about having to leave the case open."

Like hell something more urgent came up! Wren may have been reborn last week but being dead for twelve years didn't make her daft. And rats are rather noisy when they come scratching at walls they have no business lurking within.

"So, Lionheart didn't find anything?" Wren asks. Mishka shakes her head in answer.

"The two days he was in town, there were no incidents. When he left, he said it was possible that whatever was causing the attacks may have moved on. We hoped the incidents would stop, but last night two of my younger students interested in beginning formal training as chrysalises were attacked and nearly killed as though whatever was behind the attacks was making up for its missed meals. And..."

The older woman trails off, chewing her lips and glancing around as though afraid they will be overheard. Wren leans in closer, hoping to assuage her worries.

"Mishka, what's wrong?"

"Some of the townsfolk have been talking. They think a witch is responsible for the attacks, but there—there aren't even any hexen in town, at least not anymore. They've already driven out the few who claimed sanctuary in the area. They weren't even living in the town proper, more like on the fringes in the countryside, and... Atalia, I'm so scared. I don't even know what to do. I can't leave my other charges. These are my students, and I can't protect them if I leave town."

"Whoa, whoa, slow down." Wren sets her hands on Mishka's shoulders. "Tell me what happened. Why would you need to leave town?"

Fear rolls off of Mishka in waves, sickly and yellow. Wren's stomach churns from the texture, how strong the woman's fright is.

"The city council came to speak to me the other day. I—I'm worried they think I'm the one responsible for my students being attacked, but I'm not. They... The mayor, he mentioned they used to burn witches at the stake for a lot less than attacking teenagers and mixing poisonous teas."

"He threatened you."

"Not exactly. He was very casual about the whole thing. Trying to scare me, I guess, but Ata, if this keeps happening..." She trails off, biting her lip as though she was about to share something very secret, very forbidden. "That's why I came here. I needed to see if someone could help me."

The woman bursts into tears, and for all the woman's emotions are already knocking around in her psyche, Wren braces her resolve and pulls her into her arms, The other woman's feelings intensify to a fever pitch, drawing tears to Wren's own eyes as she shushes her, holding her through the fit.

"Shh, shhh, shhhh... I've got you," she coos, humming under her breath the way her mother used to for her as a child, the way Wren herself once did for...

Mysterious attacks on teenagers and talk of witchcraft. Frightened townspeople and thinly veiled threats. It's a perfect storm for a witch hunt. Murder in the name of righteousness. Destruction in the name of reparation. Not that any witch hunt led by normal people ever resulted in the finding of an actual witch. That's what technomancers are for.

Years ago, she would have said if Lionheart already went in and found nothing, then it was likely nothing. A technomancer's word is definitive, after all.

Wren would roll her eyes now.

Her technomancer education may have prepared her for a lot as far as dealing with lycans, vampyres, and witches went, but after awakening her witch blood, Wren learned a whole lot more about hexen than she ever could have learned from any League sponsored education. She didn't have much of a choice really. As a hexen, one of the spell-folk of Deus, she had to learn and adapt lest she end up hurting herself and the people around her for lack of understanding and control. Wren returned to proper society as a witch with a bad attitude and the magical might to back it up, and she proved her worth a thousand times over despite her hexen blood.

Hell, they practically worshiped her for a time after she saved all of their goddamn lives. But all sweetened fruits eventually sour.

"Mishka, I want you to think. Did anything strange happen before the first attack? Anyone new come to town?"

"I don't know. I don't think so. People are always passing through. We are right off the main road to Sekhmeti."

Interesting.

Wren reaches for her locket and curses. She forgot it in Kai's study. Hikaru hadn't exactly given her time to collect all of her things, and her tarot deck had been on the table next to it. *Double damn!*

"But," continues Mishka when 'Atalia' doesn't say anything, "now that I think of it, a sweet red-headed girl stopped by the tea shop on her way through town."

"A red-headed girl."

"Mhmm, pretty young thing too with freckles. Just about your age, she looked. She was wearing a light polka-dotted sundress and a floppy sun hat."

Strikingly similar to Summer Helsdottir, sans the horns, but those could have been covered up by a hood or, if it were big enough, a floppy sun hat.

"Was she about this tall?" asks Wren, gesturing. "Skinny, white girl with dark eyes, maybe nursing an injury?"

"Well, yes. She had a rough-looking hole in her shoulder. I bandaged her up before she left, but I didn't see her again."

It's Summer alright. The hole in her shoulder no doubt the gunshot wound Wren left her during their last tango. The last Wren saw of the other witch had been on the light rail, the summoner jumping off the carriage to disappear in a void-thick wash of teleportation magic. Which, now that she thinks about it, Summer doesn't have teleportation abilities. How did she displace herself?

"Mishka, what day did she stop by your shop?"

"The 2nd. The attacks began the same night"

Merely a day after Wren encountered the witch on the light rail?

"You mean last week?"

"Mhmm, the 2nd Day in the Month of Falling."

Also the day a group of hexen wielding void-magic attacked Snowfall Palace. The day one of Wren's targets, Dr. Johannes Faust was rescued before he could answer for his crimes at the asylum where Wren was resurrected.

Coincidence? Not likely.

"Did she mention where she was going next?"

"We chatted for a bit. She mentioned meeting her husband in Sekhmeti."

Husband? Summer has a husband?

"She was sweet enough, and she gave me the idea to take a trip to Aureus. Now that it's fall, the desert heat won't be so bad, and the palm springs are to die for. But then the attacks started."

Mishka's expression is downright dour, and Wren doesn't blame her for it. Wren's only been re-alived a handful of days and already she needs a vacation from the entire world.

"I should get going. I need to be home before dark because of the curfew, and I'm sure a young woman like you would much rather enjoy the festival than the laments of a frail old woman."

Mishka turns to go, but Wren catches her arm with gentle insistence. "W-Why don't I go with you? I'm on my way to

Sekhmeti anyway, and maybe I can help you figure out what's happening."

"Atalia," says Mishka, eyes soft. "Not to say I don't appreciate your offer, but if a technomancer found nothing, what makes you think you will?"

It's a fair enough point. An incorrect point, but not one Wren can correct without giving up the ghost.

"Well, okay. That's true. I can't compete with a technomancer, but did you know the Tokiseishu Firefly program works with the Miyazaki adept training program? Fumiko–sensei is one of the greatest living technomancer teachers, and she taught us a few ways to ward off negative energy and supernatural mischief." It's a bold-faced lie, but Mishka doesn't need to know that. "At the very least, you won't be alone if the council starts threatening you again."

Mishka's teeth worry at her lower lip.

She's almost got her. She can see Mishka wavering, her fear starting to ease into reassurance. No one wants to face something like this alone. Wren knows that better than anyone.

"I don't know. I'm starting to think I'm cursed."

"You're not cursed," Wren assures her. "Besides, I'd love the chance to catch up with my *Saga*."

When a small smile quirks Mishka's lips, Wren knows she's won.

"Alright, but don't say I didn't warn you. This old lady is not the hoot she used to be at parties."

And if you are cursed, Wren thinks quietly as Mishka turns to lead her to her car. *I think I have a good idea which witch cursed you, and I owe her a visit.*

Sometimes, it takes a witch to catch a witch.

Prosthetics in Deus are less an abnormality and more of a way of life. It is not unusual to have friends, neighbors, and family members with prosthetic enhancements either due to injury or a voluntary integration known as technolyzation.

Compared to more advanced methods of technological integration such as neural nets and subdermal enhancements, this method of human+ enhancement is not only less costly but also more readily available due to an initial lack of government regulation.

Technolyze Me: How Voluntary Amputation Became Commonplace in The League

C. R. Ashworth, 1845 A.P.

4

THE HERMIT

8th Day in the Month of Falling – 9:47AM

"KAITO, YOU MISSED OUR MEETING THIS morning, and I need your mission debrief on Shinka. I am assuming you are out of the palace considering the Jade Wing's security measures have been activated. I understand you are probably upset Miss Nocturne left without your notification, but *Otōto*, please—"

Kaito deletes the remainder of his brother's voicemail unheard. He's not interested in what his aniki has to say about Wren. Hikaru lost the right to say anything to Kaito about Wren the moment the man asked his lover to meet him without telling Kaito. Did Hikaru really believe his A.I. so easy to deactivate? Kaito built AYA especially for the purpose of deflecting such attempts.

Two hours from Snowfall, Kaito stops on the doorstep of an old friend. The hedge is overgrown, the garden weed infested, and the house beyond is more aluminum than wood. Brightly colored graffiti paints the side, saying, "TeCH=DeAth. The GoDs r WA(I)tcHing." A security cam revolves lazily above the front door, slow circuits that only cover about a third of the yard, but Kaito knows better than to believe its feed is the one being monitored within. Amateur mistakes.

"AYA."

"Yes, highness," chimes the A.I. from inside his helmet.

"Is this the right place?"

"My sensory functions are unable to penetrate beyond the front gate, your highness. It is possible the network beyond is fortified against intruders."

Which means this is most definitely the right place.

Kaito hacks into the gate's security systems, forcing it open. He walks his lightcycle up the walkway and tucks it amidst the tall grasses surrounding the vegetable garden. AYA fires off warning bells in his headset, but Kai strides forward unafraid even as a hidden wall panel hisses open to reveal the blackened barrel of a turret.

"Halt, intruder. Identify!" demands a tinny, computerized voice.

Kaito's swords vibrate on his back in anticipation of battle, but he doesn't reach for them. He activates his neural tech instead. His sights whirl to life, lines of code and calculations flashing before his eyes, as he runs analytics on the weapon. Hacking into the local network, he deactivates the weapon in mere microseconds.

The turret clicks off with a fizzle.

"Is this how you greet your old sempai, Tomi?"

Surprised sputtering burbles over the comm, the turret's barrel swings wide, and the panel hisses shut, the front door sliding open instead.

"Kaito Miyazaki, you rat bastard! Did you have to disarm my one security system? It'll take me hours to get it back online."

The person in the doorway is no technomancer, not even an adept, but they are most certainly on the cyborgean end of human+ with a neural extension curling around one side of their bald head and a mechanical skeleton comprising the lower half of their body.

Tomi Nottingham, one of the most skilled hackers in Murasaki, greets Kaito with a dimpled shit-eating grin and a handshake.

"As if you don't have at least three more in perfect working condition."

"You know me too well, old friend. Come in, come in. Though I warn you, I'm not expecting company. Let alone his royal highness, Kaito Miyazaki."

"Would you have done anything had I notified you of my coming?"

Tomi's rounded cheeks jiggle through their laughter. "Not in the slightest. How's Renki doing? Kid's about to turn sixteen, isn't he?"

Tomi's home is small and full of all sorts of knickknacks. There is a television in the living quarters surrounded by gaming consoles, a stack of magazines beside the bin, a mess of schematics and empty coffee mugs on the coffee table. A tinkering table, holding a scattered smattering of computer parts and building tools, occupies an area that would otherwise be a dining room, and a curio cabinet full of glass animals and mythical beasts makes homey the farthest corner of the room from the door right behind a dining table which has probably seen more paperwork than meals. It's lived-in and cozy. Renki used to love Tomi's ever-shifting hideouts as a child, mostly for the game consoles and the curiosities.

"He is well. His remote hacking abilities have far improved since you last worked with him."

"Oh, that was years ago. The boy's a natural, but I notice he's not with you."

"No, my purpose for being here would not be suitable for him."

"Not suitable, eh?" Tomi frowns, looking Kaito up and down and eyeing the deep wine color of Kaito's tunic. "Now that I think on it, I barely recognized you through the camera feed. You've changed your wardrobe."

In the eight years Kai has known Tomi, they've never seen Kaito in anything but the grays and lavenders worn by the grieving in Murasaki no Yami.

"Any particular reason for the change? Not to say I'm not happy for you. Just curious."

"If it's all the same to you, Tomi, I'm afraid I don't have too much time for pleasantries."

"Of course, of course. My fault. So, what brings the illustrious Miyazaki-sama to my neck of the woods?"

"I need you to track someone for me."

"This humble one! Act as a tracker for Kaito Miyazaki himself. I thought the Miyazaki had a battalion of trained adepts just for that purpose." Even as they fake an aghast expression, Tomi moves to their primary office.

"Miyazaki resources are not at my disposal for this case."

"Meaning?"

"Meaning they are not at my disposal."

And this is true in a multiplicity of ways. Firstly, their systems in Shinka are still down and probably won't be fully operational for another few days. Secondly, Kaito's systems are not designed for tracking of this nature, and his brother's work is nothing to take lightly; Hikaru would have ensured Wren's falsified credentials difficult, if not impossible, to trace. While Kaito may be a master at combat hacking and coding, he is less inclined toward the nuances necessary to tamper with bureaucracy. Hence where Tomi comes in: a person he trusts who also happens to be in possession of the expertise he requires if he is going to locate his missing witch. But more importantly...

"You don't want anyone knowing you're looking for this person, do you?" provides Tomi as their lower body folds and unfolds into a computer chair.

"Astute as ever, Tomi."

Tomi's workspace is a computer programmer's dream. A wall of monitors set up around three motherboards, interconnected by a hand-built cooling system and framed by two portable laptops. The air is chilly, nearly freezing to keep the computers at optimal temp and in working order.

Kaito uploads the information he saved onto his drive when he first brought Wren to Yuki ga Furu onto Tomi's system. On the largest monitor pops the face Wren wore before her true identity was revealed to him—an Ebelean girl in her late teens, dark-skinned and round-faced but unhealthily skinny with long dirty-blond hair and hooded ebony eyes. Wren's glamour of her is less severe, healthier, the way Atalia would have looked had she not died a victim of abuse in a sanatorium.

"Atalia Vaishi? She's cute." Before his eyes, Tomi's system pulls up the woman's credentials, the majority of which have now been fabricated by Hikaru. "Ebelean citizen, nineteen years old holding a Firefly certification, an international passport, and a credit chip containing..." Tomi whistles, lowly, more than a little impressed at the amount of zeros on the value. "...a rather generous sum. She won't be wanting for clients anytime soon. So, what's so special about this chick? She about to bear Zeus his latest lovechild?"

"Zeus found himself abandoned in the old world after Hera had enough of his infidelity and his followers grew weary of him stealing into the beds of their wives and daughters."

"Oh, right! I'd forgotten. Never been a fan of the Greeks. So, is this a personal interest, then?" Tomi waggles a brow at Kaito. "Not like you to chase skirts, your highness," Tomi teases, projecting a short graphic of cartoon cat running from a skunk above his head. Tomi, for all their brilliance, is more than a little eccentric. Most computer geniuses are. "Actually, now I think of it, I've never seen you chase anything on two legs that you weren't intending on either arresting or chopping to death."

"You don't chop with a katana, you cut or stab, and I am not chasing a skirt. This woman's safety is of great import to me."

"And why would the prince of Murasaki care about the safety of a Firefly half his age? A Firefly who apparently just appeared in L'amor Lux's records at 12:37 this morning? She works fast, having earned that many credits in just ten hours."

They waggle their eyebrows at Kaito, who regards the lewd expression with a steely look.

"Alright, alright," they relent. "Your business, not mine. I'll put an alert out for her credentials. If she scans in anywhere, my system will detect it. Can't guarantee how long it will take though. She may not have run her ID yet."

"Thank you. I appreciate the assistance."

"No problem. What are friends for? Besides, it's the least I can do considering you've saved my hide from more than a few tight spots. Which... horrible idea, on your part. If his highness had any sense, there'd be less of me here to annoy you."

Tomi laughs at their own joke, and Kaito merely shakes his head.

"Hm. There is one other thing. I'm sure this will take far more of your time, so I understand if you aren't up for it."

Tomi gasps dramatically, holding a hand to their chest in faux offense.

"Do you doubt my abilities so! Woe is this poor mortal to be judged so lacking."

"Tomi. I am being serious. What I am asking will not be easy."

"You know I like a challenge."

Kaito pulls a small titanium capsule from one of the pockets on his belt. No bigger than a grain of rice but loaded with enough juice to power a satellite, S33Ds can be installed into the base of the skull flush with the brainstem where they sprout specially designed axons which integrate into a person's central nervous system until the S33D exists in perfect homogeneity with its now posthuman user. Capable of storing memories, synchronizing with computational systems, or simply acting as an ingrained comm unit, these neural augmentations are the core of the Miyazaki family's posthuman tech systems, and by extension, all of Murasaki has access to the civilian grade version of the implant. This one is frayed and burnt beyond repair, but it is intact. Tomi's eyes light up at the sight of it. The spark of his blue neural sights vibrant as he scans the S33D.

"Whose is that?"

"Mine."

Kaito sets the drive on the desk. The little thing, unobtrusive but representing a huge portion of his life, was his original S33D. The drive had been installed when he was just six years old after he'd told his mother he was ready to begin adept training.

THE HERMIT

"This was yours! Holy cow, man! How did you even salvage it? It's shot up to nothing."

"I recently discovered that twelve years ago someone hacked into my system to great destructive effect. They used the information garnered to instigate the events that resulted in my system being shut down. I ask you to figure out who the person responsible was."

"Kaito–sempai, be reasonable. You've too much faith in me. I don't think even I can manage that. This drive, it's... it's all but demolished. How the hell—"

"I thought the great Tomi Nottingham loved a good challenge. Or do you admit defeat already?"

They stutter, spouting indignities for even implying them not up for the task before snatching the drive out of Kai's reach when he attempts to collect it back.

"Admit defeat? I'll show you defeat. I have tricks that'll put your finest hackers to shame."

"I would expect no less from you."

Tomi's eyes narrow as Kaito turns to leave them to their work. "You are different."

"Tomi."

"No, you're different. I thought it was just the lack of mourning attire, but no, you're genuinely happy about something."

More like determined.

"Okay, maybe not happy, but you seem focused in a different way than I've ever known you to be. Like you found something you've been looking for a long time."

"Will you scan the drive or not?"

"I'll see what I can do with it."

"Thank you," says Kaito with an incline of his head. "If you don't mind, I'll wait until your scanner catches a lead on Miss Vaishi."

Tomi shrugs. "Not at all. Make yourself at home. I'm not exactly in a way to be hosting royalty, but you know that. I'll let you know once I get a ping on your skirt."

Kaito rolls his eyes as he turns from Tomi's computer set up.

"I await your news."

Tomi stalls him only once more as he makes his way out the door.

"Oi, sempai."

Kai angles his head back, listening.

"Love is a good look on you, my friend."

Tomi doesn't see Kai's expression as he walks out of the room, but the technomancer's smile is plain as day even if a bit cloudy.

I love you.

A sleepy whisper, murmured into his clavicle post coitus. A truth as naked as their bodies at the time. She always refrained from saying it in the past for reasons he never felt the need to discover. She probably didn't mean to speak the words aloud last night, but speak them, she did. As much as Hikaru might like for Kaito to think Wren's leaving was her choosing, that Wren was as callous and selfish as people claimed the Songstress of Lorelei to be, Kaito knows better. Even when they stood at opposite sides of a chasm in the wake of Wren's newfound nature as a witch, Wren had never been selfish.

He knows beyond an inkling of doubt that were it her choice, Wren would have stayed with him. His witch would rather have greeted the dawn with him than been sent off into the gloomtide of a moonless night.

Fourteen Years Ago – 7th Day in the Month of Planting 1863 **– Two days after Wren's return**

"Vulcan Xipilli, it is a joyous occasion indeed," announces Absko as the Alliance gathers in the celebration hall of the Abbey, the presidential home and congressional fortress of Aighneas. Madame President Morrigan "The Morrigan" Gewalt had been happy to host them in the wake of their recent victory against

Seraphim's forces. "In just two days, the Alliance has turned the tide of battle. With your glorious reclaiming of Cresta de Corail and your sister's triumphant return, we are at last in position to end the civil war and bring the Pontiflex to justice. As such, I propose a toast: to you, to Deriva, and of course, to the woman of the hour, Wren Nocturne."

A resounding acquiescence rings through the banquet hall, and an ensemble of glittering glasses rise in toast the young monarch, who bows his head in thanks to the praise from where he sits beside the president. Kai's mother sets down her glass before lifting her head to Xipilli.

"Speaking of Lady Wren," begins Mirai. "I am saddened by her absence this evening. I hope all is well."

Xipilli's face falls. Atzi answers in his stead after trading a glance with her brother.

"I am afraid our sister is quite fatigued. She opted to spend time with Zenza. She has only just met her niece after all."

"Oh?" inserts Rameses. "Surely a powerful technomancer such as your sister could present herself here for a bit. After all, she single-handedly took down Llywelyn yestereve." Someone snorts at the word "single-handedly" as though Wren's lack of a prosthetic for her amputated hand is a joke. Kaito's eyes roll to the person in question, and they cow at his steely glare. "If I remember correctly," continues Rameses, "Lady Nocturne never shied away from a good drink. Would she not rather relish in her victory than tend to a baby?"

"Haha! Wren Nocturne, a nursemaid! Preposterous! She should be reveling with the rest of us."

"Eh! Chike, be careful. Your wife may have left your heir to her death."

A round of laughter goes up around the hall. Kaito observes as Xipilli remains stern-faced and unmoved. Yes, it is quite uncharacteristic of Wren, as extroverted as she is, to turn a cold shoulder to the opportunity for drink and festivities, but the implication that Wren is incapable of caring for a child leaves a sour taste in his mouth. Atzi doesn't seem to appreciate the sentiment either, looking sadly down at her meal. Xipilli waits for the ruckus to die down before he speaks again.

"As Atzi just said, our baby sister is resting."

"Vulcan Xipilli," protests Tungsten Farqaad, a technomancer from Isis. "I know you would probably prefer to have one of your Derivan doctors tend to her, but perhaps it would be wise for her to undergo reintegration sooner rather than later to aid in her recovery. Dr. Faust here would be most honored to perform her procedure. Would she be interested in following through before our final assault? To see Mångata on the field would be a sight to behold after all this time."

"When and if my sister undergoes reintegration is not your concern, Farqaad."

A murmur goes through the congregated technomancers. Hushed speculation as the reasons why Wren may not choose to undergo reintegration.

"But she was a prodigy. Why would she not choose to have her tech systems reintegrated? Without them, she's practically an invalid."

"You heard the rumors, didn't you? About the necrotic magic that turned the tide of battle in Deriva? They say she was the source of it."

Kai focuses on the cup before him even as two Murasakan technomancers behind him converse back and forth about how Llywelyn died in a most heinous manner.

"I heard powerful witches can't integrate tech into their systems. Their magic is incompatible with it. The wild nature of it fights against the inorganic materials."

"It must be true then. Wren Nocturne can raise the dead."

"She sacrificed science for witchcraft?"

"I heard she sold her soul to an eldritch beast for the power to gain her revenge."

No one has spoken in any official manner of the happenings on the battlefield the day Wren returned. Or at the very least, no one has officially linked Wren with the undead that rose to demolish Seraphim's forces the day Llywelyn was killed, and the new Vulcan has been adamant about keeping his sister's name out of debriefs and tactical evaluations of the operation. Mirai, as the empress of Murasaki no Yama, has supported this endeavor, promising Kaito and Hikaru's silence on what they witnessed of Wren's powers.

But rumors spread like disease, and her return framed by such a spectacular display of dark magic, the most volatile seen in years, is too much of a coincidence for people not to talk, and with no one willing to risk the scandal that could unfold by formally silencing them, the rumor mill churns uninterrupted.

Unexpectedly, Fumiko, Kaito's aunt, is the one who stands up for the woman everyone is talking about. Fumiko, who at times barely seemed to tolerate Wren's inquisitive nature during the 247th Technomancer Trials, clears her voice and quiets at the hushed murmurings.

"Lady Wren has been a prisoner of war for the last year and half. It is to be expected that she would need time to recover before she even considers reintegration, and time spent with family is a balm to those who have suffered extreme trauma. Surely, with time and rehabilitation, Lady Wren will choose to have her tech reintegrated into her system. It is, after all, a privilege she worked hard to achieve."

Xipilli nods his head in thanks, and the room quiets.

"Of course. Of course!" agrees the Morrigan. "Such things do take time. Shall we offer a toast to Lady Wren's speedy recovery then? After all, I'm sure we will do well to have her blade on our side when we take down Pontiflex Catalan in a week's time."

"Hear, hear!"

The room drinks while Kaito's lips stay dry.

He walks the outdoor corridors of the Abbey to clear his head before he turns in for the night. He left the banquet early, uncaring for further social interaction. Skirting on the high of victory, most everyone drinks more than their fill in celebration of a battle they had hardly a hand in winning. It's enough to dry the wine the moment it touches his lips.

So instead, he strolls the outskirts of the fortress, passing several foot guards as he goes, when something pings his sensors. He's walked into the activation field of a spell. He draws his tanto as an ingrained precaution, curious as to who would be able to cast anything within the confines of a League nation stronghold. His sensors trace the energy to its source, somewhere on the top of the high walls surrounding the mansion.

He climbs his way up the wall with a series of jumps and handholds along the brick and mortar. Once he reaches the ramparts, he sees the spellcaster, perched on the edge of the rampant blue-green magic weaving around her in glittering spirals.

It's Wren.

It's always Wren, isn't it? She haunts his dreams, his thoughts; she chases away the quiet, and tears down his resolve. A part of him wants to hate her for it while another can't bear the thought of it disappearing again.

She sits with her legs dangling toward the ground below, not unlike how he found her in Shinka the night of their graduation. The night they danced together to distant music, the double moon eclipse making the blues in her hair shimmer. The night he kissed her for the first time. She'd been wistful, he remembers, from something dealing with her family, gazing up at the moons with unshed tears glistening in her eyes like gemstones. Only this time instead of staring up at the moon, she concentrates on a mirror glowing viridian in her palm. From where he stands, he can't make out anything on the glass, but Wren's expression is soft and open, like dew on a flower petal and terribly fond. He had forgotten just how peaceful such a look is on her, tender and beautiful, and he nearly strikes himself across the face for forgetting.

"Wren?"

THE HERMIT

The woman nearly jumps out of her own skin. Her hand closes and the green energy disintegrates into the ether, the mirror left devoid of power. She whirls around and spies Kaito with a flinch. The soft expression of before is gone. Surprise sparks in her face, but then she sees Amatsu in his hand, and even that is replaced with fear. Fear which quickly devolves into the same chilly smile she wore on the battlefield. Her indicia glows, the triskele on her forehead even more vibrant than it was four nights ago. Still, he wonders at the meaning of it on her body, wonders what he is dealing with, what kind of witch Wren has become.

"Ah, Miyazaki–sama. To what do I owe the pleasure of your sword glare?"

He scolds himself, sheathing his blade as quickly as he can. "I detected a magical presence and came to investigate."

"Ah, I suppose it would be natural for you to investigate even the most minor castings with a weapon in hand." She flings her legs up and over the rampart and jumps down into the courtyard, landing lightly on her feet, a small note on her lips to soften her descent.

Kai follows after her once he shakes off the suddenness of her movement.

"What were you doing just now?"

"I fail to see how that's any of your business."

Wren doesn't halt her retreat, making her way back to her and her siblings' rooms.

"Wren, this isn't a game."

"You're right, and even if it was, I'm not inclined to play."

Kai closes the distance between them, catches her by her amputated forearm, and spins her around. She stumbles as he pulls, their bodies colliding together. She makes a strangled sound in the back of her throat, and he glares down at her. "Answer the question, Wren. What are you doing using magic?"

"Fuck off!"

Wren shakes her arm wildly in his grasp, trying to throw him off. Her elbow lifts, nailing him in the chin hard enough stars burst in his eyes. He grits his aching teeth and stands firm even as she tries to kick his legs out from under him. He is so busy trying to keep ahold of her, he doesn't realize the shift in her body language, the difference between an angry, hissing cat and a frightened rabbit in a snare.

"Get off me!" she shouts.

The panic-tinged anger in her expression makes him immediately let go, dropping her arm as though burned. He backs up, wide-eyed and equally stricken by his own actions.

"Where do you get off demanding answers of me?! I don't answer to you. And I sure as hell don't owe you anything, so instead of hounding me for my 'misguided choices,' why don't you just leave well enough alone, disgusted with me as you are?"

There is a quiver to her voice and a glaze of tears over her eyes. What was he thinking, manhandling her like that? After everything he knows she's been through.

She curls her arms around her torso and staggers away. He does the only thing he can think of to try and rectify the situation.

"My Lady, please," he calls as withheld and controlled as he can manage through the slew of emotions crashing around in his chest. It is a small miracle that she stops and turns back to him. What she finds is Kaito, a prince of Murasaki no Yama, kneeling face down in the dirt before her. "This one acknowledges he has wronged you and begs your forgiveness. It was wrong of me to lay my hands on you without your expressed permission."

He hears her shift back and forth on her feet.

"Oh, stop it, Kai. You always take things too seriously." She gives an airy laugh, and he looks up at her. When she notices him looking, she gives him a close-eyed smile. It's forced, agonizing to look at. "Besides, I'm not worth dirtying your clothes over."

That isn't true, and he is about to express as much when she drifts away from him, quiet as the dead and equally forlorn. It is wrong, so terribly wrong. Wren should never be so quiet. She should be full of life and laughter and song. Never quiet as the grave. Quiet as the dead.

Kai rises to his feet.

"Wren—"

"Wren, there you are. I thought I heard shouting," Xipilli's voice cuts him off before he can properly start.

"It's fine, Xipilli. *Todo bien.*"

More lies. Do they not cease to fall so easily from her lips? Nothing about this is fine.

Xipilli looks over Wren's head and sees Kaito standing there, knees still dirty from the ground. The glare the young monarch sets on him is poisonous enough to wilt flowers, but Kai sets his spine and meets Xipilli's eye, impassive and unmoved by the older technomancer's renewed spite for him. A tense moment passes between the two men before Xipilli's dark gaze snaps back to Wren.

"Where have you been?"

"Around."

"You were supposed to be in the guesthouse. I was about to send Irene to look for you. It's not safe for you to be unaccompanied."

"Don't fret, brother. I won't disappear into thin air the moment I'm out of your sight."

Xipilli whirls around affronted as Wren ducks around him and disappears into the building with the barest of glances toward Kaito.

"Does the prince of Murasaki no Yama make a habit of harassing the family members of other houses?"

"I came across Lady Wren by happenstance."

"Happenstance, *mi culo.* The last thing my sister needs is you dogging her footsteps."

Kaito does not justify Xipilli's accusation with an answer, predictably angering the man further. The Vulcan pivots away with a huff.

"Consider this your last warning, Miyazaki. Stay away from my sister. You and your witch hunter family."

"Wren is not a witch."

The words fall unbidden from his mouth, and even Kaito can hear how falsely his protest rings.

"Is that why you and your brother stood as guard dogs in wait while she dealt with the man who destroyed our entire family? Because she *isn't* a witch."

"What are you going to do?"

Wren standing with a witch's athame in hand, witch's indicia on her brow, and magic curling around her fingertips as she prepares to exact revenge on a man who brutalized her.

"I'm going to destroy his soul."

The memory is heavy with newness, and Kaito can only turn away as disgust bubbles up, unwelcome in his gut. Xipilli shoots one more glare at him, the message there clear, before he too disappears back into the guesthouse set aside for the Derivan royal family. Kai lingers just a moment longer, as though trying to will some measure of understanding from the space Wren and her brother just vacated. Eventually, he relents and traces his way back to his own assigned quarters for a sleepless night.

They say denial is the first stage of grief, but what has he to grieve when Wren is right there, and he is the one who is too much of a coward to face her?

No. Kaito is no coward. He just doesn't know where to begin. How can he even begin to bridge such an insurmountable gap? A gap forged by war and trauma.

Present – 8th Day in the Month of Falling – 6:57 PM

The incessant buzzing of an alarm system going off pulls Kaito from his musings. Tomi's computational system picking up something on the network.

They lean their head out of the doorway to look at Kaito.

"I got a ping. It's your girl. She just scanned her ID at a Firefly communique in Xindi. Not sure what she's up to, though."

Kaito rises from his place in Tomi's living room.

The Hermit

"Then I take my leave. Thank you, Tomi."

Wren may be hours ahead of him, but it matters not. He knows which direction to go.

Golden banners, desert heat.

Mångata screams to life in her hands. Blood spilling. Someone taunting her.

"You truly are marvelous, my lady..."

A girl with Atzi's eyes. A weapon firing. Pain in her side. Kai shouting.

"Wren!"

Golden banners, desert heat, a spire that reaches for the heavens.

Kai before her. Raindrops trailing down his face as her life's blood seeps away.

She finally says the words, but they are too faint, too late, and too far gone to make any difference.

Golden banners, desert heat, and blood in the sand.

Wren Nocturne's Vision
8th Day in the Month of Falling, 1877 A.P.

5

THREE OF PENTACLES

WREN FIRST MET THE NAGI FAMILY WHEN she was eight years old. Vulcan Tlanextli and his family hosted Ebele's royal family in Cresta de Corail for a week to discuss very important matters of state.

Her dress, a horrendous blue-ribboned monstrosity picked out by her stepmother, had been unbearably itchy in the heat of the sun as she stood with her father, mother, stepmother, and siblings to greet their guests: Orisha Absko Nagi and his two children, Chike and Chiamaka. Chike was a year older than Xipilli and four years younger than Atzi; Chiamaka, on the other hand, was about a year younger than Wren.

While the grown-ups were busy negotiating back and forth over something entirely too trivial for an eight-year-old, Wren, ever the wild child of the villa, coaxed Atzi and Chiamaka to sneak away with her. They'd gone to the beach (It would have been a crime to waste such a day better spent swimming languishing in a frilly dress inside!) and laid out in the sun until Atzi's hair took on an amber hue and Wren's skin darkened to a deep olive shade. Chiamaka hadn't wanted to lie in the sun, but despite not knowing how to swim, she'd been happy to wade around in the shallows until her feet pruned up.

SONATA

It had been a fun week really, Atzi, Chiamaka, and Wren against Xipilli and Chike. Girls vs. boys, and the girls won almost every time even if the boys always claimed they let the girls win because it was the gentlemanly thing to do. Wren would then promptly kick Xipilli in the shins for being chauvinistic. It was all fun and games until Tlanextli, Elisabeta, and Absko announced the official betrothal between Chike and Atzi.

Atzi and Chike, who barely knew each other at the time.

Atzi hadn't taken it well. Neither had Xipilli or Wren for that matter. Atzi was their big sister. What right did Chike have to take her away from them?

It all turned out well in the end. It was years before the wedding took place, and over time, Atzi and Chike got to know one another bit by bit. Hell, at fifteen, Xipilli came back from his first technomancer trials calling Chike '*compadre.*' Neither boy passed that year, but out of their failure, the two became thick as thieves. A true bromance if Wren ever saw one; she used to joke with Atzi that maybe Xipilli should be the one to marry the prince to many a playful scolding.

Chike did eventually earn himself the title of technomancer, graduating in the same class as Wren during the 247th Technomancer Trials. Eleven of them passed that year: Wren, Xipilli, Chike, Yixuan, Selene, Jamar, Art, Anika, Irene, Bakura, and Kaito. Eleven shiny new technomancers, and within four years' time, nearly half of them would die by Wren's very hand. Wren Nocturne, the technomancer turned witch.

Wren travels with Mishka to New Osaka, a smaller town three hours south of Xīndì and closer to the Ebelean border. On her lightcycle, Wren follows behind Mishka's car, a little smart affair more cubelike than the sportier vehicles they pass on the road—economical with low environmental impact.

It's late by the time they arrive in a historic downtown district that couldn't have been further removed from Tokiseishu than a country town house. It's quaint and intimate in the way small towns tend to be. All of the businesses are local, family-owned, and each storefront has its own little pizazz of personality. But despite it barely being just past sundown, all of the shops lining the road are closed down, windows dark. The few bars and entertainment venues that should be open until at least midnight are shut down. Even the street food venders have all packed up despite the hour being early for such things.

Mishka parks parallel in the alleyway between two of the buildings, and Wren pulls up behind her to park the lightcycle. Taking her helmet off, Wren follows Mishka around the alley to a storefront that says:

"Madame Mishka—Firefly"

The windows are clear, polished glass, and the lettering is a vintage newspaper font in a gilded ink. The L'amore Lux crest decorates the front door. The hanging bell rings brightly as Mishka unlocks the door.

"There's a curfew. Quickly! Come inside."

A cold wind blows through Wren's skirts. The hair on her arms crawls, and Wren feels like she is being watched, but when Mishka ushers her inside, the sense dissipates, the shop door closing behind her with a frightened click.

Mishka's place of business is a mixture between a tea shop and a bookshop.

There is a check-out counter on the far side of the room, behind which is a floor to ceiling length rack of shelves holding colorful jars of various tea blends. She sees a jar for an earl grey, several green teas, and a few red teas as well. There's a jar label specifically "Sleep," another for "Focus," and a third for "Love." There are even a few specialty blends for arthritis and reproductive health, including a prenatal blend.

Lining the other walls are shelves of books—possibly for sale, possibly for perusal while her customers drink their teas. Fictional texts, old world stories, and romantic tales of loss and recovery. There are fantastic adventures about elves and hobbits and wizards and intergalactic travel. Many of the texts Wren would never have found on the shelves of most League mandated libraries or bookstores in her first life. Murasaki really has moved forward if they allow these kinds of novels to circulate. The only reason Wren read them as a child was because Freya procured them for her via Tlanextli's behest. She may not have been raised a princess, but there were certain things to be enjoyed as the daughter of Deriva's Vulcan. Granted, she isn't sure if Xipilli or Atzi read them, their governess far stricter than Wren's mother. Elisabeta would have thrown a proper fit if she'd caught her children reading anything that might have painted magic in a positive light.

Not all of the texts are fictional though. There's some non-fiction. Textbooks containing information about reproductive and sexual health, recipe books, music books. The collection also includes more salacious texts on how to give and accept love both physically and emotionally.

There is a raised stage on one side of the shop next to a reading nook. She might entertain in the space, singing for her patrons, or perhaps she invites others to perform while her customers enjoy their tea at the various tables elegantly dressed in soft linens and decorated with fresh flowers. And on the farthest side of the room, through a door sectioned off by a curtain and closed off from the rest of the shop for privacy, Wren would suspect there to be the makings of a more intimate space for Mishka to host clients, whether they be patrons seeking her company or women seeking her expertise as a midwife.

It's just the kind of place Wren would expect a Firefly of Mishka's age to own—the space of a woman who is likely retired from most of her previous duties, including teaching the next generation of Fireflies. Which begs the question, why did Mishka leave her place as a *saga* in Ebele?

"You have a beautiful set up," says Wren as Mishka makes her way behind the tea counter.

"Thank you, dear. Sir Lionheart was rather taken with it as well."

Oh?

"Did he stay here then?"

THREE OF PENTACLES

Mishka looks away from 'Atalia' to the ground, her cheeks darkening. How cute to see an older woman blush from receiving the affections of a younger man! "He was very kind."

Uh oh! Wren is willing to bet he was kind, and if Mishka's countenance is anything to discern from, he treated her like fine spun gold. How fascinating to find out her former schoolmate has an attraction for older women.

Handsome and smooth with words, Lionheart had been one of the most popular boys around during their trials. It earned him the reputation of a lady killer of sorts, breaking hearts left and right including one of Wren's friends. Poor Lily lost her virginity to him early on during the trials and had her heart broken by the careless boy when he had the audacity to express an interest in Wren right in front of her, not that Wren gave him a second glance. Back then, Wren—all of sixteen years of age—had been more preoccupied with earning her technomancer certification and keeping her big brother from giving everyone who looked at her the wrong way a black eye. Boys, and girls for that matter, had been of no consequence to her. Friendships were to be made, of course, but Wren hadn't been interested in, well, anyone really in a romantic sense.

Well, anyone who wasn't Kaito Miyazaki.

Though she's not quite sure her intentions were aimed toward romance back then. He'd just been too much fun to tease and annoy. It was such a fun game, seeing what sort of ridiculousness would get a reaction from him, and she always knew she had the incredibly stoic male's attention when his silvery eyes flashed with near-murderous intent. Like he wanted to strangle her but was too much of a gentleman to actually do so outside of a sanctioned spar. If she was being particularly infuriating, the little mole at the corner of his left eye would twitch. Xipilli used to tell her one day Kaito would hack into her system and deactivate her for being so annoying. But the joke's on Xipilli for that. Wren granted Kai access to her system voluntarily on their first mission together.

Wren's cheeks heat as the clicking of an appliance brings her back to the present.

"Would you like a cup of tea?"

The Firefly busies herself at a small stove turning on the tea kettle, and Wren hasn't the slightest idea how to behave. Atalia was a total stranger to her. What Wren knows about her begins and ends with an impersonal medical file. She knows nothing of her personality, her demeanor, what food she likes, what her favorite color is. Hel, Wren doesn't even know if Atalia was right- or left-handed, though she supposes Atalia had cut herself on both arms, so there's a possibility she was ambidextrous.

Whose idea was it to wear someone else's face again?

Oh, right... Hers.

"Yes, thank you."

The older woman is on edge. Tense like she is expecting something bad to happen. Considering six children have been attacked in the last seven days and the city council is looking to blame these attacks on her, she has a reason to be nervous. Wren reaches across the counter and sets her hand atop Mishka's.

"Mishka. It's going to be alright."

The woman shakes her head, unbelieving.

"Is there anything else you can tell me about the teens who were attacked? Maybe what exactly happened to them."

"Ata..." the woman starts to scold her, but Wren singsongs "Mishka" back, and she relents.

"Most of them are still in the hospital. They were all attacked in their sleep. Their families found them in the morning, blood dripping from their eyes. When they were rushed to the hospital, there was no evidence of an attack other than the bloody tears."

"If there were no injuries, why are they staying in the hospital?"

"Because they're catatonic. They don't react to the calls of their names, they have to be tube fed, some of them don't even so much as move. The first victim was only just discharged after being in the hospital for five days."

"Are they fully recovered?"

"He's fine. A little lethargic and unable to sleep soundly, the poor dear, but can't say I blame him."

Several days of total catatonia but once recovered, the victims are perfectly fine. At least, whatever is attacking them isn't deadly. Or rather, it hasn't killed anyone yet. Hard to tell what it might be with so little information, but a rogue vampyre would need to bite the victims, and a wraith would have outright killed the teenagers. When wraiths get agitated enough to do harm, they usually go full speed ahead into bloodshed, and wraiths don't typically target multiple children either, so that's out.

"Does he remember anything about the attack?"

Mishka shakes her head.

"Nothing. Just being unable to move. Gods! What if something happens tonight? My poor students."

"They'll be okay."

"I know, but what if it gets worse? The council already thinks I'm the one responsible."

"Even if something happens tonight, I'll be here to testify that you had nothing to do with whatever might happen."

"Then they'll just burn us both for witchcraft."

"They can't do that. Murasaki is a sanctuary for hexen."

"You think the laws will keep people from behaving irrationally? They're frightened, Atalia. And when people get frightened, they get violent. And the city council is not going to stop them."

And isn't that the even bigger problem with humanity as a whole? The town's paranoia already threatens to come down on Mishka's head, looking to find someone responsible for a phenomenon they can't explain. It's happened before. There are whole textbooks written about the phenomena, warnings against making the same mistake again. But mundane humans are nothing if not predictable when it comes to repeating history. Accusing someone of witchcraft has always been an easy means by which to justify killing someone. Whether or not the accused actually was a witch is usually the least of anyone's concern. Once a group of frightened humans decides someone is guilty, nothing short of a new target will divert their attention. They're almost worse than hexen and human+ in that regard.

It's why the League, for all that they are prejudiced against hexen of any kind, installed the rank of technomancer, setting up a rigorous vetting process to weed out anyone unfit for the title and privileges the rank can offer. Were there a technomancer on the case, they could hold dominion over the whole town, ensuring that a thorough investigation was carried out before any justice (or injustice) could be wrought. Hehe... If Kaito were here, he'd give one glowy-eyed glare to the city council and the cowards would probably piss themselves. This town is after all within Murasaki no Yama's borders, and Kaito's not just any technomancer, he's their crown prince. Oh, he might even turn on his sights, the lavender glow of his neural tech as intimidating as looking down the barrel of a loaded gun to a mundane.

But Kaito is miles away, and there are no technomancers here, the last one mysteriously summoned away. Thankfully, Wren is, in fact, one of the monsters that go bump in the night. It'll take more than a few humans with pitchforks to tie her up at the stake a second time. Being burned alive once is quite enough for her taste, thank you.

"Well, the best way to fend off fear is with knowledge. We'll find a way to make them see reason. After all, is it not in our training to calm agitated hearts?" she asks with a forced smile on her face. Judging from Mishka's expression, it probably isn't very convincing. She should spend some time in front of the mirror testing Atalia's expressions if she wants to play-act her emotions better.

But who is she kidding?

It's a ridiculous statement. Mishka knows it, and she knows it. No amount of Firefly training will make fending off an angry crowd any easier. In fact, it's probably one of her weakest points, more likely to scream herself hoarse or blow somebody up than actually calm anyone down. Unless you can frighten them into submission, angry mobs only listen to the loudest voice they agree with, and no amount of reason can penetrate the skull of someone who finds no value in logic.

Wren has quite the history with that truth. A girl can talk herself blue, bend over backward, possess every degree she could ever achieve, and still she'll be called into question because for some reason people still believe penis envy is a thing and women are too "emotional" to be logical. Hence, one of the main reasons she avoids crowds at all opportunities.

Well... that and her empathy.

"And who knows?" Wren continues. "Maybe we can work a little love magic and get them all to fall head over heels in love with you?"

Mishka's mouth quirks up in the tiniest of smiles at her joke. Well, at least, Wren's brand name humor still works.

"You always did excel at the more empathetic side of our arts."

She and Atalia have that in common then. Mishka turns around to assemble their tea service as the kettle begins to whistle. Two cups, a teapot, and a sachet of what looks like a red tea with rose hips and lavender in it. Such blends are good for calming nerves and inspiring sleep if Wren's Firefly training serves her correctly.

"Why did you leave Ebele?"

The question pops out of her mouth unbidden, and glass shatters as a teacup slips from Mishka's hands. Wren hurries to help clean up the shards, but Mishka stalls her.

"No, Ata, it's alright. My fault."

Wren stops her from bending over.

"No, I'm sorry. I didn't mean to startle you with that question. Let me."

At her insistence, Mishka relents, allowing her to pick up the shards.

"You didn't startle me. I just..." She folds into herself, uncomfortable. "You might not remember, Ata. You were so distraught I had to sedate you, but I saw what that wretched man did to you. I hoped Chiamaka would hold him accountable for attacking you, but when she dismissed you instead, throwing you out as though it was your fault an animal attacked you, I left."

An ugly memory surfaces in Wren's heart. "Animal attack" a fitting description.

"Oh, Mishka. Surely, you didn't have to—"

"Yes, I did. You think I could stand for one of my students being brutalized by a rabid dog? A dog that wouldn't be put down in the aftermath despite my witness statement for having cleaned you up. You were fourteen, for goddess's sake."

Wren had been seventeen when a pack of man-shaped dogs made her a spoil of war, and when she was eighteen, she made sure every last one of them paid for biting her. Only one escaped her wrath, protected by a system that put more value in a man's potential than a woman's suffering. Heh, she'd gotten him in the end though, him and the people that protected him.

"I tried to relocate my students elsewhere," Mishka continues, "but before I could make the motion through Lux, they dismissed me from court."

"And you've been here since?"

Mishka nods. "You know, I've never been much for small towns, but they have their charms, and this one is so close to the border that there's a good mix of folk around, though I can't say there's much by way of hexen. The council encourages them to 'move on' if they ever pass through. Since my arrival, I've seen them drive out three hexen families, two lycan families and a pair of djinn who sought sanctuary from Sekhmeti. The few that remain in the area live on the outskirts of town and keep as low a profile as possible, so it's pretty safe. Or at least I thought it was, but anyway, after what Thames did to you, I couldn't stay in Ebele."

Wren jolts, nearly slicing her palm open on a sharp edge. What Thames did! Thames is the son of a bitch who raped Atalia.

Donarick J. Thames, the current Primarch of the League and the son of Seraphim's spiritual former leader, Pontiflex Catalan— the man who thought it his divine right to laud over the whole of the League.

THREE OF PENTACLES

However, toward the end of the war against Seraphim, Donarick betrayed his father, killing the pontiflex and cementing the Alliance's victory. The decision earned him the title technomancer despite his previously failed examinations. From what Wren remembers of the man, he'd always been a rather subdued character. A loyal puppy, with no bite and even less of a bark, shadowing behind the other world leaders who appointed him a mere figurehead to replace his father in Seraphim. That was the last Wren really heard of him before her defection and self-imposed isolation. He hadn't even been present at Wren's trial by combat.

"Oh, darling, you've cut yourself."

The older woman drops down to grab Wren's wrist and holds a tea towel to 'Atalia's' bleeding forearm. Only the bleeding isn't coming from any glass mishaps. Damn it! The curse mark is bleeding again. That's the second time today.

"Oh, that's alright, Mishka. It's actually an old cut. I can take care of it."

"Nonsense," she declares, holding firm. The pale pink cloth turns red surprisingly quickly. "Here I have a first aid kit under the sink."

Mishka scrambles up to grab said first aid kit and leads Wren to sit at one of the tables. She unwinds the bandage from around Wren's wrist and starts cleaning the wound without comment. Mishka wipes the blood from Wren's wrist gently enough, but there is a strange look in her eye. She brushes the blood away again and again and again as though mesmerized by its ebb and flow.

"Mishka?" calls Wren.

The woman's head leans forward, nostrils flared, as she wipes the blood from Wren's arm again, lips parting.

The chime of the front door opening yanks her focus from the wound.

"Madame Mishka?" calls a sweet teenage voice as Wren draws her hand out of Mishka's grip. Whatever trance the sight of Wren's blood lulled her into has vanished into thin air.

"Eun-ji, it's close to curfew, dear. What are you doing here?"

A young lady of maybe fifteen or sixteen, wearing everyday jeans and a sweater, steps through the door. She has a sachet at her side, and she's left a bike next to the front door. She's pretty. A sweet-faced girl with black hair cut in a bob and chocolatey brown eyes, but despite her cheerful disposition, there are deep bags under her eyes. Purple bruises contrast sharply with her porcelain skin.

"Sorry, Ms. Mishka. My dad's run out of the tea for his arthritis, and I was hoping to pick some up before dark. I'm not intruding, am I?" asks Eun-ji, glancing at 'Atalia' warily.

Mishka smiles gently. "Of course not. This is an old student of mine. Atalia graduated with her Firefly certification from Tokiseishu. We were just catching up. Ata, this is Eun-ji. She's actually just begun her own Firefly training."

Wren, who is presently tying a clean bandage around her forearm, raises an eyebrow at that.

"Really?"

The teen bows to Wren, hands clasped before her.

"Yes, ma'am. I was inspired by what Madame Mishka did for my father. He's getting on in age, you see, and his joints give him so much trouble that he barely leaves the house. The doctors and biomechanics were considering joint replacements, but no one in this town has the kind of money that would have been needed for such a procedure, so we gave up hope on him ever leading a normal life again. But when Madame Mishka arrived in town a few years ago, she made him a tea that helped ease the pain a lot. He lives almost like normal now."

"That so?"

Eun-ji beams as she nods, but something about that doesn't strike Wren as right. If the man was suffering so badly from his ailments that biomechanics were involved in his treatment plan, then there is no tea in the world that could possibly give him an "almost like normal" life experience. That is, unless, it's not the tea helping his pain.

"Here, Eun-ji. I had a parcel all set for him."

The teenager rushes over to the counter, and Mishka checks her out.

"Thank you, Mishka. I'm so sorry to barge in like this, but my father is in great pain."

"It's no trouble, dear. Give your father my regards. Remind him: one cup in the morning. One cup at night."

"Yes, ma'am." Eun-ji bows to Mishka and, on her way out the door, shouts, "Nice to meet you, Ms. Atalia."

Wren waves as Mishka closes and locks the door behind the youth.

"Her father has arthritis?"

"Yes, some of the worst I've ever seen. It's just Eun-ji and her father. They don't have much, but they have each other. The tea really does help him. It surprises me how much."

Yes... It certainly is surprising that a simple tea would have the power to ease a man's crippling arthritis like that.

Mishka yawns, long and weary.

"Oh, sorry. I guess I'm more tired from travelling than I thought. You're welcome to stay up later if you'd like, but I think I need to turn in for the night."

"No, it's alright," says Wren. "You've had a stressful week. You should sleep."

"There's a bed through that curtain. It's where I normally tend to my clients, but with everything going on... Well, the sheets are clean in any case."

Without another word, Mishka makes her way out of the main shop and up the stairs to her personal quarters no doubt. As she goes, she holds her head as though suffering from a headache.

How curious...

Wren dreams of the past.

Of summer days in Deriva, playing in the sand with her brother and sister. Of singing lessons with her mother. Of sparring with Kaito by the lake in Shinka. Of making love to him. Of chasing Fae, still unsteady on her toddler feet, through fields of fireflies while Silje tried to bat them out of the sky. Of corpses rising at her command. Of painting the roses red. Of fire licking at her nerves until they blackened with death.

Then, she's dead again, nothing but an essence drifting beneath the waves of eternity. The tides pull her along, low tides and high tides, minutes and eons all wound up in one. It's peaceful. Simple. A lulling score of rising and falling hymns to keep her soul quelled.

But the silence is interrupted.

The witch has yanked her from the deep and tugged into sunlight, into her remade body, but just before she could settle in her skin, clawed hands sink into her chest. She tries to lift her arms, but they are stuck fast like she's been paralyzed. She can't even open her eyes.

Her unseen attacker pries open her ribcage, shoving itself inside. It claws its way into Wren's meridians like a worm, chewing its way through the fibers of Wren's being to nest in the heart of her magical network and leech her power from her.

"Give in..."

This thing thinks it can attack a witch who has seen the other side of death and win!

Wren fights back. Dipping into the chakra point at her lower belly, she unlocks the energy pooled there and releases it from its confines. The magic in her blood sings into overdrive—a vibrating aria in a razor-sharp key.

Wren's ghostly magic courses unchecked through her system, cold as death. Necrosis seeps into her own living tissue, self-inflicted and agonizing, like she's rotting from the inside out. The parasite shrieks as Wren's necrotic magic rips through her body, encompassing the darkly creature that so foolishly trapped itself inside her. Nowhere to hide, nowhere to go but out, and it scrambles its way to freedom in a panic. Wren screams awake as the creature rips itself out of her.

Wide-eyed and breathing hard, she all but falls out of bed, shakily crawling her way to the mirror on the far wall, desperate to see her own face after experiencing her own skin rotting from her bones.

'Atalia's' eyes close as she releases the glamour. The other woman's face fades, and when her eyes open, Wren Nocturne stares back at herself, curly blue-black hair, skin the color of sun-soaked wheat, and bright blue-green eyes glowing a bioluminescent green. Her witch's indicia pulses erratically at her brow. The triskelion—three interlocking spirals swirling away from each other at the center of her forehead, an old mystical representation of three parts of a whole—outright vibrates with the force of the magic she just unleashed on herself, and from this symbol, a cascade of wild script descends to glow a brilliant viridian along her face, neck, and arms.

Kaito's fingers had tickled slightly as they traced the patterns that shimmered down her back just the other night. He'd never done that in the past, too wary of her newfound nature to touch them so tenderly then. She exhales, touching her own face in relief, and laughs aloud at herself for how freaked out she'd been.

"Bleeding pixies! What was that!"

Well, she did not in fact turn herself into a walking corpse. Hell, she isn't even sure she has the ability to do that to herself, but she'd rather not find out. Melting flesh isn't a good look on anyone, and she's met her fair share of zombies. Thoth! She's made her fair share of zombies, and even the fresh ones are about as ugly as they are stinky.

The little room toward the back of Mishka's shop is clean and quaint. Along with the small bed she's just thrown herself out of, there is also a nice table, comfortable seats, a swanky Victorian bathtub complete with lion's feet, and a dresser/cabinet holding various accoutrements for tending to patrons: massage oils, candles, incense, and, ahem, accessories for the art of entertaining more carnal pleasure seekers, but there are other more mundane things including a supply of pens, paints, and ink.

One of Mishka's patrons is a rather talented artist, it would seem. A canvas sits unfinished with the initial rendering of Mishka's outline posed rather coyly on the bed: her hair tossed about her head and a silken kimono-like robe laid loose around her form, doing nothing to cover her. The only thing preventing the portrait from being obscene is the unfinished nature of it, the lack of detailing providing the illusion of a "safe for work" rendering. Wren imagines when it is done it will be quite the work of art. A very "not safe for work" piece of art, but maybe something that could be hung in an art gallery and admired.

There is no tech painted into the woman's skin. No augmentation seams or power nodes or even the tiniest of ports for upload and download ability. Either the woman doesn't have any technolyzation or the painter had not yet gotten to those details either.

The only thing Wren dislikes about the room is the complete lack of windows. Not even a frosted one. Not that Wren is claustrophobic or anything, but in the wake of her nightmare, it makes the space a bit oppressive, especially considering she has been enjoying the freedom of riding in the open wind most of the day.

Wren sags sideways onto the bed.

She sorely wishes she could simply lie down and go back to sleep. Why did she even bother to sleep in the first place? Wren and nightmares are bosom buddies, have been for years. It's just one of those things, really, and despite her independent nature, she's always slept better when sleeping next to someone, usually her sister or mother when she was a child. As an adult, when the rare opportunity arose, Kaito would share her bed. More of the time, in his absence, Fae and her feline familiar Silje slept with her those last few years of her first life—not that the toddler would have been a very fearsome opponent against any of Wren's night terrors, but having the little girl close kept a lot of Wren's anxiety at bay. Silje, on the other hand, was a frightful deterrent for any night-time demons.

The sense of being watched weighs heavy on her back, and even though no one is around—not even a lurking, lifeless soul—she has the distinct sense she is not alone.

She wonders if the burning woman is haunting about somewhere nearby. That might explain her sense of unease, but it's doubtful. Wren would sense the ghost's presence if she was, and the neat/cursed thing about being a medium is that ghosts need to work to hide themselves from her. If she is haunting Wren, she'll be back at some point, but for the moment, the faceless woman seems content to spook about elsewhere. At least, she hasn't shown up in her nightmares. Regular nightmares are one thing. Nightmares driven by restless, vengeful spirits are another thing entirely.

But this felt different.

Less like a nightmare and more like a psychic attack, and when she calls the bottle of water across the room to her hand via her telekinesis, it's like moving an overworked muscle. Which begs the question: if the teenagers around town have all been attacked in their sleep, did Wren's experience—whatever it was—qualify as one of those attacks?

Bang Bang Bang!!

A loud banging pulls Wren from her musing, and she barrels for the door.

A Firefly is more than a courtesan. She is more than an entertainer. She is more than any outsider can even comprehend unless they choose to look past the beauty and elegance of the Firefly before them.

She is an advocate for the voiceless, a balm for the injured, and a crutch for the broken. In this chapter, we will be looking at Fireflies known throughout history for their ability to affect change within political circles, and we will begin with the Firefly, Helen De Santos: the prophetess who turned the tide of war with a single cup of tea.

An Excerpt from *Love Bugs: Deus' Fireflies and their influence in World Politics*
By Madame Kali De Vrie, 1747 A.P.

6

FIVE OF SWORDS

W REN REINSTATES ATALIA'S GLAMOUR before throwing aside the curtain that blocks off her little corner alcove.

"Madam Mishka! Madam Mishka, please!!"

A middle-aged gentleman, frantically waving his arms, stands outside the shop door holding a young girl to his side—a girl bleeding profusely from her eyes. The girl is Eun-ji.

"Mishka!" Wren calls up the stairs as she goes to open the door and let the pair in.

No answer comes.

"Who are you? Where is Madame Mishka?"

"I'm a friend. One of Mishka's former students. What happened?"

"My daughter! She... Something attacked her. I—I don't know what to do."

"Bring her here."

Wren gestures to the backroom and helps the man carry Eun-ji to the bed. She's in a bad way. Her breathing is shallow and raspy, her ribcage straining to draw as much oxygen into her system as possible like something had been trying to strangle her to death.

"You said something attacked her?" asks Wren, checking the girl's vitals. There are no visible wounds, only the blood dripping from her eyes, tear trails of blood like she'd been crying the most harrowing cry that could be cried.

"Yes, I—I couldn't sleep, so I thought I would check in on her. When I went into the room there was this—this thing sitting on her chest. It hovered over her face like it was—like it was..."

The man trails off, too horrified to put words to what he saw. He might even be going into shock.

"Wait here, and don't let anyone in until I'm done."

"What are you doing?"

"Saving your daughter's life."

She pushes the concerned father out of the room despite his protests and turns her attention to the girl on the bed. She's dying, her lifeforce drained to almost nothing and her every breath a perfect imitation of a death rattle.

If Wren is going to save her life, she needs to do it quickly.

Wren finds the girl's ribcage nearly caved in as though something sat on her chest and bore down hard. Cthulhu below! Why didn't her father just take her to the damn hospital?! Wren sets her hands on the girl's brow, prodding for her lifeforce and realizes why he sought less scientific aid. Her essence is completely shredded, a splintered thing fluttering like a tattered flag in a storm wind at the center of her being, flighty and frantic and rapidly disintegrating.

Merde!

Wren chews on her lower lip.

Necrotic in nature, Wren's magic is not suited to healing. She can heal. Jessabelle's medicinal teachings were the first magical spells she learned outside controlling her telekinesis, but she gets along better with dead things.

Mere weeks after Jessabelle found her half dead and newly awakened as a witch, Wren picked up a dead bird and unintentionally brought it back to life. Sounds cool, sure, but undead things are terrible, empty husks of fabricated life, pale imitations of what they once were. A chirpy thing in life, the little sparrow should have sung for the sunrise every morning, but in the days after Wren reanimated the creature, it never made so much as a tweet. Eventually, Wren decided to put the poor thing out of its misery, giving Silje permission to eat the decrepit thing. The cat had been eyeing it ever since Wren brought it into the house. The bird didn't even try to fly away when Wren set it on the floor in front of the hungry feline.

Despondence... An old bedfellow of Wren's.

The months between Jessabelle saving Wren's life and her return to the warfront had been flooded with it. And a lot of the time, Wren felt like that bird, a dead creature coaxed back into some illusion of life. Unable to sing or fly or love, Wren drifted around the house like an empty husk of a person, capable only of existing. A shell without a ghost yet capable of breathing half-life into dead things.

But this girl isn't dead yet. Dying, yes, her breath stolen by whatever entity attacked her, but not dead.

Moving to the bathtub, Wren stoppers the base and turns both faucets on at full blast. She adds salt to the water, and before it can get too full, she swipes mint, eucalyptus, and baby's breath from Mishka's tea stores and sprinkles the mix of dried leaves into the water because not only are the herbs good for easing respiratory distress, but Dried Leaves = Dead Plants. Eun-ji is surprisingly light in Wren's arms as she manipulates her into the warm tea bath, not bothering to undress the teen.

Careful to keep the girl's airways above the water, Wren unravels the bandage at her forearm, reopens one of the curse cuts, and shoves the now bleeding wound into the water. The salt burns into the cut, but Wren grits her teeth and begins a songweave.

The notes sink into the water, vibrating under the surface and pulling the inner essence out of the dead foliage, creating glittering green ripples. Where Wren's most comfortable chord structures typically settle in the F♯ minor key signature, Wren forcefully retunes herself into a different major key, a comfortable A Flat. The sharps become naturals or flats and the unchanging tones soften, the whole of Wren's essence twisting into a gliding legato rather than its usual high-strung allegros. *Poco Agitato* is great for summoning the undead, enough energy to get the lazy bums up and kicking. But healing takes more nuance. Every note is as lengthy as the time it takes to coax a single cell into repairing itself, every held pitch dipped in vibrato to stitch sinew back together, the frequencies as important as the magic weaving through the score itself. And Wren, while practiced in both the musical and magical techniques, has never been at home in an adagio and her natural witchcraft doesn't lend to it either. One sour key and she could boil the water, crush the girl, or even drain the living essence out of her.

It takes time and a lot of concentration, mending the damage done. Splintered bones crack themselves back into place under her song's direction; bruises clear from lung tissue as Wren coaxes the pooling blood out. And the most difficult task, stitching together the torn fabric of her spirit into some semblance of whole.

For twenty minutes, the witch pours magic into the girl— twenty minutes of sustained output toward an aspect of witchcraft she is not naturally attuned to—but eventually Eun-ji draws a full unaided breath. Expanding properly once more, the girl's chest rises and falls in steady, life-sustaining, inhales and exhales, and the color returns to her face.

Fatigue blankets Wren's limbs as she closes the songweave with a lulling decrescendo. Heavy and weighted, she groans as she lifts herself from the floor, and the room spins before she drops back to her knees.

Ugh! Andale, Wren. Si, se puede. This girl still needs your help.

Taking a clean cloth, she dabs the blood from the girl's face. Bloodstained tears. What could have caused that? She's heard of a banshee's scream causing the capillaries to burst in the eyes of their victims, but Eun-ji's eyes are unharmed, and her mental-scape is scraped up, like something was feeding on her thoughts or emotions. Could be something vampyric? But vampyres, even psychic ones, have to break skin to feed on their victims.

Five Of Swords

Mishka said that whatever had been attacking the teenagers hadn't managed to kill any of them yet, so why is this attack on Eun-ji so much worse than the others?

Wren reaches for the incense on the vanity and lights several sticks at once, using the smoke to further clear and stabilize the psychic damage done to the girl's lifeforce. It may seem superfluous compared to the blood and music and immense outpouring of Wren's power to piece the child back together, but the oldest practices survive for good reason. After a good smoke cleanse, she'll be able to sleep off the bad juju. A longer sleep than normal, sure, but it will be the slumber of the living rather than the eternal sleep of the dead. For now, at least. Here's to hoping whatever attacked her doesn't return.

Wren goes to speak to the father.

The man sits wringing his hands at one of the tables. He rises the moment he sees 'Atalia.'

"Is she alright? Is she going to be okay?"

"She's not in immediate danger anymore."

"Thank heavens..." The man sighs, slouching in on himself. "Eun-ji, she's—she's all I have left."

Wren leans heavily against the counter. The man's relief is enough to make her want to sag into a nearby chair herself, but now's not the time.

"Mr...?"

"Keng."

"Mr. Keng, do you have any idea what attacked Eun-ji?"

He pales, and there it is: fear. Cold and sickly, it coils around his heart, like a python winding itself around and around the beating organ in an attempt to paralyze it.

"No. I—I've never seen anything like that before."

"What did it look like?"

"I didn't get a good look at it, but it looked like a hunched-up person, almost like... like an old woman, but it can't have been. It glared at me with glowing white eyes and then disappeared out the window."

Wren hums in understanding. So definitely not a vampyre. They're ageless after all, and people past a certain age don't handle the shift very well.

"Do you—do you think a witch attacked my daughter?"

Wren's mood darkens. Always with the witch paranoia!

"Witches don't typically smother teenagers in their sleep."

The man flinches. Wren's voice is probably a bit darker than necessary, but she won't apologize for it. Irrational fears gets innocent people killed.

"But it looked like an old hag. Just like hexennacht decorations with hooked noses and pointed hats."

"Decorations are decorations. Gimmicks drawn up to make a joke of something people are afraid of. They're not representative of the real thing."

And besides, "old woman" does not equate to witch. Seriously, whose idea was it to portray grandma as dangerous? Oops! Sorry, can't go over to your abuela's today. You might come back with a wart on your nose and boils in your knickers.

"But—"

She is *so* not having a discussion on the wrongful portrayal and appropriation of a whole group of people by century–old propaganda right now.

"Look, your daughter needs to be taken to the hospital."

"The hospital?"

"Yes," she snips, willing herself to simmer down. "She needs medical observation and a place warded from malevolent beings. Whatever attacked her might come back, and it would be best if she were someplace where someone will be checking on her regularly. She won't survive a second encounter if it comes back."

The man swallows. "I—I understand."

"Do you have the means to take her there?"

He shakes his head. No car. Pretty common in a small town like this. People don't have much need for vehicles when everything is easy enough to get to via bicycle.

"Why don't you sit with her? I'm going to check on Madame Mishka. Perhaps we can use her car."

"She never came down."

"She was really tired from our trip. It's possible she just slept through it."

The man looks skeptical, but his daughter's wellbeing far outweighs anything else on the man's mind, so he goes easily enough, moving slowly with arthritis. That he got Eun-ji here on his own is a miracle unto itself.

Wren makes her way up the stairs, calling for Mishka as she goes. Something's off. Despite what she said to Eun-ji's father, there is no way the woman could have slept through the banging the man made trying to get into the shop. The volume had been enough to get Wren scrambling to her feet in moments. Never mind both his and Wren's shouts of her name.

The topmost stairs creak, and Wren winces at a particularly loud groan. She remembers sneaking down to the kitchens with Atzi as a little girl. The last time was the day their father announced Atzi's betrothal to Chike. Her big sister had been so upset, that not even a promise of her favorite sweets could coax her out of her room. Wren, then eight years old, had faked a stomachache to get her sister to come out and take Wren to the kitchens. They'd been caught by Wren's mother after the stairs gave voice to their super-secret mission. (How is it that stairs, perfectly silent during the day, become so noisy at night? Are they lonely perhaps? Calling for more visitors at the slightest touch of a companion? Shouldn't they be more grateful for the visitor they have?)

Freya hadn't scolded them though. Instead, Wren's mother took both girls down to the kitchens herself and fixed them each a cup of cinnamon sweet milk. Freya wiped away Atzi's tears and spoke quietly to both girls about love and marriage. Wren hadn't been particularly comforted by the conversation, but it made Atzi feel better.

The door to the second-floor apartment hangs ajar, practically drifting open for her as she approaches, which wouldn't be odd if the deadbolt weren't drawn.

Mishka's living space is a quaint one bed/one bath floor plan, but the place is not in the shape Wren would have expected for a woman like Mishka: dirty dishes piled in the sink, a few days' worth of unwashed laundry thrown haphazard on the floor right next to the hamper, and various trinkets scattered across the floor. When Wren flicks the light switch, nothing happens, the bulb above her head blown out, shards of glass glinting in the light of the streetlamp burning through the blinds.

The TV is on—a mid-sized monitor anchored to the wall across from a small sofa. The glow washes over the apartment in flickering blues and reds as a movie plays quietly. Wren doesn't recognize it, some family action-comedy by the looks of it—the family cat pouncing to the rescue to save a little boy from a rat seeking world domination. Wren pads her way into the apartment, avoiding the debris on the floor as best she can, and makes her way up the hallway.

The bedroom is not in much better condition. The sheets are rumpled, pillows thrown on the floor, empty teacups scattered on the nightstand. The window is open, the drapes swaying in the night breeze.

A book lies open on the bed, a journal of sorts with a pen left discarded in the sheets. Mishka was writing before bed, it would seem, but the Firefly in question is nowhere to be found.

Wren flips through the pages and finds something about curses written in scrawling cursive.

> It's been a week since the first of my students fell ill after being attacked in their sleep. I don't know what to do. I feel like I've been cursed. Maybe I'm paranoid, but I'm so tired. My usual sleeping brew isn't helping, and I've adjusted the recipe three times to no help. I go to sleep just fine, but I wake up more tired than ever.

Sleeping problems, thinks Wren as she continues reading the woman's trembling cursive.

I ran into an old student in Kindi. I shouldn't have let her come here. What if something happens to her, too? She's been through so much already, and she was bleeding from a cut on her arm. It looked kind of like... I don't know what came over me, but it was like I could hear the pain in her blood.

Goddess, the things that girl has been through.

But that's never happened before. I can't sense someone's pain. I'm no empath. I'm not even psychic! But it was like I could taste her suffering just by looking at the blood. I wanted to... I wanted to drink it. Not the blood. The pain.

Wren flips back a few pages to find a recipe. The notes look suspiciously more like that of a sleeping draught rather than a tea brew. Several places are scratched as though the woman had been playing with measurements and ingredients.

~~½ tbs~~ ¾ tbs of lavender
¼ tsp of chamomile
⅔ tbs of valerian root
~~1 tsp of dried skullcap leaves~~ Too dangerous. The mayor was asking if I sold it in any of my teas. I said I didn't and burned the rest of my supply. Sub with magnolia bark.
2 drops of blood
½ cup of absinthe
~~1 cat whisker~~ (I don't have a cat. Will have to substitute or take in a stray. I got the whisker for the first brew. Procured from the Withers family. They have four cats, but it didn't help, and I can't keep pretending to visit their new baby. The child is perfectly healthy, and the mother is

recovering well. At least, they haven't been plagued by whatever this strangeness is.)

Underneath the ingredients are varied instructions for boiling and steeping and how much water to add, but below all of that and added in bold lettering:

Nightshade

No measurement, no quantity, not even a cautionary note to the extremely toxic nature of the plant, just "Nightshade" written in deep black ink, a recent addition to the recipe.

There are words written in the side margins as well. Neither Ebelean nor common, the words are written in Hexen.

So, Mishka is a practicing witch, a low powered one but a witch nonetheless. Wren suspected as much. The woman has probably been keeping herself off League radar her whole life, and as a Firefly, she would be able to hide right under the noses of the very people who would persecute her.

Smart woman.

Wren looks at the teacups on the nightstand and picks one up for inspection. There are still dredges in the bottom of the cup. A potion brew, the frothy, purple liquid drips with magic. Mishka's magic. The cup is fresh. The woman probably drank it after bidding 'Atalia' goodnight. Between the recipe and the magic lacing the cup, the addition of nightshade into the mix could've made the drink potent enough to kill her. The woman should have been down for the count having drunk such a mixture.

Yet, there is an empty bed and empty apartment to go with a sleeping draught that should have, by rights, downed a horse.

"Screeeeeech!!"

Wren slams face first into the mattress as sharp talons latch onto her back. High-pitched wailing rings in her ears as her eyesight blackens. A gnarled hand yanks her head back by the hair, and Wren pushes backward, a telekinetic lash of power knocking her attacker away.

FIVE OF SWORDS

"Argh!"

Wren whirls around. Mishka crouches on the floor, coiled and ready to strike, but it isn't exactly Mishka she's looking at. The older woman's face has aged, cracked, and wrinkled like an ancient mummy, a crooked, hooked nose and sunken eyes blackened to coal. Her long pure white dreadlocks have mangled, whole chunks of them falling from her skull. Warts decorate her hands, and her rich dark skin, the color of calla lilies, has shifted to this yellowing-green tone.

Green like disease. Yellow like infection.

Wren's viridian tendrils of magic hold the hag-like Mishka long enough for her to regain her footing.

"What are you?" she demands, only to receive a snarling answer, the witch's teeth glinting red in Dei's crimson moonlight. She struggles against Wren's snare before grasping one of Wren's psychic threads and yanking. It severs from Wren's magical core, and electricity shocks through Wren's system, like having a string tugged from her body. She tumbles sideways, catching herself on the nightstand. Teacups tumble to the floor, shattering. There is a wet slurping sound, and Wren looks up to find the monster sucking down her magic like a limp spaghetti noodle.

What the hell! This thing eats magic. What sort of creature eats magic?

It lunges for her. When Wren rolls out of the way, its head meets the table leg. Wren kicks it twice in the face. It shakes itself, and on a third strike from Wren's heel, Mishka's features, a beautiful, wise woman, return to normal. Wide brown eyes imploring her, struck through with a mind-numbing fear.

"Help me..." she chokes out, convulsing in on herself as the hag's mask returns.

Mishka is still in there. Mishka is trying to fight this thing. Something inside her which feeds on magical and psychic energy using her body as a host like some magical parasite.

And the pieces fall into place.

Wren sings a lure requiem as the creature scrambles her direction—a haunting yet insistent melody she composed to call spirits to her. Ghosts are everywhere after all, and if Wren can't fight this thing with her own chaos magic, she can summon the dead to fight for her.

'Mishka' dives at her.

She wrestles with the hag, tumbling up and over. They smash into the furniture. Wren rolls over the shattered glass on the floor. The shards prick her skin, and blood seeps from the fresh cuts. Good. Fresh blood calls the dead faster.

But it also sends whatever monster, creature, or netherbeast currently infesting Mishka's system into a frenzy.

It wasn't Wren's blood that made hunger shine in Mishka's eyes earlier in the parlor. Not exactly, anyway. It had been the magic in Wren's blood, more concentrated than Mishka's, garnering the parasite's attention.

Her nightmare earlier hadn't been a nightmare at all. It had been an attack, an attempt to invade Wren's body. But it miscalculated, returning to its original host after its failure and commanding Mishka into the night to feed, no doubt weakened from Wren's subconscious defense.

Hence the attack on Eun-ji, the last person to come into contact with Mishka.

Now, it tries again to get to Wren, whose magical reserves are depleted from keeping the teenager alive. And Odin's eyepatch! Is it strong!

Wren ends up on her back. Claws dig into the apex of her shoulders as the hag sits on her chest, heavy as a boulder, to smother Wren into submission. It crushes the air from her lungs and the notes of Wren's song drift away with the wind. Fighting for freedom, Wren scratches the beast's face, her sharpened nails tearing the skin clean off. (*Sorry, Mishka...*) The creature roars in her face, spittle flying into her eyes and mouth. Foam froths around its lips and gums, like a rabies infected canine.

The first ghost, a seemingly unobtrusive ball of light, comes wailing through the window to lift 'Mishka' off Wren's chest. Her airway cleared, Wren picks up the requiem once more, directing the newly arrived spectre into holding her attacker still. The spirit hums with her, a green glow beginning to pulse at the edge of its shape as it harmonizes with her.

The entrance of the ghost panics the creature, its movements becoming uncontrolled thrashes trying to ward away the spirit as a second spectre joins the first, a familiar fiery visage.

The burning woman was nearby, and now, despite her previous hostility toward the songstress, she's come to Wren's aid. The stronger spirit latches onto 'Mishka.' The hag screams as spiritual fire snakes around her body. She smacks herself trying to snuff out flames that cannot be put out by any means in the waking world. Together, the two ghosts wrangle the possessed witch into a corner, giving Wren a clear field.

Wren opens her empathy and focuses her psychic surge not on Mishka herself but the inner workings of her magical network, specifically on the parasite which has wound itself so tightly within the woman's meridians Wren can barely distinguish where Mishka's witch magic begins and the parasite's ends. Black, viscous, and slimy, it clings to her like a cephalopod, suckered to the barely-there gleam of the Firefly's silvery essence.

But there is something tangible Wren's empathy can target: the pain. Stolen agonies circuit around the parasite in quantities greater than any single person could handle, and it's this mass of teenage angst Wren zeros in on.

Wren shreds through the displaced anguish, stealing its essence and prying the parasitic beast out the other witch's lifeforce. Incorporeal scalpels perform a psychic surgery, albeit her blades are not the most precise, and the creature's constant wiggling makes her nick Mishka's network on more than one occasion. It fights against her, squirming like an insect away from her magic, but when Wren's viridian lifeforce slashes open its side, it shrieks, tearing itself from Mishka.

Mishka's body drops to the floor, a puppet cut from its strings, and Wren tumbles backward as it evacuates itself completely from the woman's lifeforce to rip through Wren's synapsis in a last-ditch effort to save itself. It swims up Wren's magic and barrels into her chest, latching on with slim, string-like tentacles and digging into her flesh to dip into her stronger aura.

Just like in her nightmare, it tries to burrow its way into her hearth and take over. It drills into her heart chakra and finds the lock that Wren keeps on all her pain, all her trauma, all her suffering.

"Stop it!"

Tendrils oozing void pry her open and flay her alive. Painful memories flash through her: Her mother dying. Her father and stepmother murdered. Being a prisoner. Becoming a witch. Losing everything/everyone she ever cared about. Meeting Death and being rejected by even that eternal. Being resurrected. Being shunned. Heartbreak. Grief. Betrayal. Having what little she regained taken away again in banishment.

The pain-eating beast gluts itself on her every hurt. It whispers to her. It can take away her anguish. It can calm her storm. It can ease her torment. All she has to do is let it in. Let it take over from here. She's done enough. Shouldn't she have the chance to rest? It can give her that. It can give her peace.

Fire pulls her from the dream. A burning circlet around her arm, the faceless woman wraps a charred hand around her wrist. It jolts her awake like a solid slap across the face.

Wren knows what it means to erase a person's grief, and those memories, as painful as they are, they're hers, damnit!

"Innsiden!" she growls, and the spirits converge on her. Wren amplifies the necrotic element of her magic, commanding the two ghosts into her body.

Wren's teeth grind, her head exploding with noise as the two entities wedge their way into her psyche. One of them yanks the parasite from her meridians, and the other shreds it to pieces before it can dig its way deeper. Wren puts her hands over her chest, tangling her hands in slime, and physically pulls it from her core.

Electric pain screams through her nerve-endings, angry and desperate and afraid, and Wren pulls her aches back into herself, tucking back into their safe box and leaving the creature starved. It panics, rapidly extracting itself from her network.

Before it can completely leave her, Wren catches it in a cage of necrosis, death and rot and ash all threaded together in a gleaming emerald spiderweb. It bangs against her threads, a cornered animal in a trap, and when it tries to devour her magic, it can't; Wren's resolve too strong to overcome.

Wren struggles with the parasite until it sits in her hand. The netherbeast—and it is a netherbeast. It has to be. Its borderline existence between tangible and intangible is too classic an example for a creature from a different plane of existence.

It's ugly to look at—an amorphous blob of void with an uncountable number of tentacles, kind of like a jellyfish but it keeps shifting its domed head from top to bottom along its oral armaments. Pulsing and globulus with a strange viscosity atypical of most netherbeasts, its physicality is that of jelly. Wren could probably touch if she wanted to. Unlike Wren's magical essence, which is more light and mist than anything else, this residue is nigh-on completely tangible. As if its appearance wasn't nasty enough, gluttony drips off the thing in rivulets. Hunger, cloying and rabid, pulses hot at the center of the beast's focus, and within its depths, she can feel Mishka's magic swirling in its gut, pieces of the witch it managed to suck down after it latched onto her like a magical hookworm.

Parasitic little thing, indeed.

The netherbeast writhes as Wren's magic courses through it, its outermost aura withering to nothing. And just as she would any physical parasite, Wren crushes it. The humming strings collapse in on the parasite; Wren's vibrant green energy strangles it to death. The jellyfish-like netherbeast dies with a hiss and a wet squish. Magic to kill magic.

Wren stuffs the vile corpse into the empty teapot on Mishka's vanity and wards it with a piercing high note that'll peel the skin off someone's bones if they so much as touch the pot. As she does this, the two spirits who came to her call hover in front of her. She bows her head to them.

"Greetings now and parting forever," she hushes in the language of the dead, but only one of the ghosts evaporates from her sight, leaving behind naught but the faintest of chills and just a touch of ectoplasma to dissipate in the air. The second, the burning woman, shrieks silently at her before whooshing out the open window, breaking teacups and saucers on its way out.

Anubis, Hades, Hel, and Enma, please explain to her what she did to merit the anger of such a ghost. But then why did she even bother to answer her call in the first place?

Wren sits heavily on the bed just as a spine-chilling rasp echoes from the opposite side of the room. Mishka, once again the sage-like and beautiful, lies dying, straining for air.

"Mishka!"

Wren stumbles her way to the woman, already reaching for some semblance of power to feed into the other witch's damaged meridians, but it is a folly. The other witch's system is so damaged, Wren's power leaks right back out like water through a broken pipeline.

"Ata..."

Mishka's voice is withered and airy. Her eyes open, sluggishly. They shine their normal, warm brown, but the shade brings no comfort. Mishka looks at Wren from the cradle of the songstress's arms.

"Hold on, Mishka. Please. Don't die. Not like this."

The woman's head shifts from one side to the other, and she mouths the words, "My heart recognizes yours."

The witch's thank you.

Before Wren can respond, the light fades from the woman's eyes.

Democracy and Bureaucracy within the League:

While each League country has free reign to establish its own governments and method of order (i.e., Murasaki no Yama's Technocracy, Deriva's Constitutional Monarchy, Seraphim's former Theocracy), each country must answer to the Technomancer Council and Primacy.

Established in the wake of Seraphim's defeat by the Alliance, the TCP is the ruling body of the entirety of the League, and at the head of the council is the Primarch—a technomancer elected by the majority vote of the current technomancer roster. The Primarch holds absolute power over every certified technomancer in the League.

Excerpt from *Systems of Government in Deus*
Heather Ables, 1872 A.P.

7

THE MOONS (PART 1)

9th Day in the Month of Falling – Xīndì – 8:23AM

"**K**AITO, WHERE HAVE YOU GONE? WE haven't heard from you. Renki is worried. He—he keeps asking questions about Lady Wren and your relationship, and I don't know what you expect me to tell him because Hikaru sure as hell isn't saying anything. The boy needs answers, and I don't know how long I can keep him in the dark before he takes off searching for them himself."

Kaito deletes his aunt's harried message after listening to it in full. Fumiko's concerns are not unfounded. He knew Renki would have questions. It's why he left a holographic message on the boy's servers before leaving Tomi's bunker.

I know you have a lot of questions about my behavior as of late but know that bringing Lady Nocturne to Snowfall was not a decision I made lightly. Despite what the stories might say, the Songstress of Lorelei is someone who has long held my trust and would never do you harm. There has been a misunderstanding concerning Lady Nocturne, and it is imperative that I rectify it. In the meantime, listen to your uncle and great aunt. Maintain focus on your studies. Your first trials are just months away. Do not let any confusion you may be struggling with now cloud your goals. When Lady Nocturne and I return, we will answer your questions together. I promise you this.

Be Safe and Keep Strong,
Your Tousan

He knows Renki has seen his message. AYA reported to him the moment the projection finished playing. If the teen does have a response or question to Kaito's message, he hasn't replied back with said response. Not to say he isn't expecting one. He fully expects the teen to push back against being left in the dark, but Kai is balancing on the edge of a knife. The sooner he can track down Wren the better

Kaito rides through the night to Xīndì, the sleepy town just rising to begin the day. There is evidence of a festival having taken place. Various business workers take down their decorations, and yawning festivalgoers are just now making their way home from a night spent in frivolity.

But something feels off.

The air of the festival grounds is thick with tension, and the people who see him, most of them unaugmented normals, cower at the sight of his augmentations. It is an atypical response. Most people see a technomancer and scramble for a closer look, unable to get close enough even if they manage to touch him, but not this town. These people seem terrified of him. He scans for the source of their discontent, and he finds it in pieces: broken signage along the walkways, a fallen tree branch, and one of the cars boasts a shattered front window.

What happened here?

AYA has been monitoring the news broadcasts for him in case 'Atalia' should appear on any headlines, but nothing has cropped up. There have been no storms in the area, and stories of magical mayhem would make the national news in a matter of minutes, especially in the wake of a festival night. But then again, if whatever incident last night involved hexen havoc, would not the townspeople be thrilled by his presence?

L'amor Lux banners sway gently in the breeze, fine spun silk trimmed in gold and silver. This would be where Wren registered her ID. To what end though? He hopes he can find out quickly. He parks his cycle and dismounts, commanding AYA to scan the area for signs of Wren, magic, or anything suspicious as he approaches.

"Blessed Waking, good sir."

The grand dame greets him at the entry point of the park, her greeting sincere if a little strained.

"Madame," he greets. There is a bustle of activity taking place in the enclosed garden. People moving back and forth, loading vehicles, and tearing down finely set up spaces for relaxation and enjoyment.

"I'm afraid we've missed the opportunity to entertain you. We are a travelling sparkle of Fireflies. Now that the festival is over, we will be moving on."

Kaito nods in understanding, watching as one of the men controls a droid to pack up the luxurious fabrics of his tent. The robot rolls and stores the plush carpets and sturdy linens within its barrel shaped body before rolling over to a parked caravan. Kai's eyes narrow, however, when he sees charring at the center of the main tent.

"I am not here as a patron, madame. I am looking for someone: a Firefly who passed through here late yesterday afternoon."

He activates a holo-projection of Wren's glamoured self, and recognition immediately alights on the woman's features.

"Ah, Miss Vaishi. Yes, she used the communique and then continued on her way."

"Would you happen to know where she was heading?"

"Is there a reason you are looking for her? If she's done something wrong, I assure you no one here had any part in it."

That's a peculiar response...

"She's done nothing wrong, I can tell you that, but I am invested in her safety. Please, if you have any idea where she went or where she is going, I would greatly appreciate you telling me."

The woman seems to take his response with a grain of salt. "She met up with another Firefly named Mishka."

"Mishka?"

"Yes, Mishka Dara. I believe Atalia was Mishka's student at one point. They left for New Osaka together."

New Osaka, huh? Just a few more hours south in the direction of the border. What are the chances Wren spent the night there? If that's the case, he can catch up with her today if he hurries on.

"Thank you for your time, madame."

He turns to leave.

"You're a technomancer, are you not?"

Kaito pauses. "That is correct."

"Another technomancer came last night asking about Atalia."

Steel grey eyes narrow.

"Do you know who they were?"

The Firefly shakes her head.

"I'm afraid not. He was not so amiable to conversation as you, and when I refused to tell him anything of her, he threatened to carve my face open."

"Do you remember what he looked like?"

"Well, he wore a mix of Seraphim and Sekhmetian colors, but his augmentations were more akin to yours than any Seraphim I've ever met. Shorter than you, shaved head, more barrel shaped. He used these strange energy-coated knives."

Not knives. Kunai. Tanaka, the technomancer who helped rescue Faust from Snowfall's dungeons. Tanaka's kunai blades may be small in comparison to typical technomancer weapons, but his integration of anti-magic technology into the blades is nearly perfect. Tanaka's kunai were capable of impaling a magic-user and dispelling any existing magical auras around them. He can also use them to hack into a robotic system, though Kaito is unfamiliar with how that works as far as the integrated tech in the weapons.

THE MOONS (PART 1)

"What did he do when you refused to answer his questions? Did he hurt you?"

"No, I activated my distress beacon before he had the chance. My defense droid managed to chase him away, but they caused quite a bit of destruction to the festival grounds in the process, and my poor droid will need tending to by a mechanic before I can start taking patrons privately again."

So that's why the townsfolk seem so wary of him. "Was anyone injured?"

"Nothing beyond scrapes and bruises, but these people aren't used to posthumans. They have one adept in town, and she has no visible augmentations other than her mechanical leg."

"It would seem I am doubly in your debt. Thank you for this information."

"You're welcome, and I do hope you find your charge, sir."

He offers the woman a final bow before turning back do his cycle

So, Tanaka is tracking Wren. The question is how he managed to trace her ID scan through Hikaru's defensive coding. Alternatively, is he acting on his own or at the behest of someone else?

14 Years Ago – 12th Day in the Month of Planting 1863 – **The Abbey, Aighneas**

Days pass, and Kaito catches glimpses of Wren's presence: the shine of blue-black hair flitting between the guest houses set aside for the Derivan envoy. A song on the wind that fades away the moment he turns to it. Visions of wild green eyes disappearing the moment he finds them in the corridors. The light familiar footsteps of a ballerina dancing away from him in avoidance or fear, or worse, shame.

SONATA

She seems to flit in and out of existence, a presence everyone is cognizant of, but no one truly sees, save for her brother and sister. Even Chike, for all that he is her brother-in-law, tells him that he has not seen Wren in person since her first day at the compound. And in every instance that he catches sight of Xipilli or Atzi, he seeks out her form beside them with a desperate need to know he didn't hallucinate Wren's return, but she's never there.

Were he a more irrational person, he might wonder if this newfound obsession with peering into shadows, this constant looking for someone who may or may not be there is the result of a curse or spell she has placed on him, but he is not an irrational person. He knows how to dispel such mediocre curses on his own, first of all, and secondly, defenses against them are hardwired into his system. Besides, curses require physical application, either a poisoned gift or an object planted in his vicinity, and Wren has been nowhere near him or anyone for that matter.

The first time Wren appears before anyone other than her siblings for longer than a fleeting second is at a tactical meeting about the final siege against Vatidome, the capital city of Seraphim where Pontiflex Catalan lives.

When Wren appears, the idle conversation ceases, despite the fact that everyone has been murmuring about the woman on the edges of civil conversation since her return. Taking in the former technomancer, she seems strained and on edge. She doesn't speak a word, listening but unfocused as the discussion resumes, until her brother booms for silence from those assembled so she can speak. She is there at her brother's behest to deliver important intelligence about Seraphim consorting with witches. Apparently, the Pontiflex has been releasing incarcerated witches from captivity in exchange for their services to bring down the rest of the League.

"They've also been recruiting in the wilds around Lorelei and other neutral zones. Garnering support from hexen and posthuman outcasts to fuel their war. It's why their forces never seem to diminish."

THE MOONS (PART I)

She keeps casting wary glances at Rameses and Farquaad as she speaks, as though the two men pose a threat to her, and when Rameses addresses her, her jaw tightens.

"This is extraordinary information, milady," proclaims Rameses. "But Seraphim coordinating with hexen? The very basis of their society opposes such things. How can you be certain your intelligence is correct?"

Wren's response is as deadly venomous as a serpent's bite. "I've seen it."

The same menacing aura, oppressive and suffocating, which clung Wren the night she killed Llywelyn re-emerges in response to Rameses' questioning, and the athame at her hip—Lacuna, she called it—drips with necrosis in response to her rage. When she rests her hand on its hilt, her viridian aura whips around like an angry ghost's, caressing her skin like a lover and spurning all others like one scorned. The room flinches at the sight of the blade that ate Llywelyn's soul. Gobbled down by the witch's curse, there'll be no peace for the dead man, condemned to an eternity trapped within a blade fattened by his cries of agony. Kaito still hears those cries in his nightmares. Though it is not the man's pain that terrifies him; it is knowing the woman who caused it.

The pharaoh, a man unaccustomed to bowing to a woman, withdraws entirely, cowed by the poison dripping from her words and the magical might thickening the space. Even Xipilli stiffens as Wren's otherworldly essence permeates the room, and the hands of several technomancers twitch in the direction of their weapons until Mirai sets a hand over Wren's.

The touch surprises everyone in the room, and for a tense moment, Kaito doesn't know if Wren will bolt from the contact or react with violence to it. Never mind the fact that Xipilli's trident sparks in warning the moment the older woman touches his sister.

But as his mother whispers something in Wren's ear, the lines of stress in Wren's body go slack, and she corrals the manifestation of her ire back. There is a collective exhale as the oxygen returns unburdened to the room. Wren bids the empress a hushed thanks and excuses herself from the room.

Xipilli tries to stop her, but she sidesteps him, leaving without another word. Xipilli takes command of the room in the wake of his sister's intel, and the discussion resumes, a new plan forming around what Wren has told them. Kaito sits and listens for only a few minutes as another disagreement on the proper approach commences before rising himself and following after Wren. But she is nowhere to be found, disappeared like a whispered promise drowned in a gale.

Hours later, Kaito sits and stews in the overwhelming sense that something is horribly, inconceivably wrong. Wren being a witch is the least of the issue. He's never seen her so ill at ease in a room full of people. If her magic is so volatile as to manifest during a simple conference meeting, how could she even hope to control it?

"Kaito, come sit with me for a moment."

Mirai's smile is warm; her eyes twinkle in the light of his holo. Kai rises from his place, deactivating his screen and following his mother to her personal quarters. The lodge the Miyazaki family has been housed in is quaint and homey but foreign. It smells different, like diesel fuel and poison oak. Everything is characterized by hard edges and angular architecture, nothing like the smooth arches of his home. The doors open the wrong way, and the network doesn't run as smoothly. Too much metallurgy in the way. It's like living in a box that is half tin can, half xyloidinous patterned wallpaper over sheetrock to create the illusion of wood.

Mirai settles at the small dining room table, and as Kaito settles opposite her, one of the housekeeping bots delivers two glasses of water for them. Kaito drinks only to keep from sitting still. It's laughable. First, he finds himself chasing after Wren while she avoids him, and now, he can't sit still. It's like their dynamic has been reversed. She was always the one chasing after him during their summit.

"You've been doing some pretty extensive research as of late."

He stiffens. So, she's noticed his extra time spent in the cyber libraries, hacking into League mainframes above his clearance for answers to his questions. His A.I. isn't powerful enough to slush through the coding, so he has to do it himself for the barest of documents. His servers are overheated from the constant draw, working himself into overdrive. Hours upon hours he's spent digging through medical records, closed case files, and banned research, looking for any case of a witch coming into their magic later in life, to find a single explanation, and he would hardly even call it that.

"Have you discovered anything interesting?"

Yes. And no.

Traumatic awakening. A theoretical phenomenon unseen and unobserved in nature but written about by an unnamed researcher over a century ago at the height of the war against hexen. He'd been trying to weaponize magic, bottle it for League usage, and this theory came out of his experiments. The theorem rests on the basis that everyone in Deus descends from a group of common hexen ancestors. He thought someone with a sensitivity to wild magic, when put under extreme duress, could awaken their dormant power to powerful destructive effect. The primary flaw of the theorem however—no such instance has ever been recorded, and the experiments conducted in an attempt to prove it possible... Well, let's just say execution was a mercy for the researcher.

"Nothing helpful."

His mother hums, sliding a maintenance capsule across the table. A pill the size of his pinky nail, in this singular dose of medication rest thousands of biodegradable nano bots waiting to hit his system to activate and repair his tech from the inside. They're standard issue for Murasaki human+. He shouldn't need to take one for another couple of months, but the amount of coding he's subjected his mainframe to has worn on his circuits.

"You've overstretched yourself. Your network is damaged from ripping through firewalls."

There is an admonishment in her words, a gentle reprimand given more to encourage caution rather than an outright scolding. He swallows the small, unobtrusive pill, a treatment that costs more than some people make in a year, given to him freely for his position and his worth to the League.

"You know, perhaps Lady Wren might find an interest in your research. She is probably now what I would consider an expert of sorts in magical theory."

Kaito's hand tightens, and the cup shatters. The housekeeping bot rushes forward in alarm to clean up the mess of water and broken glass. Mirai doesn't flinch even as water threatens to spill into her lap. Kaito rises, calm in deference to the shards lodged in his palm, and makes his way to the kitchen. Pulling the glass out, he tosses the pieces into the bin and turns on the water faucet, sticking his bleeding hand into the stream.

"What are you going to do?"

Spirals of red circle the drain. Spirals, like the triskele on Wren's brow.

"I don't know what you mean."

"Kaito, a year and a half ago, you told me you wanted to marry that girl, and you believed she would be amiable to your proposal."

"I know."

"You have spent the last year looking for any sign of her, holding onto the hope that you would find her again, despite all evidence to the contrary that she was dead. Are you telling me that now that she is returned, changed though she may be, that the time was wasted?"

"Never."

"Then why are you poring over useless casefiles that are decades old instead of speaking to the witch you are conducting research on behalf of?"

Kaito winces at Mirai's usage of the word "witch."

THE MOONS (PART I)

"A year and a half ago, a holo-disk was delivered to the Alliance headquarters that horrified all of us, and I watched my youngest son's world shatter before my eyes. I've only seen that look once before, and it was in my own reflection when your father died."

"Tousan was killed by a witch."

Mirai nods slowly.

"And somehow Lady Wren has returned as one of the very foes we have so long fought against. Believe me, I've struggled to wrap my head around it as well. I can't even begin to understand how confusing this must be for you, but imagine how difficult it must be for her, knowing someone she once trusted is from a family of renowned witch hunters."

Shame burns through him. He'd been so busy dealing with his own tangled thoughts and feelings, he hadn't even begun to think about what her change might mean for her. How her choice to pursue witchcraft may have been as devastating to her as finding her practicing it may have been to him...

"There are some things more important than hexen and technomancers, and I like to think love is one of them."

A knot twists in Kaito's throat. The glow of the tech node on the back of his injured hand pulses heavily, a mimicry of his heartrate.

"I frightened her."

His confession is so quiet he can barely hear himself, but his mother is a technomancer, and his kaasan's breath catches.

"I came across her the other night on the ramparts. She was weaving a spell of some kind, and not knowing it was her, I approached with my sword drawn."

"Kaito."

"I was in the wrong. I know that. I just..."

For the first time in his life, he doesn't know how to behave or act. These are uncharted waters for him. He can lead a dance or accompany a singer but only if he knows the steps, only if he's practiced the score. Improvisation... That was always Wren's strong suit.

"I wish she would tell me what I need to do."

"Lady Nocturne is a woman who has survived wartime imprisonment, Kaito. She is under no obligation to guide or coach you on how to speak with her or approach her. And she is certainly not obliged to seek you out even if it was she who used to goad you into reacting when you were trainees."

Wren, with whom he has shared so much of himself, is not the same stubborn devil-may-care girl who used to incessantly tease him in the training grounds of Shinka Temple. To be fair, he isn't the same haughty teen who used to brush her off as an annoyance back then either. They have both seen war. They are both changed by it. Her change is just ever so more profound, bone deep in a very literal sense.

"I want her to be safe."

Even from him? Because isn't he, as a technomancer, hell, as a man, a threat to her?

"Then I ask you again, my son. What are you going to do to fix this?"

Except the thing is, Kaito doesn't really know if there is even anything left between him and Wren to fix. Wren hasn't exactly been receptive to his presence. Of course, he doesn't think he would be very receptive to someone who has greeted him with a drawn weapon twice in a row either. But if there is something there, something clinging to life in the space between them, doesn't he owe it to both of them to nurse it back to health?

So, he makes his decision to try again. He still has questions he needs answers to, but the last thing he wants to do is corner Wren again, and Xipilli has made it abundantly clear that Kaito is not welcome around his baby sister.

He goes to Atzi instead.

Zenza is napping in her mother's arms when Atzi Moctezumo answers the door. "Kaito–sama! What a surprise! Come in, please."

THE MOONS (PART I)

She settles him at a small table, already set with coffee and sweet biscuits.

"I do not seek to take up your time, *princesa*," he begins. "But I am troubled and was hoping to gain your perspective."

"Oh?" offers Atzi, taking a sip of her coffee. "I hardly think my perspective can offer much to a technomancer as powerful as Kaito Miyazaki."

"It has to do with Lady Nocturne."

"My sister?"

Kai nods.

"You two are friends though? Wren always spoke highly of you. Should you not go to her yourself?"

Though the sheer magnitude of his discipline, Kaito doesn't wince.

"I fear she will not receive my questions with grace."

"Mm," Atzi hums thoughtfully as though he has revealed some great secret. "And what questions might those be? There isn't very much in this world Wren will give grace to. She has very little patience for anything she deems irrelevant or overly tedious."

And does Kaito know that!

"Has Wren mentioned anything of the last year and a half to you or Xipilli?"

Atzi looks sadly at the baby in her arms. Zenza's little infant face scrunches up, almost in reaction to Kai's question. She doesn't fuss, not yet, but her mother coos at her.

"She won't talk about it."

"Nothing at all?"

"Nothing at all, and Xipilli is an enabler, telling me to back off whenever I ask. Xipilli likes to pretend her new persuasion is temporary. He's called for several surgeons, hoping Wren will let at least one of them examine her for reintegration. Like our sister is a broken doll that can be fixed... But she refuses to even entertain the idea of seeing a regular doctor, reintegration aside."

"But why?"

"I don't know. She insists she doesn't need medical attention even though protocol would dictate she submit to at least a physical. And no matter how much I press her, she just says she isn't injured, and she isn't sick. Even when she fainted, she refused."

"She fainted?"

Atzi nods.

"Her first day back."

"Any idea to the cause?"

Atzi shakes her head.

"She was fine. Perfectly normal if a little subdued. She asked if she could hold Zenza, but the moment I put her in Wren's arms, Wren fainted. She hasn't really touched her since. Though, now that I think of it, Wren hasn't touched anyone since she got back, and she is normally a rather tactile person."

And yet Kaito had the audacity to set his hands on her.

"She struggled through the meeting yesterday, and..." The prince swallows his pride. "I saw her several nights ago and handled myself poorly. During the confrontation, I overstepped, but when I apologized for my behavior, she told me she was not worth the respect she is due."

Zenza burbles, fussy noises bubbling up from her mouth. Atzi shushes the baby, bouncing her.

"You know, when my sister was born, she giggled. Most babies cry when they're born. Not Wren. Wren laughed and it was like a song resonated through the room. She's always been that way. Where someone else might cry or scream, she'll smile and laugh it away." Tears glimmer in Atzi's blue eyes. "Wren hasn't laughed once since she came back."

Kaito looks away as a tear escapes the princess's eye.

"I know she seems different, but Wren is still Wren. I can't even begin to imagine what she's been through, and I won't presume to know my sister's mind, but I do know my sister. She's terribly strong-willed, as I'm sure you know. She's always cared little for what other people think. She's a free spirit after all, but ... I can say, whatever the misunderstanding between you, I believe that his highness's initial hostility to her in Deriva has upset Wren far more than she will ever say. I'm glad to know Prince Kaito is bothered by the situation, too."

THE MOONS (PART 1)

Kai averts his eyes from the woman's honey golden gaze. He can definitely see how Wren and Atzi share the same blood and upbringing. Xipilli as well. The Derivan siblings, for all their differences, were not the kind to take opposition lying down. Atzi, for all her mild mannerisms, regards him with the kind of look that offers both a warning and a blessing: a warning against hurting her sister and a blessing should he attempt to mend the rift between them.

Atzi hums, gently rocking Zenza. Her voice is a higher pitch than her sister's, a fairy-like soprano as opposed to Wren's flowery alto. Kai bows his head to the woman.

"Wren is important to me. Thank you for your advice, princess."

Atzi bows back to him as Zenza begins to truly cry for her mother's attention. It is at that moment that Wren walks into the room.

"Atzi, Zenza's fighting her nap again, do you want me to sing to her—Kaito?"

He is on his feet before he can even process the shock on Wren's face. The woman takes a step backward and turns to her sister.

"What is he doing here?"

"Wren," Atzi takes a scolding tone with her sister. Zenza's cries increase, hitching hiccups fast approaching a full fit.

"I was just leaving. Excuse me."

Kaito thanks Atzi once more and excuses himself, and while he walks at a controlled pace, he feels like a thief running from Wren's gaze.

According to an old-world fairy tale, when Sleeping Beauty fell into her enchanted sleep, only a kiss from her soulmate could wake her. In the Brothers Grimm's version of the story, they write that a handsome prince woke her from her cursed sleep with true love's first kiss. They never talk about how, in reality, countless men came from around the kingdom to offer their hearts to the slumbering princess. But it was all for naught.

Because, in truth, the princess's soulmate was no mortal prince but the witch herself, so wounded by her own battered pride at being denied the barest of friendships with her destined, she destroyed them both in a fit of anger, and while her princess slept on for eternity, the witch's heart darkened and withered until naught was left but hatred.

Excerpt from *Fairy Tales Known, Unknown*
Lily M. Esquire, 1874 A.P

8

THE MOONS (PART 2)

13th Day in the Month of Planting – 1863 – The Abbey Gardens

THERE IS A HEDGE MAZE IN ONE OF THE gardens. Kaito loses himself within. Settling himself in a dead-end clearing, he folds himself into a lotus seat and meditates. He clears his mind, focuses himself, and puts worldly troubles away until the sun begins its descent, and the shadows stretch around him.

He only opens his eyes when a fierce presence enters his frame of reference, volatile with chaotic energy. Wren rounds the corner, a whirling ball of rage, her eyes glowing green. How did she find him?

Witchcraft—the word comes unbidden to his mind.

"How noble you are, highness, sniffing around other royal houses for the sake of what your esteemed family considers good and righteous and decorous."

He doesn't have the wherewithal for this. Not yet. Not until he figures out how to handle her.

"Not now, Wren."

"Yes now. Right fucking now!"

Atzi must be mistaken. Clearly, Wren is set on making it abundantly clear that his presence is both unwanted and uninvited. He rises from his place in the grass, moving to jump the hedge and leave. But when she sends a pulse of telekinetic power flicking at his heels, he whirls around, Tsukuyomi drawn. He meets her, blade flashing. Her eyes widen in surprise even as she stalls the blade in midair just long enough to dodge out of the way. He parries again. She flits away, ducks down, and swipes at his legs with a kick. He jumps to avoid her attack, slashing again. She twists away from him, and he sends a pulse of saibāki through the air to destabilize her magic. As she lands, the glow in her eyes flickers like a lightbulb about to die.

She stumbles.

He whirls forward, Wren's eyes close, bracing herself for the strike, but Tsukuyomi's blade stops inches from Wren's throat. Kai's silver gaze burns with molten fury, boring down at her. She opens her eyes, and he silently dares her to make a joke of this situation. She does not disappoint.

"Too bad there's not a lake nearby," she says, tilting her head to the side, lips quirked at him. "You're cuter when you're wet."

He chokes on his own spit and yanks Tsukuyomi from her throat.

"What's the matter?" she coos, eyes glinting venomously. "Not going to finish it? I thought the Miyazaki were proud witch slayers. Or is this the part where you start demanding answers? Maybe you should wax on about one of your aunt's lectures on the evils of witchcraft and tell me how much of a monster I am."

"I do not think you are a monster."

"But I am a witch and in some ways that's worse, isn't it?"

He sheathes the katana, turning away and fuming at himself for indulging her this much. Atzi's words aside, in the face of Wren's naked hostility, he is unprepared, and if he doesn't leave right this moment, he will do something he'll regret.

"Believe what you wish. I'll have nothing of it."

He turns his back on her.

THE MOONS (PART 2)

"What! Too disgusted and horrified to even look at me. I thought you wanted answers!"

He does want answers. He wants them badly, but if she wishes to accuse him of untruths, let her. He is too tired, too angry, and too hurt for this conversation. Maybe after the war is over, he can figure out how to deal with her. To make her see logic and reason and listen to him. Some way to relate to her again the way he wants to, so that he doesn't hurt her. So that she doesn't hurt him.

He walks away, leaving her behind.

"Don't ignore me!"

More than anger, there's pain in her voice. A cry unlike anything he has ever heard from Wren. He turns as she attacks him. Her eyes shine, and it isn't with the viridian glow of chaos magic.

He nearly takes an elbow to the nose.

"That's enough, Wren."

"No! You come at me demanding answers, you kneel down in the dirt for touching me wrong, and now that I'm here in front of you, you don't want to deal with me. Are you such a coward you would rather go to my sister who is still healing from childbirth?"

He pulls his attacks, only allowing himself to defend against her. She notices when he lands a hit to her stomach and a blow that should have rightfully winded her, only pushes her backward.

"Stop pulling your punches!"

She wants to fight; her body language screams it.

"Fight me, already! Go on. Hit me!"

She wants him to hurt her. Self-destruction and she is trying to make him the trigger.

Her hand comes up to slap him across the face, and he purposely doesn't block. The blow connects, a sharp sting that actually scrambles his servers, but he catches her wrist and holds, the small bones in her wrist grinding together in his hand, and she hisses.

"Stop this, right now." His voice is dark as he growls at her, a low warning.

He'd forgotten Wren's tenacity for bold defiance. Is reminded of it now as she stares up at him, her shoulders set and her chin tilted to the side. There will be a handprint on her wrist tomorrow, proof of his touch. Proof of her new fragility. It horrifies him and exhilarates him at once, dark and twisted and terribly obvious to Wren. Wren who smirks up at him as though this is all a fun game to her. Maybe it is.

"Make me," she taunts.

She moves to kick him, bite him, hurt him any way she can even though it's unnecessary. Her very presence hurts him.

But her endurance is beginning to wane, her breathing grown ragged in rage. He shoves her, and she missteps, thrown off balance. Kai pushes her back against the hedge column, shoving hard enough to lift her off of her feet. Her legs come up and wrap around his waist, squeezing tightly. Her leather clad back drags harshly along the marble as her legs pull him farther into her. She twists her hand out of his grasp, and both her forearms come down on his shoulders.

He grunts from the hit but holds firm at her waist; her hand grips the collar of his shirt to yank him forward, resistance an afterthought against her.

Teeth crashing, their mouths ram together in a bruising kiss, chock-full of anger, frustration, and longing. It's messy and painful but so fitting for the circumstance, and even as arousal pools in his belly, horror floods his being. He struggles to take control, reign himself back in, but her teeth close on his bottom lip, so he grabs a fistful of her hair and tugs. The resulting gasp forces her to release his mouth. When she tugs again, challenging him with her eyes, he pushes forward, pulling her head back by the hair, and his teeth close around the apex of her shoulder and throat.

She cries out and stills, his teeth holding firmly onto the bare flesh of her neck while her nails dig into the skin of his chest. They stand frozen in place, the tension coiling around them taut as a spring-trap. Her hand is still fisted in his shirt, her other arm wrapped around his neck. His heart pounds; heat, insistent and blistering, aches in his core despite the blood in his mouth. Wren's legs tighten around Kaito's waist, enough that his lower ribs creak, and Kai releases her shoulder. Already he can see the outline of his teeth, pink and purpling on her skin. Even through their layers of clothing, the firmness of him pressed against her center cannot be lost to her. She confirms as much when she presses down into his hardness.

Wren shifts, and desire coils in the pit of his stomach as her lips ghost over the shell of his ear. "Kaito," she murmurs darkly into his ear. "Why are you holding back from me?"

The springs tighten between them. Kai's hands close around her forearms and press them back against the stone as he tries to control himself. His forehead drops to her cheek, and she makes a noise in her throat as though trying to hold herself back from weeping. He grinds his teeth together, screws his eyes shut, swallows around his bone-dry throat, and forces his resolve to maintain itself.

"I," he pants, "do not want to hurt you like those bastards did."

Wren flinches in his hold, and why shouldn't she? She probably didn't know anyone knew what happened to her. And by the heavens, he wishes it wasn't known because Wren before anything else is a survivor, has survived a brutality that no one should ever have to endure. He knows she has suffered. He can never know the full extent of how much.

But then, she wilts, softening in his arms the way she used to.

"You can't," she whispers against his jawline. "You won't. I missed you too much."

Kai jerks his head up. Wren's eyes shine with desperate, unshed tears. Kai's own darkly desire reflected back at him in those blue-green pools, naked and yearning. Kaito's hands tighten around her waist, and the gasp that rolls through her whole body flashes through her indicia, otherworldly and ethereal, sparkling like a vein of emeralds in the sunlight before disappearing back into her skin.

"You won't break me."

Once again, her indicia pulses as wild as the woman herself, and Kami! It is beautiful. More radiant than her tech ever shone even in the darkest of underworlds. The rational part of his mind forgets why the marks glow against her skin, and he shifts forward into the witch offering herself to him against the cage of his arms and the stone at her back.

"Wren—"

"Kai," she begs and snarls and sobs, viridian glowing in her gaze. Kai's own violet sights flash on. "I needed you... I never stopped needing you. Even if you don't need me, could you just pretend? Just for a little while that you might need me, too."

Wren makes a broken sound in the back of her throat as though a rejection from Kai would break her more thoroughly than anything else she has already overcome. As though he could shatter her right here and now, break her to pieces and leave her, no, leave them both broken in the dirt.

He shifts a hand to her jaw, tilts her face up to meet his and captures her lips with his own. Tender and gentle, unlike any of the lead up that brought them here, he soaks her in and drinks deep of Wren's lips, stealing her breath and claiming it for his own. She is fire and ozone, lightning and wind bundled together into something he can hold on to. He sets his hands on her body once more, and she opens at his touch like the petals on a lotus bloom. A proper reunion kiss. Grief—long-bottled and ignored. Relief—untainted by horror and fear. A "welcome home" and an "I missed you" rolled together even as the strain of their frustration boils beneath the surface.

"I do need you," growls Kai, kissing her again, fervor building. "I never stopped needing you," he says, remembering a night spent trying to forget, trying to move on, trying to pull himself out of his grief to no avail and shoving it aside in favor of stealing the breath from her lungs so he can breathe again for the first time in over a year.

"I could never stop needing you," he confesses his greatest sin, his greatest avarice.

The Moons (part 2)

Wren moans, insistent in the back of her throat. "Then take me." It echoes in the fibers of his soul. "Break me." Her fingers unfasten his belt, finding his want. "I was yours first."

Kai's resolve unravels.

"No, I was yours."

He twists her around. Her front meets the granite, and Kai throws aside the belt that keeps her skirt tied to her body. His left hand winds around her throat while the other shoves past the waistline of her skirts. She is already soaked with arousal, her walls flexing around his digits as he begins to work them inside her, stroking for the treasure within that will unravel her. She cries out when he finds his mark, but he swallows her gasps with a kiss.

"Wren," he gruffs.

"Kai," she sighs as he plucks the correct chords buried in her folds.

She is warm and wet and so glaringly present. Being able to call her name and have her respond in kind, it's like falling into a dream.

"Kaito!"

A shouted demand.

He pulls her by her hips from the pillar, and she pulls him down to the ground in a fevered kiss before arranging herself in his lap, her back pressed flush to his front as he tips her forward. The damp earth cushions her knees and dirties her skirts even as he shoves them out of his way. She braces herself on her elbows as he unbuckles the rest of his trousers, quaking around him and mewling as he presses into her depths, warm, tight, and familiar after all this time. No dream could encompass what it feels like to give himself to her, to bring their bodies together for the first time in nearly two years.

They make love, right there, in the dirt, and it is rough and violent and every pent up, vile, desperate feeling they've been so carefully nursing since their reunion. Fervent passion to exorcise the malcontent between them; it unfolds, like the petals of a spring daisy after a hurricane, into a healing bloom.

SONATA

Time is lost to them. It could be thirty minutes, it could be an hour, it could be longer even, before, together, they reach the height of their passions, his release ripping through his system as she clenches around him. All he knows is that dusk is falling, the sun's dying glow casting the world in hues of orange and red. He inhales harshly through his nose, fingertips bruising into the soft curve of her hip, her skirt still pooled around her in silky dark-blue waterfalls of fabric, before lowering himself down, carefully, on top of her. His arms wind around her torso, and she embraces him in turn, her amputated forearm across his back, her hand in his hair, now damp and disheveled from his efforts.

He does not pull from her, not right away, soaking in the heat of her body for as long as she'll let him, long enough for the place where they are joined to become uncomfortable, both from their fluids and from the growing soreness that will surely greet the both of them come the dawn of the next day. She wriggles a bit underneath him, and he lifts himself up and off of her. Kai rolls them over, cradling her to his chest after tucking himself back into his pants and pulling her skirts back down. She stays, resting her head against the line of his pectoral.

He lays on his back, one hand under his head, the other warm at her waist, wrapped around her loosely enough that she doesn't feel trapped. He is calm in a way that he has not felt in nearly two years, and he allows the feeling to settle over him (them?) like a blanket.

The silence stretches between them like a cat waking from an afternoon nap; it's peaceful. She breathes steadily against his chest, and he wishes for a long sun-warmed moment that he could forget what they were fighting about to begin with. A silly thing really considering how serious the whole situation is, but he wants to forget. Just lay here and watch the clouds overhead, their fluffy, sunset-pink curves floating and changing as the minutes wander by while she stays curled into his side. It is as a misty curlicue wisps its way out of a fluffy cumulus that he notices the fabric of his shirt beginning to dampen.

THE MOONS (PART 2)

"Wren," he calls, rising up onto his elbows to get a better look at her face. Panic sets in as he sees the tears clinging to her lashes, rivulets of escaped drops damp on her cheeks. Did he go too far? Was it too much for her? Gods be damned, he should have controlled himself better. What if she wasn't really ready? What if— "Did I hurt you?"

She shakes her head.

""No. Sorry, sorry. I—I don't know why I'm crying. I just..."

He cradles her face in his hands.

"Was it... Did I..."

She sets a finger at his lips, smiling through her tears.

"No, no. You did nothing wrong. You were perfect. I just got a little overwhelmed, is all."

He doesn't understand. Not entirely, but when Wren lowers her head back into the folds of his shirt, he simply pulls her in tighter and begins drawing shapes over the skin of her arm. He waits and Wren calms. She sniffles one last time into his shirt collar and clears her throat. Kaito draws back to look at her.

"Why did you go to my sister?"

"I am worried for you."

"If you were so worried, perhaps you should have come to me instead."

"That would be difficult considering not even your own siblings are able to find you half the time."

Wren cows a little at that.

"You don't need to worry. I'm fine."

She is not. That much is very, painfully apparent, written into her skin in glowing patterns that hum as he passes his fingertips over them.

"Don't lie to me, Wren."

"I'm not lying," she insists into his collar. "At least, I'm as fine as I can be when I'm constantly being slapped in the face by everyone else's stupid emotions. I don't know what my own are anymore."

For a moment, these words don't make any sense, but then it falls into place. Her newfound reclusiveness, her avoidance of everyone other than her brother and sister where before she used to relish in being around people. Her reluctance to touch anyone despite her tactile nature. How she nearly dropped her infant niece in a faint when the child was placed in her arms for the first time. Her hostility to a man who questioned her merit.

"You're an empath." She looks down, her face shadowed from him as her hair falls in front of her eyes. "You can feel other people's emotions."

"To put it mildly. It's worse when someone touches me. If anything is going to drive me mad, it's going to be that. It's easier to just stay away from everyone." She laughs, darkly and ironically. "It's funny though. I can't get a read on you at all. Must have something to do with all of that high quality tech in your head."

"That would be unique to my family and our neural hubs. Our systems guard us against psychic attack. We would have to override them manually to drop the firewalls."

She hums in understanding. "That must be it then. How ironic that the only people who I can tolerate will have nothing to do with me? I already knew your aunt hated me—"

"My aunt does not hate you."

"—But since Deriva, I might as well be hell spawn to her. Though I guess witchcraft is kind of at the top of your family's worst evils list. Your mother takes it all in stride though. She's the only one of you with any amount of sense. We had a good conversation the other day."

"You spoke to my mother."

"She came to speak with me, yes."

"What about?"

"She offered me the option of having a Murasaki surgeon perform my reintegration procedure."

Kai's eyes go wide at that. Such an offer is unheard of. For his mother to offer Wren such a thing—

"Don't get excited. I turned her down."

"Why?"

"Kai..."

"Tell me."

THE MOONS (PART 2)

She is silent for a long tense moment, gathering her words. "They shut down my system."

And he understands.

"They shut me off like a computer, and I couldn't do anything about it. I never want to experience that again. I do not want to undergo reintegration. Besides, I'm sure I don't need to remind you that tech and witch blood are not very compatible."

He angles his face toward her and tries to keep his knee-jerk impulse to anger and judge out of the conversation.

"I don't understand how it is possible. You were—you are a technomancer. That witchcraft was an option for you to choose should have been an impossibility."

"I didn't choose this, Kai."

He doesn't say anything to that, so she continues, her voice a little more subdued, a little more vulnerable not unlike when she first ever so gracefully confessed to him in the catacombs.

"I had a choice between surviving and dying, and I chose to survive. This," she says, holding a green tendril of energy in front of her face. It is a credit to his self-discipline that he doesn't flinch at the sight of it. "...is the consequence. Do you think I should have let them kill me instead?"

Kai takes in her admission steadily. He can't decide which is worse: that he thought she did this to herself or that it wasn't even really a choice for her to begin with.

"I am glad you did not let them kill you."

The silence stretches between them again. The tension in Wren's face tightens as though she is wrestling with something. He leaves her be, sinking into his own thoughts on this whole fucked up situation. He remembers the recording from Llywelyn, his own experience encountering Wren in cyberscape, the mysterious happenings around Seraphim operations that helped them maintain their advantage, knowing implicitly that Wren was behind those happenings, and finally encountering her again to the sounds of Llywelyn's death in the background.

He thinks back to a simpler time—to Wren calming him in the dark, to her holding a hexen baby on her way to return it to its mothers. He thinks of the time he held her hair back from her face while she was sick, of Wren smiling in the light of the rising sun on a dock as he saw her off, of keeping that memory in mind as he sought his mother's approval to court her, all of what should have and could have been had reality not proven its potential for cruelty.

"Do you hate me, Kai?"

Wren's question breaks him from his musing. His eyes slide to her, and the answer comes easily, even if it frightens him to say as much.

"No, Wren. I do not hate you."

"Despite what I am now?"

Despite the witchcraft, the strange and dangerous powers she has, the fearsome potential for destruction she now has, the terrible reality that she is now in a tug-o-war with her own sanity, a duel every witch with even a modicum of the abilities she has demonstrated has lost to catastrophic result.

"I could never hate you, Wren."

"Then what is it?"

"Wren, these powers you have. There are reasons they are spurned. They are dangerous and damaging to your being. You cannot sustain this. I am afraid you will end up just like every other witch who has ever achieved such abilities, driven mad with magic-fever and put down like a rabid dog."

"That won't happen."

"How can you know that?"

"I'm still me, Kai. I haven't changed. Not really. Don't you trust me?"

He sighs, all at once exhausted and resigned. "Ride with me tomorrow."

"What for the final assault? Xipilli wants me with him."

"Talk to him. Tell him you'll ride with me instead."

So I can look after you.

Silver eyes peer into tearstained aquamarine. She blinks once at him, studying him, looking for something in him that he hopes she finds. He must pass because her eyes close to half moons as the sunny smile from their summit days dawns across her lips.

"Alright. I'll tell my brother that the esteemed Prince Kaito insists on suffering my presence."

Kaito's own lips quirk at the jest. "You know, Xipilli is going to have a conniption over it."

"My condolences to any hair he loses."

Wren laughter rings out as bright and clear as wind chimes in the crisp mountain breeze.

When a witch dies, her magic will spill into the world, an uncontrolled outpouring of pure chaos known as an Echo.

An Excerpt from *Hunting and Identifying Hexen*
by Finnick Lockecraft, 1852 A.P.

9

ACE OF SWORDS

WREN NEVER WANTED TO GET MARRIED nor had she ever wanted to have children. She once promised herself she would never fall in love, would never chain herself to any man, woman, or person either through marriage or a child. At the tender age of eight, she knew that she would never suffer childbirth for a selfish, self-centered man when one of her mother's friends lost the battle with postpartum depression and took her own life. The "grief-stricken" widower remarried not two months later.

Therefore, she chose to become a technomancer, and if she couldn't be a technomancer, she could be a Firefly just like her mother. Bound only to her own heart with the privilege to choose who she spent her time with and how she spent her time with them. She could dance and sing and play music. She could keep company for the lonely, act as an advisor for those needing guidance, and if she so felt like it, offer more for patrons she found worthy of more intimate attentions. That had quite appealed to her eight-year-old self.

Yes, Wren had decided all of this at eight years old. No to marriage. No to children. No to tying Cupid's noose around her own neck.

Wren could laugh at herself now, considering everything that came to pass afterward, everything that's happened since her resurrection, but that would be unfair to her obstinate childhood self. It just goes to show how little she understood as a girl.

A fond smile quirks her lips as she remembers, clear as day, rolling with Kai in the grass, tumbling under and over him as he took her beaten and battered self and accepted it, as he took everything she had to offer, all of the anger, the pain, the regret, and returned it tenfold. She'd let him invade her and want her, and relished in the loss of his control, basked in the torrent of his passion, a flood washing away her carefully built defenses with ecstasy and unfettered honesty. A nineteen-year-old Kaito embraced her beaten, battered soul with wanting hands rough enough to banish the self-loathing, rekindle her spirit, and make her feel safe in his arms, showering her with potent kisses that reflected back to her the same all-consuming need she felt for him.

The scars of the last year and a half of her life peeled open to bleed poison onto the mud during their heated reconciliation. Like the rebreaking of a poorly mended bone, a wound inflicted with the purpose of correcting and repairing damage once thought irreparable, she allowed him to reset the break and issue forth proper healing. That was the day she truly allowed herself to love him.

It was embarrassing, she remembers, crying in front of him in the afterglow of their tryst, but in the waters of those tears, her heart, a cold, withered thing in her chest, began to beat again—not just for Kaito, either.

An hour outside of New Osaka, Wren pulls off the main road into a thicket of thistle and palo verde. The change in foliage acts as a testament to the changing climate as she makes her way from the temperate forests of central Murasaki to the western deserts that begin on just before the border into Sekhmeti. Her flight out of town had been harried, but thankfully, no one tailed her. She doesn't have time to be caught up in whatever investigation the local adept force will want to open now someone has been killed. Mishka... Dead on the floor because a parasite invaded her system at the command of a witch with a penchant for summoning nasty beasts from beyond the void.

With the sun coming up, the events of the previous night feel like a fever dream. A vivid nightmare, really, but they were real. Mishka's dead body, chilling in her arms, Mr. Keng's cries of terror and the subsequent mad dash out of town after stuffing the warded teapot in her cycle: it all brings to point a certain nostalgia from a lifetime ago that Wren would rather forget. Another death added to the blood on her hands. Another innocent life taken because she wasn't enough.

The teapot leaks with void magic. A familiar signature belonging to a witch she owes a visit to. Summer has never been opposed to hurting other hexen to get what she wants. She once killed five hexen babies trying to make chimera in Lorelei.

But why Mishka? The woman helped her, treated her wounds, and gave her a place to rest after Wren left a bullet hole in her arm.

"And she paid you back by cursing you with a parasitic netherbeast," Wren hushes aloud. "Killed for your kindness." Bullocks! And why? What does she gain by setting a pain-loving monster loose in such a small town in the first place? Why curse a woman who took care of her? Why curse a fellow witch at all?

It doesn't make any sense!

Wren's killed her own fair share of witches, so no point in being hypocritical. However, she's never hurt someone who didn't hurt her first, and she would never hex anyone who did her a solid. So, what did Mishka do to deserve a fate so terrible? Eaten from the inside-out by a magical parasite.

Cauchemar, Mara, Pisadeira, Kanashibari.

The creature or phenomenon goes by many names depending on what part of the world or culture a person grew up in, but in the common tongue, it is known as The Nightmare—a netherbeast who feeds on pain and suffering as it strangles its victims in their sleep. Wren studied it briefly as a teenager. The League teachings describe The Nightmare as a witch or hag seeking to harm young people, draining their being to gain power or favor with whatever entity they are seeking privilege from. The witch steals into a person's bedroom, usually an adolescent youth or young adult, and assaults them in their sleep, riding them until it's filled its gullet.

But, as with most things concerning hexen, the truth is far more complex.

The Nightmare is not a witch at all. It's barely even a netherbeast. But in the way worms are considered animals, the Nightmare is considered a netherbeast. Parasitic in nature, the Nightmare nests inside the magical network of a witch, enslaving the witch and riding them for its nightly feeds on sleeping children and teenagers. The Nightmare uses the possessed witch's body as a conduit to paralyze its victims and drain all of the sorrow and hurt out of its meal. With a witch of Mishka's magical pool, the victims would recover eventually, left merely catatonic for a few days after the attack. Though Wren doubts any of them will ever have a good night's sleep again.

(Poor dears. She wouldn't be surprised to find an upswing in the dreamcatcher trade again. Granted, they probably aren't illegal in Murasaki anymore, what with the hexen sanctuary thing.)

However, as terrible as the fates of the slumbering innocents are, the ultimate victim is the possessed witch. Eventually, the witch's body gives out, the parasite draining their pool of chaos magic until there is nothing left but ash, or caught in the act of "riding" a victim, the witch will be executed by the League or, as Mishka had been afraid of, by a mob of frightened townsfolk for crimes not their own. You would think that this would kill the Nightmare, too—the death of the host resulting in the death of the parasite, but ironically enough, the Nightmare profits from the witch's death as from the remains will arise not one but two newly hatched Nightmares.

A disgusting cycle of life, death, and rebirth.

ACE OF SWORDS

This one made the mistake of trying to cement Wren as a host for its soon-to-be-born young and wound up destroyed by its prospective real estate. With Wren as a host, a witch with a stronger magical network, the vampyric creature would have killed its victims, Wren's natural affinity for necrotic magics capable of draining every last drop of lifeforce from a person. It was the sole reason none of the teenagers had died during the attacks, Mishka's magic too weak to do more than temporarily cripple them. If it had just run its course through Mishka's body and allowed its young to fend for themselves, it would have two healthy spawn capable of disappearing into the closest magical network to continue the cycle.

Without interference from another witch, there is no way to evacuate a Nightmare from a witch's magical essence, the victim doomed to carry the infestation to term without any knowledge of the grisly offspring forming in her core. That is, of course, only the case if the witch doesn't kill herself in a mad fit first.

There is something to be said for being driven insane by dreams and nightmares. For a long time, Wren believed she survived the war only to lose herself in night terrors—that one night, she would leave her bed in a lucid dream and drown herself in the ocean waves just beyond her bedroom window in Cresta de Corail.

"Thankfully," Wren muses. "Most nightmares are survivable."

"Only if you aren't alone."

Wren jerks her head up, looking for the source of the voice, a whisper both familiar and not, but no one is there. She is totally alone.

It must be the fatigue getting to her.

Two days in a row now, she has woken up after a few scant hours of sleep. Not to mention the heavy spellcasting she did to banish the curse on Shinka Temple—wow, was that really only two days ago?—and the energy she drained saving Eun-ji's life just hours ago. If she isn't careful, she's going to crash.

Wren shakes herself out of her stupor and rises. Time to get back on the road and out of Murasaki before someone comes after her. It's bad enough Mishka's Echo is going to have every adept within a five-mile radius barreling over to investigate the massive surge in chaos magic; worse still that Eun-ji and her father were there in the very heart of the witch's territory when said magical outburst occurred. She winces, remembering how Mr. Keng had been flung backward out of the room when the release occurred. Hopefully, he wasn't injured too badly in the blast, but she'd been too busy getting the hell out of dodge to check on him. The man looked like he was about to call the witch hunters on 'Atalia' before he got a face full of magic. Thankfully, no one has seen her real face. They'll be chasing a ghost should they deem to come after 'Atalia' for justice against Mishka's killer.

Nevermind that Wren did her damndest to save the woman's life...

The teapot full of Nightmare husk gets shoved as deeply into her bag as possible, to be, henceforth ignored for as long as possible. Ick! The thought of touching it still wigs her out. Once it stops oozing magic, she'll get rid of it, but the last thing she wants to do is drop a magically radioactive parasite into a toilet for a ride down the waterslide into the town's sewers.

The wind whips through her hair as she rides. Despite her lack of sleep, Mishka's wakefulness potion keeps an alert buzz through her system. Were it not for Mishka's tea, the easy hum of the lightcycle's motor may very well have put her to sleep instead. She is far more accustomed to the steamcycles and searunners of Deriva. Those motors are steam and electricity powered, and a strong draw on the clutch makes them roar like angry lions. Wren used to love the sound of a revved engine before the war. But after... Well, let's just say the sound of an engine growling is not her favorite sound, especially not if the rider is a technomancer out for her blood.

ACE OF SWORDS

There are two legal ways to cross the border from Murasaki to Sekhmeti: the light rail and the river crossing in Chairomura, a border town at the southwestern edge of Murasaki. And considering everything that happened on the light rail the last time she set foot on it, she'll take the bridge, thank you very much.

With hours of road behind her, Wren approaches the checkpoint on the outskirts of the city limits to find a huge traffic jam blocking her way: lines of cars and semis as far as she can see. There are even a few grounded hovercraft sitting in the grass off the side of the concrete. Many of the drivers have shut off their vehicles. One gentleman sits leisurely smoking an e-cigarette; another woman reads a book or at least she attempts to while her toddler wails for her attention in the backseat. A whole family sits playing a game of some kind on a tablet, and one of the semi drivers seems to be enjoying a gourmet meal right on his dashboard. Every-so-often they'll be allowed to inch forward, and the A.I. operators programmed into the car will allow the vehicle to creep up without even needing to notify the person sitting behind the wheel.

Unwilling to sit in a bumper-to-bumper line up, Wren pulls her cycle into the space between vehicles to cruise her way to the checkpoint officials, and suddenly the drivers who hadn't been paying the least bit of attention to their surroundings perk up at the sight of her skipping the line, and she rides past them to resounding chorus of angry car horns. A few people even make offensive hand gestures at her. Hah! No matter how advanced the cars get, road rage never changes.

One of the patrol officers flags her down as she gets to the inspection station. She can barely tell if the person is male or female. They are so heavily armored, and a gas mask covers the entirety of their face.

"Ma'am, you can't enter the city." Filtered through the mask, the voice rings like an aluminum can. All metallic percussion and no wind. "All vehicles must turn around or wait until clearance is granted."

Hmm... Time to see if Hikaru's hacking skills are worth his salt. He did say she would have the rights of a private citizen under the royal family.

"I have clearance."

"I highly doubt that, ma'am."

She presents Atalia's passport and ID. From the officer's left middle finger, a scanner alights and pans over her credentials. They make an affronted noise as the red light of the holo turns a crisp, ready-steady-go green.

"I take it I have clearance."

The documents are thrust back under her nose with a scoff.

"Yes, you have clearance, but ma'am, please, it isn't safe in the city. An outbreak of disease has afflicted the entire population. If you enter, I cannot guarantee your safety."

A disease outbreak? In Murasaki? What kind of disease could bring a city located in a country as technologically advanced as Murasaki no Yami to its knees? And if it is so bad here, why hasn't it spread to the surrounding cities? She filled up on gas in a small town just an hour away from here and didn't hear anyone so much as cough. An hour of distance is nothing for a plague.

"Just how long has this been going on?"

Before the officer can answer her, an indignant complaint drifts over from the far side of the station. A complaint made by a very familiar whiny voice.

"I have clearance. I just lost the papers during the crash. You have to let me into the city. If you'll just call my uncle, the Vulcan of Deriva can—"

"I do not take orders from the Vulcan of Deriva, Princess."

Wren looks over to see a young girl in Derivan battle garb huffing at a very tall patrol officer who stands arms crossed as he regards her through his mask. Her hair is different from the last Wren saw her, let loose from a confining ravel of braids to halo around her head in a full afro, but there can be no mistaking Wren's niece from the way she stamps her foot and demands for something she is not being given—not to mention the very large rifle strapped to her back: Agni.

"Whether you had authentic seals or not doesn't matter if you cannot present them to me in person. I could be held for criminal neglect if I allowed you into a disease-ridden city without proper validation."

"But my—"

Another girlish voice, not Zenza's, responds.

"Please, sir. We are travelling to Sekhmeti on behalf of the Emperor. We'll only be passing through to get to the border. Surely, we won't get sick in that short amount of time."

"We also have filters to wear," a slightly deeper voice adds. "We are trained to handle situations like this."

Wren walks the lightcycle around the central dividers to see a girl and boy in the battle leathers of the Miyazaki family. The girl has her hair done up in a tight bun with a few flyaways around her face, and the boy's hair is slicked back from his face in a slightly longer crew cut. They both look windblown and travel dirty, and the lightcycle between them is dusty, far dustier than would ever be acceptable on vehicles kept by the royal family. It's Akari and Renki.

Who let these teenagers off their leashes?

"None of you are certified. If you think I am going to let a bunch of teenagers—"

"They're with me."

There's not much in this world that glitters that isn't cold. Metals sap the heat from your fingers. Diamonds sparkle brightest in the frozen depths of the sea.

No, there is not much warmth to that which sparkles. So much truth to this fact, it's a wonder the dead don't sparkle and shimmer in the moonlight. Perhaps that's why magic sparkles, because for all that we like to think fairy tales are warm and fuzzy, they're really just chilly reiterations of life's boundless horrors.

Taken from Wren's Book of Shadows
Lorelei Forest – 1862 A.P.

10

SEVEN OF SWORDS

9th Day in the Month of Falling – Chairomura
Checkpoint – 3:45PM

W REN'S VOICE CARRIES LOUDER THAN SHE intended, but it gets the point across, and the three teens turn to look at her with mixed response. Akari's eyes bulge at the sight of her, first in confusion then in recognition, and while the girl's mouth drops open, nothing comes out. Hopefully a fly doesn't go in.

"You!" Zenza's shout is laced with no small amount of unhappy surprise. Right, the last time Zenza saw 'Atalia,' she'd been throwing lightning at her uncle in a train car.

But Renki... Renki not only looks happy to see her; his whole face seems to brighten at the sight of her, a wide smile dimpling his cheeks. It reaches all the way to his bright green eyes.

"Lady W—I mean, Miss Vaishi."

"Hey, kids," she greets as she approaches them.

"We're not kids," mumbles Akari.

"Right, you're teenagers. So much worse."

"These three are with you?" The officer's frown is spectacularly dented. Like a canyon right between the man's eyebrows.

"I don't see anyone else with them, do you?" Wren responds, one hip cocked to the side, hands on her belt. The wind rustles her skirts around her boots, wide set in a powerful stance.

"If you're their chaperone, how come you've only just arrived?"

"Do you see the traffic back there? I had to suffer the wrath of at least a hundred car horns to catch up with these three. You wouldn't believe how bad teenagers are about following traffic laws. Speed-racers, the lot of them."

Renki chuckles while Zenza opens her mouth to protest, but Akari elbows the princess in the side, bearing the brunt of the girl's hazel glare.

"And you're telling me you have clearance to enter when these three don't?"

Wren shrugs as the officer who checked her over originally answers.

"She's got clear credentials, sir. Unlimited access by specification of the crown."

"The crown! Well, I'll be damned. Fine. Take them and go, but don't come crying to me when you see the state of things in there."

"Not at all, officer. We'll be through and through as fast as a bullet. Come on, you three."

Zenza opens her mouth, probably to protest or complain or something else equally annoying, but Akari takes her by the elbow and pulls her onto her lightcycle. Does Zenza not have her own transport? How'd she get here? What are any of them doing here for that matter?

There's an awkward moment as all three of them try to pile onto one single-rider cycle. Why is there only one lightcycle between three teenagers? Wren shakes her head and tugs Renki to ride pillion with her.

Akari and Zenza follow behind as Wren pulls out of the checkpoint and into the city proper.

Renki is quiet behind her, holding onto the rail of the cycle rather than her, but his posture is easy. Maneuvering the cycle with him as a passenger is a bit finicky at first, considering the teenager is taller than her, but Wren adjusts to his extra weight easily enough, and the kid knows enough about the physics of riding pillion enough to help her out.

There's not much of a skyline. Chairomura is not a sweeping metropolis like Tokiseishu, its tallest building standing maybe twenty stories tall. But it is still a city, and where Wren expects to find a few pockets of rush hour traffic or at least a few stray buggies zooming along the highway, the streets are deserted.

"What the—?" she hears Renki gasp behind her.

Abandoned cars line the road. A few vehicles scratched up as though something attacked the outside of the cars. None of the businesses are open. There are no people. The only sign of life comes and goes in the wail of a siren in the distance.

Despite the strangeness of the cityscape, the drive to the bridge is uneventful. Crossing into Sekhmeti should be easy enough. They'll present their passports to the border patrol and be waved across, easy as blowing a dandelion. In and out of this city in a handful of minutes. Only when they arrive at the bridge, not only are the scanning systems dark, but the bridge is down, the entire midsection blown to high heaven. Not even a beam of construction cabling is left to climb across, and when she looks down into the river, the water rushes riotously over the piles of debris submerged.

Even more off-putting are the armed robots trudging back and forth on the far side of the estuary. She doesn't see any operatives though, just machines: a pair of bulky bipedal robots with large, anchored rifles aimed and ready to fire on anyone who might attempt to cross. Wren dares to inch further forward, and one of them fires a warning shot just shy of her front tire. Renki makes a shocked sound behind her, and she immediately backs up lest the machine take a true shot.

Wren doesn't know what is going on here, and she is not about to find out. Not with three teenagers now in her charge.

"The checkpoint officers didn't mention anything about this," Renki yells as she turns the cycle around.

"Does Sekhmeti normally keep armed robots as sentries?"

"Yes, but the weapons are usually inactive. The entire system is automated, so we don't keep people stationed here, and neither do they. Typically, our surveillance drones interact with their robots pretty amicably. For them to fire on us just for approaching..."

"Tell Akari to follow me back through the last exit," she tells Renki over the sound of the wind, and he hums in affirmative. Wren dips the cycle onto the exit ramp, carefully avoiding a car flipped against the safety railing. She sees Akari follow in her right-side mirror.

Coming off the highway, the city streets are not in much different condition. Scatter cars abandoned in the streets, but she does see a few pedestrians slinking along in the shadows. They scurry away at the sound of their engines, and not for the first time, Wren wonders what the hell kind of disease has run rampant through this town.

They ride through an older downtown area, filled with buildings which may very well have been erected when Murasaki was still a hexen state, maybe long before technomancers even existed. The sign on one of the buildings affirms it reading, "Built in 803A.P."

She pulls into an open parking lot and stops the engine. She and Renki dismount as Akari pulls in behind her to park her own cycle. Zenza jumps from the cycle before Akari has even come to a complete stop, already racing away to Dei knows where. Akari curses and takes off after the other girl, nearly toppling her cycle onto its side in the process.

Wren sighs, praying for the patience not to psychically yank these kids into the air by their ankles. But Atalia's not a witch, remember? She's just a normal, non-magical Firefly babysitting a bunch of augmented teenagers. She can do that without magic, right?

Hah! ...Yeah, right...

Wren kneels, and a tendril of magic slithers along the ground toward Zenza's retreating back.

"Stop," Wren commands, and the viridian whip lashes at Zenza's boots.

The girl freezes like the devil just nipped at her heels—which it kind of did considering Wren just whipped her ankle with a bit of magic—Akari nearly bowling her over.

"Return."

The pair turn to look at her and march themselves back, Akari looking smug, Zenza looking cowed. "Now, explain to me why I just found you three arguing with a border patrol officer."

"We don't owe you an explanation," mumbles Zenza, only for Akari to shoulder the younger girl.

At Wren's side, Renki shuffles his feet, seemingly embarrassed. "Well, we were trying to sneak past the checkpoint and got caught."

"You got caught? And why, pray tell, are three adepts-in-training trying to get into a disease-ridden city illegally?"

Renki and Akari share a shifty glance.

"Well, we're together," says Akari, gesturing between Renki and herself. "Looking for Renki's dad..."

Renki's dad? Who's Renki's dad?

"...and we just so happened to run into this brat."

"I am not a brat!"

"If it weren't for you, we wouldn't have been caught."

"It's not my fault the patrol recognized me."

"Everyone knows who Princess Zenza is," says Akari. "The gossip columns are still printing articles about you and your family more than five years after the co—"

"Right," drawls Wren. "And what exactly is the crown princess of Deriva doing sneaking into a Murasakan bordertown unaccompanied?"

"You sound like my uncle!" Wren actually reels back at the vehemence in the accusation. Wren sounding like Xipilli? Please, goddess, no! "I'm not a baby. I can take care of myself, and I know how to get around plenty on my own. And who are you to ask me any questions? Aren't you the crazy woman who nearly blew up my uncle on the light rail?"

Well, yes, but it was an accident.

Surprisingly, Akari puffs herself up ready to answer.

"You, brat, this is you're au—"

Renki elbows Akari in the side. Wren cuts in before the two can give her away to her niece.

"My name is Atalia, princess, and yes, I am the one who almost blew up your uncle, so maybe you should answer my questions before I decide to blow you up, as well."

Zenza pales.

"You really are a witch."

Oops...

"Not exactly."

"Not exactly?" asks Zenza, eyebrows arched skeptically at Wren. Well, this is just becoming more and more of a shitshow.

"Answer the question, girl. What are you doing here by yourself?"

Zenza huffs, crossing her arms over her as yet undeveloped chest.

"A case appeared on our servers. I intercepted it before my uncle could see it and decided to take it on myself."

"You stole a case from your uncle?"

"He grounded me for firing Agni in the light rail and said he was going to put my training on hold until I could prove my ability to be responsible, but when this case popped up, I... Look, it's none of your business why I wanted this case, and I don't have to answer to a lunatic witch like you."

So, her niece is not only headstrong and stubborn; she's a mischievous little rascal to boot. Wren would be proud were she not positively livid first.

"So, running away from home with a stolen case is the best you can come up with to get your way? Have you no sense of your own mortality?!"

"I didn't run away. I told him I was taking a case. I just didn't listen when he told me not to go anywhere."

"And he hasn't come after you yet?"

"Well, I didn't tell him which case I was taking, and there's a good chance he doesn't know I'm gone yet. He was kind of busy with the conference coming up in Aureus, and he does this thing where he automatically assumes people jump to follow through when he makes a declaration. It works most of the time, but I'm his niece. I don't have to listen to him."

Wren blinks. How did this girl end up being more like her than Xipilli or Atzi? It makes her feel surprisingly fond.

"Okay, so then how did you get here without a steamcycle?"

The girl looks down, sheepish. "I, uh, I kind of crashed it trying to outrun the patrol."

Wren blinks. *This girl!*

"Yeah, she crashed it into Renki's lightcycle, and now we're stuck with her," Akari snips. Wren takes the time to really look at the teenagers, and they look worse for wear than long-distance travel might justify. Renki's clothes are dirty, the lavender sash at his side stained with oil, and while his battle leathers are scuffed up, they did their job protecting him from the pavement. With just a few scraps across his hands, he appears mostly unscathed. Zenza is in much the same boat, favoring her right side, and the left side of her helmet is scratched beyond salvage, but her injuries are superficial cuts and bruises.

Loki's mistletoe! Thank every eldritch horror in the cosmos, the two were wearing proper gear.

"How injured are you?" she asks them.

Zenza turns her head to the side with a scoff. Wren can feel the irritations dripping off the teen in rivulets. It's amazing how similar her aura is now compared to when she was a baby. She felt exactly the same as an infant, crying for nothing more than attention. Stubborn little thing, she was. Wouldn't sleep anywhere but in her mother's arms or, on the rare occasion, Wren's when she was feeling indulgent or wanted to get a good grip on Wren's psyche.

Technomancers don't realize this, and Wren will never point it out, but the best way to down an empathic witch is to shove an infant into their arms. The first time Wren held Zenza, the one-month-old latched on so tight to Wren's psyche the witch blacked out. It was like Zenza knew her aunt would be able to understand her every want and need without her ever having to cry for it, and she had not wanted to let go. To call the ferocity of the unwitting glomp "unexpected" is an understatement, and up until then, witchy Wren hadn't been around any babies other than Fae. And Fae was different in so many ways, a constant little presence in her head, overwhelming in its own way for the first few months but manageable.

"I already took a stim. You don't need to lecture me."

Faced with the same temperamental aura of a one-month-old in a now fourteen-year-old body, Wren is unamused.

"If I was going to lecture you, I would be ranting about how you could have killed yourselves. Instead, I am asking if you're alright and thanking the moons you both had enough sense not to drive without your helmets on. So, tell me again I'm lecturing you, princess, or answer my question properly before I drag you to the nearest hospital while I notify your dear uncle of your whereabouts. And I have a feeling he won't be nearly so indulgent about rectifying your lack of awareness for your own mortality."

The girl flinches.

"My steamcycle landed on my left leg when I skidded. It hurts, but nothing is broken, and I took a medi stim already, so the bruising is going down."

"Thank you. Renki?"

"I was able to jump from my cycle before impact. I just landed funny and scraped up my hands. I'm dirty because I helped the princess get out from under her steamcycle which had been leaking oil onto the ground. Both of our bikes were left inoperable from the collision."

"Wonderful. Now, I am going to check you all into the nearest hotel, and you are all going to contact your guardians and supervisors immediately. Then you are going to wait there for them to retrieve you."

"But—"

"You will not be going to Sekhmeti, not with hostile robotics ready to fire the moment you step too close to them, nor will you move from that hotel room once I've made sure it is safe, and I will lock you in it if necessary."

"But you got us through the checkpoint. What was the point if you're just going to leave us behind while you go through the border?"

"I took you through the checkpoint, so you all didn't end up arrested for ornery behavior toward a patrol office following getting caught red handed trying to bypass a sanctioned international checkpoint. I was going to take you across, but with the bridge down, I can't take you with me. Your supervisors will have to collect you themselves. Hikaru and Xipilli will arrive and deal with whatever the hell is going on here. The city will be saved, they'll sort out whatever is going on with Sekhmeti, and I can go on my merry way without a group of teenagers mucking up everything I need to do."

Renki's face falls, and Wren feels just a little bad about his dejection, but it's the truth. He doesn't have a lick of an idea what she's doing, and she's fairly certain if he did, he would stop looking at her like she is someone to be admired.

It's a bitter thought—one that has her turning away from the trio to access the GPS system in her lightcycle and looking for a hotel suitable for three teenagers closely affiliated with the royal families of their respective countries. The sooner she can get these kids somewhere safe and sound, the better.

Behind her, Wren can hear Akari and Renki going back and forth in their native tongue. She catches a few words here and there. "Finding," "together," something about her followed by "leave."

"What are you two whispering about?" asks Zenza.

"None of your concern, princess."

Zenza's anger flares to life, skirting electric over Wren's empathy.

"Don't you know it's rude to exclude someone from a conversation when they're standing right next to you?"

"Don't you know it's rude to butt in on a conversation that has nothing to do with you?"

The two girls bicker back and forth while Renki attempts to cool them both down. Wren just shakes her head and continues trying to figure out the damned search function on the GPS. She's tech savvy, for sure. She would never have made it to technomancer rank in her past life if she wasn't, but whatever updates they've done to their GPS satellites in the last twelve years has really thrown the system for a loop. The map just keeps spinning in circles, unable to pinpoint a location for her.

"Um, hey, crazy witch lady!"

Zenza, can we, please, not shout things like that? Wren thinks. *Wait, when did the bickering go quiet?*

The lull of three teenagers going back and forth has diminished entirely. Wren looks up to see what has caused the temporary quiet between the teenagers. All three teens are looking at something on the far side of the lot that Wren can't quite make out from where she's standing. In the last few minutes, the sky has darkened substantially. It was already a cloudy day but not this cloudy. And the texture of it is wrong.

"What is it?"

Wren leaves her place to get a better look at what they are seeing. She feels the fear before she sees its source. A seeming family of five runs down the street away from something out of their line of sight. The man at the front of the group yanks open a car door before nudging the two older children inside while his partner circles around to the passenger seat with a baby in her arms. The engine revs to life and they skid away down the road in the direction of the city outskirts.

"What was that?" asks Akari.

"Renki," calls Wren. "How far out does your mapping reach?"

"About a kilometer in front of me."

"Do you see anything over there?"

Renki's sights wink on, spiraling golden in his eyes as he sets his field.

"There is another group of people walking this direction."

"What do they look like?"

"I can't tell exactly. They're obscured and moving so slowly I can barely do a motion read."

The wind picks up. Atalia's blonde hair whips around Wren's head as thunder growls overhead, and hurricane sirens begin to howl. Lightning flashes across the sky, but instead of brightening the darkness, the void-like black streak seems to suck the light from the world. The void-lightning is quickly followed by an accompaniment of thunder.

There's a distant scream and the crash of broken glass.

Something is coming.

Maybe the feeling of electricity she felt earlier hadn't been Zenza's emotions at all but something much more sinister. Another bolt of black lightning is followed by the same thunderous boom, but this time when the light returns to the world, a group of people stand at the edge of the lot.

Wren's eyes narrow.

They seem off. Shambling more than walking, their faces blackened by some strange substance, their bodies shaking with unstoppable shivers. They cough and snort and hack their way toward them.

"Draw your weapons, now, and stay by me."

Renki draws his katana, Akari her smaller chisa katana, and Zenza pulls her father's technomancer rifle, Agni, from her back.

"What are you going to do?" asks Renki.

Wren clears her throat and sings.

Lacrimosa dies illa
Qua resurget ex favilla
Judicandus homo reus

A requiem for the dead, Wren stretches her magical might to knot her will around the small group of undead staggering toward them. It's a songweave she's woven hundreds of times, but something is off. They don't fall under her will.

"What are you doing?" Zenza asks again, panic growing in her voice. "Nothing is happening!"

"Be still," says Akari.

The closest shambler is about a stone's throw away, and Wren can make out the boils lining its face. Its eyes, pitch black, cast in coal, are shuttered by void magic. It opens its mouth, teeth gnashing in their direction, and Wren flings a chord of psychic magic at it. It shouts "no" as it flips over and lands on its head with a squelch. But the undead don't speak, and the reason they aren't falling under her will grips Wren with horror.

"Get on the cycles, now. We can't fight these things."

"What? Why not?" asks Renki.

"They're just walking corpses."

"They're not corpses," she hisses, grabbing Renki's wrist and tugging the teen with her back to her lightcycle. Akari follows, but Zenza… Trigger happy Zenza…

"I don't care what they are. They don't scare me."

The teen raises her rifle, a charge already humming as it loads. Wren whirls around and curls her fingers toward the gun's barrel.

"Zenza, no!"

She bears down on the trigger as Wren casts the barrel skyward. The shot flies into the ozone, and the kickback sends Zenza careening to the pavement. Wren yanks her back up onto her feet.

"Why'd you do that? My aim was perfect."

"They aren't dead, you foolish girl!"

There's the crux of it. Wren's magic holds no jurisdiction over the living. She is not a controller of minds. These are living, breathing people, infected by some horrible affliction, and Wren is not about to let these three teenagers get blood on their hands.

Zenza's eyes widen to comical size as she stutters to repeat Wren's words back to her. Another streak of lightning rips across the sky, blackening the world, only this time it is accompanied not by the boom of thunder but by the screech of a raptor. The darkness clears and a great buzzard swoops down from the sky, its talons outstretched and twitching toward them, and Wren and her charges barely hit the deck as it flies overhead, narrowly missing Wren's back.

The booming sound hadn't been thunder at all but the thunderous beating of wings. The wings of a gigantic netherbeast.

A *blixvi*—A Lightning Bird.

"Get on the bikes!" she shouts, and the three rush to obey.

Wren runs backward, pushing the shamblers off their retreat and keeping an eye on the lightning bird as it circles around for another dive. Probably the size of a car, the bird is a sickly yellow and blue color, its feathers dipped in black void-magic. Thick talons extend toward Wren, and a curved beak snaps for her face, sharp as a pair of garden shears. Wren sings a sharp staccato note that hits the bird right in the chest. It barrel-rolls through the air before righting itself and spiraling back into the sky.

Preoccupied with the bird, she doesn't notice the shambler on her flank until its diseased stench curdles in her nose.

"*Gaaaaahhh!*"

It lunges for her, but a katana coated in golden saibāki glances off of the shambler's teeth, and she flings another pulse at the shamblers, throwing them backward. When she turns around, Renki looks at her in askance, his sword at the ready.

"Good work. Now let's go!"

He nods, and they run for the lightcycle. Akari and Zenza are already clamoring onto Akari's when the netherbeast stoops again, diving for the girls.

"Zenza!"

"Akari!"

Zenza drops to the cement, but Akari makes the mistake of drawing her pistol. The shot goes wide. The blixvi catches her in its talons and jerks her into the air. Its beak snaps at the girl's face and neck.

"Akari!"

Wren whips her intention forward like a lasso and catches the bird by its tail, halting it from carrying the teenager away.

"Zenza, shoot it!"

Zenza bolts up, Agni at the ready. She takes aim and fires true. The bullet hits the netherbeast in the side. It releases an angry caw and drops Akari. Renki dives forward, catching his friend before she hits the cement.

"Alright, come here, you," snarls Wren, pulling hard on her magical tether to the blixvi. It flutters in the air, angrily snapping at her as she tries to reel it to the ground. "Zenza, fire again."

"On it," says the girl, a smile in her voice. Agni charges and fires, but just before the shot hits, a surge of black magic dispels Wren's hold, and the blixvi soars into the clouds despite the blood dripping from its side.

A hooded figure appears in a flash of darkness.

"Förstöra!"

A massive wave of energy bursts through the atmosphere. Wren magically yanks the three teenagers to her and pushes outward with everything she has to keep herself and the three teenagers from being blown to bits.

Zenza's screams ring in her ear as the dust clears. Wren looks up to find the hooded figure twisting a teleportation spell.

"Faulen!" sings Wren, and dusty emerald light swirls from her fingertips toward the witch, but before her spell hits, the hooded figure disappears in a spiraling burst of void-stricken mist.

Wren's spell hits the wall of a storefront, and within moments, the brick crumbles, the glass chips and discolors, and a decaying ruin is left in the wake of previously healthy brick and mortar.

"What in the name of gadgetry was that?"

Akari's brown eyes are dilated beyond normal from fear and panic, the blue glow of her inlaid tech flickering like an emergency light. She managed to keep her face from being pecked, but she grips her upper right arm where blood oozes in slow rivers to the ground—blood as black as the diseased shamblers vacating the lot.

Depending on the witch's abilities, Echoes can be incredibly dangerous and should thus be carefully contained. These Echoes left unattended can morph into ley lines, fonts of magic, or, in cases where the witch died of unnatural happenings, volatile hauntings.

An Excerpt from *Hunting and Identifying Hexen* by Finnick Lockecraft, 1852 A.P.

11
THE SUN (PART 1)

Present – 9th Day in the Month of Falling – New Osaka– 10:27AM

KAITO REACHES NEW OSAKA AROUND midday. The streets are bustling with activity. People going to and fro on their daily tasks. The local academy is brimming with activity, students taking an early lunch outside in the cool sunshine. He finds Madame Mishka's tea shop easily. It's hard to miss considering the enforcer vehicle pulled up on the walkway in a defensive parameter. The adepts gathered around it have weapons drawn.

Shimata!

Two of the adepts immediately bolt to attention as he pulls up. A third, younger and greener, nearly fires off a round in surprise, but Kaito deactivates the laser pistol before it can fire with a burst of saibāki. The lad is so young, he probably hasn't even been to his first trials yet, which means he isn't a certified adept yet and should therefore not be touting a weapon through the streets.

"Put that away, you idiot," spits the senior-most officer, slapping the youngster with the twitchy fingers upside the head.

"I swear to everything on this planet, I'm going to demote you back to trainee if you don't start controlling yourself."

"But this is a crime scene. Shouldn't we secure it?"

"Not by firing on civilians. We already have two that have been taken hostage by a goddamn building. Don't make me toss your sorry behind through the window."

"But the plants—!"

"Enough about the plants!"

While the trio squabble, Kaito only sighs. Typical for a local force. Older adepts, long retired from active duty, will often take up local peacekeeping positions in smaller towns. In such places, they have the ability to serve as not only law enforcers and justices of the peace but also city council members and mentors to the next generation of adepts. Really, it's just a convenient way to fatten their pensions and their paunches. They haven't even asked him for identification yet...

Rubbing his eyes, the technomancer dismounts his lightcycle. Despite his state-of-the-art visor, they feel gritty with dust and road. In his helmet's internal comm, AYA pipes up.

"Miyazaki–sama, your monitoring systems are showing signs of fatigue. Do you require an adrenal boost?"

"No, AYA. I'm fine for now."

"Yes, sir."

And he strides forward, completely ignoring the adepts as he makes his way to the door.

The building is saturated with magic. Wren's necrotic aura ripples through the woodwork alongside another which pulses unchecked through the building's very foundations. It's out-of-control and volatile, rapidly accelerating like an orchestra without a conductor. An Echo. A magic user has died on these grounds.

Kaito's feet hasten to the door only to be blocked by the head adept.

"Sir, this is a restricted area under strict investigation. You can't just—"

THE SUN (PART I)

The adept, an old soldier whose organics have gone to seed and whose augmentations are at least 20 years old, shuts up when Kaito's swords flash, sights spinning.

THIS BUILDING IS NOW UNDER THE JURISDICTION OF THE ROYAL FAMILY OF MURASAKI.

The order flashes through the adepts' integrated systems, a warning not to interfere any further, and heed it they do, for they now know exactly who is delivering the command. Who could mistake the lavender sights of the silver-eyed calyx of Murasaki?

As they stumble over themselves, frantically trying to make themselves more presentable and ducking into various levels of kowtow, Kaito examines the shop's front door: stuck fast, not by lock or bolt or shield, but by an overgrowth of plant life.

Vines twine their way along the edges of the door, crisscrossing over the window in rigid brambles. If he turns his head ever so slightly, he can imagine runic shapes emerging from the cacophony of flora. Extending a hand toward the foliage triggers a tightening on the door frame. The plants coil and writhe with a liveliness he has only ever seen in enchantments, and on his scanners, a silvery glow pulses from their vein-like centers—wild magic settled at the very heart of the plants.

"We've been trying to get in for hours, but these plants are possessed."

Kaito turns his attention back to the head adept. The human+ takes it as an incentive to continue.

"Every time we try to get it, they attack us. I've already sent one of my adepts to the med techs with a nasty infusion of some kind of poison. Made her skin break out in hives and boils so bad I thought her skin was going to peel right off."

Kaito's sights spin as he runs analytics on the adept's system: Hakimm Bakura, possessing a prosthetic right hand, dermal armor graphs, and an ocular exoskeleton at least 15 years out of date. Barely qualifying as a cyborg by today's standards, the man may very well have retired not long after the war.

"There are two heat signatures inside," Kaito states.

"Yes, they've spoken to us over comms. Mr. Keng and his teenage daughter. The girl seems to be in a bad way; something about being attacked by some hag in the night. She mentioned something about a woman who saved her life."

Kaito's pulse jumps.

"What woman?"

"Another firefly, I think. Some stranger named Atalia, who came in with the madam yesterday, but we haven't seen hide nor hair of this woman. Mr. Keng says he saw her kill Madame Mishka."

Brow furrowed, Kaito turns back to the door. That doesn't sound right. Why would Wren kill a woman she came here willingly with?

"Not sure I believe him though. The man was in hysterics over the comm, saying crazy things about ghosts and hags and witches. Apparently, his daughter was attacked last night after coming into contact with her, but the girl seems steadfast that whatever killed Mishka wasn't human, but who knows, really? Not like we've seen the so-called angel of life and death since we arrived."

"Do we know what attacked the girl?"

"Probably the same thing that's been attacking the other teenagers around here of late. Honestly, we all thought Mishka was the one behind it. All the attacks were kids connected to her shop, but now she's dead, so who knows? The old man is worse off than the girl. The shock of finding the firefly who owned this place dead triggered an attack of some kind. They both are in dire need of medical attention, but these damn plants..."

Kaito turns back to the door with a hum.

"Vacate the premises. I will take it from here."

"But the witch—"

"Is no longer your concern, captain."

The man bites his tongue and bows. "Yes, highness."

Kaito waits until the patrols have left, leaving him alone at the center of the barricades, before he turns back to the door. There are scorch marks on the plants as though the adepts tried to burn their way in—to no avail. He extends a hand, and the plants react accordingly, writhing with agitation. He draws back before he finds himself whipped across the knuckles by a particularly spiney rose.

Looks like these plants have just about as much love for him as they did for the local adept force. Unsurprising really. Now the question becomes: does he fight his way through the foliage or seek to pacify it? With two civilians trapped inside, the prospect of further irritating the hostile plants doesn't sit well with him, and were this any other occasion, he would have no choice but to resort to a forceful entry. However, this is not any other occasion. In his possession is something none of these other adepts would have had. He only hopes the aura surrounding it is enough to calm the plants or at the very least coax them into believing him a friend.

From the confines of the pouch at his belt, Kaito pulls Wren's locket. Even a day away from the witch who enchanted it, the piece of jewelry holds strong to his songstress's essence. Within his sights, a small pool of data coils around the body of the locket, spiraling patterns of 1's and 0's. Positive values in the 3rd, 102nd, and 437th variables indicate the presence of magic both boundless and necrotic in nature. Empty values at the 52nd and 111th place indicate a nonlethal nature independent of the original castor, so unlike the protection spell Wren placed on his signet ring, the enchantment will hold regardless of the distance between itself and its maker. The few negative values he can find tell him the enchantment is not infallible and will weaken without magical refreshment over time and use.

For now, however, the spell is perfectly potent.

Careful not to disturb the enchantment, he winds the chain around his fist and holds it out to the guarded doorway.

"Pray peace," he calls. "I am a friend and mean no harm to you or the people you guard."

He isn't entirely sure if he is speaking to the plants, the dead witch's echo, or both, but a response comes regardless. The vines withdraw, the door opens, and Kaito steps in unencumbered.

Well, by the plants, anyway... as he steps over the threshold, he has to duck to avoid a teacup saucer flying at his head.

"Who are you?! Go away! No more witches!"

"Baba! Stop it!"

"Stand back, Eun-ji. I'll handle this—argh!"

A middle-aged man, near the beginning of his twilight years, crumples to the floor, clenching tight to his right knee. When the leg gives out entirely, the youth behind him barely manages to keep his head from cracking against the back of a chair, pulling him sideways so he lands in a heap on the carpet instead.

"Papa! I told you not to move. Your arthritis—"

"Damn it all to my arthritis! If this old fool can't keep his only kin safe from devils, what good is he?"

Kaito steps fully into the room, hands held aloft.

"My name is Kaito Miyazaki, technomancer ID: 876921B."

"A technomancer," whispers the girl, Eun-ji.

Her father forces himself up to his knees, a broken chair leg in hand. "I don't buy it. How'd you get those blasted plants to let you in without magic, eh? Those adepts have been trying for hours—eh!" The man cuts himself off as Kaito's sights spin.

Scanning the two for injuries, the prince approaches the pair with a placating gesture. AYA confirms their identifications: Keng Jung-Hoon and his daughter Keng Eun-ji, both civilians, both unaugmented. Jung-Hoon is largely uninjured; however, Kaito's scanners are sharp enough to see the telltale signs of the osteo-arthritis running rampant through his system. He must be a stubborn old goat indeed to defend his child so steadfastly.

The girl, on the other hand, hasn't any business being conscious. Eun-ji's rib cage is beyond battered, rife with bruises as though freshly healed from multiple fractures, and there is an unsettling void within her aura as though pieces of it have been sucked from her. However, lingering around the torn portions of her aura and physical injuries is the familiar emerald glow of Wren's magic, working to heal and correct the damage caused by whatever attack managed to do such damage. This girl should be resting. Once Wren's magic dwindles away, she'll hardly be able to stand, let alone calm her riled-up father.

THE SUN (PART 1)

The man lets out another cry of pain, and Eun-ji is quick to shuffler into the small kitchenette behind the counter. There is a hiss of steam and the sound of bubbling water. When he looks over, the girl is ruffling frantically through the cabinets for something. Kaito has no idea, so he addresses her father instead.

"Keng Jung-Hoon, I understand you and your daughter have been through an ordeal, but I assure you, I am here to offer aid."

"Well, thank the heavens for that." Jung-Hoon's tune changes instantly. He holds his chest as though overcoming a heart attack. "That witch killed Mishka and would have probably killed us, too, if I hadn't caught her defiling the madam's body."

"She didn't kill her, baba," Eun-ji chides her father once again. The girl's fists clench at her sides.

"You didn't see what I saw, Eun-ji. Mishka deteriorated into nothing, and right before that woman ran off, the whole building shook. Then the plants came to life, and we got trapped here."

If the firefly was a practicing witch, the shaking of the building very well may have been Mishka's echo. Her death would have released the wave of power which brought the plants to life and flooded the shop with the silvery essence AYA's systems are now tracking through the space.

"Why would she save my life if she was only going to kill Mishka? It makes no sense."

Her posture speaks of pain riddled through her torso, hunched as she is. His scans, too, pick up magical residue all over her being. A familiar magic currently working to heal her injuries even as it fades into the ether.

"I don't know, Jiji."

Jung-Hoon's shoulders sag. Kaito waits patiently as the pair's conversation dies before addressing the teenager. "Do you have any idea where she might have gone?"

Eun-ji looks at him in surprise.

"When I met her earlier, she and Mishka were talking about Sekhmeti. Maybe there?"

"Hn."

It would make sense for Wren to head for the border. Hikaru no doubt made it clear she was no longer welcome in Murasaki no Yama. But why Sekhmeti? Wouldn't it have made more sense for her to head to one of the hexen zones? New Chernobyl was only a few kilometers farther south, and Lorelei also sat on Murasaki's border. Even Deriva would be a better choice. It is after all her birth home and where the last of her known kin live, her brother and niece.

Well, Wren's reasoning aside, he'll have to hurry if he is to cut her off at the border. He turns back to his charges.

"You are both in need of medical attention. It would be best if you came with me to the nearest hospital."

"But my father can barely walk without his tea."

His tea?

Seeing Kaito's raised eyebrow, Eun-ji explains. "Madame Mishka had a special brew just for my father's arthritis. I've been trying to find it, but I don't know where she keeps it or if she only mixes it when we need it, and with Mishka gone..." A sob chokes off the girl's explanation.

"Oh, Eun-ji. This old man can manage alright without. What's a little bit of pain?" Jung-Hoon staggers to his feet with a wince. "See, right as rain."

A new energy signature crops up to his left.

The storefront window shatters half a second after AYA pings an alert. Kaito draws his tanto and the steel clangs against a glinting blade a blink before it can impale the man in front of him. Jung-Hoon falls back to the ground. The impact of his skull on the floor rings loud in Kaito's ear.

"Get down!"

Eun-ji drops as Kaito whirls on their attacker.

On the sidewalk, another technomancer stands with a spare blade in hand. His monocled visor reflects silver in the sun, the targeting crosshairs on the lens lit up in a flickering orange. He wears the battle leathers of an adept from the southern region of Murasaki, loose fitted gafeng pants and a leather vest, but they are the wrong color. Instead of the deep wines and violets of Murasaki, he instead wears a mix of Seraphim red and burnt Sekhmetian gold. Fitting for a traitor.

Tanaka Ryu. The rogue who helped a group of hexen attack Snowfall Palace seven days ago.

"Miyazaki–sama? Fancy seeing you here. Consorting with a new witch, I see?"

He points the kunai in his hand to Eun-ji. The teen crawls backward, and Kaito's eyes narrow.

"There is no witch here."

"I beg to differ. This place reeks of heathen, and this little strumpet is covered with magical energy. I wasn't expected to find one so green, but I won't pass the opportunity to add a new trophy to add to my wall."

"You hunt witches yet lead a vampyre and a shifter in attacking Snowfall."

"Mere tools to be used to an end. I follow orders. Perhaps you and the rest of Murasaki should learn to do the same. Mixing yourself up with another witch? Really, Miyazaki-sama? Didn't you learn your lesson twelve years ago? Not to worry. Why don't you just stand down while I hunt her down lest you suffer second embarrassment?"

Kaito's eyes narrow. *So, he's after Wren.* And Kaito draws his steel.

Tanaka's crosshairs rotate and the man lunges through the broken window towards Kaito. Kaito twists to avoid the sharpened edge of the kunai, cutting up with Amatsu, engaging the other Murasakan technomancer in a dance of blades. But it is not the steel in Tanaka's hand he has to worry about.

REMOTE HACKING DETECTED

The notification scrolls across his sights. Tanaka is trying to inject a virus into his tech system.

ACTIVATE FIREWALLS

On his command, AYA revs to life the firewalls embedded within his interface.

Tanaka shoves one of the tables over, reclaiming his first kunai from where it landed at Jung-Hoon's feet while the man scrambles backward as fast as he can. Kaito parries around both blades, narrowly avoiding one as the other slices past his right eye. Lavender sights spin as he targets Tanaka's systems, and their blades lock in front of their faces.

DESTABILIZE MAINFRAME

Tanaka pulls back, stabbing for Kaito's stomach. The tip of the kunai glances off the leather of Kai's armor, a thin trail of blood seeping into the cloth. Tanaka grins.

"First blood, prince. Do you yield, or shall we keep on? Which do you think will happen first? Think I can bleed you dry before my virus hits your system or will your network fall under my control? Either way, I'll be sure to let your little witch whore know you were looking for her before I slit her throat."

Kaito spins forward. Amatsu clangs against Tanaka's kunai as AYA's cloaked systems invade the other technomancer's interface. Tanaka's eyes screw shut as Kaito's command operation takes effect.

"Gah!" shouts Tanaka as an electrical surge rockets through his body. The man flails, twin daggers glancing off Kaito's sword. The crosshairs on his monocle go dark and his inlaid tech flashes wildly on and off. Kaito cuts downward, opening Tanaka's shoulder. The man swipes blindly at him in response; a surge of electricity shoots through Kai's body as the kunai stabs into the meat of his bicep. He grits his teeth and kicks the man into a nearby table. The man rises with a feral growl and thrusts his blade toward Kaito's head, but as Kai raises his tanto to block, glass shatters against Tanaka's face.

Boiling water splashes across tender, now melting skin.

"Argh! *Biǎo zi!*"

THE SUN (PART I)

Eun-ji stands at the counter holding a tea cozy. The porcelain shards of a teapot litter the floor.

"Get back," shouts Kaito as Tanaka throws one of the kunai, but Eun-ji, too slow to dodge, stands stock still in shock as her father dives in front of her. Eun-ji screams as both father and daughter tumble to the floor. Kaito lets loose a volatile pulse of saibāki toward Tanaka only to have it implode in on itself, his servers scrambled from the virus clashing against AYA's firewalls.

"I'm going to enjoy ripping your witch to pieces, Miyazaki."

Tanaka lunges to stab Kaito in the stomach but is stopped short when a vine whips out to wind around his arm and yank him off his feet. He lands in a pile of glass as another bolt of pain electrocutes Kaito's system.

He drops to a crouch, pain lacing through his neurons into his S33D, shutting down his sights. It would be crippling had he not survived worse once before...

SYSTEM FIREWALLS REINSTATED

...and redesigned his tech for just such attacks. Lavender light returns to the center of his eyes.

"Tanaka!"

"Baba!"

Kaito is moving to end the rogue technomancer when he hears Eun-ji's cry. He turns. The kanai... The blade has sunk deep into the man's back. Tanaka brutally summons the weapon back, rending flesh and organs. Blood pours from the man's wound, staining his clothing.

"Purity for Deus," snarls Tanaka before he rips the top off a combustible. "Your witch cast her last spell when she relieved your family of the curse that should have destroyed you all."

The fuse sparks and hisses, filling the room with smoke. The fumes burn Kai's eyes and nose. His organic vision blurs, leaving naught but cyber-lined reality as Tanaka scratches his way out the window onto the street.

"Tanaka!"

He takes a single step forward and the combustible detonates. Fire and flame sear through the room. Kaito, lunging toward the two civilians behind him, throws a last-ditch pulse of saibāki to deflect the blast. Glass shatters and wood crumbles as he uses his own body, alight with technolyzed energy, as a shield. It isn't enough to save him the bruises and burns, but it keeps the blast from automatically destroying the entire shop with him, Jung-Hoon, and Eun-ji inside.

Kaito draws his katana and starts running after Tanaka when he hears Jung-Hoon choke on smoke. Eun-ji shouts to her father in their native tongue, panicked and scared as the fire leeches its way toward them.

Torn, Kaito stalls. One foot poised to race after the traitor hunting his soulmate and the other urging him to rescue the pair behind him lest they perish in the fire, it seems like an impossible choice.

But it isn't. Not really.

Leaving these two to die is the last decision he would make. Even if his own conscience didn't demand such, Wren would never forgive him for choosing her over the lives of innocents. Kaito pulls Eun-ji and her father toward the back room, away from the unnatural flames.

Stepping through the curtain is like walking into an alternative space.

Here Wren's magic is even more potent. The air is cool and calm despite the inferno blazing its way in. Water drip, drip, drips from the faucet into the half-full tub. There is a note of peaceful slumber on the air, like a lullaby sung for the restless dead. Healing magic permeates the walls and the furniture, and his spine tingles as the coils of latent energy sink into the burns there. It feels like home and happiness, solemnity and sadness at once.

She was here. His witch. She saved a life here. Tried to save two lives here but lost the second battle to her own horror and grief.

The heat pulls him from his musing. Fire lays claim to the curtain, and in his early daze at being surrounded by Wren's magic, he realizes the fatal error he's just made. There is no window in this room and therefore no way out.

Kuso!

That's when the deck of tarot cards in his back pocket begins to vibrate. A tendril of magic pulls from it a single card: the sun. The card drifts upward to a spot on the wall and hovers there, swaying from side to side as though waiting for him to react to the message. Kaito doesn't read tarot, knows little to nothing about it or any meaning he may garner from the cards. Why the sun? Because of the fire behind them? Because it's presently daylight outside? Wait... daylight. Is the card trying to get outside into the daylight?

Drawing Tsukuyomi, Kaito summons a net of saibāki around the blade and hurls it directly at the card. The card flutters away, and the katana impales itself into the wall, and when he calls back the weapon, the thinnest sliver of sunlight peeks through the hole.

That's it. That's their way out.

The sun card was pointing him in the direction of the sun so they could escape.

"Get in the water," he commands Eun-ji. "Try not to inhale the smoke."

Eun-ji nods, shuffles herself and her father to the small bath. Kaito makes sure the pair are settled in the tub before going to work, unleashing on the wall until a hole big enough for them to pass through is made. Smoke clogs his nose and mouth. His respiratory systems work in overdrive to clear the toxins from his chest, tapping into as many filters as he possesses to keep the grit out and the oxygen in.

He ushers the now soaking Eun-ji through first. Then, flinging Jung-Hoon across his back, he follows the girl through the new opening in the wall. And when his feet touch the pavement, fresh air billows through his lungs.

He pushes Eun-ji forward around the block, toward the street where already a firefighting crew have converged to combat the raging fire. When they reach the sidewalk, he turns, relieved to find Eun-ji unharmed.

Her father is not so lucky. He's lost a lot of blood and lies heavily over Kaito's shoulders, pale and barely clinging to life. Kaito takes a medi stim from his belt pouch and injects it into the man's belly.

"AYA, call for an ambulance."

"Yes, your highness."

And Kaito waits for time and tech to heal the battered body before him.

The same cannot be said for the storefront, now engulfed in flames. The plants scream at the intensity of the flames, and the lingering magic of the Mishka's echo evaporates into the ether with a shudder Kaito feels all the way through the nanotechnology grafted into his very marrow.

But how? Does it even matter?

Eun-ji, anxious at his side, asks him a slew of questions, but he doesn't have the strength or energy to reassure her. He is too tangled in his own bitter emotions to offer comfort. He came here looking for Wren and found instead a trail of death and destruction. One he couldn't even put a proper end to.

By the time the flow of blood stops, Tanaka is long gone, but Mr. Keng will live to see tomorrow's dawn. He knows that with a surety. The person he isn't so certain will make it to tomorrow, however, is far beyond his sight and rapidly getting farther away as danger rides on her heels. Weariness seeps into his bones, and the ache in his chest returns full force; only this time it is laced with dread.

Kami, he hasn't felt this alone since the weeks following his mother's death, and even that paled in comparison to when Wren died.

The Sun (part i)

The Alliance forces approach from the north and the south, the contingent divided in two to better siege the Pontiflex's basilica, a palace carved out of the very ice it rests on.

Wren rides with Kai on his lightcycle much to Xipilli's dismay. As they approach the compound, Wren becomes increasingly restless behind him, the fur coat she wears rustling with her every move. Kaito's mapping system is picking up a field of power hovering just in front of them, steadily strengthening as they approach. The ominous feel of it becomes suffocating, and Kai continues to run analytics only to come up on wall after wall after wall until Wren lifts herself up to look over Kai's shoulder. She tenses with a choked inhale. She activates the comm in her helmet and shouts to their forces.

"Stop!"

Three adepts, too far forward to react on time, ram headlong into an invisible barrier. Their vehicles explode on impact and their human+ bodies are thrown into the barrier. They writhe in agony. Blood pours to the ground as their augmentations are pried from their bodies; flesh, organs, white matter, and bone displace as their fleshy parts disappear through the barrier, leaving nothing but tech behind.

The barrier, actively glowing with a neon fluorescence during impact, settles back completely invisible. To the untrained or unaugmented eye, one would never guess there was anything there, only miles of uninterrupted snow and ice. Not even the bodies of the three adepts are visible on the other side, a perfect illusion for a deadly trap.

The Morrigan calls the convoy to a halt.

Military tanks and armored robots stop behind the cavalry vehicles where most of the technomancers ride, including Hikaru, Xipilli, Irene, The Morrigan, Kai and Wren, and a few other technomancers. Hikaru dismounts his cycle and approaches the remnants of the three unfortunates on the ground. After a quick scan, he turns back around.

"All of the tech has been fried. Salvage is not an option even if there was a chance they survived having their parts ripped from their bodies."

"Nocturne, what is this?" asks the Morrigan.

Wren dismounts from behind Kai and steps toward the barrier, her boots crunching through the snow. She removes her glove with her teeth, raises her hand to the ward hovering in space, and pushes her awareness out. Tendrils of viridian power curl from her fingertips before hooking into the ward. The sigils around her face glow, and her hair shifts in the otherworldly breeze kicked up by the flexing of her magic. Several of the technomancers and adepts behind her take a step back, having only heard of her abilities and never witnessing them first-hand, but Wren ignores the whispers, closing her eyes to concentrate on her task.

Xipilli comes up to her, questioning what she's doing. He cuts himself off mid-sentence when she shoves her amputated arm through the barrier.

"Wren, what the fuck!" shouts Xipilli.

Nothing happens to her arm. She doesn't even flinch. All they can see is a neon glow where her arm enters the field. The limb on the other side of the barrier is invisible to the human eye.

"¡Estás loca o qué!" Xipilli continues cursing colorfully in Deriva as he yanks Wren's arm out of the barrier himself. She graces him with a quirked eyebrow and an eye roll as she takes back her limb before addressing everyone.

"It's an anti-tech field. A filter as it were. It won't allow anything inorganic through, even going so far as to shred a body into pieces if an augmented individual were to try to enter."

Wards are commonplace when dealing with wild magic users, but this—this is something new. And this something could only be invented from a cooperation between science and witchcraft.

"So, we cannot get through?" asks Hikaru.

THE SUN (PART I)

Wren shakes her head. "Not if you don't want your head ripped apart."

The witch walks along the parameter of the ward, tracing and seeing where and if it curves or changes variation. A crackle comes through on their comms. The other group to the north, led by Mirai, Fumiko, and Absko, has also encountered the ward, losing several adepts to the field as well. This implies the ward is circular, having a central origin point; Kaito's theory is further confirmed when Jamar orders several attack drones to try and enter over the top of the barrier. None can manage it, and one of them is now scrap metal after touching the ward. It rolled down the side of the dome in a fit of sparks and busted circuitry after contact.

"So we are at a standstill," comes Absko's voice.

Rameses curses. "Damnit! All of our planning kaput because of these cursed magic users."

Kaito dismounts before approaching Wren, who has so far been quietly contemplating the barrier. Her lips are half twisted, half pursed into a grin, and her brows are furrowed together. He knows the look she gets about her when something is brewing in her head, especially when it is something dangerous and potentially insane. She wears the same look now.

"What are you thinking?"

"Most magical barriers are held up by a central group of casters. There's probably a coven keeping it active at its center. If we could get to them, we could dismantle the barrier."

"And how are we supposed to manage that? We can't get in," growls Rameses.

"You can't, but I can."

Xipilli turns to his sister.

"Absolutely not!"

"We don't have much choice, Xipilli," she says, already unstrapping the various mechanical accoutrements adorning her. Her headset, her pistol, even her utility belt which holds her comm unit. "I'm going."

Kai looks on quietly as her brother rages.

"With that body! Are you insane?! You'll be unarmed, unaugmented, and basically defenseless."

"I'm hardly defenseless, Xipilli," she says ominously, the triskele's glow reflecting in her eyes. He's never seen Xipilli flinch so violently.

"Vulcan Xipilli," calls the Morrigan, interrupting. "This may be the only route available to us."

"This is my sister's life we are talking about!"

The glow of Wren's magic softens as she sets a hand on her brother's shoulder. "I'll be fine, hermano."

"And if you're not? How will we know if you end up dead? You have no vital monitors, no comms, and no way to call for help."

"Give me an hour. If the ward isn't down by then, you'll know it didn't work."

"And you just expect me to leave you behind again? Not happening."

She sighs before pulling her athame, her Lacuna, from her boot sheathe. The bone dagger shines obsidian in the cold sunlight. Her magic unfolds around her as she wills it to hover over her palm before she draws it across the meat of her hand. Xipilli looks on in horror as she kneels, drawing an array into the frozen ground. The snow steams with the applique of blood.

Kai tracks her actions with calculating eyes. When she rises back to standing, she pulls her hair free of its tie. Black tresses fall around her shoulders in silky waves, and she separates a piece of hair from the nape of her neck. She uses the dagger to cut the lock of hair free and winds the ribbon around the sachet of hair with her magic. When she finishes, she floats the locket over to Kai. He holds out his hand as the green ribbon settles in his palm, her hair nestled within.

"There's an inscription on the ribbon. If I'm not back in an hour and the ward isn't down, read the spell, throw it into the circle, and it'll summon me back."

The locket rests in his hand like a promise. He forgets to breathe as their eyes meet. She is going to do this, and he is not going to stop her. He nods to her, an acknowledgement her trust will not be misplaced.

"Why are you giving it to him?" spits Xipilli.

"Because you, brother mine, won't wait long enough," hisses Wren. She shakes her head, handing Xipilli her tech for safekeeping. "I'll be fine, Xipilli. Trust me, okay?"

Xipilli looks like he wants to keep protesting, keep dissenting, keep making up any excuse to keep her in his sight, but with Wren's determination unwavering, he relents.

"Keep your head down, and don't do anything stupid. If you get caught, I'll never forgive you."

She quirks her brow and laughs. "If I get caught, you'll just summon me back out."

"Brat!"

"Love you, too."

She steps toward the barrier.

"Wren," calls Kai. She turns to him. "Be safe."

"Always," she says, then disappears into the ward.

The barrier surrounding the Pontiflex's fortress falls exactly fifty-two minutes after Wren enters the field.

Ludo Ex Machina—The League's Trial by Combat

Not unlike the gladiator games of the past, the Ludo ex Machina is a long-held human+ tradition among their own. A means by which to judge the guilt and appropriate punishment for any posthuman who has stepped out of line or wronged another. These games are duels to the death with the victor going free for bringing divine justice down on the head of their opponent.

—<u>On Technomancers and Adepts: A History on Human+ Soldiers</u>
By E.X. Icarus, 1812 A.P.

12
THE SUN (PART 2)

**Three Days Later – 21st Day in the Month of Planting –
Vatidome City**

KAITO READS ALOUD FROM AN EBOOK OF
one of his mother's favorites: *I Am a Cat*. An old-world
novel by Sōseki Natsume.

"*Wagahai wa Neko de Aru.* As yet I have no name. I've no idea
where I was born. All I remember is that I was miaowing in a
dampish dark place when, for the first time, I saw a human being."
(Natsume 3)

Passages taken here and there from different places in the
book. He reads them at random.

"The autumn leaves, arranged in two or three scarlet terraces
among the pine trees, have fallen like ancient dreams. The red and
white sasanquas near the garden's ornamental basin, dropping
their petals, now a white and now a red one, are finally left bare.
The wintry sun along the ten-foot length of the southwards-facing

veranda goes down daily earlier than yesterday. Seldom a day goes by but a cold wind blows. So my snoozes have been painfully curtailed." (Natsume 16)

He never understood why his mother enjoyed the tale so. So much of it, a ruthless portrayal of the unkindness animals suffer at human hands and how utterly mundane humans are even though they believe themselves to be the masters of their own destinies, and the ending... The first time Mirai read him the full story, he cried, and after calming his tears and talking out his thoughts and feelings, she sat him down and told him all things end in death.

"There is nothing in the world more pleasant than to eat something one has never eaten, or to see something one has never seen before. If my readers, like my master, spend thirty or forty minutes on three days of every passing week in the world of the public bath, then of course the world can offer them few surprises: but if, like me, they have never seen that spectacle, they should make immediate arrangements to do so. Don't worry about the deathbed of your parents, but at all costs do not miss the grand show of the public bath. The world is wide, but in my opinion it has no sight more startlingly remarkable to offer." (Natsume 241)

His mother titters, a small smile gracing her face at a simple kitten's proclamation of a bathhouse being the most important sight to be seen in the world.

"*Akachan,* read me the passage about how he knows what his owner is thinking."

So, he scrolls through the pages.

"I am a cat. Some of you may wonder how a mere cat can analyze his master's thoughts with the detailed acumen which I have just displayed. Such a feat is a mere nothing for a cat. Quite apart from the precision of my hearing and the complexity of my mind, I can also read thoughts. Don't ask me how I learned that skill. My methods are none of your business. The plain fact remains that when, apparently sleeping on a human's lap, I gently rub my fur against his tummy, a beam of electricity is thereby generated, and down that beam into my mind's eye every detail of his innermost reflections is reflected." (Natsume 349)

As he finishes the passage, Mirai's eyes slide shut. This morning's dose of medicines have taken their toll on her, but the doctors are hopeful with this new approach.

Kaito, however, isn't so sure.

He shuts down the holo and leaves his mother to rest.

When Kaito was a boy, his aunt once read to him the story of a sleeping beauty, cursed to eternal sleep until true love's first kiss woke her. He doesn't quite remember the moral of it, ever dubious to the idea any kind of love can form between two strangers when one of them lies catatonic in a magical slumber, and Fumiko always pressed that acts such as kissing another person should be done with the other consenting to the contact. He can't help but think of it now as his fingers dance over the holographic keys of a piano.

The sound is synthetic and electrical, a pale mockery of the true ringing of mallets hitting carefully tuned strings, but it is the best he has available here, away from home and seated across the room from his own sleeping beauty.

Wren sleeps.

Overly pale and devastatingly small, Wren lays nestled under several blankets. They had a scare yesterday when Wren's body temperature dropped all of a sudden, hence the warming blanket now folded over her torso. Her hair, carefully brushed by her sister, lays across a white pillowcase in a dark halo around her head. At the center of her brow, the triskele has yet to quiet. It glows a dull greenish blue, like lightning trapped in a tinted bottle even if its edges are now unrefined, like paper torn at the edges. At least, this coloration he can call beautiful, reminiscent of the clear waters of Wren's home, and a reassuring antithesis to the virulent, moldy green it darkened to during the siege.

Kaito shudders, remembering what caused the shift of color.

In order to defeat the coven of witches at the heart of the forcefield, Wren summoned a long-dead witch into her very marrow, losing all sense of self to gain the power necessary to win against the Goblin King, Yggfret. The infestation tainted the natural viridian emerald of her magical markings. Kai tries to forget the color, grotesque as it had been oozing from Wren's indicia like poison from a wound.

She would have been lost to him were it not for the locket of hair she left him. Upon reciting the spell, Wren's eyes, which were black as soot under the influence of the foreign spirit, cleared to reveal familiar blue-green, and she collapsed into his arms sick with spell fever.

Three days later, Wren still has not woken. He wonders, if he had been but a few minutes later, would he be sitting next to a coffin rather than a bed? She lies comatose, her price to pay for the sheer magnitude of magic she invoked, while the Alliance sings her praises—the hero who made possible their victory over Seraphim. The Alliance's diamond, currently under the careful watch of her brother, her sister, and Kaito Miyazaki.

In the times when he is not tending his duties or sitting at his mother's bedside, Kaito holds vigil, playing music, and Wren is a silent audience. The barest flutter of her lashes, the soft sighs of her breath, and the steady rise and fall of her chest all the reaction he receives for his efforts.

Her hands at her sides, an IV drip feeds fluids into her system, keeping her hydrated as she recovers. A monitor beeps steadily at her bedside, keeping track of her vitals. It serves as a metronome for Kaito's music.

THE SUN (PART 2)

Originally, several doctors scrambled for the opportunity to tend the Alliance's hero. Despite Atzi and Kaito's concerns, Xipilli, unsure what to do, had allowed a small group of them to treat her to near cataclysmic effect. Not only did Wren's magic lash out against them in her sleep, subconsciously protecting her from what it interpreted as an attack, but when one of the doctors did manage to follow through on a procedure, the witch went into cardiac arrest, an experimental adrenal injection meant to rouse her doing far more harm than good to her hyperactive magical network. Afterward, Xipilli banished all of the doctors from tending to her. Wren's body is not that of a technomancer's, and their personnel do not know enough about her system to safely treat her. For all the League knows about how to kill a witch, they know next to nothing about how to help one suffering from chaos fever.

A sudden clatter breaks the quiet.

Kaito pauses on a chord and looks up to see a black cat perched on Wren's windowsill. The animal stills, looking at him with large green eyes, as Kai's sights whirr to life, scanning the creature. Roughly the size of a housecat, there is something off about the feline. Its edges undefined, its fur seems to shift and sway like mist. There is magic about it, not witch magic per se, nor fae magic. It is wilder, more chaotic, like a netherbeast's, a suspicion made more plausible when he finds he can't pinpoint it into his VR-scape. But what would a netherbeast be doing here? It has one paw lifted as though planning to jump onto Wren's bed but stalls, eyeing Kaito as though assessing whether the man is a threat to it or not.

Kaito holds still, and a single paw reaches down to settle on Wren's forehead.

The resulting reaction is unlike anything Kaito has ever seen save once: the singular occasion of a waylaid mission into cyberscape. At the featherlight touch of the cat's paw, Wren's indicia pulses. The tattered edging of the symbol repairs itself, becoming more whole, more akin to before Wren disappeared into the barrier.

Kaito stands in alarm as Wren's magic sings to life. An ethereal echo of the piece he was just playing hums through the room. Wisps of chaos glide around him, twining through his clothing and over the holo of the keyboard, a phantom hand caressing his skin. It feels like her, knows it's her presence down to his very marrow.

"Wren?"

He approaches the bed, but just as he is about to take her hand, the door behind him opens and the moment breaks. The cat's paw lifts from Wren's brow, and it darts from the room, gone in the whispered padding of lithe footfalls. Gone in an instant and had he not recorded the whole instance, Kaito would question whether it even happened.

"Miyazaki-kun," a soft voice calls from the doorway. He turns to see Atzi. Wren's sister has been a constant presence by her side, always there to greet Kaito with a smile when he comes to call even though Kaito never smiles back.

"Princess," he greets with a bow of his head. She returns the gesture with a small curtsy.

"Is everything alright?" she asks, noticing his sights are on. He deactivates his tech, glancing out the window. No sign of the cat.

"Nothing to be alarmed about, highness, but you haven't seen any stray cats around the compound, have you?"

"Stray cats? Not that I've seen."

A medical droid zooms in behind her, and Kaito moves out of the little bot's way as it flits over to run a scan on Wren. The droid will also clean Wren's linens and wash her for the day once Kaito leaves which will be soon now Atzi has returned.

The keyboard holo shuts down at Kaito's command, and he collects his swords from the nearby table.

"How is your mother?"

Kaito stalls in the doorway.

In the days following the fall of the Pontiflex, the Alliance celebrates. Banquets are held in honor of the victorious, drinks poured for the new generation of war heroes, and public executions held to exuberant media coverage. With plenty of

THE SUN (PART 2)

witches and other hexen caught aiding Seraphim, there is plenty of magical blood to be spilt. And for the posthuman traitors, the Ludos ex Machina begin to much fanfare.

Tch! Fights to the death between prisoners... Such a distasteful tradition, but one held in high esteem nonetheless by the majority of their peers.

In the wake of Seraphim's defeat, the Alliance followed with this tradition, hosting a slew of Ludos ex Machina as a means to divvy out punishment for those who betrayed them. Broadcast throughout the League, adepts and technomancers on the losing side of the war enter the arena to fight for another day of survival. Betting pools are assembled, fortunes made and ruined in the games, and fresh corpses feed the hounds of war.

But it is not all the joy and avarice of victory. Funeral pyres are held nightly. Countless lives lost because of one man's greed, and even more lay infirm, fighting for their lives in hospital beds. Among the mortally wounded is Kai's mother. The Empress of Murasaki no Yama lies cursed by a witch's spell, dying while the best doctors in the League fail to cure her of a curse working to destroy her from the inside out, a magical wasting disease of the blood, and the Miyazaki family abstains from the vast majority of the celebrations in observation.

He left her side this morning after she fell asleep while he was reading to her. She holds on, talking with him, Hikaru, and Fumiko when she can, but her weakness only grows.

"She fights the affliction, but the doctors are at loss for how to treat her."

"What about the Dispel Corps?"

Kaito shakes his head.

The droid begins its scan, hovering over Wren's chest. A blue light pans over her, starting at the crown of her head. Atzi looks at her sister sadly, blinking before looking back at Kaito.

"It's slow going, but I believe she's regaining her strength. Maybe once Wren wakes up, she'll be able to banish your mother's curse."

If Wren wakes up... It could be weeks, even months before the magic in her system disperses enough for her to wake. He knew the witchcraft would do her more harm than good. He just didn't expect it to happen this quickly.

He fights down the need to touch her hand. There is a reason only the droid is allowed to tend to Wren. Physical contact aggravates her condition, her magic stirring up like an untamed beast in response to any person's touch, even her siblings, should they overstay the boundary of their welcome. Instead, he conducts his own scan of her with his sights, committing to his databanks her current condition. She is stable and still. Even the magic in her blood seems to be sleeping, lulled to rest by his music.

"Thank you for allowing me to visit her. I will take my leave now."

"I'm sure my sister appreciates your presence, highness."

Kaito bows his head and leaves.

While Aighneas is metallurgy and gasoline, Seraphim is concrete dressed as marble, steel dressed as wood, and nuclear decay masquerading as clean energy.

In the wake of taking over the Pontiflex's basilica, the Alliance settles to recover and reorganize in the city surrounding Vatidome. With most of the city underground as a means to conserve warmth in the face of the tundra, the little above ground is reserved for those able to pay the cost of heating and electricity against the frosts. Xipilli opted to have his sister housed in an above ground cabin separate from the rest of the compound where sunshine and forest will aid her recovery, but Hikaru had chosen to keep their family in the main compound of the frozen basilica. It means the trek from Kaito's rooms to Wren's is a short ride on his light cycle through the snow lest he decide to make the walk on foot.

THE SUN (PART 2)

Hikaru and Fumiko are seated, nursing cups of tea when Kaito returns.

"They've decided to give Donarick jurisdiction over Seraphim."

"Donarick Thames? But he is the son of the former Pontiflex. How can they trust him?"

"He killed his father. Were it not for him—Oh! Kaito, you're back early. How is Lady Wren?"

"Unchanged."

"Thus we see the true nature of magic. It does naught but destroy. Even its own practitioners."

Kaito makes no comment. What can he say against truth?

His mother and Wren, both in hospital beds, were put there by magic. Wren's condition entirely self-inflicted.

A circle of bodies lay around the array. Witches, all of them. The glows of their indicia flicker and die as each draws their last breath.

At the center of it all, a volatile pool of necrotic magic.

"I suppose he'll be a mere figurehead. After all, he isn't a technomancer."

His brother gives an uncharacteristic sigh, pinching the node at his left temple between his thumb and index finger with a wince. Kaito can empathize. He's had a stress headache for two days.

"Rameses has rectified that. Honorary advancement for his service."

Wren's eyes are black as pitch. Not a trace to be found for clear aquamarine. And when she sings, the texture is mottled and nasally, not anything like the songstress he knows.

"The witch on us who turns her back, will burn until her bones are black. A witch left with no one to trust, shall crumble til she's naught but dust."

"Wren," calls Kaito. "Fight it off!"

"Ah! The lover... Poor Wren. Twice damned. Once by fate. Twice by love. Poor thing, my poor child, and you pass judgement like the pack of cowards you are. So called witch-hunters. You think you can kill my children. You can't. Not while my darling Wren is alive."

"Wren doesn't belong to you."

In the present, the conversation around him continues.

"How did you vote?"

"I didn't dissent, but I didn't vote yes either."

"Oh, you poor, poor thing. Still think you can turn back the clock. None of us has such power. She speaks the elder tongue with ease. It sings through her blood, her body, her spirit. Will you play her accompaniment, prince? Or will you too seek to end the song?"

"Wren, come back to me."

"She's not listening, boy. I've put her to sleep, and she so needed the rest."

"Wren!"

The lock of hair in his hand burns with magic.

"And then, there's Deriva to worry about."

At the mention of Deriva, Kaito tunes back into the conversation. "What about Deriva?"

Hikaru turns to him. "The other countries are vying for Xipilli's favor. I'm sure I don't have to tell you why."

Wren—the magical wild card currently sitting in Xipilli's hand.

"Xipilli continues to hold firm his sister maintain her technomancer title, and any who ask of her are briskly told she is fine, merely recuperating, and to mind their own business. I'm sure I don't need to tell you it doesn't sit well among the more conservative technomancers for a witch to have such autonomy, but who could speak out against the witch who made our entire victory possible? They can't touch her so long as her brother protects her lest they risk war with Deriva, and your Wren is enough of an unknown they are afraid to speak against him."

"Wren is not mine, Hikaru."

Hikaru segues around his statement.

"They discuss the number of ways her magic can be used as a weapon for the new Technomancer Council. They speak openly of her like she is some finely forged weapon if only Xipilli will comply."

An object to be used like she is no longer human while at the same time Kaito hears all of the whispers lingering in the air of her witchery. It leaves a foul taste in Kaito's mouth: technomancers willing to leech the benefits of Wren's power while condemning her in the same breath.

"Whether Xipilli complies or not matters little to Wren. She is not a tool, nor is she bespoke to her brother. She doesn't follow orders blindly, and her allegiance is to herself and her loved ones, not any country or contract."

"Which puts her in a very dangerous position," inserts Fumiko. "If she demonstrates they cannot control her, they will view her as a threat. One to be eliminated."

Heat flares in the pit of Kai's belly, his fist clenching around nothing. Wren isn't even awake right now. How dare they discuss her while she lies vulnerable in a sick bed! The cowards.

Hikaru raises a hand before Kaito interjects.

"We don't want that to happen, and I'm sure once Mother is able to add her voice to the discussion, she can squash their ridiculous ambitions. It's okay, *didi*. Everything will settle. Everyone has already decided not to put the election of primarch to a vote until Kaasan has regained her strength."

Hikaru's optimism is admirable, but Kaito holds a half-empty cup. All he can do is bite his tongue and sit helplessly at the bedsides of two of the most important women in his heart, his mother and his lover, and hold onto the hope both of them will wake to see him once more.

The next morning, Kaito sits by his mother's side while Fumiko plays her koto on the other side of the room when Mirai's voice rasps through the room.

"Fumi…"

Fumiko rises from her place by the window and approaches the bed. Kai's mother is wan: her hair hanging limp around her head, the pallor of her skin a sickly grey. Even her eyes, normally bright with vitality despite their dark hue, have dulled, the whites of them reddened with burst capillaries, evidence of the internal struggle taking place within her body. Her tech strains to expel the curse ripping through her living tissues and even in this venture the doctors question whether her defense systems are doing more harm than good.

"Mimi..." Mirai lifts her hand to her twin sister, at the call of the old nickname, and Fumiko is careful as she grasps the fragile-looking limb.

"Where is Hikaru?"

"He is attending a conference in your stead."

"Will you bring him to me?"

"Onēsan?"

"It's time, Fumi–imōto."

Kaito starts as his aunt stifles a sob. What's wrong? Her vitals are reading just fine, and she isn't having any sort of fit.

Fumiko presses her lips to Mirai's forehead. When she pulls back, her sights are on. Mirai winces, struggling to force her own tech to activate. The sisters look into each other's eyes for a long, quiet moment. Fumiko blinks a tear out of her eye before rushing from the room to collect Hikaru, shutting the door in her wake.

"Kaito. My baby."

Kai takes his mother's hand, and when he finds it cold to the touch, he understands. His mouth dries, and the walls close in. His hands and feet go numb.

"You've grown up so quickly. I feel like I've blinked and now suddenly you're a man."

He feels like he's suffocating.

"No, Kaasan, hold on just a little longer. When Wren wakes up, I'm sure she can—"

Mirai shakes her head, a barely-there side-to-side. "It is done, Kaito. And even if Lady Wren did wake up in time, my life or death is not a burden she should have to bear."

Kaito chokes down the protest on his tongue, and his mother's hand, mangled by black magic, brushes over his cheek.

"I'm glad you found her, and I pray you never lose her again."

"Kaasan—"

The Sun (part 2)

Mirai pulls her son down and hushes him. "You're so much like your father. He was always so sure of who he was, too. So much more than I ever was. Never doubt yourself. Even when the whole world screams otherwise. It takes a strong will to stand against the storm where others might be swept away in the downpour."

Even the press of her lips against his temple is cold.

"Okaasan!"

Just then Hikaru enters the room.

"Hikaru," hushes Mirai. "My eldest."

Kaito's brother comes around the other side to hold their mother's hand.

"I'm leaving you a terrible burden, Hikaru. And you are going to make mistakes. You are going to misstep, and most of all you are going to be angry at me just like I was angry at my father. And it's okay. It is all okay because you will learn from those moments, and with every lesson comes wisdom more precious than gold.

"Most of all, and this is the hardest lesson to learn as a leader, so I hope you can learn it early, but the truest mark of strength is not in your ability to stand, it is in your ability to bend."

"Mom, why are you saying this?"

"Because it's time, sweetheart."

Mirai holds tight to her boys' hands. Kaito's palm folds around his mother's, and while her hand is too small to fully encompass his anymore, she winds her fingers strong and secure around his thumb and forefinger. Surely, this isn't the grip of a dying woman. It's too real, too solid, too firmly tethered in reality. That hand taught him to write, brushed his hair as a child, and showed him how to hold a sword. His mother's hand, always open and ready to take his own in his times of need to steady him, trembles. The tremor, so unnatural and out of place, rockets through him like the shaking of the earth beneath his feet.

"My sons. My pride. Take care of each other."

Kaito's vision goes blurry as the cool lavender glow of his mother's tech fades to black.

In the times of the most ancient civilizations, medicine men and women used to ingest poisons and venoms as a means to make their very blood a poison and an antidote in a single potion.

Who would have thought thousands of years later, we would discover that exposure to magic can do the same with the proper augmentations and a predisposition to magical affinity? In a process fatal to more than 85% of participants, adepts are put through hours and hours of magical radiation until their lymphatic systems become highly specialized sources of anti-magic capable of dispelling curses and magical maladies. Those who survive the process become members of the elite Dispel Corps—adepts who exist solely to counter the effects of witchcraft on the technomancer body.

Excerpt from *Magical Maladies: Epidemiology in Deus*
Dr. Franklyn N. Stein, 1684 A.P.

13

THE SUN (PART 3)

Three Days Later – 24th Day in the Month of Planting, 1863 –
The Abbey, Aighneas

MIRAI MIYAZAKI'S PASSING IS MET WITH somber acknowledgement by the whole of the Alliance. The flags are flown at half-mast. People wear the mourning colors of their respective countries, a piece of lavender hung from their belts or scarves in honor of an empress who may not have been their own but who was a solid ally through thick and thin. And blanketing over them like a shroud is Change.

Change comes like a thief in the night, his mother's death bringing with it an unrelenting shift of obligation.

Fumiko, his obaasan and sensei, a woman considered wiser than many of her peers within the League, defers to him as he takes over the tasks that were days ago hers. She is no longer the younger sibling to the monarch of Murasaki, the Calyx to Mirai's Peony Crown. The title now falls at his feet, Crown Prince Kaito Miyazaki the newly appointed Calyx to Hikaru's flowering bud, answerable to none but the new emperor himself, the blooming peony of Murasaki no Yama. He now bows to his brother, Hikaru taking on the burden of the crown and Kaito doing all he can to keep his brother from being crushed under its weight. Kaito receives condolences, acts as a liaison between the new emperor and the adepts and technomancers under their banner, organizes funerary rites, and keeps a vigil over his aunt and brother.

Fumiko grieves for her sister, a careful eye kept on her lest she follow her elder twin to the grave:

"Your mother always loved a good race. She beat me by mere minutes when we were born, always racing to the future, eager to cross an undrawn finish line. That's where her namesake comes from, all of our father's hopes for the future coming to fruition in her. Mirai, always looking to tomorrow while I embraced the lessons of the past. She found her voice first, lost her baby teeth first, became a woman first, found love first. The only time I beat her at anything was in graduating as a technomancer first. She got so mad; she didn't talk to me for two months after I graduated. We were teenagers, your mother hot-tempered and impatient. She didn't speak to me again until I ended up injured on a mission. It was superficial, but it was a kick in the butt for her. She made me tutor her while I was recovering, and she passed her exams the next year because she wasn't going to let her imōto get in trouble alone. I should have known she'd beat me in this race, too."

Hikaru, aged nearly a decade in a matter of days, accepts prayers for long life with grace and dignity:

"I'm not ready. I thought we'd have more time before..."

Hikaru never finishes his thought, drifting into a silence Kaito lacks the words to break.

Yet even in the wake of bereavement the political machine continues to churn out steam.

"We cannot put the vote off any longer."

"We must pass the new legislation. The longer we wait, the more risk we have of it all crumbling down."

Kaito and Hikaru, instead of being able to grieve for their mother in peace, sit in the conference hall with the rest of the assembled technomancers.

"We must elect someone to the primacy."

THE SUN (PART 3)

"Hold on just a minute. We haven't even decided to create the position of primarch, let alone elect someone to it."

"Well, then we make the decision. Sitting on our hands isn't going to help our countries rebuild."

"Hikaru, what is Murasaki's stance on all of this? Should we or should we not elect into position someone who can call to arms all technomancers as needed?"

Hikaru stiffens at his side. Up until now, he has made a point to stay out of the argument, content to listen and wait as others present their arguments. This is the first time he has been asked to speak rather than Fumiko, and the gravity of which is not lost to him. Kaito meets his brother's eye.

"It is difficult to say. We have always governed ourselves by the merit of our own democracies and dynasties. A major change to that hierarchy would have unforeseen benefits as well as consequences."

Hikaru's non-answer is unsettling to say the least. Not even within their own country does one person get the final say on major political decisions. Mirai always consulted with her ministers and the other state technomancers before making decisions, and her decisions could at any time be challenged should a majority of their adepts find fault in her logic. As the new Emperor, Hikaru's position would be much the same, so why doesn't he say as much? For one single person to be able to unquestionably call to arms every technomancer in the League regardless of nationality or allegiance—it's asinine.

"I disagree."

Rameses turns to Kaito.

"Prince Kaito, I didn't realize you had such strong predilections against this."

Kaito regards the man coolly. Without his usual headdress and royal garments, Rameses is far slighter than he would normally appear. The man, easily three times Kaito's senior, is wrinkling despite his technomancer augmentations; his hair, normally dyed black as crow's feathers, is in need of touch up, the gray peeking through around his temples and widow's peak.

"No single person should have such power."

"Young prince, this means of power is designed to prevent a technomancer nation from ever attacking an ally again. The position is in itself a check against imbalance."

"What my nephew is highlighting," inserts Fumiko, "is your failure to take into account the repercussions of an abuse of power. Say a technomancer does not agree with a decision or assignment from the primarch. The primarch then has the ability to denounce the technomancer for noncompliance, creating dissension. It could completely dismantle the League's entire cause for existence."

A murmur traces around the room, and several of the technomancers communing remotely nod their heads in mute understanding.

"So, we set up a check and balance protocol." Farqaad rubs his hands together like he has just reinvented the wheel. "There! Easily fixed."

"And who is going to draw up such legislation?"

"It doesn't matter!" Xipilli's voice booms out over the hall. "We cannot take a vote until all registered technomancers are accounted for. That is the law."

Farqaad makes a show of looking around the room and checking the communications log.

"Xipilli, who is it you are referring to? By all accounts, everyone remaining is present."

"My sister is still in recovery."

"Ah, yes. Lady Wren, the hero of the hour," agrees the Morrigan. "Have we any idea when she might wake from her ailment?"

Before Xipilli can respond, Absko speaks up. "To my understanding, Lady Wren shows no signs of waking anytime soon. As such, I have to motion we carry out the vote without her."

"Father," protests Chike.

"It's unfortunate, son, but we have already put off this decision for too long, in deference to the hope Her Excellency, Mirai Miyazaki—rest her soul—might partake. I see no logical reason to hold off any longer especially when we do not know if Lady Wren will even wake from this awful affliction."

Jamar puts his fist down on the monitor with a subdued laugh. "Che, don't you mean especially since the technomancer in question is barely even a technomancer anymore?"

"What are you insinuating?" demands Quetzal, one of the Derivan technomancers.

"The lady lies catatonic from magic fever. What do you think I mean?"

Xipilli rises to his feet. "My sister saved your miserable life, you ungrateful bastard."

An outburst of noise as the hall erupts into argument. People calling Jamar ungrateful, people praising Wren, people agreeing with Jamar's assessment, people cautioning Xipilli to be more reasonable since Jamar was only stating a fact.

"Enough!" shouts Gewalt, subduing the assembly. "This entire alliance owes Lady Wren a great deal of gratitude."

It is enough to cow the Sekhmetian, Aighnean, and Ebelean sects, and Xipilli and Irene and the other Deriva technomancers all settle at Gewalt's acknowledgement.

"However, speaking of your sister, there is something I wanted to propose to you, Xipilli. It pertains to the Goblin King."

"What about him?"

"His execution must be scheduled, and as with any occasion, the decision on who will carry out the sentence has come up several times between myself and a few other members of this assembly." She looks sidelong at Rameses, Lockecraft, and Absko. "We propose Lady Wren carry out the sentence. When she is well, of course."

Xipilli's brow darkens.

"Even if my sister were in perfect health, Madam President, she is not an executioner."

"Yes, I know, Vulcan, but think. She is owed vengeance against this fiend more than anyone in this room. Would it not be a triumph for her first act upon rousing be to finally bring an end to a witch who has brought so much strife to all of us?"

SONATA

"President Gewalt, it is highly unusual to ask a member of the court to perform such an act regardless of baser motivations," inserts Fumiko.

"Yes, Grandmaster, but please, allow me to summon forth my specialist. He is a most popular director and live broadcaster. I'm sure you will find his ideas rather intriguing."

At this, Gewalt gestures to the front of the conference hall. A gentleman steps inside, escorted by two adepts. He wears a smart business suit in a sunny sky-blue shade, terribly loud considering most of the room is wearing mourning colors, blacks, greys, and whites. This man enters with all the flourish of an A-list actor with exuberant hand gestures and a booming voice. It grates on Kaito's hearing, how off key it is. He has a rather interesting augmentation about his head: an ocular lens over his right eye, outfitted with a microphone threaded through the skin of his jaw. Broadcasting equipment, all the world seen through a camera lens and filtered through an auto-tuned white balance.

A squat man trails in after him holding a bulletin board almost twice his size. The broadcaster snaps his fingers at the man, and he hurries to set the board in the middle of the room, nearly tripping over his own feet in the process.

"Your Majesty, Winston Vaishi. It's a pleasure to address you today," he greets Xipilli, swinging his arm so wide he nearly hits his man in the face. "Tell me. Have you ever heard of the Broken Heart?"

Xipilli regards the man with an icy stare.

"I have not."

"It is a popular method of execution among hexen folk," continues Vaishi, gesticulating to a hand drawn figure on the bulletin board. "The victim or sacrifice is chained to kneel on a raised dais while the executioner cuts away the flesh of their chest, rips away the ribcage, exposes their lungs, and then pulls their heart from their chest to place it in their mouth. It is a method used on only the most vile of sinners. A statement against their crimes and the suffering they ought to endure for it."

Rameses stands in outrage.

THE SUN (PART 3)

"Director, we of the League have never and will never employ the use of such barbarity to make a statement."

"Of course, Pharaoh, but these are extreme circumstances we find ourselves in indeed. Seraphim, a sworn member of the League of Industry, has consorted with and employed hexen into their military ranks. He sent the Goblin King himself to destroy an entire royal family. Barbaric though the punishment may be, is not Seraphim's betrayal and the crimes committed against all of our nations so extreme as to warrant the showing of such a statement?"

King Absko and Pharaoh Rameses, seemingly swayed, nod their heads as several leaders of the smaller nations do the same. In fact, the majority of the chamber seems to lust for blood as much as any vampyre or lycan Kai has ever seen. The director continues.

"World leaders, please. Picture it. The Goblin King, Yggfret Bloodfang, the lord of all practitioners and creatures of the dark arts, a war criminal, convicted and brought to justice to answer for his crimes, kneels on a darkened platform under our lesser moon. Out of the darkness steps a beautiful young woman, dressed entirely in white. It is Lady Nocturne, alive by some miracle after having been supposedly killed in the most unsightly of ways by the very being who kneels before her, and not only she is alive, she stands above him, a conquering hero. She is ethereal and fearsome, a vision of benevolence. A witch who wields her magic for our just cause.

"She asks the witch king for his last words, and when he finishes, she lifts her blade from the nearby table and begins. Her blade descends and with each cut, each hack of her athame, her gown turns crimson. By the end, baptized in the blood of her enemy, she transcends us all, mere mortals presented for the first time with but a glimpse of the divine. This angel of death, this goddess of justice, the witch who stands as a symbol of our righteous cause. None would fail to answer our call at such a display, and you, Vulcan Moctezumo, will have solidified Deriva as a true world power."

Xipilli is quiet for a long drawn-out spell while the rest of the room explodes in an uproarious agreement.

"Xipilli, you cannot consider this."

Hikaru, sitting next to Wren's brother, implores the man to dismiss the idea, but Xipilli doesn't respond, doesn't even glance Hikaru's direction.

"As I stated earlier, Mr. Vaishi. My sister is presently in recovery. I will not presume to answer when there is yet a possibility she may never wake."

At this, the man seems to understand his misstep and bows deeply.

"Of course, sir," he stutters, looking at Gewalt. "Perhaps we can revisit this topic once she has recovered?"

"Perhaps."

Xipilli's lack of an outright rejection does not sit well with Kaito.

"Miyazaki–sama." Atzi greets him at the door to the quarters where Wren sleeps. She bows at the waist, a black lace veil over her face. "We're so sorry about your mother."

He bows in return to the princess, garbed in mourning black. This woman has lost both of her parents to this war.

"This war has taken many from us all."

She and her kin can truly mourn now, a luxury denied them by the demands of war.

Atzi leaves him alone with her sister as usual, as though he hasn't been absent these last few days, and Kaito settles himself at Wren's side. It has been three days since his last visit. So much has kept him away: his duties, his grief, and the shadowy hand of self-doubt. Three new companions to replace those now out of his reach.

And the silence...

THE SUN (PART 3)

The wretched, unending silence should be filled with the voices of the people he loves most: his mother who is gone, his brother who wraps himself in mourning silence, his aunt whose quiet sobs are no less deafening than gunfire, and Wren who lies at death's door.

She is pale, paler than he has ever seen her, and when he touches her hand, the chill of the limb is unsettling, especially considering the number of blankets draped over her. How much more of this can her body take?

Setting a beacon on the nearby table, Kaito's holographic keyboard unfolds in a wash of light. The keys, translucent and alight in a luminous orchid shade of purple, are the standard for a baby grand. They don't feel like anything in particular as he warms up, playing through various scales and arpeggios as he considers which piece he'd like to play. It isn't the same as having an actual piano or keyboard under his fingers, but the longer he plays, the warmer the projection becomes, similar to how an old-fashioned reading lamp might heat up the longer it is used. Terribly inefficient things. When he was seven, his mother pulled one of the ancient things out for him during a lesson on thermodynamics. The halogen bulb had gotten so hot that when Mirai guided Kaito to spray some water on it, it emitted a strange fizzing noise before his mother pulled him back as the bulb burst with a loud pop.

"When the temperature inside contrasts too greatly with the outside, the glass will shatter," she'd told him.

Would the same happen to Wren? Would her body eventually give out from being forced to exist like this, dependent on the heat and nutrients fed to her by machines?

As his fingers hover over the first chords of his chosen piece, a scraping sound at the window draws his attention.

When he pulls the curtain aside, he finds a cat pawing at the pane. It's the same cat from the last time he was here. The one who placed its paw on Wren's forehead, the animal who brought his witch's magic to life.

SONATA

It looks at him, and he looks at it: wide, green amber to his silver. The animal meows at him, pawing once more at the glass, imploring him for entrance. Atzi mentioned they started closing the window two days ago, the chill from the outside worsening Wren's condition.

"Have you been trying to get in this whole time?"

Another mewed response, and Kaito slides the window open. He is wary, muscles tensed in the event the creature does something to injure the slumbering witch, but it merely hops onto the bed, lithely dances its way around the various tubes and wires connecting Wren to the life support, and settles itself on Wren's stomach.

Almost immediately, the animal begins to purr, whether from pleasure or annoyance, he can't be sure, but it blinks slowly at him before curling into its own little ouroboros, its long tail draped over its nose. It rubs its head into the witch's covers, sinking deeper into the soft downy comforter, before closing its eyes.

While he isn't entirely sure what he was expecting to happen when he decided to allow the animal in—perhaps something akin to what happened the last time he saw the cat touch Wren— he didn't think it would come in just to take a nap on her. But the cat or netherbeast, whatever it is, isn't doing any harm. It even made sure to step around the medical equipment.

So Kaito leaves it be, returning to his holo-piano. At the very least, the cat will act as a space heater, giving the witch a little extra body heat.

Kaito plays one of his favorite compositions: a suite composed at the turn of the 17th century. There is beauty in simplicity. The musical embodiment of the sepulchral, the score breathes with lungs found in the spaces between notes. Notes tinkle down, cascading through the room like the gentlest of rainfalls. Misting through the space to dampen everything in cleansing, purifying water.

The element of life.

It hasn't rained since his mother died. It should be raining. His mother loved the rain. She used to run out into the mid-summer showers with Kaito despite the unending pile of paperwork requiring her attention. Walking the streets of Tokiseishu, able to do so without any guard, because the downpour kept away the thicker crowds, she would always start with her umbrella dutifully held overhead, but before long, the item would end up discarded in favor of running through puddles, letting the wind pull her hair from it carefully styled knotting while the water tangled it.

The first movement ends on a hanging chord, not quite dissonant but not quite a resolution either. Perhaps it's a denial that the gentle fall must end, or maybe an invitation for something darker to take its place?

A breath later, he begins the second movement, heavier, darker, and during this movement, the rain clouds darken to thunderclouds. The storm builds between the notes, complete with moments of grumbled thunder and clashing lightning.

Kaito's eyes close, and he loses himself, letting the rhythm wash over him. It cards through his hair and clothes, dances over his skin, soft as a sigh, and sinks into his lungs. Hands steady, measured despite the building storm within him, he wraps himself in the feel of the music.

The rains of summer's end.

These are the rains of the warring seasons when the bitter chill of northerly winds rushes south to shatter the spine of summer. A subdued anger, chilly, served cold... An anger that ends not with an explosion but with a whimper carries straight on into the third movement.

So immersed is he in his playing, he doesn't notice the beginnings of glittering magic weaving around him.

Call and response... A conversation unfolds in the music, two opposites carrying on back and forth, alike but ever-so-slightly different, asking for different things. Neither is willing to compromise in a way fitting for the other until one is forced to yield—a lopsided bargain never meant to be fair. The conversation unravels around him, a song of two rather than one, amethyst and emerald tangled together but unable to merge. The storms of winter blanket the world in ice and sap the color from a painting, but it is not until the fourth movement when true rain falls.

Droplets of water dance over his hands to fall through the keys.

A constant downpour, the heavens opening up to rain down sleet and hail and snow. A long winter laid over the land like a curse. Desolate and bitter, the cold teems with loneliness and abandonment.

It aches. This movement. Like a thorn dug deep into his chest taking root and seeding the most constricting of vines around his lungs. His breath stutters but his hands carry on undeterred, soldiers marching through war and famine, pestilence and death, to come out on the other side with some pale semblance of peace. And as his heart freezes in the unyielding rains of sorrow, an unexpected light parts the clouds.

The solstice candle alights, blooming a crisp blue green. He reaches for this light, fingers grasping for the final series of notes, the longest winter night gives way to the yawning warmth of spring, and the frosts begin to melt.

In the last movement, acceptance arrives, the minor key returning with the same lighthearted texture of the first movement, only brighter. This kind of rain always comes complete with a rainbow. The small ray of sunshine to inspire hope despite the clouds still weeping around the sunbeams. The frost-flecked buds of flowers poke through the ice, hinting at new life, at creation and the birth of spring. They wait for the sun to coax them into unfurling, so they can show the world that life recovers from the cold, dark, ugliness of winter, temporary even though it feels unending.

Violet and green slot together as the final chords come to a sleepy, bittersweet resolution. And as he strokes the last descending arpeggio, he imagines for one broken second he is accompanied by the fluttering melodies of a songbird.

The cat meows. His only applause from an audience of two, one who cannot understand, the other unable to, trapped in a prison of her own mind. Wren couldn't clap for him even if she wanted. With a heavy sigh, he deactivates the halo, wiping his damp cheeks with his sleeve and letting the final notes of his song fade into the silence.

"Kai."

The barest of whispers, hushed as the last note of the score dies.

And when he turns toward that soft, familiar voice, the bluest of green eyes meet his.

His lover opens her eyes for the first time in six days, and the smallest ray of light penetrates the ever-shifting rains of grief.

So, what is the difference between a magical disease and your usual run-of-the-mill virus or infection?

Simple. While microorganisms are the cause for the common cold, and cellular imbalances are the cause for certain cancers, magical diseases or curses are rooted in something far less substantial: Thought.

They may have physical symptoms, some may even be treatable with constant and careful planning and medication, but the source of the ailment remains intention; therefore, only magic can treat magic. Because of this "fight magic with magic" compendium, oftentimes the best solution is annihilation of both witch and victim to prevent further spread.

Excerpt from *Magical Maladies: Epidemiology in Deus*
Dr. Franklyn N. Stein, 1684 A.P.

14

FOUR OF WANDS

AKARI IS COUGHING. ACHING, HACKING coughs wrack her entire body, and the sight of it is so disconcerting Wren banishes Zenza and Renki into the other room. This way, she can tend to Akari herself in the little storage closet away from the eyes of her young companions.

She has the girl laid out on several bags of flour and grain and covered with several table linens. Barely an hour since the attack and already the wound from the blixvi festers, a putrid blackening creeping up from the broken skin like a mold. It blisters through her flesh, itchy like a rash. Akari started scratching seventeen minutes ago, and five minutes ago, Wren knocked her out, singing her into a magic-induced slumber to keep her from tearing apart her own skin. Now, the girl wheezes in her sleep, tossing and turning with fever, and Wren curses the fact she doesn't know more about lightning birds and the magical maladies they spread.

A Blixvi—a witch-summoned netherbird known for raining pestilence down on its nesting grounds. Thunderbird, Izulu,

Firebird, Strix, La Lechuza... all cousins of the blixvi and not dissimilar to its disposition for controlling the weather or, according to frightened humans, doing the bidding of a witch. Wren has never encountered one personally, but she's heard of them. Magical birds of immense size, some of them are cursed witches and bloodthirsty familiars while others are worshipped as gods depending on regional/cultural beliefs.

She doesn't know how long she has to cure Akari before she turns into one of those shamblers. She doesn't even know if she can cure Akari. Healing damaged tissue is one thing. Ridding a body of magical infection is a whole other discipline, one best approached with tonics and medicines. That had always been Jessabelle's forte. The older woman had been a medicine woman first and a witch second, kind of like Mishka with her teas... The thought comes and goes with a pang of grief... But Jessabelle had been so much more than a potions brewer, her healing powers comprising the very essence of her magic. In the early days of Wren's magical awakening, Jessabelle tried to soften the blow by teaching the young witch potion work, not that it took...

¡Pinche, Wren! ¿Por qué no escuchaste mejor? But no! She'd been too busy feeling sorry for herself to bother. Hindsight.

She replaces the damp cloth on the girl's head with a frustrated sigh and leaves to check on the other kids where they sit in the dining area of the restaurant they've commandeered as a safe haven.

A cozy place by the name of Feliz Bordello Cafe, the local dive appears to specialize in the melting pot of border-town cuisine. Falafel, desert goose eggs, pan dulce, gongzi, steamed buns, mudcrust curry... There's even a little dancing mascot, though she isn't quite sure if it is supposed to be a dancing burrito, a dancing gyro, or a dancing eggroll, and it's wearing a sombrero, holding a horsetail whip, and has bells jiggling around its ankles. Food with ankles?! Now that's terrifying... This is the kind of family-owned place where the menu is for tourists and the regulars bring their own ingredients if they ever want something outside of the usual fare. Well, she hopes it's local. Either that or the owners are a bunch of appropriators, not to say none of the locals aren't white, but... the joke on multicultural cuisine is less funny when it comes from a *gringo*.

From the door to the kitchen, she can see Renki and Zenza in one of the booths. The pair huddle over Renki's holoscreen, no doubt researching the blixvi themselves.

"I cannot believe you're listening to her." Zenza has her palm unit out, and she uses her index finger (she must have a manipulation implant) to tug information back and forth from the boy's screen to her own. "We should be grabbing Akari and getting the heck outta here. Not sitting here following the orders of a witch."

"Zenza," chides Renki, "she saved Akari's life and kept you from killing a bunch of innocent people."

"And! She's still a *bruja*. How do we know we can trust her?"

Wren closes her eyes in frustration. Right, Xipilli, with his hatred of all things hexen, has probably ingrained wariness to the evils of witchery into their niece. Thou shalt not suffer a witch to live and all... never mind how crappy a translation the quote is from the original text.

"She knows what she's doing."

"Didn't you find her in a sanatorium?"

"Well, yes, but it's not... Look, Miyazaki–sama trusts her, so, so do I."

"Miyazaki–sama? You mean your Prince Kaito. My uncle can't stand your prince. What do I care about whether he thinks she's trustworthy?"

A frown creases Renki's features.

"Zenza," calls Wren. The girl hiccups in surprise, whirling around to look at 'Atalia.' "I can't give you a reason to trust me other than my word. You're grown up enough to make your own decisions as to whether or not you want to believe me, but right now, I'm more concerned with chasing down this bird to heal Akari than with your judgement of my character."

Zenza sits back on her hands, a pout on her face.

"Renki, have you found anything?"

The boy nods. "Well, it's definitely the cause of the disease infecting the town, but it shouldn't have the ability to bring a city of this size to its knees. Not without someone feeding it magic."

"So the witch from earlier has it chained to her will." Three guesses who the witch is. Void-magic, summoned netherbeasts, and general mayhem—this has Summer's name written all over it. She's probably syphoning magic through it to infect the city, but why a sleepy little bordertown like Chairomura? Why is Summer doing any of this? What does she have to gain other than watching the world burn? "What else have you found?"

"It's a bringer of pestilence, and it feeds on the bodies of the people it kills, like a vulture. There are only a few recorded cases of them attacking towns. The most recent case was fifty years ago."

"Does it say how they cured the disease?"

Renki shakes his head. "They didn't. So many people got infected, they had to purge the town."

"Purge the town?"

"Bomb it," provides Zenza, and Wren scoffs.

"They didn't even try to cure it, did they?"

Zenza shrugs.

"It was a smaller Seraphim town," explains Renki. "And the Pontiflex didn't want to risk the disease spreading countrywide."

Naturally... If you can't beat it, blow it up.

"Anything on how to kill it?"

"Other than dropping a ton of napalm on the town where it's nesting?"

"Zenza," says Wren, exasperated with the girl's attitude.

"What? That's what they did. And it's 'princess' to you!"

Grrrowl!

Zenza's stomach growls loud enough to challenge a train horn.

"Hmm, and when was the last time her highness ate?"

"Shut up!" pouts the teenager.

Then, Renki's stomach growls as well.

"Aha... Akari and I haven't eaten more than ration bars since we left Snowfall."

"And how long ago was that?"

Looking sheepish, he answers, "About twelve hours ago."

Arms crossed over her chest, Wren shakes her head. So much high-quality tech in their bodies and still only human. Teenage humans at that. Sustenance = very necessary.

"Well, then," she says with a clap. "It's a good thing we hunkered down in a diner. I don't suppose either of you knows how to cook?"

The two look at each other first and then back at 'Atalia.' That'll be a no then, and she can assume any supplies they brought with them went up in flames with their cycles. At least, Wren still has her pack.

"Come on, you two," she says, hands on her hips as she strides back toward the kitchen.

Despite the electricity being out, the main refrigerator is on a generator, and inside are stocks of fruit, vegetables, fish, and meats. There are bags of rice, oats, and flour. She picks her way through ingredients, throwing out anything too brown or too limp for her comfort. A large amount goes into the trash, but she does track down a few vegetables and a pack of ground beef she judges to be the appropriate shade of red.

"Mind chopping these for me, princess?"

"Onions?"

"And bell peppers." Wren nods, holding out the vegetables on a carving board. She fully expects the girl to scoff and complain about lifting a finger to help, but contrary to the bratty princess-ery Wren has learned to expect from her, she merely sighs, takes the offered items, and does as 'Atalia' asks, leaving Wren to start browning the meat. Or she would, anyway, if she could figure out how to turn the damn stove on.

Renki has to help her, reaching over and turning a dial before inputting an uncomplicated series of numbers on the oven's pin pad—look, twelve years is a long time when it comes to kitchen appliances, and the numbers and text are written in a mix of sanskrit and hanasu which Wren cannot read. Not to mention, it's one of those touch-activated, high-tech ones like a tablet or holoscreen.

"Ooo! Can we make chile rellenos?" asks Zenza, holding up a string of dried chilies.

She gives the princess a deadpan expression. While Wren has eaten plenty of rellenos in her lifetime, she's pretty sure making them involves a whole lot more than ground beef and chilies. Also, not dried chilies either...

"What?" asks the girl, affronted.

Now, listen. Wren is in no way, shape, or form savvy in the kitchen. She can boil water and heat something up, but do not ask her to produce any kind of culinary treasures. It isn't going to happen.

"I don't know, Zenza. Can 'we' make chili rellenos?"

"No," she says sheepishly. "But I know how to make tortillas."

Wren blinks more than a little impressed.

"What? My uncle taught me how."

Ah... right. Xipilli and Atzi were the ones who loved experimenting in the kitchen even though Elisabeta made it clear they had no business there. Wren couldn't stand it. It got too hot and standing at a stove just made her feel antsy.

"It's unexpected, but tortillas sound fabulous. What else do we know how to make?"

"There's a rice cooker over there. My dad once showed me how to use one," says Renki.

The two teenagers gape as Wren turns a full-fledged smile on them. "Tortillas, rice! Sounds like a start. You two work on those things. I'll get the meat and veggies cooked up, and we can have tacos."

"Tacos?"

She nods. "I know it isn't a Tyrsday, but yes. Tacos."

Well, it's no gourmet meal. The tortillas are lumpy, the rice is just this side of undercooked, and the meat and vegetables are kind of bland, but it's food, and picante sauce makes everything tolerable. Renki doesn't complain, and Zenza's hunger outweighs any disgruntlement.

The teenagers fed, Wren sends them to coax some rice and strips of tortilla into Akari and commandeers the space, not for cooking but for brewing. Willing any and all latent memory of Jessabelle's lessons to surface in her head, she sets about brewing a potion that will hopefully help Akari's system fight off the blixvi's sickness, but a few scattered lessons on potion craft between almost dying and truly dying does not a potion master make.

Forty-five minutes and a headache later, a pot bubbles angrily on the stove top. A mess of herbs sits laid out across the counters next to a knife, freshly wiped of the blood she drew to activate what was supposed to be a healing tonic. A concoction she is now trying to figure out what to do with considering when she spilled some of it on the counter it burned a hole through the metal. When the single droplet of her blood landed in the concoction, it turned the previously orangey liquid an alarming shade of lime green.

She's pretty sure the color she is going for is red.

So she starts over, getting a bigger pot and putting twice as much water in. She also simplifies which herbs she uses.

"What is this?"

"Ah!"

Wren just about jumps out of her skin at Renki's voice. This kid! When did he come back in the kitchen? If he keeps sneaking up on her, she is going to put a bell on him.

"Sorry."

"It's fine," she says, turning back to the unused pot. "And don't touch that."

"It looks like it's about to become sentient," he says, warily lifting the lid she put on the acidic mixture.

"I'll show you something sentient if you don't leave it alone!"

The teen drops the lid. Thankfully the liquid within doesn't splash everywhere. Small mercies.

"Where's Zenza?"

"She's with Akari. She was sleepy."

Ah, yes... Zenza always did go right to sleep after mealtimes as a baby.

"So, what are you doing?" asks Renki.

"Trying to figure out a potion to stabilize Akari."

Forget about curing the ailment—she'll aim to magically strengthen Akari's immune system enough to slow it down. So she pulls out lemongrass and orange peel, apple cider vinegar, mint, and star anise. All safe ingredients which should stave off the affliction if she does this properly. It won't do anything for the child in the long run, but she's not about to risk poisoning Akari by accident.

"Can I watch?"

Renki's eyes are a dusty green in the light of the kitchen's generator, wide and open and far too eager.

"Not sure your instructors will like you looking over a witch's shoulder while she stirs a figurative cauldron."

"Fumiko–sensei says we should learn at every opportunity."

Yeah... Not sure the grandmaster meant that in relation to witchery.

"You can watch. Just stay back. Last thing I need is a trainee without a nose if this mixture decides to blow up."

"There's a chance of that?"

"Do you see the hole on the counter?" She points, his gaze follows, and the teen immediately pales. "Magic isn't a science, kid. I can't just follow a recipe and expect it to turn out the same every time. Too many unknown variables, especially considering none of this is my own equipment."

"Unknown variables?"

Wren nods. "The age of the herbs, the state of the soil where they were grown, or even if it all comes from the same source. I don't know if these pots are pure steel, what's been prepared in them in the past, or if the person who handles them cleans them with a hand towel or a sponge. It all affects the balance in ways I only somewhat understand."

Four Of Wands

Never mind the unpredictability of her core ingredient, even if it is the one ingredient Wren knows best how to deal with.

"Witchblood is the main ingredient of any potion," Jessabelle had said so long ago. "The more saturated with magic, the more potent the potion. I normally use about three drops per brew. You'll only need one. Any more and you might find yourself with an adverse effect you weren't counting on. Potions meant to repair tissue can become cancerous, sleeping potions coma-inducing, and if you ever find yourself brewing something malicious... Well, I guess, I don't need to warn you what using too much blood will do to those potions."

Wren diligently checks and double checks her measurements, affirming her portions are correct before reaching for the knife. This time instead of dropping a bead of blood directly into the potion, she nudges a bit onto the edge of the blade and stirs it into the mixture. The effect this time is a much nicer auburn, and the rolling boil settles as, by literal magic, her blood cools the elixir.

She'll take it as a testament of success when she dips a wooden spoon in, and the spoon doesn't immediately dissolve into nothing. It's even better when she doesn't go into convulsions after taking a sip. In fact, the pressure behind her eyes vanishes. She's been ignoring it since she shielded herself and the teenagers from the blast of power meant to delete them all.

"That's about right."

Renki, who has been quietly watching her work, perks up at the sound of her voice.

"Can I try?"

"Do you want to be turned into a toad?"

The boy flinches, sputtering while Wren chuckles.

"Kidding, kidding. It shouldn't hurt you. Might even help some of the bruises from your earlier crash."

The pout she gets in response is probably the most adorable thing she's ever seen. Almost as adorable as the death glares Kaito gave her for being a total shithead during their trials. Ahh... Simpler times...

Renki steps up beside her, and she finds herself amazed by how tall the boy is. He's only fifteen and is at least five inches taller than her. He's probably not even done growing yet. Judging by how much the teen ate earlier, he's probably fixing for another growth spurt. She wonders how tall his father is.

Renki dips the spoon into the potion and takes a small sip. His tech flashes golden, a visible zing racing from his feet to his ears, and he makes a sound like an exhaust tank being put on ice.

"Whoa! I feel like I just took an energy stim."

Hmm... Revitalizing properties then. "Any weird feelings?"

"No. I mean, I was achy earlier from the crash and then the witch attacked us, but I feel just fine now."

Wren nods.

"Don't go getting excited. It's only a temporary boost. You'll crash once it wears out."

"Kind of like a caffeine crash."

"Of sorts."

Wren ladles out two shot-sized glasses of the potion and hands them to Renki.

"Here. Have Zenza drink this and see if you can get Akari to swallow it as well. This is for her more than us."

He nods and hurries away, leaving Wren once again alone in the kitchen. The lime green potion still bubbles despite being off the heat for over thirty minutes, and it shows no signs of stopping. What the heck did she make? Better yet, how can she make use of it? She carefully tests to see if a glass cup will be eaten away by the liquid. No dice. The vessel shatters on contact, so she tries one of the coffee cups, instead, finding that, yes, she can store it in something made of ceramic. Not that a coffee mug is ideal transportation, but oh, yes! The teapot! Corked, warded, and safely tucked away in her satchel.

But the Nightmare....

She clicks her tongue, pondering whether what she is about to do is a bad idea, decides it is and does it anyway. She digs the pot out of her bag and opens the lid. Still leaking void-magic, the Nightmare's corpse lies limp at the bottom, the jellyfish-like creature in the early stages of decomposition. She hums the starting notes of her un-funeral march, and void-tinged tendrils twitch, reaching for freedom. She shifts her tuning, and the Nightmare rolls over, her magic weaving into the void to lull newly woken undead into some semblance of calm. (It almost looks pretty glittering with her emerald signature.)

She then pours the philter in the pot.

The undead don't speak or moan or even feel pain, but she imagines, by the way the tiny zombie writhes, it's screaming—or laughing. The draught bubbles, furious, and Wren backs out of the splash zone. The lime green color shifts, darkens, and then settles on a muddy purple tone. Hot to the touch, Wren coaxes the lid back onto it telekinetically and wraps the teapot in a thick towel.

"¿Qué es eso?"

Renki and Zenza are in the kitchen doorway. Zenza frowns at 'Atalia.'

"Nothing you need to worry about, *princesa*. Renki, were you able to get Akari to drink?"

Renki nods.

"I think it's helping. She fell right back asleep afterwards."

"Good."

"You've been brewing in here."

Zenza is a teenage hurricane of indignation. She stands one hip cocked to the side, arms crossed over her chest. She looks just like her grandmother, Elisabeta. Amazing how much can be inherited through blood alone. Wren's stepmother used to take the exact same stance right before assigning Wren extra chores or punishment exercises, but Elisabeta was actually frightening whenever she took on the "mom" stance. Zenza is too much of a round-faced adolescent to pull it off. She hasn't come into her hips yet, her shoulders as yet are too narrow and unburdened, and Wren has seen too much in her life, past and present, to be intimidated by a fourteen-year-old throwing a tantrum.

"I'm glad to see the healing draught perked you right back up, highness."

Wren tucks the wrapped teapot of—well—of something toxic in her bag.

"Renki told me it was medicine. I wouldn't have taken it if I knew it was a witch's brew."

"It is medicine, princess. How do you think your various pills, serums, and vitamins come to be? Herbs—boiled and cooked to make medicine. The tonic you drank is the same thing minus the laboratory, synthetic chemicals, and warning label." It just has a little something extra in the recipe most chemists would balk at.

"If I turn into a frog, I swear my uncle will—"

Akari screams, and Wren rushes past Renki and Zenza to the sick girl. Akari convulses on the makeshift bed.

"I thought you said she drank the potion."

"She did," answers Renki. "I gave it to her myself. She drank all of it."

Wren drops to her knees, turning the girl's head to the side. Foam bubbles dark and purplish around her mouth.

"Renki, go get me another cup of potion!"

He darts out of the room.

"It's your stupid potion did this!" Zenza yells. Did it? No, that's not right. Nothing Wren put in could cause a seizure like this. Wren tugs the neck of Akari's shirt down. Before her eyes, the infection spreads up her arm. The girl's skin grays and wrinkles, blackening with a waking decay. The tech nodes around her collar and temples flicker erratically, her mechanical systems doing nothing to counteract the malady ravaging her body.

"Here!" Renki reappears, a glass of the elixir in hand, and Zenza has the gall to slap it out of his grip.

"You're going to kill her if you give her more of that poison!"

The glass goes flying. Wren stalls its descent before the liquid can slosh everywhere, siphoning it into her hand.

"Stop it, you crazy witch!"

Renki cuts the princess off before she can lunge for Wren, tackling her to the ground.

"What the heck is wrong with you! Don't you see she's going to kill your friend?!"

"If that were true, then why are we perfectly fine? We would be dying, too, if it was the potion, and I saw Miss Vaishi take a sip of it herself. It's harmless."

"You don't know that!"

"Zenza, enough with your paranoia!" shouts Wren. "Now shut up and let me focus."

Zenza balks at the command, but Renki shushes her, letting the witch work.

But what is causing the adverse reaction?

Akari coughs up bile and quite possibly some of the contents of her stomach onto the floor, and the potion which was bright red is now a garish burgundy. As she keeps coughing, spit flecks black on Wren's hands, burning hot, and the little bit that touches the elixir hovering above her fist turns portions of it a burnt orange.

Her saliva! Her saliva is burning through the potion. The infection must be affecting her digestive system making drinking the potion ineffective. She'll have to feed it into Akari's body like a syringe, coaxing the liquid into Akari's system via the wound in her arm.

Bit by bit, Wren coaxes the healing draught into Akari's veins, breathing a sigh of relief as, when the last of it is gone, the rot setting into Akari's tissues diminishes, retracting back to the origin point to reveal healthy skin. Well, mostly anyway. At the wound point, a jagged ring of necrosis remains, just itching to spread once more.

"You—you saved her?"

Zenza's voice is flooded with disbelief. Wren turns to the princess, still held firmly by Renki even though she isn't fighting to tear out Wren's throat anymore.

Not yet, she hasn't.

"No," Wren answers, truthfully. "All I've done is hold off the affliction. Eventually, without a proper cure, she'll succumb to the blixvi's disease." She turns back to Akari, the girl's tremors subsiding. "Akari," she calls, gently, stroking the child's brow. "Akari, open your eyes, love."

The Murasakan girl's eyes flutter open to the barest of slits. The whites of her eyes are coal black. She's so weak, the light of her tech barely more than dulled embers in a dying fire.

"Hey. There you are. You're okay. I've got you."

"M–miss N–Noc–"

The girl chokes on her own spit. Wren turns her sideways, patting her back as she coughs and heaves. Sweat beads at her brow. Fever sweat, and not a normal fever either. *Maleficarum et detraxi*, curse of the life blood, the salty dew saturated with dark magic. Wren holds the child to her breast as the fit subsides. Her raspy breath is wintry against Wren's collarbone, a stark contrast to the heat of her skin.

Is she going to fail here, too? Is Akari going to die because of Wren's wanting?

No, thinks Wren, screwing her eyes shut. *I will not let another child die under my charge.*

"Renki, find some more linens, and take them into the kitchen. Akari cannot control her body temperature. Zenza, help me move her. We'll use the heat from the ovens to keep her warm."

The two teenagers do as she asks, and once they have Akari rearranged on the kitchen floor, Wren cranks up the oven, cracking the door to let the heat spill over the sick girl. Still she shivers, the chilly touch of death working to take her over again.

¡Pluma de Serpentino! How long does she have to figure out how to nullify the sickness before it's too late? This girl is barely sixteen years old, damnit! For good measure, she siphons another cupful of elixir into Akari's system.

"Is she going to be alright?" asks Renki, adjusting the linens over his friend as Wren finishes coaxing the second dosage into the girl.

"She's stable for now, but who knows how long that will hold."

"Is she going to die?" Zenza's voice trembles.

Not if Wren can help it.

"You two stay with Akari. Give her a spoonful of potion every twenty minutes, and do not miss a dose." Lest the disease progress so far her body nullifies the potion once more.

Four Of Wands

"Wait! Where are you going?"

"Bird hunting."

Wren rises, strapping her satchel around her shoulders and pulling her cloak over it.

"Bird hunting!" shouts Zenza. "You're going after it by yourself!?!"

"Akari doesn't have much time, and I'm willing to bet when I find it, I'll find the witch who summoned it."

"But the witch teleported away. She must be miles from here by now."

"Not necessarily. Teleportation is taxing on the body, and very few witches are capable of such magic naturally. Unless she's feeding energy from a familiar, she won't have gone far, and even then, the ability is limited by her connection with said familiar." Silje once teleported Wren several hundred miles to safety in light of an attack on her life, but Silje had been a displacer beast, accustomed to dimensional travel. The same cannot be said for other netherbeasts. "Zenza, for all that your timing is questionable, you got a good shot in. It's injured and will need to feed, and if it doesn't do so soon, it'll be in trouble."

Zenza blushes at the praise, her ears pinkening as she ducks her head to hide her face behind her bangs.

"Th–they—" Akari bolts up. She isn't awake, not exactly. Her eyes are open but rolled into the back of her head. Her mouth opens and closes, sounds falling from her lips as though her vocal cords were grinding together like sandstone. "Th–they arrr..."

"Shh, Akari. It's alright. Lie down."

"They're c–coming!" the girl gasps and falls limply back on the makeshift bed.

Thunder rumbles outside, the overhead lights flicker out, and the banging of fists against glass echo through the restaurant. Wren, Zenza, and Renki jolt to their feet. Loud raucous thuds and angry bangs boom from the dining hall, percussive and foreboding before the sound of shattering glass breaks the cacophony and the heavy beating falls flat into a resonant silence.

Hunger tickles Wren's awareness.

Zenza moves for Agni sitting on the opposite counter, but Wren stops her. She grabs both teens. Ducking down, a hand over each of their mouths, Wren pulls the pair with her to hide on the far side of the kitchen. Zenza mumbles against her palm. Something along the lines of "What are you doing?" but she cuts herself off as glass shatters in the dining hall. They each make a strangled sound against her palms until the moans of the shamblers reach them.

Both teens stiffen. The whites of Zenza's eyes are stark around her irises and her breath stutters against Wren's palm. Wren's ears twitch, listening as hard as she can. Shuffling feet, the scrap of table legs on the floor, the thump of a saltshaker tumbling to the floor. How many are there? Do they know they're here? The door to the kitchen rattles, and Wren focuses her magic. Renki's breathing stills as wild script appears on 'Atalia's' hand. The dishwasher disconnects from the wall and nudges itself into the swinging kitchen doors silent as the grave. Thank Sigyn this place doesn't have an open serving counter.

There is another roll of thunder, darkness folds around them as the generator powers down. In the wake of the booming thunder, the silence on the far side of the kitchen door is deafening.

There's a bloated snarl, and the kitchen doors bang against the dishwasher. The pair tense in her grip, but they relax in increments the longer the quiet extends until another bassy bang echoes through the kitchen. The pounding repeats rhythmic for a solid seventeen seconds before quiet unfolds once more, the banging giving way to moaning and shuffling, no less worrisome.

Merde!

Renki says something, but with Wren's hand over his mouth, it sounds more like a whimper. Wren draws Agni over to Zenza.

"Renki, draw your sword. Zenza, power up your rifle but don't shoot, and stay quiet." They both nod and Wren lets go of their faces. Renki draws his sword, and Agni lights up orange. The whir of the rifle powering up is loud as an engine comparison to the pregnant stillness of the kitchen, and Zenza winces.

"It's alright," she hisses, reaching over and shifting the silencing nodule on Agni's barrel to active. The powered-up weapon quiets.

"How did you know Agni has a silencer?" Zenza whispers in surprise.

Because the one time Chike fired on her with Agni, she never heard the shot coming. Only felt the searing pain of a bullet ripping through her stomach. The slug didn't kill Wren, but it was the last shot her brother-in-law ever fired. *Berserkr.* Not that she's about to tell Zenza that. The princess still thinks she's Atalia Vaishi.

"Hush."

There's an emergency exit door toward the back of the kitchen. Wren hasn't checked where it leads, but she imagines it opens into a back alley.

"Renki, are you able to set a boundary ward?"

"I have two beacons on me, but if I set them, you won't be able to use your powers."

"I know; that's why I'm going to go out the back door," she whispers to the teenagers. "Barricade it behind me and set one of your beacons."

"But you'll be locked out."

"It will also lock every magical/supernatural being out, including people too far gone from the blixvi's affliction, which is exactly what we want."

"Y–you're not t–taking us with you?" asks Zenza, looking chalky around the gills.

"No. Akari can't be moved. I'll circle around and draw them away. Then you set your second beacon at the front of the restaurant. It should keep you safe while I'm gone. I'll be back once I kill that damned bird."

Zenza shakes her head. She doesn't want to be left alone.

"Yes. If any of those things manage to push their way through before I can get around, you are to shoot to kill. I don't care if they're your favorite babysitter. Do you understand me?"

"But you said—"

"I know what I said, Zenza."

The girl's scared. The fear drips off her in nauseating waves. This is probably her first time in a situation like this ever, and her uncle isn't here to bail her out. Hel, the only person here to save her is a witch she doesn't even trust.

"That was then. This is now. You keep yourselves safe and if anything comes through those doors, you shoot it down. Do you understand?"

Zenza nods.

"Renki?"

The boy doesn't look frightened, his expression calm and serious, but there is a tremble in his free hand. He nods.

"Good."

And Wren rises. She slinks her way along the floor, staying out of view of the windows on the kitchen doors, to the exit. Pushing down on the latch, she checks through the crack if there is anything outside. It's clear, a yawning emptiness juxtaposed by the vociferous bangs behind her.

Renki and Zenza huddle close together, armed and looking at the kitchen doors. Zenza flinches with every bash of the doors against the dishwasher. Wren winces as the heavy appliance nudges slightly to the left. Time to go.

The door closes behind her with a quiet slide of metal.

The alley is dark. There's a fire escape hanging over a dumpster. Flies buzz past her face, and the stink of waste burns her nose hairs. Water drips somewhere, and someone tagged a yellow smiley face with Xs for eyes on the opposite wall.

"Lady Wren."

Wren nearly leaps out of her skin.

"Renki, get back inside!" she hisses at the boy whose foot is stuck fast in the door jamb.

"Let me come with you."

"No. Set the beacon and close the damn door."

A gale wind rips through the narrow alleyway, nearly tossing Wren off her feet. A car horn wails. The nearby traffic lights go on the fritz followed by the squealing of tires. Renki steadies her before she can smack into the wall, and she uses her magic to ground herself firmly upright. Lightning strikes, taking all of the color from the world, are followed by the thunderous beating of wings.

"Get back inside, right now."

"But—"

"Get inside, Renki. I can't deal with this and worry about you getting infected, too."

The boy's brow furrows.

"But what if you get infected?"

"I'm a witch, kiddo. Magical ailments won't affect me the way they'll affect you."

He looks as though he wants to protest, chewing on his lip and staring at her, all too reminiscent of Kaito. Aya yay! Stubborn Miyazaki boys!

"Look, you're smart, and you know what you're doing. Your Kaito–sama has done a good job training you, but this isn't about your ability. I need to catch the blixvi, so I can cure Akari, and I wouldn't be comfortable doing that if I couldn't count on you to take care of them. Akari and Zenza need you more than I do. We can't leave them alone."

His ears turn pink, her words putting responsibility and obligation on his shoulders, two things she knows he understands implicitly from his Miyazaki teachings. It's a manipulative thing to do, but she does mean it, and when he hurries back inside, she closes her eyes in a grateful prayer.

She stays just long enough to feel the surge of saibāki coat the door and hears the teen shove something heavy against the door.

There's a good lad.

Kaito, you've done good with this brat.

She smiles fondly and turns to the mouth of the alley. Time to go bird hunting.

Netherbeasts—Monsters of the astral plains.

Witches are capable of many things. Some of them are even capable of reaching through space and time to draw out creatures which have no place in our world. Netherbeasts summoned to Deus are volatile and dangerous. They are magical essence incarnate, unpredictable and treacherous, but easily bound to a witch's whims. However, if you can break the tether between the witch and the beast, it will turn on its master.

After all, what slave wouldn't seek revenge against its oppressor?

An Excerpt from <u>Hunting and Identifying Hexen</u>
by Finnick Lockecraft, 1852 A.P.

15

FIVE OF WANDS

Chairomura Checkpoint – 8:48PM –Kaito

THE EVENTS FOLLOWING THE BURNING OF
Mishka's shop are tedious. Police reports, hospital check-ins,
and evidence gathering... all jurisdictional hogwash. It not only
wastes Kaito's time but drains him of the last of his energy. Enough
so, he has AYA initiate a system sleep-regeneration command so
Kaito may rest for at least a few hours undisturbed.

When Kaito wakes, rejuvenated and fully powered, he rides
to Chairomura. Where he expects a smooth flow of traffic, he
finds instead a stretch of parked cars with people idling outside,
sitting on their hoods and tailgates and shooting the breeze as
though it were a summertime barbeque. This, coupled with the
complete lack of vehicles leaving Chairomura, spells out exactly
what is going on.

"Is there a reason the city is in quarantine?"

To say the officials are surprised to see him would be an
understatement. They jump to their feet, sorting out their
uniforms and saluting him.

"Your highness, we weren't expecting you."

"Answer my question."

"An illness, sir. We've locked down the city in an attempt to stave off the spread, but we've still had a few rogues enter despite the quarantine."

"Rogues?"

"Well, she had clearance. A Firefly with specialty designation from the crown. She took three trainees into the city with her. The Derivan princess and two Miyazaki teenagers."

Two Miyazaki teenagers! As in Renki and Akari. *Tā mā de!* So much for telling the boy to stay put. Renki has always been obedient, filial, and attentive to Kaito's wishes, but with Wren thrown into the mix—a wild card the boy doesn't fully understand—he probably should have expected a change in behavior.

"Tanaka–san has already arrived to deal with the situation."

"Tanaka?"

"Yes, sir."

"How long ago did he arrive?"

"Not long. Maybe half an hour at the most."

The officers flounder as, without warning, Kaito pulls his cycle into the lane heading for the city. This is not good. Wren and Renki are in a diseased city with a rogue technomancer on their heels, and they have no idea.

Feliz Bordello Cafe – 8:21 PM – Wren

The rancid reek of disease permeates the diner. Piss, shit, sweat, and puss. The once pristine glass of the restaurant's front windows is shattered and stained, torn pieces of blackened flesh dangle like macabre garlands from the jagged edges. The front door hangs off its hinges, the frame dented and scratched. The neon light bulbs of the open sign halfway snapped off leaving only the bottom tail of the 'p' and the loop of the 'e.'

There is no sign of the blixvi, though evidence of the beast can be found: feathers, talon scratches, and, of course, the disease-ridden humans.

Twelve shamblers amble aimlessly within, bumping into tables and chairs. Occasionally, one will trip over a leg, hitting the linoleum with a splat. They lie still and moan for a beat before staggering their way back up and continuing their ambling drag, one heavy footfall at a time. One of them, a pox-ridden male, bangs on the kitchen doors. His hands leave smears of oily black with every hit, and his teeth bite divots in the metal. More than a few pearly whites lie broken on the floor, but he can't get in, the dishwasher obstructing his goal.

A tin can, suspended in mid-air, floats into the restaurant. It circles the shamblers' heads and whacks the one smacking the doors on the side of his skull. He growls in annoyance, turning around to trudge after the floating lure. The can hovers at the center of the diner, the shambler reaching to nab it when it begins to shake wildly. The rocks inside rattle loudly like a cheap maraca.

The other shamblers twist to attention, all thirteen groaning after the lure as it zips out of the diner into the street. Once all of them are out of the building, the can arches across the parking lot, disappearing across the street, and the diseased humans chase after the bait.

Thunder rumbles above Wren's head, the clouds thick gray blots against the purpling horizon. Renki's ward goes up as another flash of dark lightning blackens the sky, and Wren heaves a sigh of relief. She's thrown the makeshift lure as far from the teens' location as she can manage, which is a ways away as far as telekinesis is concerned. Renki's ward will do the rest as far as keeping the kids out of trouble while she's gone birding— provided of course she doesn't take too long.

Wren pulls her hood over her head and ducks into the cityscape.

SONATA

She's read about how in the old-world days, people used to go bird hunting for sport: lines of rich folks all lined up with boom sticks aimed at the horizon. They'd send a dog to frighten the fowl then shoot the birds, too slow and fat from human caretaking to fly away. Some people would even go hunting for a prize fowl to slap on the dinner table for special occasions. One particular country made popular a holiday where they would slaughter these fat gobbling birds called turkeys and serve them in a celebratory dinner. People would gorge themselves on the feast, and then nap the rest of the day away before putting an annual sporting event on these boxy home television sets via this network called cable. Archaic and crude compared to their current networking systems, but it was two thousand years ago.

The practice of shooting/hunting birds for sport grew out of fashion for most countries in Deus though Aighneas and Seraphim still organize sporting events for their upper class. Not turkeys though; turkeys went extinct ages ago—the birds couldn't handle the magical radiation. In Deriva, she used to go fly fishing with her family every summer. Tlanextli once caught a sail-finned white shark; the apex predator was on board long enough for their domo to get measurements on it. Nose to tail, it had been eight feet long—its sail stood as tall as an eight-year-old Wren at the time—and while she doesn't remember the exact measurement of its jaw, it had been wide enough to easily fit a fat watermelon inside. One of the scientists tagged it, and Tlanextli then pulled one of its teeth before returning it to the water alive and flapping.

Wren climbs the fire escape of the tallest building in the area. It's no skyscraper, maybe fifteen stories up at most, but it'll do. The rooftop gives her a better vantage point, and she sees the lot where their cycles were obliterated. Just beyond is the border crossing where Sekhmetian robots tread, prepared to fire on any movement, and ambling about the veritable maze of steel mountains between are scores of diseased humans. They stagger through the streets as dusk settles over the world. She had to dodge around more than a couple on her way here.

No wonder they shut down entry into the city. Living zombies. How ghastly! To turn the once healthy into mindless, toothy monsters. She wonders if the blixvi's disease is only contagious via bite or if the pestilence can be passed merely via airations or water contamination. How many people are infected? How many more are healthy enough to leave but can't?

The groans of a shambler greet her ear. To her left, a shambler waddles his way toward her, following a second tin maraca. Her bait. She had it follow her up the fire escape. It's Bang-bang-Knock-knock, the one who tried to tear down the kitchen, lagging behind the others Wren emptied out of the diner. Even at this distance, she smells the stink of him. It curls her upper lip. Swollen like a water-logged corpse, his skin bulges from his face and throat. His mouth hangs open, lips flapping like fleshy laundry on a loose line. The shambler swats at the tin can like a cat swatting at a teaser toy, a gangrenous dollop of skin slushing off his hand.

How much longer can he survive this disease, wasting away in front of her as he is?

Blixvi are carrion feeders. It spreads its disease for the purpose of garnering its next meal. If she is going to lure the bird out of the sky, she'll need a freshly dead corpse. That is, after all, why she chose this one—a man close enough to death killing him would be a mercy.

But the decision is taken from her as quickly as the thought comes and goes.

He takes four more steps in her direction and then crumbles, quite literally. His skin flakes from his face, and with choked breaths, he lolls to the ground, leaving a greasy smear on the pavement, his moans so loud they echo in her stomach.

Eventually, the sound, along with the infected, dies.

Well, that makes her life easier. Poor guy. She wonders what kind of person he was in life. Was he an asshole or a gent? Did he have a family? If he did, was he an all-round family man or a deadbeat? Regardless, she'll never know. Not unless his ghost decides to pay her a visit, but it hasn't popped up yet, so either he's decided not to engage her or he's moved on, easy as that: no big flash of light, no tunnel to the heavens, just a quiet fade away to the other side of the veil.

Well, people like to think death is quiet. Wren's had been anything but, and this guy's sure as hell wasn't quiet or peaceful.

Lightning strikes the ground to her right, and she dives out of the way as a massive, feathered shape swoops down. Its talons sink into the fresh corpse, its wings spread in a dark mantle over the kill, and a sharp beak clamps down on the man's skull with a sickening crunch, slicing through bone and brain matter as easy as scissors through paper.

On the ground, the bird is easily two feet taller than her, its hulking shape twisted in favor of its uninjured side. The evidence of Zenza's marksmanship, a rotund bullethole, drips crimson onto the ground. Its vulture-like head boasts a nauseous yellow crest while its midnight blue eagle-owl body is spotted through with jagged, black streaks reminiscent of lightning. The bird's beak, a crisp sky blue, stains with the juices of its feast.

It hasn't noticed her yet, too invested in its meal. Wren draws a breath and peers around the edge of an exhaust pipe. In the quietest pianissimo, Wren breathes life into a rousing tune.

A penny for a spool of thread
A penny for a needle
That's the way the mulberry burns

POP! The corpse's head splits from its body, spine still attached—a Slithering Skull—one of Wren's more gruesome undead.

Goes the weasel...

FIVE OF WANDS

The bird screaks as Wren's disembodied skull attempts to strangle the netherbird. The column of vertebrae tightens around the bird's throat, spiny ridges digging into the pestilence-ridden fowl like tiny daggers.

The blixvi's beak catches the undead's tailbone and rips it away. The blixvi smacks Wren's slithering skull into the ground like a flail. Shaking its head back and forth, it looks kind of like the mascot on one of those old-world flags—an eagle wrangling a serpent.

Flinging her intention forward, necrotic magic ensnares the bird's foot in a vice.

Discordant notes fall from Wren's lips, vibrating up the coil of magic, and the bird's feathers shrivel and fall from its body in molt while Wren draws her knife. She doesn't know which part of the bird she needs to brew a cure, but she'll carve it into tiny pieces if she needs to.

Consider yourself plucked, pinche pajaro, she thinks, raising her blade.

"Rafvæða!"

The shouted spell crackles out with the same void lightning as the blixvi. Wren releases her hold and dodges sideways, narrowly avoiding the curse. Wren's bag slips off her shoulder and skids across the lot, the towel-bound teapot of potion clattering across the cement of the roof. Her slithering skull is not so lucky. The undead is struck, vertebral tail clanking like a xylophone's keys as Wren's spell dissipates, and the skull falls limp to the roof.

Rest in peace, Nameless.

The netherbird shrieks up, wavering back and forth as it attempts to fly into the clouds despite its significant lack of feathers.

"You meddlesome bitch!"

At the edge of the roof, a hooded figure unfurls from nothing. Looking like a flamingo with one leg braced against the other and their hip cocked to one side, the robed figure stands at the center of a blackened array: two interwoven squares and at their periphery are the scrawled runes ᚱ and ᛏ. The runes for journey (raiðo) and necessity (nauþiz). A teleportation array.

"My poor birdie. Did this wicked witch hurt you?"

A sickly sweet baby voice coos at the bird as though it were a beloved pet rather than a harbinger of disease and decay. Unable to properly fly, the blixvi plops down on the roof at the witch's feet, and the bird ducks its head and nuzzles its master. The gale of the bird's massive wings rustles the hood from the witch's head to reveal braided red hair and spiral goat horns.

"Summer."

The summoner stands opposite 'Atalia,' a twisted smile on her face. It pulls her freckles in oblong directions. Looking so much younger than she actually is with curled ribbons dangling from her horns—horns she had sewn into her own head in a grotesque homage to Dr. Frankenstein. Or maybe she's paying tribute to the horned gods of old: Cernunnos, the horned one and lord of wild things or mayhaps Chernobog, the demon of ill fortune.

"I must admit, I am at a disadvantage. You know who I am, but I haven't the slightest idea who you are."

"And it will stay that way."

"But this is our second time meeting." She draws her athame, a scimitar-like blade as long as her forearm. "Are your manners really so poor you won't introduce yourself? Hiding behind a glamour like a coward?"

Ha! If this woman only knew who she was talking to.

She draws the blade across the meat of her brachialis and offers the bleeding limb to the netherbeast. Wren's stomach flips as the bird laps up the witch's blood, flapping its wings and tittering happily, the grotesque version of a bird flitting about in a watering fountain.

"I save my introductions for people I don't intend to kill."

The bird's feathers regrow, and with a wave of the witch's hand, it takes off into the air.

"You plan to kill me with a kitchen knife?"

Wren glances down to the aforementioned "kitchen knife" in her hand. She didn't forget everything in Kaito's rooms. It's the same blade Wren used in Shinka, slightly curved with a toothy edge, perfect for carving meat.

"It is a meat carver."

"You're delusional."

"And you're outclassed."

She just doesn't realize it, yet.

"Hn! We'll see."

Summer extends her free hand, obsidian dripping from her fingertips. Wren braces herself, her own magic coursing around her in glittering spirals of wild magic, but the attack comes from behind with a shriek.

A pair of razor-sharp talons slice into her shoulder. The blixvi clamps down and lifts her off her feet. Wren twists in its grasp, kicking skyward and nailing the bird in the throat with the heel of her boot. It lets out a hacking caw and drops her, landing on a satellite to gather itself. Wren tucks and rolls through the landing. Hopping back up, she crosses her forearms in front of her face to keep Summer's boot from smashing into her nose.

"Those were some rather adorable teenagers with you earlier. Did 'Mummy' put them in time out while she goes to work? How's the little one my Søren got a few good pecks on? She hasn't eaten the other two yet, has she?"

She's never heard a monologue with quite so many questions therein. Kaito used to call her insufferable? Imagine him sitting through this!

She pushes the woman off and reclaims some space between them.

"Four against two is a little unfair," Wren says with a sneer. "Thought I'd give you a handicap."

"Right because I need a handicap from the likes of you," Summer scoffs. "Maybe I'll pay them a visit after I rip your face off. They're just the right age to act as vessels for a demon or two. Think they'll sit still long enough for me to call one up from the underworld?"

The woman slashes for her face. The kitchen knife rattles in Wren's hand, clanging against the witch's athame.

"You won't touch them."

Wren lets go of the knife, sending it flying into the blixvi's side. The bird thrashes wildly, black blood dripping down its flank to sizzle on the ground.

"You bitch!"

Summer slaps 'Atalia' across the face, and Wren tumbles sideways, elbows clanging against the cement. Pain, whitehot and sharp, starbursts behind her eyes as her temple meets the corner ledging. Her vision blurs on impact, the world losing color and definition. Wren blinks the stars away, hearing an ugly command fall from Summer's lips. Two worlds come into focus, one in high definition, the other in grayscale, as Summer makes her way to her bird, thrashing in a heap on the ground. She yanks Wren's blade out and drops it to the ground.

"Get up you useless thing before I put you in the oven!"

The blixvi bolts upward and dives for Wren, its talons snatching through her hair as Wren sends it rolling sideways with a blast of magic. Summer clicks her way toward her.

"I admit you are talented. Tell me who you are, and maybe I'll name one of my pets after you."

Pets? How disrespectful! To call a creature like the blixvi a pet! Summer's never given a lick of care about her beasts, each one just another summoned monster bound to her will, little more than slaves. Years ago, Summer pieced a bunch of chimera together from the bits and pieces of enslaved netherbeasts, sewn together in a mangle of bloodthirsty bric-a-brac when they'd outgrown their use. Silje had been one of those beasts, and Wren set the captured feline free, saving her from a fate worse than death. Disgust rises in Wren's throat at Summer, once again cracking a whip in the face of a creature as powerful as a blixvi—a creature once worshipped as a god by non-magical humans—as though it were a beast of burden.

"Netherbeasts aren't pets."

"They're my pets, and I will do with them what I will. I don't need your permission."

Wren tackles Summer, shoving her shoulder in the other witch's stomach. The two women land in a heap on the pavement. Summer gnashes her teeth at Wren, thrashing her head forward and back. One of the horns catches Wren in the side of the mouth as Wren's elbow meets Summer's cheekbone. The other witch stunned, Wren takes the opportunity to spit in Summer's face. With a high-pitched whistle, the necrotic magic in her blood-laced saliva freezes through Summer's skin. The resultant scream is nothing to laugh at, but Wren laughs anyway.

"You've always had little respect for the creatures you summon."

A sharp heeled boot rams into her stomach, and Wren rolls backward.

"*Juksemaker!*" Summer slashes low at her ankles, and Wren jumps to avoid the blade. "As if you actually know anything about me."

"I know you're as much a butcher as you are a keeper. That bird is not yours. It holds no loyalty to you, and when I free it from your will, I will laugh as it tears you apart the way your Nightmare tore Mishka apart."

A phantom hand snarls the fabric of the other witch's cloak. Wren's ghostly touch yanks the woman off her feet and throws her into the side of the next building.

"Argh!"

Brick and mortar flake off the building's side as Summer tumbles to the street. Wren follows, shimmying down the side of the fire escape. The blixvi's talons clang against the metal grating, trying to peck Wren in the thigh.

It catches her boot and tugs.

Her feet swept out from under her, her chin slams into a ladder ring. The skin scrapes from her arms and the ground disappears as the giant fowl tosses her into the air. The sky becomes down and the pavement up, and a sharp beak snaps toward her. The bird's uvula waggles from side to side as it caws up at her, waiting to crunch down on her bones.

Wren whistles.

An emerald cord of magic knots around the bird's beak, snapping it shut. Wren lands on top of it, catches its head, and latches psychic claws into the bird's essence, grabbing for the diabolical tether binding the animal to its master. Wren's knife finds its way back to her hand, and Wren slams it into the thick meat of the bird's back.

"Liberar."

The release spell she etched into the metal glows to life the moment it touches the enslaved creature's skin. Her power digs into the creature's chained core and finds the tether connecting it to its master. Now all she needs to do is—

The blixvi flings its head sideways, flipping Wren off before she can finish carving her way through the binding spell. The bird takes to the sky as Wren lands flat on her back. *Ouch!* She coughs, wheezing for air around her bruised ribs.

"You can't release my spell. The bird is my—"

Except, as Wren finds her feet, the blixvi circles back around and dives, not for Wren, but for Summer. The horned witch ducks back into the debris as the bird's beak slices open her cheek. Maybe Wren managed to relinquish some of Summer's hold on the beast?

"What are you doing?! Get off me!"

The other witch wrestles with the netherbeast presently hellbent on pecking the flesh right off her face.

"Förslava!"

Summer shouts another curse. Darkness blackens the alley for the blink of an eye, and in a flurry of feathers and magic, the blixvi rears back, flitting up with a thunderous clap of its wings. The force of the gale knocks Wren to the street as it disappears into the rumbling clouds overhead. A shift of ozone, an impossible darkening of the sky, and Wren's awareness tingles, narrowing to a fine point.

Something is about to change.

The first raindrop hits Wren's forehead, and despite her glamour, the triskele flashes bold in the dark. The heavens open up. Blond hair darkens to black as the locks billow around her head, water runs in rivulets down her face and arms, her wild script flickers into nothing, and Wren's magic washes down the drain.

What the—! Rain that can banish magic!

"You!"

Summer wheezes, blood dripping from a cut over her eyebrow. A finger thrusts toward Wren's face as she coughs.

"Impossible! You can't be back!"

The redhead rises from the rubble of Wren's forceful push with a cough. She clears her throat and hocks a wad of dirt-crusted spit onto the pavement. With a flex of magic, Wren pulls the other witch off her feet.

"Tell me how to cure the disease."

She dangles a foot off the ground for but a moment before Wren's magic snuffs out in the rain, and she drops back to the rubble.

"Get bent!" Summer spits. She raises a hand to throw a curse at Wren, but the magic fizzles out before it covers even a quarter of the distance.

Groaning erupts from the mouth of the alley, and Wren glances over to see a group of shamblers dragging their feet toward them at an alarming rate. Wren disengages Summer, ducking under a slobbering pair of human jaws and jumping onto the closed dumpster. Behind her, still on the ground, Summer screams.

"Get off me! Søren, you blasted chicken, you!" she yells at the sky. "Get down here and call off these wretches!"

But the bird doesn't appear, in defiance of its mistress. And Summer, for all her power, is unable to fend off a horde of her own making. Though, it isn't really her horde anymore, is it? With the blixvi out of her control, they'll devour anything in their path.

There's a small rectangular window above Wren's head. A twitch of her fingers pushes it open, but it's too far out of reach. *Merde!* Already the palms of several shamblers slap at the hood of the dumpster. *Double merde!*

"Søren, you wretched bird! I'm going to pluck you and use your feathers as a boa. Ahhhh!"

The woman's scream curdles Wren's blood, and Wren makes the mistake of looking back. The shamblers converge on Summer. The witch calls spells to no effect, her magic pushing back one only for another to take its place. One of them grips Summer by the head. Another's teeth close down on her shoulder.

They're going to eat her alive.

"Help! Please, Songstress! I don't want to die!"

Summer's eyes, which had been black as pitch up until now, clear to a bronzy brown, and as Wren's watery-green meet the other witch's, a single thought derails any and all plans she had in relation to this witch.

Summer's eyes are terribly, inexplicably human.

Before she can rethink it, Wren whistles, and just as the shambler's teeth are about to close on Summer's bared throat, Wren's magic pushes it off. Before she has time to think too hard about it, Wren drags Summer out of the shamblers' hold, summoning the woman toward her.

"What are you—I thought you wanted to kill me!"

"Just shut up and climb!"

Summer doesn't need to be told twice, grabbing the ledge, setting her foot in Wren's offered hands, and hauling herself up while Wren staves off the shamblers trying to mount the dumpster. They snap at her boots and tear at the hem of her skirt. Summer disappears through the window, and Wren turns to follow, relieved to find Summer's hand extended down to help her up.

The bleeding redhead pulls her through, and Wren snaps the window shut on shambling fingers.

About two hundred years after our ancestors migrated to
Deus, their languages began to shift. Our scholars believe the
shift began when magic began to peter out in some parts of
the population. Witches sought a way to communicate with
one another without cluing their non–magical counterparts
to their activities, and this strange mix of languages from
every cardinal direction would eventually become known
as hexenspeak.

Excerpt from *How Witches Transformed Our Tongues*
By Catherine Degasperi, 1575 A.P.

16

SEVEN OF WANDS

North Chairomura – 10:17PM –Kaito

T HE CITY IS NOT A GHOST TOWN. IT IS A hive—a hive of infected, shambling bees.

Chairomura groans with disease. The empty husks of abandoned cars slide by as he rides into the city. And between each mechanical husk, infected slink through the streets moaning for help and sustenance. He's never seen a situation like this. Living zombies! And somewhere in this cesspool of disease are three adepts-in-training and a witch. Thank the goddess Wren took jurisdiction over them before they ended up killing themselves.

"AYA, run a scan on the area. I want to know if either Wren or Renki are nearby."

SCANNING IN PROCESS...

SCANNING...

SCANNING...

NECROTIC MAGIC DETECTED AT 24 DEGREES SOUTHWEST, 53 KM

He angles that direction, exiting the freeway and leaning into the accelerator. The digits on his helmet display climb. He can make it to her location in fifteen minutes. Here's hoping whatever Wren is using her magic for is something mild. He takes comfort in the fact the city's generators haven't given out, something which would only happen in the most dire of situations. The streetlights are on as normal, warding away the dark of night, and more than a few apartment windows glow with the blue-tinted light of computer monitors.

"AYA, run me a status report on the Chairomura's energy usage. I want to know how long the generators have been sustaining the city."

"Yes, highness."

A laser beam bounces off the front of his lightcycle, and the wheels skid out from under him. A virtual shield erects as he careens sideways. He jerks the handles and lets the cycle go down. It lands heavy on his left leg, but he releases his grip before he can end up a skid mark on the pavement. He rolls away, crouching down to avoid a second beam, shot right over his head. The lightcycle grinds down the exit ramp, sparks flying before slamming into a stalled semi.

Over on his auxiliary systems, AYA runs a parameter analysis.

Kaito draws his swords, saibāki coating Tsukuyomi and Amatsu in amaranthine, and deflects a third blast toward a blurred heat signature. The redirected shot strikes a cloaked drone and drops it out of the sky. It crashes in an explosion of scattered parts and broken metal plating.

Across the way, a group of three shamblers make their way over, attracted by the clanging of steel.

"Hungry..." One of them rumbles out, and Kaito gets a good look at the infected for the first time. Boils, welts, and crawling mold decorate their bodies, like the black plague took up residence in a fungus and figured out how to release spores.

A second drone, in Sekhmetian colors of gold and desert amber, buzzes over, unfolding to reveal an automatic rifle. He hears the click and takes off running, juking out of the line of fire and ducking under a horse trailer. The bullets ricochet off the metal, shattering a few nearby windows. The shamblers are not so quick. Bullets rend through them, and three bodies drop, their faces splattering on the concrete, one of them rattling around like a fallen jack.

What is a Sekhmetian drone doing on this side of the border? And why is it firing on him?

The hacking center in his left eye twists, numbers trailing down in lines of zeroes and ones. He inputs his codes, ripping down firewalls to take ownership of the bot's command system.

DEACTIVATE OFFENSIVE SYSTEMS

The response comes a breath later.

ACCESS DENIED

A command away from gaining total control, electricity shoots through his synapses, blacking his sights out long enough for the drone's master to push him out.

"Miyazaki–san, how terribly droll to see you in town!"

An EMP grenade bounces under the trailer. Barely avoiding the blast, Kaito rolls into a rain of bullets. The shock of blunt force throws his arm aside. A shell glances off his armor as Amatsu leaves his hand spinning to cleave a third, newly arrived, drone in two. Two chunks of metal crash to the asphalt.

From atop one of the buildings, Tanaka laughs, weapons in hand and a visor over his face. The second drone zips around, taking aim at Kaito again, but it never opens fire. Not on Kaito at least.

ACCESS GRANTED

Thank the matrix for AYA.

The drone shifts allegiance and opens fire on Tanaka. With a shout, the other technomancer throws himself from the top of the building, ducking under a nearby awning. AYA chimes as the man sets a field, but Kaito is too quick, hacking into his systems before he has the opportunity. Tanaka tumbles forward, gripping his head as Kaito overcomes his defenses. Amatsu's coil drags the man by the ankle until he rests at its master's feet.

Lightning rips across the sky, so dark it saps the light from even Kaito's night vision. A dark shadow descends from the clouds, barreling downward before arching back skyward, its movements coupled by the thunderous flapping of massive wings. The bird disappears into the cloudline, and thunder rattles the very ground he stands on. And underneath the heavenly cacophony scraps the scuffling footsteps of shamblers.

Tanaka's laughter floods the street as the angry rumble dies. "I wonder if your whore will let me fuck her before I kill her."

"Urusai!"

He backhands the man across the face, sending him rolling into a streetlight. Amatsu returns to Kai's left hand as Tsukuyomi slices into the skin under the man's chin.

"Speak again and it will be the last syllable you utter."

The man flinches, and Kaito presses his blade in harder. Lines of code unfold, and, as Kaito's sights whirl, his servers plow into Tanaka's mainframe. A jumble of memory scans unfold before his eyes.

12*th Day in the Month of Ice*, 1872

Tanaka's breath stinks of alcohol.

"It's hard to believe the Miyazaki used to have a reputation for being ruthless witch hunters. I thought becoming a technomancer of Murasaki would bring me the opportunity to find glory and fame, but here I am, two years a technomancer, and I've yet to take on more than a domestic dispute between fairies and humans. Machines be damned! The most action I've gotten was a skirmish on the border between some

androids and a group of goblins, and my orders were to resolve the issue peacefully! Hikaru's gone soft. If it weren't for his neural nets, somebody would've dethroned that poor excuse for a ruler and thrown the lot of them in prison for betraying the League's mission."

"Tanaka–san, you really shouldn't speak in such a manner." A red-lipped, pale faced Firefly pours warmed liquor into a cup for the man. *"His Excellency—"*

"His Excellency is a cad and a coward! Letting hexen take refuge in our great country. It's a sham!"

"But isn't it a good thing? After all, an alliance with a witch is what allowed the Alliance to take down Seraphim all those years ago."

"And we paid for that alliance in blood! Or have you forgotten the number of people who are dead because of the bloody Songstress? My parents were killed by that bitch!"

The Firefly screams as the table upends, food and drink spilling everywhere, and Tanaka's behavior gets him thrown from the establishment.

28th Day in the Month of Dirt, 1875

Time passes. Tanaka's bitterness toward Hikaru and the Miyazaki regime grows, but his outlet diminishes. He follows his orders, handles his cases without err, and avoids the Firefly houses. Even the brothels of the red-light district refuse him entry for his brash unruliness.

"I have a dream of a world free from magic."

On the television, Primarch Thames gives his annual State of the League speech. This is not Murasaki. After Hikaru vacated his seat on the council, he restricted the spread of League propaganda in Murasaki, opting instead for the more traditional isolationist perspective on media sources with a particular emphasis on banning xenophobic speech, and Thames' prose is indeed full of radical, bordering on chauvinistic, anti-hexen sentiment. Wherever Tanaka is in this memory, it is a nation under heavy League influence.

SONATA

"I have a dream of a future where our children need not go to bed at night fearful of the boogeymen under their bed. A future where there is nothing to be afraid of in the dark. A future where the only worries for them are whether they've finished their homework and what time is dinner. I have a dream for a future where parents need not pray for solace on a double full moon, where they no longer hang garlic from their front doors, where our keys are not hidden by fairies, and where we no longer worry that our neighbors might one day see fit to bury a hex bag in our front yard.

"For centuries, we suffered at the hands of witches and their ilk. They enslaved us. They killed us. They tortured us all because we lack the same blasphemous abilities as they. But finally, after centuries of war, we have established a true peace. A peace without magic. Eleven years ago, we killed the Songstress of Lorelei and her followers. We re-wrote the hierarchy between science and magic, and in ten short years, we have driven them to the brink of extinction. We are so close to achieving our goal. One last push, and we will be rid of those who have plagued us for so long. I dream of a world emancipated from magic, and for the first time since my primacy began, we are so close to our goal, I can taste it.

"But we need allies. We need your support. We need people brave enough to challenge the status quo. Brave enough to put their foot down against passivity. Brave enough to make a stand where others would fall."

17th Day in the Month of Songs, 1875

A glitched figure speaks to Tanaka.
"Do you understand your mission?"
Lines of code block Kaito's visual of the person speaking. They are at once tall and short, dark-skinned and pale, male, female, and neither. A voice augmentation keeps Kaito from distinguishing anything about the speaker other than the words they are saying, spoken in the most formal of commons, a complete lack of regional/ethnic accent or pitch/tonal markers preventing any identification of nationality, age, and sex.

"I do."

"Good. Make no mistake, Tanaka. You're making the right decision."

Tanaka's gaze travels through a strange room. Inside three fluid-filled tanks, hooked up and wired within each, are the same two hexen who attacked Snowfall. The vampyric woman and Zero the shifter. The third, one he doesn't recognize, is smaller than the other two, but the same blurred coding obstructs this sleeping figure as well.

Experiments on hexen?

A bullet ricochets off the pavement in front of him. Kaito's sights go black. Something grips his ankle, and pain erupts in his calf as a shambler sinks its teeth into his leg. Kaito kicks it away. It rolls into the brick wall, plaster crumbling on impact, and lies dead at the base.

"Tsk, tsk, Miyazaki–san. Don't you know these poor souls are merely victims of a witch? The poor sod may have had a chance at survival if you hadn't just killed him."

Tanaka pulls a pistol. Shots ring out as Kai rolls sideways. The drone under his sway opens fire on Tanaka, but the technomancer fells the bot with a thrown kunai. It crashes into a gathering horde of shamblers. The explosion scatters the infected, leaving several with missing feet and knees. Gurgling screams of pain echo through the streets as their blood drips onto the asphalt.

"Teme!"

The laughing technomancer pulls from his pocket a strange, cylindrical device, and within, a moldy green liquid swirls. Kaito's scanners zero in, trying to identify the hand-sized mechanism. A fogger of some kind, capable of converting a liquid into a mist.

"Did you know the venom of some breeds of nether spider have the ability to dispel a witch's magic? We've been experimenting with it as a means of curing infected individuals."

"Infected individuals?"

"Witches, hexen, anybody whose systems are reliant on witch magic; the venom eats away the magical network the way scorpion venom attacks the nervous system. We've been trying to see if we can cure hexen of their afflictions by injecting the venom directly into their meridians. Give them the chance of a normal life, as it were."

"Magic isn't a disease to be cured."

Without a working magical network, hexen will die. In fact, he's not sure anyone could survive such a toxin. After all, what is a magical network if not just another, chaos-driven version of a technomancer's lifeforce?

"We're still in the developmental phase, of course," Tanaka continues as though Kaito hadn't spoken. "Lacking test subjects, you understand. If this had been around fourteen years ago, it might very well have saved your mother's life. We managed to save a woman after a nasty run in with Koi lycan. We rid her of the curse. Certifiably human once more despite a bite to the torso which would have undoubtedly turned her. Unfortunately, she died a few days later when her body failed to filter out the venom, but at least she died uncursed."

They didn't cure her. They killed her. The same way the puritans once burned the devil out of accused witches or tossed innocent women into water to see if they could swim. The pure souls drowned, cleansed of all their sins, and the ones who floated were fished out and murdered anyway in the name of curing them of their wickedness. Same concept, different execution. A witch could have reversed the curse's effects or given her a means of controlling it.

"We haven't been able to check what kind of effects it might have on a witch, whether it would be lethal or not. It's meant to be directly injected into their magical cores, but we have need of your witch's skills before we can cure her of them, so I've modified this little baby to evaporate straight into the ozone. I thought it would be best used as a gas or a fogger to destabilize her magic, but since the weather is amiable, let's see what happens when I release it into the sky right before it falls. Think your witch's magic can stand up to acid rain?"

The clouds darken.

"Oh, I do hope she remembered to bring an umbrella. I would hate for her little glamour to evaporate into thin air in front of the wrong person."

Kaito slashes forward, and Tanaka phases away as the mechanism ratchets skyward. It disappears into the cloudline, and a burst of white light follows, streaking across the sky like lightning.

"Enjoy the shamblers, prince!"

The man flips onto a hoverboard and flits away along the rooftops.

Kaito looks down where blood seeps through his pant leg. The bite is already festering. With a frustrated hiss, he drives a medi stim directly into the wound and takes off after the fleeing technomancer, dodging shamblers as he goes.

And as he runs, the sky opens up, and toxic rain pours down.

11:07PM – Downtown Chairomura – Wren

"Wren fucking Nocturne. The Songstress of Lorelei back in the flesh."

Summer crouches at the far side of the little storage room they've found themselves in. Shamblers pound on the small window they squeezed through, locked the moment Wren closed it on the fingers of the man nipping at her ankles. The digits twitch on the floor with the last dredges of dying neurons as Wren slides down the wall, dizzy and more than a little nauseous from the earlier blow to the head. Not to mention having her magic virtually power-washed into the sewer has wreaked havoc on her sense of balance.

"You really do have dominion over death, don't you? And here I thought I'd seen everything."

"Odd thing for you to say, considering you look like you're about twelve."

"I do not," snubs the woman. "I am much older than I look, as you well know. Older than you by more than a few years, not counting the ones you lost as worm food." Her nails click as she flicks dirt out from under them as if she isn't covered in grime from head to toe. "So, how'd you do it?"

"Do what?"

Summer rolls her eyes skyward. "How did you crawl out of the grave?"

"I didn't."

Wren gets her feet under her, rising to check the door on the far side of the room.

"Bullshit! You expect me to believe someone else brought you back?"

"So, what? I raised myself from the dead out of sheer spite."

"I wouldn't put it past you." Summer cocks her head sideways, lower lips puffed out. "No one has ever managed a true resurrection. And there aren't any witches left strong enough to even dream about attempting it."

"So I've heard."

"'So you've heard,'" Summer mocks. "You should know—you killed most of them."

Yeah... She did. And the League annihilated the rest trying to kill her.

Predictably, the door to the storage closet is locked from the outside. No matter. Opening plain wood doors is child's play when she isn't drenched in mysteriously anti-magical water, anyway. Thankfully, there are towels in the closet.

"So what? Death make you soft or just daft? We were trying to kill each other a moment ago. Change your mind or have you just got one of those odd personality disorders? I hear they are working on treatments for Borderline Personality Disorder."

Possibly, but that's neither here nor there.

"Unfortunately, you are the only person who may be able to help me cure the blixvi's disease."

"Haha! Is that all? You should have stuck to your guns and let them eat me. Like hell I'm helping you save a +ie from a fate they deserve."

Wren growls, cursing her own bleeding heart and the concussion building behind her eyes. Summer's right. Why did she even bother? Because the woman begged for help? What a laugh! There are others far more deserving of her help who she failed to keep alive, yet here is Summer, laughing at her for showing mercy.

Stop it, Wren. Think about Akari. You have to save Akari.

But what about Mishka who didn't deserve the death she was served? Oh, her head is killing her!

"You know. Most people say 'thank you' when someone saves their life," she spits instead.

Wren doesn't expect any such thing from Summer, nor does she even really want her gratitude, already regretting rescuing the woman. She should have let her be eaten. She very well could've signed her second death warrant by taking the risk of saving Summer. Summer may not realize it, but by giving Wren a hand up, she inadvertently saved Wren's life as well. She could have easily decided to leave her outside to be eaten. It was a stupid gamble to make. Summer is a bloodthirsty bitch, irredeemable and deserving of whatever end fate has decided for her; it's pure luck Summer decided to pull Wren through the window in return. Curse her bleeding heart!

"I'm not most people."

"Yeah, well, I'll carve you up myself later after we've found a cure for the plague." "Well, by all means, don't let me stop you. Not like I'm going anywhere anytime soon."

"If you expect me to believe you powerless, you're crazier than I thought."

Summer dropped her athame outside, but just because she's weaponless doesn't make her even remotely harmless. She is still a witch, after all, even if she isn't looking very good at the moment. Summer leans against the doorway, one hand cradling her torn-up shoulder. Her skin is pale and blotchy, yellowing around the places where the blixvi got a few good pecks in.

"Not crazy. Just hopeful my opponent is as idiotic as I first assumed. The Songstress of Lorelei wasting her magic helping infantile posties. What a travesty!"

Right ... because she knew who Wren was when they started in on each other. What a waste of magic saving Summer's life! If she weren't feeling so absolutely wretched, she'd take the knife and go looking Summer's kidneys.

"And you waste yours terrorizing a meaningless city?"

Wren blasts the door off of its hinges.

Chairomura Garden District – 11:37 **PM** –Kaito

Kaito loses Tanaka.

In the flurry of bodies and rain and disease-ridden cityscape, the man escapes his boundaries, and not even AYA is able to pick up the slightest ping of Wren's energy signature. It's as though the entire city has been washed of lingering wild magic. It swirls down the storm drains like refuse mixing with the taint of death and destruction.

It does nothing to help those infected by the corruption. If anything, the rain worsens their condition.

Smoke rises from somewhere nearby, soaking into the rain like acid, defiling the fragrance of petrichor, not that it wasn't already tainted by the venom released into the atmosphere. An electrical fire, maybe, or perhaps the attempt of some survivors to keep themselves warm and save generator power. Whatever the source of the smoke, it sticks in his nose like the stench of iron after a nosebleed. It's almost worse than the battering sound of shamblers banging, banging, banging at the steel paneling below him.

After losing Tanaka, Kaito takes refuge from the rain on the balcony of a clothing boutique while shamblers coalesce on the sidewalk. Despite the nanos rapidly trying to repair his injury, his leg is on fire. The bite refuses to close even if the bleeding has stopped, the skin around the wound turning an alarming gray. It doesn't seem to be spreading past a three-centimeter radius, though, so at least it's contained for the time being.

He has AYA running analytics on the wound. Whatever contagion is spreading around the city, there's a good chance it's bloodbound, liable to spread by bites and scratches. Which means he's infected, and there's no telling how long his immuno-support system can fight off the affliction before he becomes as mindless as the shamblers currently gnashing their teeth in his direction.

"The infection will be contained for the next three hours."

"And after?"

"Rapid deterioration of organic material, muscle-cell death, and psychotic unravelling."

Comforting.

"Prospects for a cure?"

"The disease is magical in nature, your highness. My databases have no record for prospective cure."

Kuso! He curses and starts a clock, telling AYA to keep a close monitor on the wound and his internal systems. He needs to find Wren and the kids. To think they are somewhere in this death trap... and with Tanaka hunting Wren, she has no idea the danger she is in.

Clearing his sights, Kaito notices the banging below him has ceased, replaced by an eerie quiet.

"مدد کریو!"

A panicked cry breaks the stillness, and the groans and moans of shamblers drift away from Kaito toward the shouted call.

"Help us!"

The voice sounds young, akin to that of a prepubescent boy, cracking at the top the way Renki's used to when he was eleven/twelve. What is a child doing running around these cursed streets alone? And judging by the increased volume of the yelling, the boy is running straight for him, and therefore straight for the shamblers ambling on the street level.

The technomancer draws his sword and leaps from the balcony. He lands on his good leg but grits his teeth when the bite wound makes itself known with a singing jolt of pain.

The boy comes into view as the first shambler reaches him: a hobbling old woman who grasps for him with gangrenous hands, the fingers all but eaten away.

Kai flickers forward, snatching the child by the waist and pulling him out of harm's way. The child screams, pressing hard into Kaito's shoulder, as those decaying hands miss him by a hair's breadth. When he sets the boy down, he looks at him with panicked brown eyes.

"My–my sister. اﮩی نﮦ یک قتل کرﯼ رﮦیا آن»

Kaito blinks. The child speaks a language he doesn't understand. A branch of Sekhmetian by the sound of it, but he can't quite grasp the origin, the boy is so strung out, and paired with his broken common, Kai can barely make sense of the child's pleas.

"تُ چاﮦ Come quick. Help! My Sister!"

He pulls on Kai's hands, pointing to a nearby shrine, tucked away behind a tall iron gate. Kaito scoops the injured boy up and follows.

The shrine is new, probably no more than five or six years old. In front of the gate is a pair of statues. The first on the left is of the goddess Chang'e and beside her a banner painted with a rabbit spirit. The second statue is of the undead mother of creation, Izanami. A goddess of the moon next to a goddess of the dead and between them an earthly shrine.

The iron gate hangs ajar, and enraged shouts spill through the gate.

"Burn her!"

"Burn the witch!"

"Cleanse the evil!"

The enraged chanting of a panicked mob within. The little boy shouts something in broken common about his sister and fire, and putting two and two together, Kaito runs faster with the boy in his arms.

What he finds inside will fuel his nightmares for weeks.

Within he finds the source of the smoke from earlier, and with it comes the stench of burning flesh. A charred corpse lies limp at the center of the blackened remnants of a bonfire, and on either side of it a twin pair of as yet untouched pyres.

Crudely built, the pyres are less firewood, more picked apart furniture, table legs and torn cushions. Handcuffed and tied down at the center is a young girl who can't be any older than Renki. She shouts and fights as a pair of men anchor her down, her words foreign to him but recognizable: Sanskri—the language of Sekhmeti.

"What's going on here?"

Could the elimination of witches lead to the destruction of technomancers as well?

Arguably, technomancers wouldn't even exist were it not for witches. Which really makes them no different than lycans, vampyres, and other spell-folk. Biologists argue that the only reason technomancers are even capable of technomancy is because of their removed lineage to witches. We do all come from a group of common ancestors, after all.

But the League teaches "no." Technology is superior to heathenry in every way, shape, and form. The world would continue to spin and the stars continue to shine without magic, but is it not equally true that it will continue without science? There is nothing in this world, the universe, or the cosmos that would fail to exist without them. Though they are made of stardust, even the stars are meaningless in the scope of eternity, and the endless rule of death will claim everyone and everything—every plant, every animal, every human, every posthuman, every witch, every god, every goddess.

That said, what if hexen and human+ were able to achieve a true symbiosis of sorts? We've spent so many years trying to kill each other. Wouldn't it be interesting to see how we might otherwise be able to aid each other?

Excerpt from "A Theoretical look at the Relationship Between Hexen and Human+" His last publication - E.X. Icarus, 1842

17
TWO OF SWORDS

Downtown Chairomura – 11:20PM – Wren

THE DOOR SHE'S BLASTED OFF ITS HINGES opens into a reception area: a high front desk, a seating area with nice leather-cushioned seats, and a large digital clock over the front doors, glass-paned with floor to ceiling windows on either side and rattling as more shamblers attempt to come in. Slipping and splatting and leaving smears of bodily fluid, they slide down the glass like drowned noodles. Perhaps they had an appointment? Sorry. Building's closed. Come back tomorrow.

"So why this town? Did the people here wrong you somehow?" Wren spits back as she investigates the area.

"Not at all. Unfortunately, bystanders end up casualties of war all the time."

What war? The one between science and magic that ended when the League dropped anti-magic bombs on Lorelei? The Vanquishing killed countless magic-reliant people and creatures: fae, hexen, netherbeast, and even humans with an affinity toward magic. It's a wonder any magic-folk survived at all. Wren hadn't, even if the explosions hadn't been what killed her.

"Why target Murasaki? They offer sanctuary for hexen."

"Sanctuary? Sanctuary! You call pretending to be a human sanctuary? Weak-willed idiots afraid of their own natures so they hide in their hovels and caves. They serve tea to the people who would burn them at the stake and teach their children how to harness a branch of magic so diluted by misogyny no one knows its true potential. Love Magic—what a laugh!"

Wren glances back as Summer barks out a laugh. There's bitterness there, dripping off Summer like spoiled milk, dreams turned to nightmares. Mishka said Summer mentioned a husband. A soured marriage? Why else would she feel such resentment toward love? Not that Wren can't understand. Just days ago, she'd thought Kaito responsible for her death, a lie to poison her against him. She wonders if their goal had been to have Wren kill Kai in the long-run—two birds with one stone. If so, it hadn't worked. Kaito survived, and despite his efforts, Wren died alone, insane, and in flames.

Walking around, she starts to think maybe this place is a little more high profile than a simple administrative building. A waiting area with cushioned seats, various cubicles outlined in wooden paneling, desks with holo-projection nodules and computer motherboards. There's an upright water fountain for refilling cups and bottles framed by a tall countertop with various slips and forms tucked into neat cubbies. This must be a bank or upmarket. There are barred windows behind a cue line advertising augmentations and a credit exchange kiosk. Wren treads over and finds various locked cabinets and medical equipment on the other side of the bars.

"Is that why you killed Mishka? Because you think she's a sell-out?"

One hand on the wall, Wren's blue-green magic yanks the bars from their place. Wren jumps over the counter and starts looking through the drawers and under the counter.

Come on. Surely, there's a worker paranoid enough to stow a gun back here.

"Mishka deserved to be neutered of her pathetic magical pathways for her weakness. The humans used to worship us as gods and goddesses, but then they rediscovered technology and our ancestors were too weak willed to destroy it when they had the chance."

"That's not what happened. The hexen monarchs were frightened magic would die out, so they made non-magical people third class citizens. Some even orchestrated mass genocides of people who couldn't use magic. So people turned to technology for protection. If they had just accepted normal humans, none of this would have ever come to be."

"Your technomancer upbringing is showing. The cyborgs started the attacks first after they figured out they would never be able to mimic magic via their technology. Their scientists couldn't explain our abilities, so they sought to snuff us out. That's always the case. You yourself have seen it happen. You, once the League's diamond, were crushed when you became uncontrollable."

Wren forces open the bottom drawer of a filing cabinet and bingo! Nestled under the pile of messily strewn paperwork is a laser pistol. She checks the firearm's settings, flicks the non-lethal setting on, and unclicks the safety. Perfect for shamblers.

"I suspect the truth is somewhere in the middle," says Wren, setting the weapon on the counter. "We'll never know what really happened. The history has become too warped over time. Warring opposites will only ever teach their people the history which paints them as benevolent and just. No one wants to frame themselves as the bad guy. In the meantime, people just grow more stupid and uninformed. It's all a bunch of mindless killing anyway. Science and magic do not need to counteract each other. Mishka understood that. Every hexen who seeks to co-exist with +ies understands that."

"Are you so childish? Science and magic cannot find balance. They can only be opposites. One ruling over the other to keep everyone in line. And since The Vanquishing, we've all been struggling under the League's metal boot. Yggfret would be rolling over in his grave to see how far we've fallen."

"Yggfret got himself and the rest of Koven wiped from the face of the earth by cavorting with Seraphim."

"Yes, and who is the one who killed them?"

Wren bites her tongue. The answer is fairly obvious. Summer laughs, then coughs as she chokes on her own blood. When she finishes her fit, she wipes her smirk clean with the back of her sleeve. "I will say, though, the number of technomancer kills to your name was a triumph."

And what was that number exactly? Wren doesn't remember. Not that she lost count or anything so arrogant. Too many blurred memories to sift through... Out of her mind with grief and magic fever, she'd gone on a rampage. They destroyed her family, so she destroyed them.

"I wasn't trying to break a record, and I didn't kill out of glee."

"Such was your downfall. You could have been a queen among hexen, and you wasted it on futile wishes for peace."

"Is that why you plague meaningless cities and tea shop owners? So you can crown yourself queen?"

"Che! What's the worth of being the queen to a bunch of mangy low-lives?"

"Those 'low-lives' are people, Summer."

"How banal of you... Well, Ms. Selfless Hero, what are you planning to do now? That knife of yours still screaming for my blood, or are you planning on shooting me dead now?"

The witch stares pointedly at the gun in Wren's hand.

"Unfortunately, I need you to call down the blixvi. I need it if I am going to make a cure. This is for the shamblers when they get in."

"Why not just kill them? Your powers are fearsome enough."

Wren Nocturne may have a reputation for being a bloodthirsty killer, but despite the ghost stories and rumors, she's never killed anyone who didn't try to kill her first, not consciously anyway.

"They didn't do anything to me, and if it weren't for your wretched bird, they would be living their lives bothering no one. Once I make a cure, I can treat the whole city."

"What if I told you there was no cure?"

Two Of Swords

The cursed cut on her arm throbs. She's bled through another bandage. It probably won't stop again until she quenches its thirst. Blood for blood.

"For your sake, Summer." Ice creeps into Wren's voice, her eyes steady as she regards the redhead for the first time since the start of the conversation. "There had better be."

Every curse has a counter-curse just like every affliction has a remedy, even magical ones. And that's what this bird-borne disease is: a magical malady. One simply needs the patience to discover it.

Summer is poised enough not to physically flinch at Wren's threat, but not even she can fool an empath. The spike of fear in her aura is all Wren needs to know her words have not been misinterpreted. Indignation, however, blankets Summer's expression.

"And I suppose if I help you, you'll consider letting me live. Pff! Please!"

"I'll consider killing you quickly."

"Hmpf, how magnanimous of you."

The backroom is full of various medical supplies: bandages, antibiotics, rubbing alcohol. There are also more valuable goods including medi stims, comm units, and neuropozyne. At the sight of the needles, capped in plastic though they be, she cringes. She's experienced too many forced injections to ever want to suffer the bite of a needle again, even one meant to heal.

"You should stop pretending I care about your opinion," says Wren, tending to her arm. While two of the curse marks still slumber, open but clotted, the third is not so demure. The cut is ugly to look at, her body's magical healing factor unable to staunch the flow. The curse scar is hungry for an offering, weeping blood and necrotic magic—not her own brand of the deathly energy but the remnant of the inexperienced coven of lost souls who gave their everything to resurrect her.

Reluctantly, Wren takes one of the stims from the locker, and before she can think too much on it, rams the needle into the meat of her deltoid with a hiss. She watches as the flow of blood diminishes, becoming manageable once again. What made it increase its flow? Is she running out of time? Or is it something else?

Just as she's about to relax, tossing the used stim into the bin, the burn starts: a terrible, itching fire originating in her veins. She forces herself to breathe, sweat beading at her brow and reminds herself to breathe. Taking a medi stim won't kill a witch, but it isn't the most pleasant of experiences. She'll survive, this pain just a short sufferance in exchange for additional healing factor.

She never had this kind of backlash from the nanos before her witchy state of being. As a technomancer, she used stims all the time. Hel, they even made her a little giddy, but with the awakening of wild magic in the blood came an intolerance to technological integration. It's why so few witches tamper with any kind of tech. Jessabelle used to get headaches just from having the radio on for too long.

So, she grits her teeth and bears it, and as with all things, the pain passes, fading away to a churning discomfort, not unlike being drunk on the wrong alcohol.

A pathetic moan against the counter draws her attention.

Summer's in bad shape, the bite on her shoulder bleeding profusely. It doesn't look like Akari's. There is none of the black corrosion of infection spreading from the wound. Either witches can't contract the ailment, or it isn't spread via zombie bites. Take that, plague bringer!

The pecks, on the other hand, have festered alarmingly fast. Wren sighs, picking up the first aid supplies. "Take your shirt off."

"Excuse me!"

"I said, 'Take your shirt off.' I'm going to treat the bite, and I'm willing to bet the blixvi got you on more than just your face and arms. You look like you're about to topple over, and I'm not a babysitter. Any of those shamblers get in here, you're on your own."

Summer looks at Wren, eyes darting from side to side as she shifts from foot to foot. Discomfort, thick and choking.

"Look, I may be attracted to women, but you're not my type. Just let me get a bandage on, and I'll leave you alone."

"It's not that. It's…"

Summer growls, then reluctantly starts to tear off her outer garments. The cloak falls to the floor, tattered and torn from the blixvi, and her top follows not in much better shape, leaving the woman in nothing but a bra, and what Wren sees gives her pause.

Bruises, green and yellowing with age of varying degrees, decorate the other witch's torso. There are small ones, no bigger than a fingerprint, bigger ones like Wren has received herself getting a kick or two in the side during combat, and one long straight bruise that starts at her hip and ends at her ribcage like she was struck by a rod or a cane. The area around her lower ribs is purple and splotchy, and when Wren sets her hand on the area, Summer flinches away. Broken ribs.

"Who did this to you?"

"Are you stupid? You saw the shamblers attack me, and you kicked me earlier."

"Exactly, earlier. Some of these are days, weeks old. Who—"

"Shut up and mind your own business. If you're going to do something, just do it, and butt out of my personal business."

Wren, taken aback, bites her tongue but sets the ointment and bandages down. She works quickly and cleans out the bite wound with rubbing alcohol, careful not to aggravate the bruises as she winds a bandage around Summer's torso. One of the bruises has a unique pattern to it. Dark in some places and lighter in others, almost looking like the outline of an animal of some kind. The crest of a signet ring? There are other peculiarly shaped bruises. Hollowed out circles scattered in the midst of a deeper circle, like she was punched by someone with augmentations.

She's seen markings like this before. Usually on the ghosts of dead women. Women who lost the war of the heart the way men lose their hearts in war.

When she finishes tending to what she can of Summer's injuries, she collects her things and retreats back to the supply closet.

"I know what you're thinking."

"What do you care what I'm thinking?" Wren turns to look at Summer, already buttoning her shirt back up.

"You have no right to judge me."

"I'm not judging you."

"Right. You're pitying me."

She would be lying if she said she wasn't. Wren shakes her head, turning back to the equipment lockers when a disease-ridden hand clamps down on her shoulder. The shambler, hiding in a locker, snaps for Wren's throat with crooked teeth, blackened with plague and infestation. She blocks, her nails sinking into the human's boil-bloated face as it shoves her. She trips over something and tumbles to the floor.

"Hel–help me!" it rasps at her, its breath stinking of putrid poultry. It scratches her across the face. "H-hungry!"

"Argh!"

Those putrid fingers grope for her face, teeth snapping for her throat, but she lifts her hands to wrestle them away. Bile flies into her eyes, and she can't let go long enough to wipe the foul-smelling shit out lest she wants teeth in her vocal cords.

"Get off her!"

With a cracking sound, it barrels sideways.

Summer steps over Wren's hip, having kicked the shambler into the wall. The infected human collapses, head facing the wrong way.

"You killed it."

Summer hovels her way over to the shambler, giving it another kick for good measure. "Yeah, well it was going to kill you. Sorry to disappoint your delicate sensibilities."

With a wince, Wren pulls herself up, bracing herself against the counter as she cleans the gunk out of her eyes. Loki's mare, that happened fast. Too fast.

"Thanks."

Summer holds up a hand. "Don't. We're even now. You saved my life. I saved yours. We can go back to trying to kill each other now."

"Fair enough. Are we starting now or are we going to wait until we get out of this wretched building?"

Summer purses her lips. "Peace until the warhorn's call."

While some feuds can never be forgiven, they can be set aside until the proper time for war is come. Summer invokes the old magical adage: a saying as old as Deus. When witches were the only hexen of this world, the differing cultures of magic users learned they had to work together in order to survive rather than fight one another.

"Peace until the warhorn's call."

Wren dips her head and tosses Summer the laser. She can make do without a pistol.

"Non-lethal shots only."

"Spoilsport."

"I mean it, Summer."

"You still haven't told me how you're back from the dead, by the way. Planning on sharing anytime soon?"

"Nope."

"Bitch."

"No. 'Witch.'"

"That makes two of us then."

The banging at the front door intensifies, the glass rattling in its frame. A crack starts to thread down the center of the pane. Bad news.

"You think there are any upstairs?" Summer asks.

"No idea, but I'm thinking roof access is the way to go."

"I can lure the blixvi from the roof."

"You're going to help me lure it out?"

"The overgrown chicken tried to kill me. You honestly think I don't want to deep fry it, myself?"

"I thought it was your pet."

"When a dog bites its owner, it's time to put it down."

Wren hums in understanding and turns to the now dead body at her feet. No point being wasteful.

SONATA

Betwixt the Moon and Stars Temple – 12:17PM –**Kaito**

"What's going on here?"

Kaito's demand is met by a mix of surprise and horror. Quieting at the sight of a technomancer, the crowd is composed mostly of human+ individuals, a few nearly-cyborgs sporting prosthetic limbs, other transhumans with minor implants around their eyes and necks for aesthetic and behavioral analytics. The few unaugmented people remain closer to the back of the group, hiding behind their augmented neighbors. None of them hold a candle to Kaito, whose augmentations gleam a sharp purple in the dim light of the temple.

"Kaito Miyazaki!" someone exclaims. "The highest ranked technomancer in Murasaki no Yama. We're saved!"

A cheer goes out among the crowd, celebratory applause and laughter, as they completely disregard his question. One of the men has a blowtorch in hand, the flame spitting and aimed at the pyre. He waves it around as he dances with glee, the blue flame menacing as it passes dangerously close to the pyre.

"I asked a question," booms Kaito. "What is going on here?"

A woman steps forward. Older but possessing an artificially maintained youth, she appears to be in her mid to late thirties while her presence speaks to that of a woman old enough to command a room full of younger men. AYA reads her tech signatures as charisma and beauty enhancers. They glow a limey green at her temple.

"Your highness," she says bowing. "Sarah Lee Fitspatrick. I'm the head of the school board here, and I'm happy to report we've found the witches responsible for this plague."

"Witches?"

"Yes, your highness. These children and their witch father snuck across the border illegally just days before the start of the pestilence. We have already taken care of the man, who was found carrying a rabbit's foot. The flames attest to his guilt, though he would not confess to his part in these dark times."

Smoke coils from the extinguished pyre, nothing but skeletal remains left of the man accused of witchcraft.

"As such, his salvation relies on his children. We were about to reunite them, but the boy escaped. It's a good thing you brought him back. Now that you're here, Miyazaki–sama, perhaps you can help us deal with the problem at hand. This girl has already proven more forthcoming than her father. She confessed to her witchery just moments ago."

"Because you tortured her until she couldn't say 'no' anymore!"

A woman, wearing the traditional garb of a priestess or shrine maiden, stands chained to a column. She must be the caretaker of this temple. She shouts and pulls against her bonds, the exhaust ports at her jawline steaming and glowing orange in her desperation.

"These children are under my protection. You can't just come in here—"

A man slaps her across the face. "Shut up, wretch, before we burn you for harboring a witch."

In total disregard of the violence behind her, Sarah Lee addresses Kaito calmly, shoulders squared with authority. "There's a witch's mark on the girl's shoulder. Proof enough if you ask me."

The "witch's mark" in question sits exposed on the girl's shoulder, brown and crescent-shaped like a waning moon, but Kaito's scans read no magical energy. Not an indicia, not even close; a true indicia either glows with power or disappears into the skin entirely. No layman's eye would be able to see an indicia unless the witch were actively using her powers. It's nothing but a birthmark, insignificant and benign.

"This girl is no witch."

"Then explain this plague! Explain to me why my husband killed our little girl. We were left here to die! No one was coming to help us, so we helped ourselves."

The quarantine. These people have been caged in a dying city for however long. Naturally, desperation and a lack of authority leads to anarchy.

"Even so. This girl is innocent."

"I'm telling you she confessed."

And judging by the crooked angles of her fingers and the crushed bones in her feet, it was a confession pulled from her throat under threat of irreversible bodily harm.

"A confession given under duress is not a confession."

"The primarch doesn't think so," she argues back to a rally of "here, heres" behind her.

"The primarch is not the ruling authority of Murasaki no Yama."

"Well, Miyazaki–sama, how about you do your job then, and kill the witch? Oh wait, I forgot, Murasaki doesn't condone the slaying of hexen anymore. You'd rather let us all die!"

"That's not true!" shouts the shrine maiden. "Hexen are afforded the same rights as you or I. That means a trial before punishment."

"It is true," spits back the lead woman. "It's the reason we're even in this mess to begin with. Every other country has a zero-tolerance policy toward hexen and for that they enjoy true peace, yet the emperor would have us wave a white flag and invite them into our homes."

Peace? Peace, meaning countless impoverished, families separated, destruction rained down on innocents just like these children.

"Peace forged from war is not peace. It is merely an elimination of the opposition."

"Well, then, his highness will just have to forgive us poor and uneducated for putting an end to the opposition we currently face."

The nozzle of the blowtorch dips down, and the pyre ignites with a violent burst of heat, and Kaito jumps into the flames.

TWO OF SWORDS

11:42PM – Wren

Wren's poppet stinks more than a little, and its augmentations clang something awful every time it bumps against the wall. The ex-shambler-now-zombie trudges heavily up the stairs ahead of Wren and Summer acting as a canary if you will. A scapegoat extended in front of them in case of shamblers hiding in the stairs. None yet, but the zombie's presence is a comfort to Wren as much as it is a warning to Summer.

"Can we stop a minute? I need a break."

Wren stops a few stairs up as Summer hunches over to lean against the guardrail, settling herself gingerly on the stairs. With a pinched whistle to her poppet, Wren sets her pack on the step above the redhead and leans against the wall herself as her undead begins a paced circuit up and down the staircase.

It's been slow going. The other witch is having a tough time breathing, winded from climbing the stairs. Unsurprising considering her broken ribs. Though, Wren supposes, they've made decent headway, seven floors up with only a handful left to go. She considers, not for the first time, giving Summer one of the medi stims she took from the locker downstairs, but she's already been too generous to the woman who is, by all means, her enemy.

"Did we have to choose the stairs?"

"Would you rather shimmy your way up the currently broken elevator?"

Because Wren wouldn't. Been there, done that, and she's still sore from the endeavor.

"I'd rather not be trapped in a building with a witch who shouldn't even be alive right now."

"This coming from a woman who was supposedly executed five years ago..."

Summer leans her head against the wall with a grunt. "We all have to survive somehow."

Is Summer feeling talkative? Perhaps, if Wren weaves her words wisely, she can get the woman to slip. "You belittle Mishka for seeking refuge among humans, yet you call living like this surviving?" Wren looks pointedly at Summer's covered torso and the ring-shaped bruise hidden beneath.

"We don't get to choose our soulmates."

"Yes, but there is no force in the cosmos that can force us to love them."

"Only our own traitorous hearts."

Summer's lopsided smirk pulls at her face in a way far more disconcerting than the horns stitched to her head. Like she's stitched her lips there the way she used to piece her chimera together, part by twitching part.

"I'm not some victim of circumstance. He loves me. I would be dead without him."

"Some might argue dead is better than living in hell."

"You would know, wouldn't you, Songstress? Back from the dead and thrust into this living hell of ours. Wouldn't you rather go back to the other side of the veil where you'll be left well enough alone?"

"I don't know. I don't much remember what being dead was like."

Maybe it was peaceful. Maybe it wasn't. Maybe it was nothing. Maybe it was everything. Regardless, death is neither here nor there for Wren right now. There won't be a second afterlife for her, not unless she completes the resurrection contract.

"He protects me from the League."

But does he protect you from himself?

"He's human+, isn't he?"

"None of your business."

So probably... Someone powerful enough to shelter a witch hiding in plain sight. A technomancer, maybe? Member of the council? Summer wouldn't be the first witch to give her heart to a witch hunter; Wren can attest to that. But the bruises on her? Not even during their worst fights had Kaito ever laid hands on her like that, nor had she ever hit him as such in turn. And Summer's patterns... it's like she was curled up trying to protect herself, not even fighting back.

"Is that how you wound up on the roof of a light rail trying to break a mad scientist from his temporary jail and risking being killed by a slew of technomancers? Survival?" Summer's lower lip disappears between her teeth, and when she doesn't speak, Wren carries on. "So, what have you done with the good doctor?"

"You know perfectly well I don't have Faust. If I did, you think I'd be in this shithole town with the likes of you?"

Wren's eyes narrow. Does she not know Faust was rescued from Snowfall? "What do you mean?"

"Well, the best way to catch your prey is to lure it into a trap."

"So, you were hoping that by spreading some mysterious disease and ailments through Murasaki, you would inspire Emperor Hikaru to bring the doctor in to make a cure. Even putting yourself at risk in the process."

"Naturally. My husband doesn't appreciate failure." What does Summer's husband want with Faust? "No mistakes this time. I didn't count on you showing up and interfering, for the second time, if I may add. Miserable pest, wearing a dead woman's face."

"Well, I'd hate to break it to you, but Faust is long gone from Miyazaki custody."

"You're lying."

"A pair of hexen and another technomancer flew the coop with him last week. Surely, you knew?!"

Summer looks at Wren stunned. "Do you think I'd be here if I did?!"

She huffs, looking away before muttering something in a language Wren doesn't understand.

"Guess your husband isn't the know-all you think he is," laughs Wren.

"Che! What were you doing on the light rail anyway?" Summer sneers, changing the topic. "Seems rather stupid for a witch to get herself trapped with a bunch of technomancers on a moving train."

Ouch...

What was she doing on the light rail? In hindsight, the light rail was quite possibly the worst place she could have gone trying to avoid Kaito or any other technomancer on the face of Deus, yet to the light rail she'd gone. Why?

"Running."

Running away... Running towards... Trying to get lost... Trying to get found... It doesn't really matter, anymore. She's here, neither lost nor found, neither running away nor running toward. Just running.

A shiver runs up her spine, like an electric zing. Her skin breaks out in goosebumps, and the chill sweats out of her pores.

Wren stands, leaning over the rail with a frown. When they'd passed by the emergency exit door to the floor below them, Wren hadn't sensed anything off, but now something dark skates over Wren's synapse. Something dark and hungry. ¡Mierde! *Los mórbidos.*

"Get up."

"Oh, come on! I just sat down."

A bang on the door a level below sends the redhead to her feet followed by a furious chorus of booms and bams like fists banging on a steel drum or timpani. The corner of the steel door waggles like a flapjack, and on a particularly loud bang, the corner yawns wide enough for a pair of hands to reach through, followed by another pair, then another, all of them covered in black boils.

"Go as fast as you can. To the roof. Hurry!"

Summer doesn't need to be told twice, taking off up the stairs. Wren folds her magic around herself, palms spread wide, and forces the door shut again. With a keened note, her poppet stutters forward to keep the door closed as long as it can manage before she takes off up the stairs herself. Her feet pound on the gritty cement, the stitch in her side tightens, and metal clangs some floors below her. The intensity of the horde's combined malevolent intention catches her feet, and she trips as the first one rounds the corner. As its gnarled fingers reach for her, a tranquilizer finds its throat.

"Hurry up!"

The shambler topples over, tripping several others, and Wren climbs her way up, taking the steps two at a time after Summer. As she gets closer to the top, she hears Summer banging against the door.

The roof access is locked.

"I can't get it open!"

"Out of the way."

With a flare of power, the door swings open, and both women stumble through. Wren's intention flings the door shut again, and she presses her magic into the door as the first shambler runs headlong into the metal.

"Can you set a ward?" Wren presses her back against the now broken door.

"Yes."

"Then set one."

Summer nods and ducks down to begin tracing an array on the ground. The shamblers bang on the door, rattling Wren's ribcage with every pump. Her head spins, sweat beading along her brow as she whistles, commanding her poppet still inside to deflect and push back the shamblers.

"Summer, hurry up!"

Her feet skid across the concrete, scrambling for purchase as another bang dislodges her.

"I'm working as fast as I can."

Wren's magic flickers in the air. Teeth clenched, head pounding, she's running out of steam.

"Well, work faster!"

"Patience."

The chalk scratches over the cement in an intricate pattern. Wren can't quite follow the lines or symbols Summer is drawing, but it's far too complex for a simple locking ward. What the hell is Summer doing?

The metal of the door folds and a blight-coated hand reaches through the frame, waving wildly in the air until it catches Wren's shoulder.

"Summer!"

"I've got it!"

The chalk array closes, and obsidian magic leaks from the sigils, expanding up and outward like a lightning strike. There is a pop of ozone and a thunderous boom, and the hand attempting to strangle her to death disappears. The banging behind her head ceases, the moans of the shamblers descending as they back away from the door. They're gone. Whatever spell Summer cast worked, and she sags against the cool metal of the door.

"Thanks."

The woman smirks at her.

"Don't thank me yet."

What?

The shriek of a bird rips through the sound barrier. Razor-sharp talons extend from the clouds as the blixvi plummets from the sky, shrieking as it descends.

"I'm sorry, *min dronning*, but consider this the war horn's call."

And as Wren's eyes widen, Summer's bleed to black.

I lost myself one night to fancy.
To a woman in my dreams.
She swept me up in eyes uncanny,
A witness to my screams.

For when the sky cries, "Moondrops,
Behold my weakened soul,"
'Cross the wondrous fields of Nox
No star shall they console.

And so I gift my heart, beguiling
To those of old, lost lore.
For in my time of dying,
Let lovers mourn no more.

"The Last Night"
An Unnamed Witch, circa 240~ A.P.

18

THE HIGH PRIESTESS

Fourteen Years Ago – 25th Day in the Month of Planting, 1863 – The Vatidome, Seraphim

A GIRL HE DOESN'T KNOW OFFERS HIM flowers.

Kaito waits outside his mother's final resting chamber, the quiet padding of aggrieved footsteps and the rustling of plain fabrics the only melody to Mirai's wake. It is almost time, everyone but his most immediate family having given their final farewells to the late empress. Many of them greet him as they pass, giving their condolences one final time before disappearing into the evening.

He greets a family of two, a father-daughter pair, as they enter. Wearing Murasaki colors—the father Kaito recognizes as a Murasakan technomancer named Orson—they bow to him before making their way inside, come to give their offerings on this the final day of his mother's wake. Orson's teenage daughter is the one who presented him flowers, looking at him shyly through her lashes. She is probably right around Kaito's age, with unnaturally wide eyes, impeccably straight blonde hair, and minimized skin pores. Her beauty augmentations do not disservice her, but aesthetic enhancements are not purely cosmetic, an inability to sweat and difficulty adjusting to varying strengths of light leave her vulnerable to overheating and impairment at both ends of the dark/light spectrum.

He doesn't take the flowers, indicating she should place them instead with the other offerings by Mirai's open pyre. Her attempt to mask her disappointment fails, but he is gracious enough to ignore it, casting his gaze back to the path leading to the central compound of the basilica.

He is not waiting out here for them.

Inside, his great uncle, Genjiro Miyazaki, who Kaito hasn't seen since the start of the war, embraces Fumiko. He is here with Kaito's second cousin, her husband, and their young daughter, Akari, just about to reach the age of two. None of them are technomancers, though the little girl seems absolutely taken with Hikaru's augmentations. They speak softly in Hanasu to Orson. The daughter, now looking somber, stands silent and thoughtful to the side. They stop next in front of Hikaru, the technomancer kneeling to pledge fealty to his brother, the girl mimicking her father's movements before following him to pay their respects to the dead. They kneel, dipping their heads to the floor in kowtow, once in greeting, once in parting to the empress's pyre before rising to take their leave. Bowing again, they pass Hikaru and Fumiko. They are the last visitors outside of their family to come to call. Their departure will signify the closing of the wake to the public.

They bow once more to Kaito on their way out, and he thanks them for honoring them with their visit. As he rises from his own bow farewell, the person he is waiting for arrives at precisely the time he told her.

Wren, her hair pulled back in a somber knot, offers him a small smile from under the sheer fabric of the black veil she wears. She followed his instructions perfectly; wearing a floor-length lavender dress in a simple cotton fabric, she seems to float along the ground. The long dark veil drifts around her, a proper meld of Derivan mourning attire mixed with Murasaki colors. Despite the cut of the dress being obviously Derivan, the sleeves long but loose and the skirt A-line, it is demure and modest, and melds well with the attire he himself wears, a specialty multi-layered robe, a cross between the old-world hanfu and kimono, worn specifically for funerary attendance. When she asked what color she should wear to Mirai's wake, he'd told her to wear primarily lavender rather than black as would typically be expected of Derivan or Aighnean visitors.

Wren bids her escort goodbye as she steps past the gate. The Derivan adept looks wary at the prospect of leaving her side. She is still in recovery after all, the IV needle still taped to the crook of her elbow, a bulge under her sleeve, but she waves him away, saying she'll be fine, and he salutes her before taking his leave.

She walks up the path, passing Orson and his daughter as she goes.

"Public visitation is over, Miss."

Not seeming to realize who Wren is, the Murasaki girl has stopped to caution Wren away, and the witch's steps falter at the girl's thin address.

"Gyta," chides the technomancer to his daughter. "Step aside."

"But—"

"Wren."

With a call of her name, Kaito offers his hand to her. The girl blinks owlishly as Wren continues toward him, and Orson ushers his daughter aside with an apology. When she reaches him, she folds her arms around him, and he becomes weightless. She is a soft comfort along his side. She smells like mint, clean and cool. It nearly covers the hospital scent, disinfectant and sterilized equipment, still clinging to her hair and skin. When she pulls away, Orson and his daughter are gone.

"Hey," she says, fingers gently cascading down his face, pausing briefly at the pressure point at his brow. "How're you holding up?"

"I am here." He catches her hand in his, pulling it down, fingertips glancing over his lips. "I'm glad you made it."

SONATA

"I'm glad to be here." Her teeth worry at her lower lip. "Kaito, are you sure this is alright?"

"The Miyazaki will invite to witness any who they deem worthy."

"Anyone else in your family bring a +1?"

She means it jokingly, but the nervousness in her voice makes it obvious she is looking for reassurance. It's her age-old coping mechanism after all. There is the smallest of tremors in her hand.

"I want you here."

"*Aquí estoy, mon rivage.*"

He hasn't heard the endearment from her lips in so long. This is the first time she's truly used it since her return. Given to him on their last mission together before the war when he said she was as untamable as the sea. "*Well, if I'm the sea, then you must be the shore. Ever present, ever steadfast.*"

So he responds in kind.

"*Ore no Kaiyo.*"

He ushers her forward, and they enter together.

The Alliance's funerary house, the Last Dwelling, kept and equipped for a variety of funeral rites and traditions across the different cultures of Deus, has seen many farewells since the start of the war. First erected in Shinka, he remembers attending a ceremony to honor the late Vulcan and Vulcana after Deriva fell. Tlanextli and Elisabeta's bodies had not been on display, their bodies never recovered from the attack on Cresta de Corail, but portraits had been hung, Xipilli and Atzi carrying out the symbolic act of setting their parents spirits to rest by having their portraits laid in water and burned. Upon such a time as the new Vulcan was able to return to Deriva, a proper ceremony of returning their spirits to the sea would take place.

Many asked why Xipilli chose not to honor Wren in the same ceremony, his half-sister at this point believed to be dead. His response had been simple. "My sister is lost but not forsaken, missing because she chose to save my life. Until such a time as she finds her way home or I see my sister's corpse alone, Deriva will keep the lighthouse lit."

THE HIGH PRIESTESS

For the Derivan funeral, the space had been stylized with the colors and textures of an island ruler's burial at sea in blacks and navies with candles and seaside hymns. The windows opened to invite in the orange shine of the sunset.

Since bidding farewell to the Vulcan and Vulcana, it has been dismantled and re-erected in Aureus, The Abbey, and now here in Vatidome City.

For Mirai Miyazaki, the decor has been transformed to fit their culture, silken curtains in gray and lavender. Offerings of flowers, fruit, and incense sit carefully arranged around the room. The lights are low, the majority of illumination stemming from the scattered candles in the deepest purple around the room and the violet glow of Mirai's pyre, plated in gold and shimmering under an arrangement of winter peonies and chrysanthemums. At the heart of the arrangement is his mother's imperial headdress, the Fate Stay Diadem, made for her by Kaito's father for her coronation. Rose gold and inset with glittering diamonds and amethysts with a central lavender diamond, the headpiece's wings fold out and around. Long strands of gold chains accented with purple beading would dangle just to her shoulders whenever she wore it.

"*Aniki,*" calls Kaito.

Hikaru turns, looking drawn but offering Kaito a thin smile. He's ready for this process to be over. They both are. His brother hasn't cried. Not in front of Kaito. It is worrying, but it also isn't his place to tell his brother how to grieve.

"*Otōto.*"

Beside him, Wren bows to Hikaru. "Hikaru, I mean, Miyazaki–heika."

Kaito's brother smiles warmly at Wren's deference, holding his hands out, bidding her to right herself. "It is good to see you recovered, Lady Nocturne, and you are gracious to accompany Kaito this evening."

Wren offers her own wilted smile and bows once more this time to Fumiko at Hikaru's side. "Sensei."

"Miss Nocturne."

His aunt's eyes are red rimmed, and she folds her prayer beads over and over again in her hand. Their hollow clicking, wooden and earthy, is strangely grounding—percussive but unobtrusive interruption to the boundless quiet blanketing their lives.

"I'm so sorry for your loss." Wren gives them her condolences. Her voice is thick with sadness, refraining from crying herself even as a sob escapes Fumiko's throat.

"She would appreciate your vigil," the woman says and then turns her face away, drying her tears once more. Hikaru sets a hand on her back, giving a nod to Kaito. He has already discussed this with his brother and Fumiko, and both of them have supported his wish. Touching Wren's elbow, he moves to his mother's pyre where their chosen priest waits for the cue to begin the final rite of cremation, and Wren follows.

The rest of his family, aside from Hikaru, have already prostrated for the last time, and his brother will approach last and be the one to close their mother's pyre window. The hands of the new emperor closing the eyes of the previous.

But first Kaito, the second son of the monarch, must give his final goodbye, and he has chosen not to do so alone.

"Kai, are you sure about this? I don't want to misstep."

And the significance is not lost on Wren.

"Just do as I do."

Beneath her veil, the greens of Wren's eyes are muted, a forest green yet somehow even more watery.

Mirai lies pristine, her body carefully washed, prepared for cremation, and dressed in a simple gray burial robe, the panels crossed in the direction opposite what would normally be worn in life. Dark sheets of hair frame her head and shoulders, the makeup brushed over her face makes her look like she is sleeping, and strings of prayer beads lay over her throat and hands to be burned with her.

He lowers himself to kneel on one of the cushions while Wren follows, carefully folding herself to kneel on the other beside him.

Unburned incense sticks sit in a wood-carved holder to the left of the low to the ground table. At the center is a bowl of Murasakan pomegranates, his mother's favorite fruit, and on either side are the incense holders, a pair of plain ceramic bowls filled with salt and rice. Framing the entire set-up are a lit pair of pure white candles for lighting the incense. Already four sticks burn, stuck upright in the bowls.

Taking two from the holder, he passes one to Wren. She takes it carefully, and mimicking him, lights it on the candle to her right. When the flames flicker out, leaving twin smoking tips, he offers it to the pyre before planting it in the left-hand bowl, Wren mirroring his actions on the opposite side.

He brings his palms together in front of his chest. Wren, unable to make the full gesture, presses her cloth-covered wrist into the palm of her right hand, and as he tilts forward to touch his head to the tatami, so too does Wren. Returning upright, he and Wren repeat the kowtow a second time. He hesitates for but a heartbeat looking at his mother's face and then tilts forward once more, leading Wren in a third bow.

Behind him, Fumiko's breath hitches with another sob.

They gather together as the priest begins the funerary rites. Flowing prayers in lilting Hanasu unfold through the Last Dwelling. Another kind of magic, nameless and universal, designed to heal and comfort and aid the deceased on their journey to the world beyond.

When the time comes to activate the pyre, a chill weaves through the air. The machine powers up with brilliant lights which shimmer through an ombre kaleidoscope of purples along the seams of the coffin. Across the room, Fumiko shivers, either with the cold or grief or both. His brother wraps an arm around their aunt's shoulders, and the slighter woman leans into Hikaru's side.

"And thus we bid farewell to our empress, henceforth known as Mingyi Tennō. Mother, Wife, Sister, and exalted Empress of Murasaki no Yama."

Sonata

The funeral musicians begin the traditional farewell hymn of their people, and it is then Kaito's tears fall. A gentle touch on his hand, comfort folding into his palm...

Wren's fingers are warm threaded through his.

When the first witches made the pilgrimage to Deus, they brought with them some of the comforts science afforded them, placing restrictions on the study of it to prevent the threat of nuclear winter they fled from in the old world. They didn't expect science to progress alongside their magic as well as it did. And the evolution of technomancy caught every witch of the time by surprise.

Excerpt from *Transitions: From Earth to Deus; From Witchcraft to Technomancy*
Heather Ables, 1870 A.P.

19

THE PAGE OF CUPS

SUMMER'S EYES BLEED TO BLACK AS THE BLIXVI descends, beak aimed for Wren's throat. She ducks toward the pavement, talons whistling overhead.

"You always were too trusting for this world. Too willing to make mistakes. Too willing to barrel your way into a brick wall you couldn't break!"

Summer full-body tackles her. Her fists knotted in Wren's hair, she attempts to smash Wren's face into the ground. Wren bucks her off with a howl, flinging the woman across the rooftop.

"At least, I always face the consequences of my decisions even when running away is the easier option. You, on the other hand, could have been a track star, you're so good at sprinting away."

"Is that why you killed yourself, then?" sneers Summer, rising to her feet. "Dealing out punishment for yourself since no one else could?"

"I didn't kill myself."

"Liar!" Summer aims a punch at Wren's face. "It's your fault none of us are left!"

"My fault!?"

Her form is sloppy, untrained, and amateur. Wren feints to the right, and Summer loses her balance when her strike goes wide.

"This coming from the witch who sics Nightmares on witches who only want to live their lives peacefully." Swinging a hand out, Wren tosses a block of concrete at the witch, who dives to the ground to avoid being crushed. "How many witches have you killed because hubby-dearest demanded it of you?"

Summer rolls like a fallen log downhill until her back meets the lip of the roof, panting there like an overworked hound. She's running low on gas, her magical tank almost empty, but then again, so is Wren.

"Shut up!" she screams as the blixvi dives a second time.

Wren deflects the bird away, bending its wing backward with a hollow snap. It lands in a puddle near the edge of the roof where Wren's satchel still lies, and just beyond is the teapot of vile potion with the Nightmare's husk sleeping inside. The blixvi squawks, flinging water everywhere, the now broken wing limp at its side. Wren grips her right hand into a fist, and the bird shrieks in pain as her magic flattens it to the cement, an invisible weight locking it in place.

Wren flings her left hand up and the teapot swings from the ground, shattering against the bird's head. The potion spews, a sluggy, purple mixture dripping with void and necrosis. It splashes into the blixvi's eyes, and oh, the sound it emits... A keening wail, sharp and pitched like a dying insect but enduring like the yowl of an injured hyena.

"Søren!" Summer screams for her netherbeast as the bird thrashes in agony, its eyes melting from its face. The Nightmare's animated corpse latches onto its face and beak, suffocating it.

"You should keep better track of the beasts you summon."

Another block of debris flies across the rooftop, hitting Summer's injured side. The woman goes down in a crumpled heap.

THE PAGE OF CUPS

With a smirk and a heaved breath, Wren steps to the blixvi to finish what she started.

Wren stands over the flailing beast, knife poised to descend. She doesn't know what part of it she needs to brew a cure, but she'll take the whole damn thing if she must. The acid has done its due course, and the Nightmare clings to the larger netherbeast's face. She's not sure if the undead parasite is trying to burrow its way in or if it's just trying to strangle the bird at this point.

Either way, she's going to put the damn thing out of its misery.

She draws the blade up, kneeling to drive it into its heart, and pain explodes at the back of her head. Wren crumples to find Summer holding the butt of the pistol above her. Her head pounds, her earlier concussion flares back into action. The other witch takes a silver syringe and rams it into her thigh. Wren looks down at her hip. The extra stim she hung on her belt is missing. Summer must have grabbed it while they were wrestling.

Summer sneers down at Wren, tossing the freshly used stim aside.

"You have no idea what I've been through. What I've overcome. Sorry, *min dronning*, but some things just have to be done."

The redhead takes the bird in her arms, banishing the cryptid from the bird's face with a curse. Wren's vision narrows as Summer begins to chant. Swirling void spirals around her and the inky patterns of a teleportation array form at her heels. She's going to teleport away, and she's taking the damned bird with her.

No! Akari!

Teeth gritted, Wren forces herself to move. She closes her eyes when the world spins and listens for Summer's anger. Every step rattles up her spine. The side of her face is wet and sticky. Summer's chanting reaches a fever pitch as Wren tilts forward, throwing herself in the witch's direction. Her face crumples, prepared to eat concrete as she sees Summer two feet to her right. She's missed. ¡Mierde! She falls to knees and elbows, scraping them raw on the jagged surface. But then, to her surprise, her hands snatch into Summer's cloak. The outside folds in, and the inside expands out.

When things return to right, the sky is gone, replaced by a metal braced ceiling and the rattling pipes of a storm bunker.

Where are we?

12:57AM – Betwixt the Moon and Stars Temple – Kaito

Kaito cuts the free girl of the flames.

"What are you doing!"

"She needs to die!"

Slinging the teen over his shoulder, he jumps from the crudely designed witch-burning pyre.

"Stop!"

One of the men tries to intercept him, but Kaito kicks him out of the way. The young boy cries, huddled close to the ground as Kaito sets his sister beside him. The girl is unconscious but alive. Too much smoke inhalation. A few hours on oxygen and she'll be fine. Fine to live as an orphan, her father burned to death for a crime he never committed. Fine enough to raise her brother alone.

With a swing of Tsukuyomi, a wave of saibāki slams into the remaining pyres, scattering the kindling about and snuffing out the flames.

"Th–thank you," the little boy tells him. Kaito nods, telling the child to look after his sister in a rough translation. The boy nods enthusiastically as footsteps approach. Without looking, Kaito swings Amatsu. An arc of saibāki pushes the crowd back, knocking the more proximal men and women to the ground.

Kaito rises and turns to the cowering townspeople, fury spinning in lavender sights. "No one is to come near these children."

"You'd put a witch's life before ours!"

"Traitor! Traitor! Traitor!" A chant begins, civilians, his people, calling him a traitor over and over and over again. A call of ignorance and fear roused by the very people he swore to protect. These are the people he has protected his whole life, reason and logic lost in the face of terror.

"You may be stronger than us," says Sarah Lee, fury burning in her eyes. "Your augmentations may be better, but I'm willing to bet even you can't hold us all off!"

The mob rallies, household tools and weapons thrust toward him as they move at the woman's command. Boots squared in a battle stance, Kaito wields Amatsu and Tsukuyomi, ready to end this, but the townsfolk never make it to him.

An explosion rocks the foundations of the temple.

12:44AM – Unknown Location – Wren

"You just don't know when to quit, do you!"

The blixvi flutters lopsidedly into the rafters as Summer kicks Wren in the face. She lands on her side, still dizzy from the jump and the concussion. Summer's boot presses into the side of her head.

"You'll have to let me know which is worse: suicide or having your head crushed by my boot—Argh!"

Summer staggers away, tripping over her own feet to land flat on her back. Wren lifts herself up, looking for the woman. She writhes, face scrunched in pain, gripping her side. Summer's indicia, the rune ᚾ nauthiz, blackened at the hollow of her throat, pulses as the nanos invade her system. No doubt the same pain that plagued Wren earlier is coursing through her now.

"I take it you've never taken a medi stim before, huh? Husband not interested in erasing his good work?"

"Sod off!"

All the answer Wren needs. Stims always have a delayed reaction on first use. Summer's eyes go from black as pitch to brown and then shine red around the cornea.

Wren laughs, despite the ache in her temples.

"I guess no one ever told you what's in those things. Nanos. Thousands of tiny, microscopic robots all racing through your bloodstream to make you good as new. Not the best thing for a witch, especially when you aren't used to them."

"When this stops," Summer hisses through her teeth, "I'm going to butcher you."

"I'd pay to see it." Wren magics Summer off the floor to hover before her. *Thaloc! Even just this hurts.* "Now tell me. Who is hubby dearest, so I can make sure to pay him a visit on your behalf?"

"...Mew..."

Wren drops Summer, startled by an all-too familiar sound, and as Summer groans, Wren finally looks around.

There's a boiler in the corner, a stack of dusty old furniture against the far wall, a moth-eaten sheet draped over a window, and wooden stairs with more than a few broken steps leading up to the tilted cellar door. The air is stale, stagnant like no one has come through in ages, but in the center of the basement is a blood-painted array.

And at the circle's center lies a small heap of black fur. Pointed ears pinned back against a triangular skull, long torso curled up in a crescent, a tail twitching meekly on the hard tile—it's a cat roughly the size of a beach ball. Viridian mist drips off its fur in ringlets of ethereal magic.

The animal keens, iron chains clamped around its neck and all four paws. Wren's heart skips a beat as familiar green eyes open, winking at her weakly.

"Silje?"

The cat mewls, a pathetic little sound that sparks tears in Wren's eyes.

"Silje!"

And Wren races for the array, smearing the edges and crawling her way to the animal's flank. The chains binding Silje's legs rattle to the floor, thrown as Wren psychically forces them open. The cat lays limp on her side, her tail giving the barest of twitches and expelling the tiniest of mews as Wren traces a hand over the shivering little body. Silje's fur is matted with neglect, her whiskers limp around her face.

She's so weak. An ounce of lifeforce acts as the only thing tethering her to life. How could a witch do something like this?

"What did you do to her?"

Wren's question rings hollow and angry in the dark, damp of the basement.

"It's just an animal."

Silje is far more than "just an animal."

Silje bound herself to Wren as a familiar, a true witch's companion, a bond of mutual devotion which transcends life and death. A netherbeast who chooses to bond with a witch will bind themselves to not only the witch but also the witch's family. Silje saved Wren's life on more than one occasion and when Wren could not, Silje protected Fae.

And when everything went to hel, Silje paid the ultimate price for her loyalty to Wren. Tumbling down the ramparts of a clocktower in a magic-binding sack to her death...

...or so Wren had been led to believe.

Staged. All of it staged, a cheap trick like a magician sawing a person in half.

How long has this been happening? Summer torturing her familiar, thieving her magic. Silje, a displacer beast who has killed technomancers, the companion who saved her life more times than she can ever repay, being treated like a fucking battery. Her familiar, chained down and leeched off of. How dare this woman taint the sanctity of the relationship between witch and familiar! To hell with a dignified death. She should have let the shamblers eat her.

"What did you do to her!"

A whip of Wren's magic strikes the other witch across the face. Summer topples sideways, but just as Wren is about to converge on her, the blixvi lands in front of her with a deafening shriek.

It pecks Wren's hands, breaking skin and drawing blood.

"*¡Vete pa'l carajo!*"

She grabs the bird by the throat, and the note that spills from her mouth, off key and sharp enough to peel the skin off teeth, reverberates through the beast's skeleton. The bird's feathers turn to dust, its flesh melts off its bones, and it falls to pieces, decaying in her hands. Closing her eyes, Wren squeezes the magical pestilence out of the creature's bones. That is after all where magic begins, in the heart of the bone where blood seeds.

Remédier, she thinks, *contrarrestar*.

Marrow drips from the creature's bones, cradled by Wren's magic, dissolving into mist and spiraling away. Where it goes, she hasn't a clue; all she knows is she is focusing all of her will on repairing the damage done by the creature, all the damage caused by a witch who cares more for herself than anyone else.

She tosses the corpse aside. It lands with a wet splat on the floor, and she rounds on Summer, currently cowering on the floor.

"You don't understand. You were dead. You abandoned us! I had no choice!"

"You think I give a serpents scale why you've done any of the things you've done in the last decade?"

"I did what I had to do!"

Summer yanks on her lingering hold on Silje, and the displacer beast writhes in agony.

"Stop it!"

Wren reaches out, not with her arm or her weapons but with her mind. Wren's empathetic powers slam into Summer so violently, the neural networks in her brain shatter. Her surface emotions split under Wren's assault, and all of Summer's bloodlust, her hurt, her pain, her mad thirst for revenge, they part around Wren. It's so strong it suffocates Wren. She drowns in Summer's anger and as much as it hurts her, the assailant tearing through another's psyche, Summer, her victim's pain is much, much worse.

No, it's not enough. She pushes harder and falls into the sound of laughter.

THE PAGE OF CUPS

Her skin grows hot, tightening around her bones. The walls are closing in, but it isn't the walls at all; it's her own flesh and blood, quavering into nothing, losing elasticity, sucking the air from the room, drowning her in the putrid stink of mortality, yet this body is capable, perfect, enduring, the proper vessel, if only it would let go... *let go*... let go of that silly thing called sanity. *Just let go, Songstress. You can do it; just push a little more, a little harder*—the vice loosens, and laughter echoes in her ears, resonant and wicked, short high-pitched cackles like a hag.

It's her laughter.

SMACK!

Wren, horrified, chokes on the sound of her own cackles. Her cheek and palm sting from slapping herself. What the fuck is wrong with her? Why is she laughing? She was in pain. She was screaming. Why was she laughing? She's still screaming. The sound grating on her eardrums. No wait. Those aren't her screams.

They're Summer's!

"Ahhhh!" The other witch writhes on the floor gripping her head, flaying about like a fish on a hot stove. "Make it stop! You stupid witch, get out of my head! Ahhh!"

Horror splits Wren's bloodlust. *Not again!*

Wren grabs Summer's head—her hair matted with blood and dirt. Forcing her still, she dives back into the redhead's psyche. She works as fast as she can, reconnecting shorn aura points, binding together ripped emotions with nothing but her will, repairing what damage she can to Summer's frayed synapse until the woman shoves her away. Wren rolls across the floor, landing at Silje's limp paws.

"You stupid, witch!" Summer laughs, manic, the whites of her eyes shot through with blood, fury resonating off her hot and volatile. Summer bites down on the flesh of her wrist and draws an array in blood. Void-magic gathers around her in a swirling pit of potential energy, all of the power she stole from Silje ready to combust.

Madness ripples in the air. The foundation cracks around them. She's going to kill them both!

Waves of black surge and coil around the room, whipping out in volatile strings of nothingness. Wren gets up, the skin of her hands and knees torn and scraped, to... to... she doesn't know what. To do something! Throw a dagger or dispel Summer's magic, anything to stop Summer in her tracks.

A cat's meow calls for her.

Wren throws herself on Silje, pulling the vulnerable feline into her arms. Her paw twitches and Wren sings, all her intention focused on getting herself and her vulnerable familiar out of Summer's suicidal death trap. Shining emerald spirals swirl and spin. They caress Wren's arms and legs, her face and thighs; Wren's magic cards through Silje's fur, around her paws, and alights in slitted pupils.

"*Förstöra!*"

As Summer screams her spell, Silje's magic roars to life and the basement prison disappears. Wren lands on her knees in the gray light of dawn, elbows slamming hard into the pavement to keep from dropping Silje.

BOOM!

The force of the blast shoves Wren off kilter, rolling her across the pavement until her back meets a metal pole. Shrapnel raining down around them, she ducks toward a parked truck, a heavy-duty thing designed for dirt-roading or hauling fifth wheels, yanks the door off its hinges, and dives into the backseat, curling around Silje as debris pounds on the roof and slides off the vehicle.

For minutes, metal, steel, and splintered wood rattle and thud through the streets. The air floods with smoke, and the heat of black flames radiates from the cement.

When it all finally quiets, Wren lifts her head to bear witness to the destruction through a cracked, dust-encrusted window. The building they just teleported from lies in ruins, destroyed in a void-powered explosion, possibly Summer right along with it unless she used the magic she siphoned off of Silje to teleport herself out in time. She has no way of knowing, buried under a dome of rubble as she is.

THE PAGE OF CUPS

Her breath hitches, her head pounding and her vision going fuzzy around the edges. She is spent. She doesn't know if it was her magic or Silje's that got them out, but either way, the teleportation has sapped her reserves. She coughs, bile and blood coming up as she hunkers down in the seat.

Summer's gone. The blixvi is gone. Her magic evaporated. She closes her eyes and breathes. Limbs heavy, brain cottony, she sinks down into the very depths of the cushioned seat. The warm arms of sleep fold around her, and Wren allows herself to drift, cocooned under a mausoleum of stone, metal, and shrapnel.

In her arms, a little furry body starts to purr.

Outside, a true rain sprinkles from the sky, and as Wren sleeps, a viridian mist curls into the cab.

Netherbeasts—Monsters of the astral plains.

We've discussed the consequences that might unfold when a witch enslaves a netherbeast. Don't forget to use such knowledge to your advantage. But not all witch/netherbeast relationships are master and servant.

Beware the netherbeast who chooses to bind itself to a witch, for they are loyal beyond comparison and will kill anyone who threatens their chosen witch.

These are the familiars.

An Excerpt from <u>*Hunting and Identifying Hexen*</u>
Finnick Lockecraft, 1852 A.P.

20
TEN OF PENTACLES

Betwixt the Moon and Stars Temple – 12:58AM –Kaito

AN EXPLOSION ROCKS THE SANCTUARY, knocking the normals off their feet.

"This is it. This is the end. The witch is taking her revenge on us."

The ringleader goes into a tizzy. She jumps onto her feet, a crowbar in hand and scrambles toward the unconscious teen on the ground, not even mindful of Kaito standing steady as a statue entirely unaffected by the ground-splitting quake. The fanatical woman raises the bar over her head, looking to bring it down on the girl's face, the little boy throwing himself over his sister.

But before she can bring down the blow, Kaito thrusts Amatsu's hilt into her diaphragm. The woman topples, lights out, to the tile floor.

The little boy looks at Kaito with wide watery eyes.

"There is no witch here."

And even if there was, it is not the place of civilians to act as judge, jury, and executioner. Kaito's sights spin, and a wall of cyber energy erects around the people who called for the blood of an innocent girl whose only crime was being a stranger unable to speak the language of her accusers. Kaito's ward shrinks down, corralling the group into a dense square of space. With a twist of his wrist, the ward locks in place, crackling with power and surging when one of the men touches the barrier. The ward pulses. The man drops unconscious.

"You can't keep us in here! There are monsters!"

The only monsters he sees here are the humans who murdered an innocent man in the name of righteousness.

"You'll be safer inside the ward, and in turn, others will be safe from you."

While dismantling the makeshift shackles binding the shrine maiden, Kaito runs a trace on the source of the explosion. The origin point is within the warehouse district, some 20km away.

"Thank you, your highness."

The shrine maiden races to the two children the moment she is released, taking the boy and his sister in her arms and whispering to them in Sanskri.

"The mob, they thought Zhou Feng was responsible for the plague just because he was unaugmented. He and his children happened to cross the border just before the disease started. He didn't speak any Hanasu or Common and neither does Zhou Lin. I tried to stop them, but..." But how can one barely augmented woman and unaugmented man hold back a mob? "Oh, poor Feng–ge!"

A pang of irritation climbs up his leg. The bite. He kneels to check it.

"You're injured."

He glances at the woman, then examines the wound. In the short hour since AYA ran her analytics, it's festered. Black, mold-like putrefaction creeps up his leg from the bite.

"Roughly two hours before infection spread, highness."

AYA's message scrolls across his interface.

"It's nothing," he tells the woman. She can't help him anyway. The only person who could possibly cure him of this affliction before it hits his system is somewhere in this city, and he hasn't any idea where.

The explosion. Was it his Songstress?

He doesn't read any of Wren's magical signature around the explosion point, but it doesn't mean she isn't nearby. He needs to make his way there before Tanaka.

"Once it's safe, I'll send people to escort you and the children to Tokiseishu. There are people there who will keep you safe per my request."

The woman nods, tears streaking down her face. "Thank you."

"I don't know how long it will be before help arrives, but," he cocks his head toward the makeshift prison, "none of *them* will be getting out anytime soon."

The woman nods.

"We'll be fine. Please, go and save the rest of the city before it all goes insane."

He nods, appreciative of the woman's dismissal. He doesn't have time to stay. His own family is still in danger.

2:25AM – Warehouse District

The explosion site is worse than he thought it would be. Complete wreckage: cracked foundation, exposed steel cabling, blocks of cement crumbled to dust, and coating all of it is a thin layer of soot. Debris has scattered as far as a kilometer from the origin point, the neighboring buildings crumbling and laced with void fire due to their proximity to the blast. Whole chunks of granite now sit throughout the area, a post-destruction rock garden. Some of them even make neat configurations around the cars and streetlamps in the area, forming little coves and piles not unlike burial mounds. How many were killed in this blast?

There are bodies on the ground, some crushed by flying debris, others blown apart, having the misfortune of being too close to the explosion.

Kaito's scans trace over the area. His virtual field automatically runs analytics on what may or may not have caused the explosion. He won't interrupt the processes, even though he no longer needs them.

Most people are pretty familiar with the concept of cause and effect. Nothing happens without a due cause. A fire starts when a spark meets an appropriate kindling. A tree falls over when it's severed from its roots. A sink floods when a clog obstructs the drain. Cause and effect. A measurable cause—something visible, tangible, and replicable—leading to a measurable effect. But what if the cause cannot be measured? What if there is no spark, no clog, no axe? What if the cause is magic, unpredictable, untraceable, and chaos-incarnate? According to arcane theory, then, there is no cause.

When it comes to magic, it isn't cause and effect; it's effect without cause.

Magic is immeasurable. Its properties too changeable, too irreconcilable, too chaotic to be measured in any way physics or mathematics might attempt. He had a difficult time understanding it at first as a child, his brother poring over books on arcane physics and theorems with him as Hikaru prepared for his first summit trials. But once he understood magic existed outside of the boundaries of time and space, it made it more palatable.

Fourteen years ago, under the theorems taught to him by his mother, Fumiko, and Hikaru, he would have gone about discovering the source of the explosion by eliminating measurable causes. Was there a gas leak? Did a machine go haywire? Or did someone set off dynamite somewhere in the building? Eliminate the measurable causes, and all that's left is the immeasurable—magic as the source of the effect. But magic is undefinable; therefore, it cannot be labeled a cause.

Thus, effect without cause.

It made enough sense to Kaito at the time. You cannot catalog and measure magic into a petri dish, so if you want to classify an effect as witchy mayhem, you have to prove nothing else caused the effect. It's a terribly tedious process but one every technomancer must demonstrate if they are to pass their trials.

It wasn't until after Wren's change in persuasion he gained a true understanding of magic.

"People who say they want to banish the world of magic don't really understand what magic is. Magic is not a void or an anomaly. Magic exists in everything and everyone. In the rocks and the trees. In the grass and the flowers, in the tiniest of insects and largest of whales, even in the most mundane of humans."

Wren told him that once upon a time, in the deep woods of Lorelei forest on a warm summer's day while children played with the birds outside Wren's little witch cottage.

"If you accept magic is neither here nor there but everywhere and nowhere at once, you start to understand its limitations and boundlessness. What sets witches apart from technomancers and ordinary humans is simply that our relationship to magic is multifaceted, capable of acting as both a conduit and a conductor. Technomancers require technology to harness and direct their natural pools of lifeforce into something tangible, the way you do with your saibāki. Witches, on the other hand, we are both originators and propagators. We have it inside us already. All we need to do is will it out, and sometimes it just stays."

He hadn't understood this at first—the concept of a witch being an origin point of magical activity is as odd a concept as a fish being the source of water for a lake. But over the course of the year Kaito spent as a welcome visitor to Wren's home and hearth during her isolation, he started to notice things.

Wren's cottage came alive.

It knew her thoughts and needs and made its own needs known to the witch, communicating through floorboards which only creaked when there was a leak in the roof or by knocking a plate from the cupboard when the fireplace was overdue for a cleaning. Wren's spells and potions because less active thought for her and more of a sense memory surrounding her. There was a day she set the dishes in the sink, and the faucet opened, dish soap already mixed in until the basin was a perfect level of foamy bubbles and perfectly tempered water. He asked Wren if she had commanded the sink to fill, and she'd merely blinked at him, saying "Oh no. The house thinks I take far too long to clean them, so it does it for me so I don't forget." The needs of the future made known in the present.

Even Wren's ghostly disposition made itself apparent after a short time. Wandering spirits used to haunt the woods around her little home, tending the gardens for her, entertaining the war orphans and widows who wandered into the forest for Wren's spells and charms, one of them even organized her closet just so Kaito would have his own space to leave a change of clothing for his visits. At least, Wren told him one of the ghosts had done it. He's fairly certain she'd been fibbing him, too embarrassed to confess outright that she cleared the space for him herself because she enjoyed his visits and wanted to make it easier for him to make the trip. She'd blushed furiously after telling him about the cleared away space, and he'd done what any other sane man would when faced with such an unspoken confession: after everyone else in the household had retired for the evening, he hung his clothes, kissed the nervous song off her lips, and let the witch guide him to bed.

Toward the end, it was hard to tell where Wren's magic ended and the forest's began. The effect of her presence not a causality but a happenstance. After her death, Kaito would visit Lorelei forest every year to lay a fresh lily on the place where he now knows Wren was burned to death, not just cremated, and even more than a decade after her passing, the forest is still alive with her residual magic even despite the Vanquishing.

But he digresses. Understanding and living with Wren's magic, no matter how short a time it had been, gave him a new perspective on finding magic. And in the years since Wren's death, he'd made it a point to code into his system a means to see magical spill, a sight meant to trace what is and isn't there, what was, is, and will be, how the very molecules of the world shift and change in response to magic, and with it came not only the ability to see magic but also the ability to trace other magical essences into his VR field, like netherbeasts and fae-folk.

His vision narrows as he activates it now. It isn't perfect. The view is patchy, and he can't scan through large areas at a time. To even attempt such would overwhelm his servers and drive his system into a hard reset.

Protons, electrons, and neutrons, they vibrate before him: the char of a burn scar, a support beam torn from the ceiling and bent at an irreparable angle, the faded lines of a blood-drawn array. Data analytics, which can only be done in a vacuum, drift into his neural net. Everything and nothing spreads out before him in numerical coding, and it is in this cellular make-up and history where he finds what he is looking for. The remnant of magical origin. A black viscous emptiness. Void magic. Entirely different from his witch's.

Wren gets caught up in the destructive aspects of her abilities. The dark necrotic energies allow her to raise the dead and rot the flesh off of bone, but the truth of it is Wren's magic pulses with the most peculiar duality of life and death. Wild and unfettered vitality laced with the inevitability of dying. He feels this aspect of her magic all the time, when she sings, when she smiles; it's in her touch, in her laughter, in her kisses. The lifegiving opposition to her death-dealing abilities. A perfect dichotomy in one witch.

No, this is not Wren's magic. Her death-domain didn't cause this catastrophe. This was void magic—emptiness surplus with destitution. The magic is familiar, scanned before in the trace of a kenku fought on a light rail. Summer's magic. Though the witch responsible is nowhere to be found.

The only thing he finds is the mutilated skeleton of a netherbird—a blixvi, judging by the lightning patterning on its skull, a bringer of storms and pestilence. *Shimata!* With the blixvi dead, is there even a chance of finding a cure? Something peculiar gives him pause. Coated with glittering dust, the skeleton glows a vibrant emerald green, and when he scans the mysterious compound, it comes back positive as residual magic from his witch, but what is it and how long has it been sitting here?

"The substance appears non-toxic. Safe to handle, highness."

"Thank you, AYA."

Taking a vial from his pack, he scoops as much of it as he can into the container. He takes another pinch of the dust and sprinkles it into the specimen-collection port in his hand, setting AYA to run analytics on it.

"Well, it appears I've missed the little lady once again."

Tanaka stands atop a slab of concrete on the ground level above Kaito. A pair of K9-D06s flank Tanaka on either side. Large cybernetic dogs, half-machine terrier/chihuahua mutts with unnaturally long prosthetic legs, steel braced jaws, and outfitted with devastating attack power, the barrels of their weapons aim at Kaito. These are military issue cyborgs, yet the dogs' augmentations do not bear the coloration of any country Kaito knows of, nor can he find the serial numbers of their origins.

"I must say, prince, it's a shame we found ourselves on opposite sides of this mindless schism. I'll be sure to give the witch your love after I pry that sample out of your cold, dead hands. I'll even go out of my way to comfort her in her grief."

Hn. Wren is more likely to tear his insides out, and she could do it with a flick of her pinkie.

"Sic 'im, boys!"

Tanaka flickers off as the dogs launch toward Kaito with all the violence of their breed and the mechanical power provided to back-up their temperament. Deadly beams of laser fire skirt past him as he rolls behind an overturned boiler. His mapping system alights, blanketing the world in code. The outlines of two K9 units and Tanaka fleeing 36 degrees northwest move like numerical ghosts through his VR interface, but these ghosts are not simple phantom spectres. The first pair of fanged jaws close down on Amatsu's blade with a snarl, and he kicks the second beast away before it can flank him. The K9 holds fast, saliva flailing from its mouth to drip down Kai's sword.

Hearing a nasty growl to his left, he flings the animal attached to his weapon directly at the second. The pair collide with clanging and barking, rolling over each other to get to him, but he bolts after Tanaka, the dogs on his heels.

The next twenty minutes are a foot race across the trashed landscape: boulders of mangled metal and concrete, bricks of shrapnel, twisted steel skeletons. His heart pounds, dodging left and right while keeping Tanaka in his sights despite the darkness. The night sky is dark not just with gloomtide but the heavy sheet of storm clouds still hanging pregnant in the sky. They rumble, true lightning crackling between them—not the darkning of before. AYA runs predictions on the K9s' movements, but just like any computer with a firewall, their software is capable of obstructing her analytics, and Kaito doesn't have the time to stop and focus on remote hacking into their systems, not when there are two of them and not when Tanaka is one wrong turn away from escape.

He dances, light on his feet, avoiding fang, claw, and laser. But there's a problem.

Kaito is flagging.

He scales a rooftop lattice, leaping from one jagged edge to another, and lands with a sharp pang on his injured leg. He goes down with a grimace. The bite pulses, fire molten in his veins. The sweat beads at his brow, hot and cold and discolored while the world around him loses color.

The blixvi's corruption seeps past his protections. His system is compromised.

The K9s converge on him. One goes for his face; Kaito feeds his bracer into its mouth instead, stabbing Tsukuyomi straight through the cyborg's chest. Sparks fly as wiring short-circuits, blood stains the katana, and the dog rolls over dead.

One down, the other zeros in on his injured leg. Teeth clamp down on his calf; however, once it gets a firm chomp on the atrophied flesh, it whines, reeling back. The dog balks and falls clean off the roof in its crazed thrashes.

"Worthless mutts!"

Tanaka.

Kaito rolls as a kunai clangs into the ground next to his head. He releases his hold on both his swords. Amatsu and Tsukuyomi fly from his grip to coil through the air led by the mechanical spines connecting them to his forearms. Together, the sister blades block and ward away the onslaught of weaponry both steel and laser.

HOSTILE APPROACHING @ 10 O'CLOCK

AYA's warning saves Kai a close shave as he flips up into the air, narrowly avoiding Tanaka's handheld kunai.

"Give me that vial!" he shouts, reaching for the bottle of witch dust.

Tsukuyomi returns to his hand, and Kaito parries the man away. What does he want with Wren's concoction?

"Miyazaki-sama, I've finished running analytics on the magical residue left by Lady Wren."

"Not now, AYA," he rasps, dodging another blow from Tanaka.

"Your highness," the A.I. continues, despite his command. "The properties within indicate a repellent to the blixvi's corruption."

Tanaka barrels toward him.

"I said give it to me!"

That's when he sees the bite on Tanaka's hand. Bitten by a shambler, he's infected. With so much of his face covered in bandages, Kaito didn't realize how far along he was, the whites of his eyes blackened, his skin bubbling with infection. Is that why he wants the vial? Does he think the contents will banish the malady?

"The dosage is highly concentrated," AYA continues in his ear, "and should be diluted for maximum effectiveness."

"Is it possible for it to be diluted enough to benefit the entire city?"

Kaito takes the bottle from his belt to study the swirling dust within. There doesn't seem to be much, the little within what he would expect a single vial of insulin to look like. How Wren managed this is a miracle in itself, magical antidotes rarer even than the maladies they cure, but if AYA is saying it should be diluted, how far can it be stretched?

"Screw the city! I need it!"

Tanaka lunges for him again, his hand reaching dangerously close to the vial. It's a sloppy maneuver, though. Kai kicks the man away even as his own vision swims. AYA sets off alarms in his head.

"By my calculations, highness, it is a possibility, but I'm afraid you are nearing the point where your own body is about to give out."

The other technomancer gnashes his teeth and tackles Kaito to the ground. Both the vial and Tsukuyomi rattle from Kaito's hand, clanking along the cracked pavement.

"You're infected, too. We could share it. I won't tell anyone. We can save ourselves and let the League take care of the rest of the town."

As in drop a nuke on it... Kaito wrestles Tanaka onto his back, grappling him into a chokehold.

"Tanaka, cease this madness!"

Thunder rumbles overhead. A single raindrop splashes on Kai's forehead, so cold compared to the fever in his bones it hurts.

"I'm mad?! You're the one who's mad. You have a cure in hand, and you want to use it on the city instead of yourself. How are you going to get it to everyone? There isn't enough to disperse to everyone, and by the time you do, how many more will be infected or even dead?!"

On the man's belt, an array of weapons and stims dangle, including the mister he used to distribute his anti-magic venom into the ozone.

The butt of Amatsu's hilt rams into Tanaka's temple, and he goes limp in Kaito's grip. The prince rips the mister from the other man's belt and scrambles to the dropped bottle of magical powder. Pulling a medi stim from his belt, Kaito drains the liquid mix of nanos and saline solution into the dust. Stoppering it, he shakes the mixture together before pouring it into the empty mister. Dizzy and nauseous, he coughs, spilling some onto his hands. It glows viridian; a soothing arpeggio of notes echoes in his head.

"What are you doing?"

The cylinder revs to life in Kaito's hands, glowing red as it goes to work compressing the mixture within. Around him Tsukuyomi and Amatsu ward off Tanaka's attacks, reaching a fever pitch now he knows what Kaito is doing, but as Tanaka's attacks intensify, Kaito's defenses waver, his energy and focus sapped as the infection takes root in his tech systems. Just a little more! The device vibrates in his hand as Tsukuyomi drops lifeless to the ground, the cabling at his wrist deactivating to conserve power. Tanaka takes the opening, kneeing Kaito in the stomach. Before he can get a second hit in, Kaito manages a sluggish sidestep around his aggressor, Amatsu returning to his hand, but it's so heavy, he can barely lift it. His tanto, his katana...

"This is the right thing to do."

He throws the blade, so weak a toss it doesn't even cut Tanaka, but it is enough to throw the man off balance. Both technomancers drop to their knees.

"You don't even know if it will work!"

No, he doesn't, but something tells him it doesn't matter. His feet feel heavy, his head spinning as Tanaka swipes an elbow across his face. He returns the blow, headbutting the man in the face. The device turns green; Kaito aims it skyward and fires as a crash of thunder sounds once more.

The device blasts with a powerful burst of air, toppling Kaito sideways. The capsule, glowing green with life, disappears into the clouds and explodes, vibrant neon greens and electric purples scattering like fireworks behind the cloudline.

Kaito lies on his back, darkness seeping in around his eyes as his night vision flickers out. When he opens his eyes, Tanaka's dagger-laden fist aims to come down on his chest.

"You're a fool, Miyazaki!"

Tanaka's shout is drowned out by a rain of laserfire. The second dog, gone rabid from the magical malady in Kaito's blood, leaps after Tanaka, opening fire and cutting off his attempt to kill Kaito. A shot blows the hinge on his mechanical knee out, and he topples sideways.

A moment later, the canine's teeth close on his arm, shredding muscle from bone. He screams, staggering back and trying to kick the dog away. Kai watches, impassive as the man struggles to keep his hand. Hn, a prosthetic hand would be a difficult adjustment for a blade-thrower.

"Get off me, you mangy mutt!"

Kaito closes his eyes and moves.

The dog releases Tanaka's arm, jaws aimed for his jugular instead, but Amatsu severs the creature's head from its shoulders first, and the K9's body hits the pavement.

Sapped of his strength, Kaito lies on his back as a new rain falls from the sky. He shakes at first, trembling with fever and illness, but as he lays there, warmth returns to his body. At first, he thinks this is Death coming for him, but no, it isn't. He warms, and his body returns to itself. His vision clears, the gray tint disappearing, and when he takes his next breath, his lungs expand unburdened. Water falls across Kaito's face, pure and untainted by the blixvi's disease, and dare he imagine it, there is magic hidden in the droplets, cradled in the gentle rise and fall of a moonlit sonata.

"Haha! Take that, you useless fleabag!" Meanwhile, Tanaka laughs maniacally on the ground, pointing at the dead dog with his mutilated wrist. "Hahaha! I can't believe it actually worked! You and your wicked, little witch actually managed to save the city. I'll be sure to applaud her from the grave. Well get on with it, highness. Kill your first technomancer and make your precious witch proud."

No, of all the witches and even technomancers Kaito has met in this world, Wren is one of the few he knows would never relish in the hubris many find in taking a life, even one so dismal as Tanaka's. His grip on his katana strengthens, and while Kaito rises onto weary feet, his stance is firm and his augmentations

SONATA

alive with violet light. Kaito sheathes his blades and turns his back on his fallen opponent.

Tanaka is no longer worth his attention.

"I'm going to summon aid into the city. The medics will tend to you, and when you are no longer in need of medical attention, you will be charged for high treason against Murasaki no Yama."

"What are you going to do when you find her, huh?" Tanaka spits red-tinted bile onto the ground at his heels. It stains the edge of Kai's boot for but a moment before the rains, too, wash this taint away. "Drag her back to your perfect palace and hide her away like a dirty little secret? Force her to live her life as someone else? A pretty little mistress you can keep at home and bring out just for special occasions?"

A shift of air, the creaking of a broken limb, the whistle of a knife.

Kaito swings blind as the man attempts to stab him in the back and feels the shick of impact. Tanaka yells obscenities, clenching the new slash across his stomach. He trips on his own discarded weapon and lands on the dead robo-dog. The resulting blowout sets fire to Tanaka's clothes, hair, and skin, a fire so volatile not even the magic of the rain can squelch it. Or perhaps, the magic of the rain doesn't want to snuff it out.

Kaito watches, impassive, as the other technomancer's system lights shift from a bright yellow to red to black. Tanaka dies in the fires of his own making.

Because these augmentations are highly customizable to the individual and their personal needs, many companies used to offer incentives to their employees should they decide to undergo technolyzation to increase their ability to perform at work. Some companies even required their staff be augmented. However, after several cases of malfunction, unsanitary practices, and an increase in post-op mortality rates, such practices were outlawed on the basis of ethical questionability and public endangerment.

Technolyze Me: How Voluntary Amputation Became
Commonplace in The League
C. R. Ashworth, 1845 A.P.

21

FOUR OF PENTACLES

**10th Day in the Month of Falling – Chairomura Warehouse
District –4:12 AM**

A LIGHT TAP ON HER CALF... FOLLOWED BY
four little touches along her thigh and hip, the padded
paws of a cat rouse the sleeping witch, but she doesn't stir until
wiry whiskers tickle her ear, flooding it with insistent purring. A
petite nose, cool and wet, nudges her hair out of the way, and she
opens her eyes to a furry black face.

"Good morning to you, too."

Silje gives a light chirrup and begins kneading the dirty cloak
tucked around Wren's shoulders. The witch lifts a hand to scratch
behind her familiar's ear and the cat practically rolls into her
palm. Outside the lulling drip, drip, drip of the gentlest of rains
taps against the window. Have the toxic rains passed them by?

"You feeling better?"

Silje blinks at her slowly, large green eyes glinting in the
darkness, obviously unable to answer, but her whiskers have
perked up and her magical signature has balanced out. It's still

nowhere near what it should be, the feline still unable to shift into her true form, not that she would in such a confined space.

Flexing her hands, Wren hums.

Were anyone there to watch, they would see a block of concrete slide clean off the side of a banged-up pick-up, followed by one of the back doors opening and a tired twenty-something woman with blue-black hair and creamy skin toppling out with something black as pitch clutched to her chest.

Her body aches and her skin feels tight. Her throat parched and her mouth desert-dry, she'll probably down a full glass of water the moment she gets her hands on one. But back under the stars as gloomtide ebbs into an infantile dawn, the air is fresh, and her muscles unwind as she fills her lungs with crisp untainted oxygen.

There are bodies in the street. Shamblers who toppled over unconscious from one thing or another. She approaches the nearest one, a woman, probably thirty-something wearing what was once a business suit, hair done up in a fraying knot. She lies still on her side, crumpled up like a discarded newspaper. Wren nudges her with her boot, checking to see if she stirs. She doesn't, but the boils and void-like fungus indicative of the blixvi's ailment are not present on this woman. She bears evidence of disease, vomit on her chin, bruises around her throat, and a wound in her calf. But it's healing. That's what's important.

Was it really so simple? Kill the blixvi and the plague disappears?

How anti-climactic...

Wren folds Silje into her cloak and begins the trek back to the kids.

When Wren arrives at the diner, the sky is just beginning to lighten. It'll be a cloudless day. Probably the first this city has seen in days if not weeks.

"She's back! Renki, she's back!"

Zenza's face greets her in the window. The girl is bright-eyed and bushy-tailed even though she probably didn't sleep a wink the night before. The fourteen-year-old smiles as she opens up the ward on the door for 'Atalia.' Yes, Wren had the presence of mind to redon her glamour some fifteen/twenty minutes ago when she knew the rain wouldn't wash her magic away again.

"Did you kill it?! Did you kill the blixvi? What about the witch? Did you take care of her—What is that thing in your arms?"

Wren might be able to put a glamour on herself but concealing a netherbeast is another matter. Thankfully, when Silje is depleted of energy, she looks just like any other black cat. No misty edges or displaced whiskers to speak of.

"A cat."

Zenza's face alights, the way Wren would expect any young girl's face to light up at the sight of a small fluffy animal, but she makes the mistake of trying pet Silje's head, and the cat immediately hisses at the princess who jerks her hand back before she can earn herself a few good scratches.

"Careful. She's not one for strangers," Wren cautions fondly, remembering another life before her death and rebirth.

Silje never particularly liked anyone who wasn't Wren or Fae, though Kaito was worthy company from time to time. The cat warmed up to the technomancer over time; it was easy considering he knew how to sit still for long intervals of time and therefore made for a comfy napping spot, and Jessabelle would eternally be good for treats off the table. Kara, however, she'd barely tolerated—the huldra too *other* compared to her witch.

Looking dejected, the girl screws up her face. "Well, I'm not one for cats, either."

"Mhmm, too bad."

Her niece, impossibly, grimaces more. "Why do you have a–a–*achoo!* A cat?!"

Wren blinks at the violence of the girl's sneeze and winces as something reflects light at the girl's neckline. Wren's eyes trace the glint of metal to a pendant which has come dislodged from where it was previously tucked away in Zenza's collar.

Her breath catches.

She'd recognize that pendant anywhere: a waning crescent moon intersecting with a half circle, meant to represent half of Deus' sun, pure silver to ward away evil, one half of a set given to the girl's proxim-parents at her Hundred-Day celebration. The private event had been held between Zenza's parents, Atzi and Chike, and their siblings, Xipilli, Chiamaka, and Wren, herself, with Xipilli and Chiamaka taking on the roles of proxima-parents to the babe while Wren held witness to the ceremony. Atzi gifted Xipilli this half of the pendant at the ceremony while Chiamaka was gifted its opposite by Chike.

Two parts of a whole. The pendant of the Deus' sun and dual moons to watch over their daughter in the event her parents were no longer able to.

How misfortune so readily comes to pass.

Wren averts her gaze and swallows the guilt.

"She's my cat."

Zenza sneezes again, rapidly backing away as Wren angles past the sniffling princess.

"Wait—*achoo!*—you can't bring that demonic thing in here!"

"Well, I'm not leaving her outside. She's hurt."

"She is?"

"Miss Vaishi, you're back!"

Renki appears from behind the kitchen doors. The boy pauses as well upon seeing the cat, but instead of looking at Silje in abhorrence, he stalls in awe. He doesn't say anything, just stares, a thoughtful look on his face as Wren settles the cat in a straw-woven sombrero shaped tortilla basket. The lid even has some tassels around the pointed bit. Her familiar gives an appreciative chirp when she sets it over the top of the basket, putting the animal in a comfy darkness.

FOUR OF PENTACLES

"Look," Zenza says. "I get most people think they're cute and there's this parasite in their pee that makes people obsessed with them, but cats make me really, really, really uncomfortable."

Really? Because she had no trouble trying to touch her a moment ago...

"I take it your uncle doesn't keep any cats around the villa."

"He prefers dogs and fish, neither of which get on well with cats."

Debatable. Silje got on just fine with Jessabelle's wolves. Of course, Silje is typically a lot bigger than any dog or wolf.

The girl sneezes again.

"So, you've never actually been around a cat."

"So?"

"So, it looks to me like you're allergic."

"I don't have allergies!"

Another sneeze follows said protest. Mhmm... Atzi was allergic to cats, too. Genetics are a thing.

"I'll make you something. In the meantime, just keep your distance."

Wren scoops up Silje in her sombrero basket and trods into the kitchen despite the sputtering teenager. Setting Silje down on the counter, she checks on Akari.

The girl is blissfully asleep. Still wan around the edges, but the boils on her skin are drying out and the color is returning to her face. When she adjusts the linens, she finds them damp and follows the wet to the back door. Rain must have seeped in during the night. She'll need to dry the girl up lest she end up with a non-magical fever next.

Wren pulls aside the damp binding around the peck from the blixvi and is pleased to note the discoloration has diminished, the black moldy spread gone, replaced with happily pink skin around the injury. It'll need to heal yet, and she'll have a wicked time recovering fully, but it doesn't matter.

She's healing, and since she was never fully infected, she should weather the side effects easily enough. Nothing a bit of pain medication and ointment can't fix.

Wren rises from Akari's side and promptly bangs her head on the stove in fright. The burning woman glowers down at her, hands outstretched toward her throat.

"You again!"

The faceless ghost lunges for her, knocking her backward, scattering pots and pans everywhere. It wrestles with her, shaking her against the tile floor until her brains rattle in her head.

"Cursed ghost!"

Wren's power flings the spectre into the nearby mirror cabinet where it falls into the glass.

"Reveal yourself!"

Wren's command rings out through the ether, and the ghost has no choice but to comply. As Wren watches, the faceless spectre shifts and shimmers in the air until Chiamaka, the girl she knew as the princess of Ebele, hovers in the looking glass, a very ghostly, very much dead princess.

Chiamaka's ghost is the perfect visage of the nightmare she had just a few nights ago. Burns mar her face and throat, her hands are charred beyond recognition, and her hair sits fluffy if not smoldering atop her head in a grand afro, just like she used to wear as a teenager.

She looks nothing like the woman who cast the curse on Shinka Temple.

Behind her, Silje hisses at the spectre. Trapped in the mirror, the ghost fumes at the cat before disappearing with a silent scream. Wren feels the scream of the dead echo through the room, and despite the netherbeast's warning having banished the dead princess from her mistress's sight, Silje ducks back into her basket, the lid quaking like the feline within is either frightened or cold.

Amidst the chaos, Akari slumbers on, entirely unknowing of Wren's frightful encounter, and Wren is left to gather her wits about her sans ornery dead woman.

This doesn't make any sense.

Chiamaka is supposed to be living the high life in Ebele, preparing to attend the grand ball in Aureus in just two days, but if Chiamaka's ghost is here...—And ghosts can't change shape. They can't pretend to be anything other than what or who they are—...who is masquerading as Chiamaka?

"Miss Nocturne?"

"¡Puta Madre a Dios!"

Wren pivots/jumps with a shriek, more than a few hairs out of place.

"Ah, sorry. I didn't mean to startle you."

It's Renki, snuck up on her again. Loki's mistletoe, somebody put a bell on this kid.

"It's fine," Wren breathes. "I didn't feel you come in."

"Did something happen?"

Wren turns her face away from the teen in favor of fiddling with the bandages on her arm. "Nothing that merits your concern, Renki."

She can practically hear him pouting.

Renki looks from Wren to the quivering basket.

"Aww, the poor thing is shaking."

"W-wait!"

Before Wren can react, the boy opens up the little sombrero basket. From inside, Silje eyes him warily. How the cat isn't hissing at him is beyond her, but he's smart enough not to touch her just yet.

Renki quietly extends his fingers to Silje's nose. The familiar sniffs his fingertips a few times, a puzzled feeling ticking over her psyche. She draws back unsure, at first, but upon a second round of inspection, one that has less to do with her nose and more to do with her magical sense, she rubs her head into the teen's hand.

Renki's entire disposition lights up. Obliging the quiet request but hesitant, he gently cards his fingers through Silje's fur.

"Where did you find her?"

"It's a long story."

As the animal relaxes, the youth grows bolder, pulling apart tangles and removing gunk hidden in the fluff. Silje blinks at Wren with tired green eyes from under Renki's palm, but the rumbling purr of a pleased housecat is unmistakable even if she looks like a dirt-crusted stray.

And as Silje starts to purr, her contentment washes away the witch's tension. Wren allows herself to deflate.

"I can help you bathe her?"

"What?"

Renki furrows his nose as he plucks a tiny black bug from the cat's tail. As though in answer, he holds it for her inspection before squishing it against the counter. Great... She'll need to give the familiar a proper bath, not that Silje will enjoy it in the slightest.

Wren crosses her arms with a shrug.

"I warn you, kiddo. It's not a walk through the water park dealing with this little demon." The boy's eyes gleam in the kitchen lights, eager and soft. An animal lover through and through. She sighs. "Alright."

The boy just smiles and turns the hot water tap on in the big industrial sink, plugging up the drain. Wren double checks the dish soap, making sure it's safe for animals, and pours a dollop into the water after finding a cloth she can use as a wash towel. Then comes the hard part: Silje.

Silje, who knows something unenjoyable is about to happen, bolts from the basket, knocking bowls and silverware to the floor with a clatter. The noise startles Akari awake, but she just mumbles and rolls back over. Renki scrambles after the cat, trying to catch her with his bare hands and getting a few nice scratches for his troubles. Wren watches, an eyebrow raised as he comes fairly close to catching her a few times but inevitably ends up making a mess of his clothes and face. Eventually, she shows the boy some mercy, catches Silje herself in a nice spiral of telekinetic magic, and without further ado, Wren plops the cat in the warm soapy water, despite the look of utter betrayal on the netherbeast's face.

Oh, the amount of spitting, hissing, and meowing she gets for her troubles!

Four Of Pentacles

Renki helps her keep the cat from bolting, though. The boy holds Silje gently but firmly in deft hands while Wren scrubs the gunk and parasites out of the netherbeast's fur. Ugh! Trans-dimensional-fleas, nasty little buggers! Eventually, she settles, whiskers drooping and a crown of suds on her head as she glares daggers at Wren for the cruel, cruel torture of a bath.

There's a familiarity to this—taking care of her familiar with another pair of hands to help her. Fae used to help her bathe Silje, too.

A knot forms in her throat watching Renki do the same now, holding Silje still as Wren drains the sink and runs warm, clean water over the cat to rinse the soap off. Once the little girl turned two, she used to sit in the bathtub with Silje and hold the house-sized netherbeast still while Wren single-handedly scrubbed a foamy sponge through the feline's coat. Though the familiar could have easily jumped away or shifted into her much larger size to escape, she never once tried to wriggle out of Fae's little toddler hands.

Occasionally, Silje would shake herself, water and soap flying everywhere, wetting Wren's hair and clothes. Fae would laugh, a high-pitched chiming laugh overflowing with delight if a little on the sharp side for Wren's ear. The toddler would splash water at Silje as recompense for splashing her, and all three of them would devolve into a messy water fight filled with the shrieks of a happy child before ending with the purring of a cat and Wren humming her way through Fae's lullaby to calm her back down.

A drop of water trails down her cheek. When did Silje flick water at her?

"Are you alright?"

Renki's question rips her from her reverie. She's been holding the nozzle in the same spot on Silje's back for Odin knows how long.

"You're quite good with animals."

"I'm okay. We have cats living on the grounds at home. Every so often *Tousan* and I have to catch one to give them a bath after they've pranced through the mud for a little too long."

As she runs a towel over Silje, Renki calls her name. "Lady Wren?"

At the call of her actual name, Wren tenses. She glances behind him, double checking whether Zenza is in hearing distance. The princess's sense of self-preservation must have finally kicked in when faced against a cat in a basket; she's nowhere near the kitchen, angrily texting someone on her comm unit.

"What is it?" she asks warily as she unplugs the drain. She throws a towel over the cat and lets Renki pat the animal dry while she moves to the cupboards. Her familiar needs a proper meal, and these teenagers could use some breakfast as well.

"I needed to ask you about something I found."

Aha! thinks Wren as she unearths a can of tuna for Silje.

"And what is this 'something' you found?"

Opening the can, Wren dips a finger in the meat and holds it out to the bundle of towel which gives a pleased 'meep' before a little black nose pokes out from the cotton followed by a pink tongue lapping up the dregs from her fingers. With the cat's apparent approval, Wren pours the rest of the tuna out into a bowl and slides it over.

Silje jumps from the towel and dives headfirst into her meal despite Wren's cautionary chide of "Don't eat too quickly," delivered as she scratches behind her ears.

"On my—on Miyazaki–sama's computer, I found a search history."

Ah... The research Wren conducted before Hikaru summoned her.

FOUR OF PENTACLES

Two Days Ago – 8th Day in the Month of Falling – Snowfall Palace – The Jade Wing – 3:23AM

The monitors around the Jade Wing's sitting room are powered down in slumber. As Wren sets foot on the tatami, a few floor panels light up.

"Mistress Wren, has something disturbed your slumber?"

AYA's mechanical voice is surprisingly gentle at this time of night. The A.I. doesn't turn on the lights, but she does initiate the starlights scattered along the edges of the sitting room.

Wren doesn't answer, busying herself instead with picking up some of the mess she and Kaito made of his desk during their earlier activities. A shiver runs up her spine at the memory. Just a few hours ago, he'd tilted her backward on this very surface, gone to his knees, and painted a portrait of worship into her body.

"Would you like me to wake Miyazaki–sama?"

"No, thank you, AYA," she answers, trying her best to make it sound like a command as she powers up one of the computer monitors. Wren opens a search engine and types in "Chiamaka Nagi." The pop-up results are to be expected. Biographical information such as family history, education, birthday, marital information, and a coronation date.

Wait... A coronation date?

Chiamaka was crowned the Orisha of Ebele? But Zenza is the rightful monarch. As Chike and Atzi's firstborn child, Zenza should have been named Orisha after Absko's death.

Brow furrowed, Wren clicks on Chiamaka's coronation date and finds the details of the events leading up to Chiamaka's ascension. Zenza was indeed crowned Orisha after her grandfather's death. However, since Zenza had been but a toddler at the time, a regent was set in place until she was old enough to rule. The regent chosen had been Chiamaka Nagi, Chike's younger sister and Zenza paternal aunt.

Chiamaka's regency in Zenza's name had not been peaceful by any means, but the woman apparently did a substantial amount of good rebuilding Ebele's economic structures after the upheaval caused by Absko's murder, not to mention the government having to deal with the countless lords and ladies vying for the throne in the absence of an heir old enough to reign. There had been enough civil dispute to warrant bloodshed, but Chiamaka stood firm her niece be named monarch, acting in her stead until Zenza reached the age of maturity.

This had been the standard for six years until a coup d'état forced an eight-year-old Zenza out of Ebele. A wretched claim began to circulate that Zenza was not truly Prince Chike's daughter and that Atzi, whom no one had seen hide nor hair of since Chike's death, fabricated the pregnancy through witchcraft. The rumor claimed that during the start of the war against Seraphim, Atzi, out of desperation to maintain political support from Ebele after the downfall of Deriva, conceived the child under a blood moon with the help of her witch half-sister. The child's conception, therefore, was a ploy to keep Chike's father from dissolving the union under the pretense Atzi failed to uphold her duty as a wife and provide Chike an heir.

"What a load of bull! Chike loved Atzi, and I was nowhere near Atzi when she became pregnant with Zenza."

"If Lady Wren would like, I can assist her in her search."

AYA's tinny voice sounds from the monitor in front of her. Wren just about jumps out of her skin at the unexpected address.

"I don't need help from someone who only exists when the electricity is on," she huffs under her breath.

Wren lifts her hands as the window she currently has open closes without her command. "Hey!"

"I suppose Lady Wren does not wish for me to pull up the exact information she is looking for then, despite saving her hours upon hours of searching through internet generated drivel."

¡Mira la! *Que chiflada esta.*

A new window pops open, and the image at the top of the page stops Wren's heart:

A beautifully decorated ivory pot, inlaid with finely carved coral at the base, painted images of colorful fish and sea life dance around the jar's belly. On top is supposed to be a lid crusted with pearl and blue topaz to remind Atzi of home, but in the picture, the jar sits open, its contents scattered on the table in a bunch of plastic baggies like evidence taken from a crime scene.

It was her wedding gift to her sister. Wren had the pot commissioned by one of the finest potters in Mareatierra, the capital city of Deriva. Wren painted the design herself to be baked into the clay. The herbs inside were a simple tea mixture designed to calm the nerves and increase the flow of blood for better comfort in lovemaking.

All of the rumors against Zenza's legitimacy stemmed from this jar of herbs brought to light six years ago. But Wren made the silly herbal mixture before magic held any part in her life. The recipe came straight from her mother's journal, one Freya favored both for her own marital bed and as a tonic for a number of young maidens on their wedding nights. Wren had even gotten the vast majority of the ingredients from the villa kitchens.

It was hardly the kind of thing for forging a false pregnancy. That kind of magic is dark and usually requires a hefty blood sacrifice, usually in the form of an unborn fetus, and most definitely could not be accomplished with a handful of tea leaves. Tea leaves! Tea leaves used as evidence of witchcraft. What year is it? 1692 A.D? Are they in Salem, Massachusetts? No! It's 1877 A.P.! Two thousand years of "progress" and they're still using boiled herbs as evidence of witchcraft!

Humans never change. They just get more scared.

"So, someone found the tea leaves I gave my sister almost seventeen years ago and decided it was proof my niece was not only illegitimate but also the product of witchcraft."

The rumors apparently laid the foundation for Chiamaka's ascent to true queenhood. A nine-month long campaign against Ebelean loyalists and Zenza's supporters in which a rather unexpected name begins to share the page with Chiamaka's: Donarick J. Thames, the current Primarch of the League. After the photo and evidence of Wren's apparent tampering with the royal bloodline of Ebele, pictures of Chiamaka always featured Thames at her side like a doting lover. It comes as no surprise to

Wren when she finds Chiamaka married Thames not two months before her coronation, a scandalously short time in which to hold two major royal events.

How inauspicious...

"I see you are catching up on what has happened in your absence."

Hikaru's voice filters in through the speakers, and when Wren clicks over, the man's face pops up on the monitor.

"Emperor," she acknowledges. Odd, it's, she checks the timestamp on the monitor, three in the morning. What is he doing still awake? "Trouble sleeping?"

He ignores her.

"Are you finding the information useful?"

Interestingly enough, there is a distinct lack of animosity in his tone. Being cordial tonight, Emperor?

"Not sure what I was expecting," she confesses. "But it wasn't this."

Hikaru hums. "Your brother nearly went to war with Ebele over it."

"I bet he did," she mumbles, crossing her arms across her chest.

"Were it not for Deriva's lack of military resources, I have no doubt he would have, but your brother is capable of making logical decisions when necessary. Instead of declaring outright war, he demanded your niece be put in his custody and named her his heir."

"Makes sense why Zenza was meeting Xipilli and not an Ebelean escort on the light rail."

"I was hoping to catch you awake, actually. If you wouldn't mind, I would like to discuss something with you in private."

A short hour later, Wren would be pulling out of Snowfall's garage under Hikaru's supervision, Atalia's credentials in her pocket, and a thinly veiled warning to stay as far away from the Miyazaki family, more specifically Kaito, as possible.

FOUR OF PENTACLES

10th Day in the Month of Falling – 7:22AM – Chairomura

Yet here she sits with one Miyazaki trainee discussing tea while another sleeps off the aftereffects of a magical malady.

Wren checks the heat on the stove, making sure she doesn't burn the oats she is now stirring into the water.

"And what of this research you found on Miyazaki–sama's computer hub?"

"Well, I did a bit more digging, and I remembered you said you saw Summer Helsdottir on the light rail." Renki devolves into an excitable spiel on his research. "The summoner was supposedly imprisoned after being arrested for several murders in Lorelei. You and Miyazaki–sama were part of the retinue that tracked her down, actually."

Yes, she remembers. It had been their first mission together, her and Kaito. It had also been their first—ahem—time together. Deflowered in a tomb... Dear stars, how fitting!

"After her capture, she was placed into General Llywelyn's custody, but when Seraphim started recruiting witches to their cause, he gave her free reign to do as she pleased so long as she helped during the war."

Wren had known about this, had found out not long after her return to the warfront, but Summer hadn't been captured during the final raid on the pontiflex.

"There are no records of her anywhere for nearly five years until The Morrigan was murdered."

"The Morrigan was murdered?"

Renki nods. "Yes, a summoned netherbeast carrying Summer's wild magic signature. Thames made a big show of hunting the witch down afterward. Her execution is what solidified his standing as the Primarch, but the timing of everything seemed off, so I looked up a video of the execution."

"Timing?"

Renki hums. "Summer was executed three days before Chiamaka publicly pronounced Zenza—" He cuts himself off, looking around and lowering his voice. "Pronounced the princess illegitimate based on herbs found in her mother's possession."

The timing *is* pretty coincidental.

"Are you implying the two situations are related?"

"I found a video of the execution, and I—I thought there was something odd about it, but I couldn't put my finger on it. Maybe you could take a look?"

Wren turns from the stove to look at the holo opening over Renki's palm.

As a public and apparently high-profile execution, the League's most important leaders are there: Xipilli, Lockecraft, Hikaru, Jamar, and Chiamaka, sitting next to Donarick Thames. The woman handcuffed on screen looks like Summer. She also sounds like her, screaming and thrashing around like a lunatic.

"Betrayer! How dare you do this to me! You're making a mistake! I'm not her! She cursed me! I'm telling you! I've been cursed! Call Nocturne, she'll tell you. Ask her! It isn't me. She's a witch, but she isn't me! I'm not a witch! I'm not a witch!"

She screams endlessly as they strap her to the pyre post. Raving screams, frantic and desperate to get someone to believe her. No one does. They light torches instead, a simple flick of a switch, easier than turning on an electric chair. Wren turns away as the flames rise.

"Shouldn't you have access restrictions on that thing? I hardly think any father would approve of their teenager looking up footage from an execution."

Renki doesn't even flinch. "Didn't you find it odd?"

"I find it morbid and unjust." As Renki frowns, Wren turns her back on the teen despite knowing exactly what he is talking about.

"But Gewalt's murder! Thames managing to capture her so quickly! And Chiamaka, well, I mean what she did to Princess Zenza right after... It would be like the Grandmaster disowning

Emperor Hikaru and Miyazaki–sama. Surely, you can see what I'm saying!"

Almost like 'Chiamaka's' personality did a 180 after Summer's so-called execution. Coincidence? Not likely.

"I understand exactly what you're saying, Renki, but..."

Wren glances down at her arm. Three cuts still mar the skin there. She's bled through the bandage again. It had been bleeding more while she was around Summer. Shit... Could it be...

Chiamaka is dead. Her ghost has been haunting her. Chiamaka is dead, and up until a few minutes ago, her ghost was a faceless burning woman, and 'Summer's' botched execution by fire took place just days before Chiamaka's personality did a polar shift. Summer swapped places with Chiamaka for the execution. Summer has been impersonating Chiamaka for the last six years.

"But what?" he asks.

She swallows. This is not an appropriate conversation to be had in this kitchen, so she smiles at the child and diverts from the topic at hand.

"And why, pray tell, have you been researching political happenings from when you were still learning to walk?"

"Lady Wren, I'm fifteen, not ten. I was already four years into my training when this all happened."

Indeed.

"I still fail to see what this has to do with you."

"My father taught me to never stand by in the face of injustice. He also taught me to never take on a situation without first understanding what you're walking into."

"Wise words. How did your father react when his son told him he would be venturing out on his own despite such words of wisdom?"

Renki's face crumbles.

"He, uh... He doesn't know I left."

Wren quirks an eyebrow up. How intriguing! A Miyazaki teenager with a rebellious streak. No wonder Hikaru wanted her gone. He has enough on his plate.

"Your old man doesn't know you're here?"

"He would have just banned me from coming, and then I would get no answers whatsoever. Hardly logical, no matter his good intentions. My uncle always says he's overprotective of me. Has been ever since my mother died, not that I remember how he was before. It's been so long."

There's a pained glimmer in the boy's eyes. The watery green reminds Wren of someone long dead, but she pushes the thought aside as her own eyes trail to the lavender sash at Renki's hip.

She notices for the first time that Kai is wearing a plain gray and lavender kimono.

"Kai, your mother?"

"She passed away four days ago."

"I'm so sorry."

He nods, his expression tight. For the first time, she wishes he didn't have neural guards, so she could wash the grief away if only for a little while. Curse the boundaries of her empathy. What good is it if she can't comfort the people she cares most about?

"Her funeral pyre is today." He pauses for a long moment before his silver gaze turns back to her. "Will you attend?"

"I thought the monarch's pyre was only to be witnessed by family."

Kai chin drops down, as a means of affirming her statement.

"The Miyazaki family will invite to witness whomever they so choose."

She bites her lip for a second, before nodding her head, the magnitude of what he is asking not entirely lost to her. It weighs heavy in her heart.

"I will be there."

His lips quirk upward, and he reaches a hand forward to touch her cheek.

"What color should I wear?"

"Lavender. Wear lavender."

Renki looks at her with too-open eyes.

"Why was she calling for you?"

And isn't that the question Wren doesn't have an answer to?

FOUR OF PENTACLES

"Something smells good! Is that breakfast? I'm starving!" Zenza's shout pulls Wren from the past. She turns from Renki to turn off the heat.

"Hope you kids like oatmeal."

"We're not kids! *Achoo!*"

Wren smiles at Zenza's shout, indignant even through the closed kitchen doors. As though to acknowledge she's the source of the princess's plight with allergies, Silje looks up from her bowl of fish, blinks, wrinkles her nose, and then returns to her breakfast.

7:57AM

There's a small tele-monitor anchored above one of the kitchen stoves. Akari finds the remote, switching the stations to a news broadcast.

"My staff and I are looking forward to hosting some of the greatest men and women of the League over the next few days. It has been too long since last Sekhmeti hosted the greatest event of the year, and we hope to do the 263rd Technomancer Trials the glory they deserve."

Jamar Sahra, looking regal and grown up in his father's regnal coat and brocade, smiles into the camera from the Shard's conference room. The pharaoh talks about how honored he is to once again host the Technomancer Trials this coming spring and gushes about how this year's planning conference will prove to be most enlightening for all in attendance.

"With new inventions to exhibit and a fresh batch of applicants to evaluate, Sekhmeti is looking forward to dazzling everyone in attendance."

The camera then pans to a man dressed in a smart white tuxedo accented with a red pocket swatch and tie. Anglo-Saxon, sporting a tanning-bed-earned orangey tan, dusty blond hair and eyes such a pale blue the irises seem to bleed into the whites of his eye, Donarick J. Thames, the current Primarch of the technomancer council, ascended to his position by flushing out his predecessor's killer.

Wren only met him a handful of times in her previous life. He flunked out during their trials and earned himself a pardon for killing his own father in the war against Seraphim. She vaguely remembers him acting as a show monkey for Rameses, sidling up to the newly elected Primarch right up until his death not four months later. To think such a meek personality elevated himself to the position of Primarch on his own standing?

Next to him, dressed in an exquisite sari and matching veil pinned to frame her face and cascade down her back, stands Chiamaka looking delicate and demure but powerful in her own right as the Orisha of Ebele.

No one would notice just looking at her, but Wren knows where to look: bruises covered by foundation around her throat and a split lip masked with the reddest of lipsticks. And the veil, anchored just so to hide the horns Wren has no doubt lie beneath the richly woven cloth.

It's Summer. She feels it in her bones. Summer is masquerading as Chiamaka, and Thames is Chiamaka's husband. Thames is both Summer's soulmate and her tormentor.

Wren's eyes glaze over. Chiamaka's undead face hovers before her, yelling at her. "Betrayer!" the ghost had shouted. Just like 'Summer' shouted on her death pyre.

Beside her, Renki refills the sink to take care of dishes as the news broadcast shifts over, and a local news reporter stands with a microphone, looking at the camera. She seems to be standing at the checkpoint outside Chairomura.

"The quarantine on Chairomura has been lifted. Reports from a technomancer inside the city confirm the mysterious disease not only contained but cured."

The broadcast doesn't name the mysterious technomancer responsible for the report which isn't unusual. Such things are usually kept top secret until a formal briefing takes place, and even then, the best technomancers care not for fame and glory. Technomancers like Kaito, she thinks fondly before shaking herself out of that particular reverie. If there is a technomancer sniffing about, she needs to make herself scarce and she needs to do it quickly.

But before she can just disappear. She has something to deal with first.

"Are you gonna finish that?"

"There are plenty of leftovers in the pot."

More accurately, she has three teenage somethings to deal with.

Akari is ravenous. So much so, if Wren didn't know better, she would worry the girl was still infected with the blixvi's disease. She isn't. Just a teenage girl taking her fill of the meager meal Wren scrounged together from oats, hot water, and a bit of the powdered cream they keep on the coffee bars at cheap diners. Probably making up for her calorie deficit the day before.

Zenza's having none of it, but Renki silently shifts his bowl over. "You can have the rest of mine, Akari."

"*Xièxiè!*"

And Akari digs in.

Wren's lips quirk up on one side. How does one keep three teenagers in one place long enough for a responsible adult to come and claim them? Silje finished her breakfast a while ago and has now taken to grooming her face and paws.

"You feeling better?"

Silje gives her a sidelong stare.

"Did your tousan ever reply back to you, Renki?"

Renki flips open his comm to check.

"He left me on 'read' again."

"My uncle's been messaging me for the last two hours." Zenza chuckles, looking at her own comm unit. "He's probably having a conniption about it even though he should be on his way to Aureas by now."

"Aren't you afraid of being punished?"

"He'll threaten me all he wants, maybe assign me extra repetitions and laps during training, but he's all bark, no bite. Even if he did ground me or something, I would just sneak out again. It drives him crazy. The first time I snuck out he got so flustered he almost called me Wr—" Zenza cuts herself off. "I mean, he said I was too much like... well like *her*."

"Who? Your mom?"

"No, my aunt."

"Chiamaka?"

"No, you dolt, my other aunt. You know, the one who killed my father."

Akari's mouth makes a perfect O. The two Murasakan adepts shift awkwardly, Akari glancing 'Atalia's' direction. Zenza for her part just sighs aloud and offers a teasing grin toward Renki and Akari.

"Don't tell me you're afraid of getting caught."

"Not afraid, exactly."

"I'm afraid. Renki's tousan is scary when he's stern."

"Look, we're not going to get caught. Besides we're with Miss Vaishi. She can get us across the border. Right, Miss Vaishi?"

Wren glances at the comm unit left unlocked by Renki's elbow and smirks at the teenager. Nope... Not quite, kid.

Wren steps out of the diner, Silje on her shoulder, with one more glance back to where she's left the kids. They'll be fine. Xipilli, Hikaru, or perhaps even Renki's mysterious "Tousan" will arrive soon to pick them up. How much trouble they end up in when they're found wholly depends on which gets to them first.

The sun is rising on the city. It smells like petrichor and damp concrete, glittering puddles of water on the ground from the night's storm.

Four Of Pentacles

Reactivating Renki's ward, Wren rubs her nose in Silje's newly clean lemon-scented flank.

"You sure about this? You're not exactly at 100%."

The mew she gets in reply is answer enough. Wren turns toward the border crossing, her pack strapped to her back. Silje wobbles ever so slightly before hunkering down across the bag on her shoulder. She's purring.

Both of them are ready to be out of this wretched city.

"Zenza Nagi: Princess or Product of Witchcraft?"

"Chiamaka Nagi Denounces Heir to the Throne—Dons the Mantle of Orisha Herself"

"Will Xipilli Moctezumo Declare War on Ebele over Niece's legitimacy?"

"Witchcraft and Nepotism: Did the Songstress of Lorelei Plant Her Protege in the Ebelean Court?"

Headlines from The League Tribunal
1871 A.P.

22

THE HIGH PRIESTESS (REVERSED)

Downtown Chairomura – 7:24 AM –Kaito

THE GRAY MOLD SEEPING FROM THE BITE wound on his leg has vanished, leaving behind clean, slightly raised skin. His scanners tell him the infection is cleared out. Not a trace left.

There are people passed out in the streets. Heaps of infected lie comatose on the ground, his readings letting him know their ailment no longer plagues them. They will recover.

With the disease cured, Kaito commands a lift on the quarantine, summoning military aid into the city, directing them first to the sanctuary where he left the townspeople locked up in a ward. His instructions for the coming guard as regards their burning someone alive are clear: investigate, arrest, and arrange for trial. Apocalyptic circumstance or no, murder is murder, and he will see to it the woman, Sarah Lee, receives the full penalty for her actions against Zhou Feng and his family.

Sonata

A message comes in on his neural net. "Downtown Chairomura, Feliz Bordello Cafe, Kitchen Storage. Please retrieve ASAP."

The message scrolls across Kai's interface, sent from Renki's comm unit. Tanaka's corpse smolders, various sparks crackle as his internal wiring melts and the fuses sizzle. Kaito closes his eyes, offering a prayer for peace over the man's body, then turns to the coordinates AYA drops into his tracers.

By the time he arrives, the sun is high enough to start drying the evidence of the night's rain.

The diner is quaint and unobtrusive. The glass front is broken, but a ward is erected in its place to keep out shamblers, a ward he recognizes as one made by Renki. He disperses the ward, stepping through the broken doorway to the sound of bickering teenagers.

"I told you she wasn't to be trusted."

"Princess, with no amount of respect, will you give it a rest? She didn't do anything to us."

Akari sounds more than a little fed up with the grumbling Zenza.

"'Didn't do anything to us'! She tied us to an ice cream machine!"

"But she didn't hurt us," he hears Renki say. "She saved our lives and cured Akari and probably the rest of the city."

"You don't know that. All you know is she left, and when she came back, Akari wasn't puking black anymore. She'll probably come back later to put us in a stew."

"Yes," huffs Akari. "That's why she fed us oatmeal and suffered through your poor excuse for tortillas."

"I didn't see you complaining when you were eating them."

"I was dying!"

"Yeah, you were quieter, too."

"That's enough, you two."

"Renki, don't you dare—"

Zenza chokes on her own spit at the sight of Kaito in the kitchen door. The three regard him in stunned silence before all of the sudden...

"Tousan! I can explain!"

"Miyazaki–sama! This was entirely Renki's idea!"

"I had nothing to do with this!"

...All three teenagers burst out to varying degrees of explanation. He lifts a hand into the air, and the sudden rush of protest ceases, the three trainees cowed by his call for silence. Though Akari still has the gall to whisper something in Renki's ear to the boy's responding "Shh!" Renki, for his part, doesn't cower at Kaito's stern stance. He instead puffs himself up, squaring his shoulders as Kaito deliberates exactly how to handle this situation.

He should, by rights, be furious. Not only did they leave Yuki ga Furu unchaperoned; they left without telling anyone where they were going and walked directly into a hot zone. They could have been kidnapped, killed, or cursed. Although, it sounds as though Akari was indeed cursed.

But he isn't. Instead, he is simply relieved. Relieved they are unharmed. Relieved they are found. Most of all, he's relieved Wren had the foresight to tie them down to one place—thank Kami the witch didn't leave them to their own devices.

"Renki."

It is neither a question nor a reprimand, just a gentle exhalation of the boy's name.

"Look I know you're probably really angry at me right now, but—"

Kaito holds up his hand again and the teen falls quiet.

"Where is she?"

"Lady W—Miss Vaishi?"

Kaito nods.

"I don't know."

"She took that beast and said something about getting across the border."

"Beast?"

"A cat," inserts Akari. "She had a black cat when she came back."

A black cat. No, it couldn't be. "Silje..."

"How did you know its name?" asks Zenza.

Without answering, Kaito rises from the floor, hurrying to the door.

"Wait! Aren't you going to untie us?"

Nope. Wren had the right idea tying up unruly teenagers so they don't get into trouble.

"When I return."

"But Tousan—!"

But Kaito is out the door, and Renki's call goes unanswered.

Stopping only to reclaim his lightcycle, scraped up and dented but still functional, he races to the border.

He sees her, standing in a circle of magic on the edge of the bridge, her familiar twining between her feet. Atalia's blonde hair whips around her head in a self-made torrent of wild magic. The river below, as though responding to her power, lashes at the shoreline. The wind whistles almost as violently as when the blixvi poured its cursed rains on the city.

"Wren!" he shouts, but his call goes unheard and unanswered as the field of magic collapses, and Wren disappears in a burst of emerald light.

Gone, and once more, his witch is beyond his reach.

Fourteen Years Ago – The Abbey – 10th Day in the Month of Light, 1864 – Summer Solstice

Days pass in a blur. Meetings and discussions, other funerals and processions, memorial services for the victorious dead. At least, now Wren is awake. When he is not taxed by commitments and responsibilities, he has someone outside of his family to meld with once more. As her strength returns, they fall into their old patterns. Carefree interactions reminiscent of their summit days, though he is not nearly as recalcitrant as his sixteen-year-old self once was.

THE HIGH PRIESTESS (REVERSED)

Words still fail him from time to time, their weight too heavy in his heart to utter aloud. In these moments, Wren, light and breezy at his side, is happy to fill the silence with song and chatter. She particularly enjoys reading aloud or tinkering with odds and ends, muttering to him about this or that as she goes. Sometimes she'll even coax him into holding or twisting something she is working with even though she could accomplish the task just as easily with her telekinesis.

He gets the aching sense she's trying to make everything as alright as she possibly can. She is not disingenuous nor is she putting on a show, her actions purely her own, but sometimes he finds her staring off into space. Like there is a cloud hovering over her she cannot banish, and on these days, when she isn't as bright, when the dark shadow of her trauma haunts her footsteps, he'll gently coax her from whatever fevered activity she is in the midst of undertaking and settle her beside him either outside in the grass or in the cool darkness of her sitting room. She'll lay her head in his lap or lean against his back, and he'll play his holoboard or comb his fingers through her hair until the shadow passes and she once more sends a smile his way.

Then there are the particularly gray days, the difficult days when both of them feel battered by the maelstrom... when neither of them can properly ward away the silence, when the ghosts seem more real than the person they sit with.

Today is one such day.

They are settled back-to-back, Wren in black and he in lavender, on the veranda of his family's guest house on this cold, gray, rainy day they share. Metaphorically "stormy" that is. Ironically enough, it is the brightest day of the year. The day of the summer solstice when the higurashi cry from the treetops and cicadas trill their mating calls. The sun is high, moving at leisure across the sky, tucking itself away behind a few fluffy white clouds every so often before returning with a blinding brilliance. Even the permafrost recedes as Ör attempts to boil the air around them, but at least, there's enough of a breeze to shush the humidity away.

One of Wren's tinkering projects rests on the step beside him, unfinished, pieces scattered haphazardly about, while his keyboard hums with purple life under his hands, cool despite it being the hottest part of the day. He half-heartedly fingers the keys in an absentminded attempt to find the will to play. He hasn't any idea how long he's been trying to decide on a piece when Wren starts humming, joining her wordless voice with his piano. He isn't sure which one of them finds the melody first, him or her, but they fold together like an unwritten sonnet. At some point, she lifts her hand toward the window and a shimmering wisp of viridian sparkles from her fingertips to dance and twine around them. It is the first time she has used magic in front of him since her waking, and as wary as he is of it, he cannot help but admit it beautiful, a visual manifestation of their duet.

Is this how we heal? He wonders. *A witch and a technomancer? Licking our wounds with song and spreading balm over the burn of war in small strokes that seem ineffectual at first but slowly coax new skin to grow?*

He watches the spell react to her songweave, lifting the various bobbles from the step and clicking parts into place. Her fingers dance and direct the instruments, a wrench twisting one way while a screwdriver spins another, as the rhythms fall into harp-like cadenzas and blue-tinged ascensions. As they make music together, the sun begins its descent, yawning across the horizon in purples and oranges. Wren's voice drifts off as the final chords of the piano vibrate through the thick humid air, and when Kaito looks to the tangle of Wren's magic, fading back into Wren's meridians, there is a mechanical bird with a wind-up key at its back.

When he winds it up, the bird's beak opens in a robotic mimicry of chirping and a sweet tune chimes from its belly like a music box but in a wind-up toy. It even walks, one metal-plated foot in front of the other, marching along like a tiny, singing, shudder-stop soldier.

The High Priestess (reversed)

"There was an orphanage in the town where I stayed after I got away. I wonder if I could make enough of these for all of the kids."

Wren never speaks of the time before her return, when she was a prisoner of war and then lost to heal and recover alone, and he never asks. She doesn't tell him how she became a witch, and to be honest, it doesn't really matter. The war is over, the magic fever is over, and she is here. They are both here despite the countless others who are not.

"Perhaps for Yule, you could send gifts for the children."

When she replies "Maybe," her lips brush against the skin of his neck.

Later that night, as the sun sets on the longest day of the year and the bonfires are lit for midsummer celebrations, the torrent of emotions in his chest begin to ebb. As the music from the festival and the noise of the crowd beyond the basilica's walls rise with spirals of grey smoke, Kaito and Wren retreat from the veranda into the privacy of Kaito's quarters, and she allows him to embrace her.

She holds him, a tether to reality keeping the numbness at bay, and hums a soothing melody. It envelops him, coating his wounds like a healing balm, and for a moment, he wonders if this is another, gentler, aspect of her magic. Life-giving and green with creation rather than death-dealing and poisonous with necrosis, but he banishes the thought in favor of sinking further into her touch. She undresses him, peeling away the starch cotton of his robes to smooth a hand over his chest and the nodes at his collarbones, alight with violet light, while he unravels the bindings of her corset and dress.

She follows him as he pulls her backward into his rooms, his hands at her waist and hips as she leans up for a kiss. Guiding him to the bed, she lifts herself up to sit astride him, the wide collar of her chemise hanging lopsided and limp around her shoulders to reveal one pert breast, untouched by the sun while the other hides beneath the fabric. She heaves a sigh as he laves attention to the mound, rounder and fuller than he remembers before tugging more cloth aside to mouth the other. His hands reach to coax her chemise from her body so he can see all of her, but she stops him.

"Wren, do you need me to stop?"

"No, it's just..." She hides her face behind the dark sheet of her hair. "I–I don't want you to see. Not yet at least."

Taken aback, a number of things come to mind that he wants to say to reassure her. That he wouldn't care. That no marks of her experience could disgust him. That she's beautiful to him regardless of any scars which now mar her body. That no matter her hardships, she is perfect.

But he says none of this.

Instead, he brushes the hair out of her face and presses his lips to hers, eliciting a surprised hiccup from her.

His reassurance is not what she needs right now. There is nothing he can say, no matter how true the words, to make her feel comfortable in her own skin. Her body is forever her own, and what she shares of it with him is her choice. So, he draws her left arm up, brings the limb to his lips, sets a kiss where Mano used to sit, and murmurs, "When you're ready."

Her relieved smile is worth so much more than the sight of naked skin.

Kai and Wren make love.

Wren's thighs frame Kaito's hips as she shifts above him in a dance of give and take. Kai's hands glide down the sway of her back as she rocks gently in his arms, his length pulsing into her very depths, hot and piercing as she embraces him both inside and out. This is the first time they've been intimate since their volatile encounter in the hedge maze, and where that encounter was a violent tearing off of a bandage, this is a soundscape to ardor. A sedate coupling more about blurring the edges of their beginnings and endings than chasing a climax.

She paints a portrait of worship over his face and chest with her lips, twining her breath with his and whispering words into his skin in a language he can't understand but can grasp the meaning of anyway. She is like the shallow waters of the reef, beautiful and approachable, a place of hidden wonders and brilliant colors yet innately connected to the vast mysterious sea, with its powerful currents and fathomless depths.

She coaxes him to ecstasy with her slow, steady undulations. As she tenses over him in her own culminating passion, he rolls her onto her back, plunging into her. She arches, breasts straining against the soft cotton of her chemise, and when her indicia manifests at her brow followed by the cascading glitter of her wild script, a vibrant blue-green dancing across her skin in the darkness, he pulls her in closer, slots his mouth over hers, and allows himself to wish this moment between them could stretch forever.

It isn't until later when they are lying in each other's arms, content in their afterglow, that he asks the question which has been needling him for the last two weeks.

"Come to Murasaki with me."

Wren, half dozing at his side, sniffles. "Hmm?"

Her voice is thick with near sleep and exhaustion, the magic she worked in junction with their lovemaking having tired her reserves, and he remembers with a pang of guilt that, though her medical accoutrements are gone, removed completely just a few days ago, she is still recovering.

"Never mind. I'll tell you in the morning."

"Tell me."

"You need your rest."

"I don't want to sleep. I want to hear what Kaito–kun has to say," she mumbles fondly into his shoulder, drowsy but still stubborn, so he deflects. Save the serious conversations for later.

"I said 'you're beautiful.' My memory banks are insufficient compared to when you're with me."

Wren sighs, a smile quaking her lips. "Kaito–kun is a flatterer. Where did you learn to say such things?"

"This coming from the girl who once said I lacked charm."

She laughs, sleepily at his joke. She is so tired. When was the last time she truly slept?

"Go to sleep, *Kaiyo*."

"I don't want to have nightmares."

"If you do, I'll wake you."

"Promise?"

"I promise."

Kaito wakes to an empty bed. Wren's flighty cursive greets him from a hastily written note on the bedside table.

My brother called a meeting. I didn't want to wake you.

It's signed with a kissy face and an angular 'W.'

He sets the note on his pillow and rises to begin his day.

With Wren's recovery, the Alliance pushes for the votes to be tallied, and the decision goes through, with Irene, Wren, Kaito, and a handful of others voting against, marginally outweighed by the votes for, and Pharaoh Rameses is elected the first Primarch of the newly established Technomancer Council. Flanked by a cabinet consisting of President Gewalt, an aged technomancer named Finnick Lockecraft, his son Jamar Sahra, and lastly, most surprisingly, Xipilli Moctezumo, the Technomancer Council begins its glorious undertaking of restructuring the League.

Proposals are made on a nearly hourly basis to be voted on by the other technomancers, and the first restructuring: the weighing of votes. Whose say has greater weight, and whose has less? A simplification on voting numbers, separated by country with country leaders gaining a percentile of the total based on how many technomancers bend a knee to their flag.

As Emperor, Hikaru takes his responsibility in this incredibly seriously, weighing the pros and cons for Murasaki no Yama, ensuring he makes the best decisions for his people, seeking counsel with Fumiko, Kaito, and the other Murasakan technomancers often, but Kaito's vote on matters becomes proxied by his brother where before he could vote his sway himself. He still has a voice within the council; he can make proposals and argue his ideas, but ultimately, he holds no jurisdiction over the decisions made by the council as a whole.

The opposite occurs in relation to Wren.

With Xipilli acting as a cabinet member, Deriva's vote falls on Wren's shoulders as the younger sibling of the Vulcan and his acting second-in-command. Wren, who never cared an iota for political matters, now becomes the sole voice of her country excepting when she gives her right to Irene or Quetzal, not that she speaks for many, Deriva's roster of technomancers nearly caput in light of Seraphim's hostile takeover. The meetings wear on her. An ever-present bottle of absinthe at her elbow during long meetings, her empathy grating on her nerves until she gives her proxy to Irene. The second time this happens, people take notice, and Xipilli plays it off as an unexpected setback to her recovery.

The next day, Wren completely shirks her duties, and when Hikaru asks after her, Xipilli rolls his eyes, stating the behavior was pretty typical of Wren.

"She's never taken matters of state seriously. At least, Quetzal is here instead."

During the midday break, his brother informs him they will be leaving for Murasaki in two days' time. "You've been more than diligent in these political affairs, but I know they tax you."

Kaito regards his brother over the edge of a recording of the morning meeting's minutes.

"It is my obligation."

Hikaru nods in understanding. An outburst from a group of Aighnean adepts, arm wrestling with their mechanical arms and causing a general ruckus, draws Kaito's attention. Hikaru tuts as the smaller of the two men wins, his robotic limb letting off a bit of steam as the boys around him slap him on the back in congratulations.

"I'm thinking we should return to Snowfall soon. There isn't much more of import to be discussed, and most everything left can be handled remotely. Many of the other nations are planning their departures as well. Besides, Mother's ashes need to be placed at their final resting place."

On Shinka's grounds next to their father's in their ancestral hall. For the time being, her urn rests on a makeshift altar, incense burning on either side. Fumiko has made a point to clean and replace the offerings daily, and Kaito and Hikaru start their day offering incense and prayers.

"You and Lady Wren seem to have fully reconciled?"

Though there is much left unsaid between Wren and Kaito, he hums his agreement. Perhaps such things need not be discussed. How easily they've fallen back into each other despite everything. There is plenty of time now, surely. No reason to rush forward, especially if she acquiesces to something he has been pondering for the last few days.

"I heard Xipilli mention to Chike that the Derivan envoy would be departing for the isles later tonight."

"Tonight?"

"I assume Lady Wren will be departing with him. Why don't you spend the afternoon with her? It may be a while yet before the opportunity arises for you to see her again. And didn't you mention something you wanted to discuss in relation to her?"

Yes, he did, but he needs to speak to Wren first.

He finds her sitting in the Vatidome's library. She's opened one of the windows and leans heavily against the pane where a black cat is perched. She runs her fingers over the animal's head, gives it a scratch behind the ear, and nuzzles its cheek with her nose. Black cats and witches. It's terribly cliche, a motif generated centuries ago to spread fear and paranoia, yet here is a black cat settled with his witch. He is loath to interrupt the scene, but as soon as he steps through the door, large ambery green eyes find him, and the animal hops to its feet.

Wren looks up to see him but instead of the smile he expects to find, she instead panics, bolting to her feet to clean off the table in front of her.

THE HIGH PRIESTESS (REVERSED)

"Kaito! Is the meeting over already?" she asks, scrambling to stack the various books and pages. The cat jumps onto the back of the chair she was in and stretches.

"No, simply stagnated by our inability to cement any decisions."

"Predictable." Now she smiles at him as she taps a stack of pages together. "Too many voices and not enough actual votes makes for a standstill every single time. I'm so done with these miserable old goats. And they are miserable, I promise you that. Half of them are worried their wives will find out about the mistresses. The other half are the wives and mistresses—Oh! Silje, don't knock that over!"

Wren's exclamation comes as the cat jumps to her worktable, knocking over a bowl. A muddy-green liquid of some kind splashes everywhere. She drops the materials in her arms, hand extended to the waterfall of the concoction.

"Oh, you meddling thing!"

The cat yowls as though in response to the witch. Kaito bends to help her clean up the mess, but she stops him as whatever was in the bowl begins to burn through the table.

"Damn it! That's not supposed to happen."

Before his eyes, the liquid seeps out of the table, swirling in a perfect orb in midair, before funneling itself into a nearby glass bottle. Wren sighs in relief, and as he looks at her, the triskele on her brow fades back into her skin.

"Thanks," she snips at the cat.

Another yowl.

"I'm not hiding anything."

An annoyed mew.

"Well, if you think so, you say it then."

Another sound from the animal.

"You can speak to animals."

Wren flinches, green eyes wide like she forgot he was there for a moment. A piece of hair sticks up at the top of her head and her mouth makes a perfect 'o.' He bends to help her clean the mess.

"No, not exactly. Silje is just—I mean, everyone talks to animals, don't they?" She laughs awkwardly, picking up the vial of potion and sticking it in her bag before hissing "*Åka på*" at the cat.

She nudges the animal away, and it jumps out the window with an irritated huff, its tail puffed up with agitation.

"Silje?"

"Just a name. Everyone deserves a name, don't they?"

"She came to you while you were ill."

"Probably for the heating blankets."

He stares suspiciously after the animal.

"Kai, it's just a cat."

Is it though?

"What is this?"

He indicates the mess of scattered papers and sketches askew across the table. Ink-stained notes and open books. She has a table propped up on the far side, the screen showing a graph of various runic sigils beside a file which looks suspiciously like someone's medical records.

"It's nothing." Wren powers down the screen, her mad dash to pick everything up renewed now the corrosive substance isn't burning through the table. A corrosive substance he suspects she concocted. "Just some meaningless research. You can forget you even saw it."

He picks up a page to see Wren has scrawled the words "Wasting Hex" across the top. Whole passages are scratched out in angry, frustrated pen marks.

Return to Sender—Mirror, mirror, mirror back. Let me cleanse this wretched act. *Let me give you what you lack.*

Banishing Beelzebub

Rot Hel's Hexes. Avenging Angels. *No, Vengeance Devils.* Kissed by pestilence.

Typical healing potions didn't work on the patients Jessabelle tried to help. Animals can't get it, and I tried to infect myself. *I can't infect myself.* Witch Blood = Cure? *No, witches are just hex resistant. Like antibodies built in the body over exposure to a disease. Can you make a* vaccine?

THE HIGH PRIESTESS (REVERSED)

Need the source of the curse. What's the source?
Bone, beak, blood, flesh. That's how one can kill a pest.
"Wren."

"I know this looks bad, but I promise I was just testing out a theory."

What's worse? The longer he looks across her workspace, the more disturbed he becomes by her studies: notes written in vibrant red, crushed and caked to the paper as though clotted, powered roots and herbs crushed up and burned around a pile of what look to be chicken bones, and lastly, Lacuna, Wren's bone dagger, resting to her right on a silver tray. The blade is stained crimson with freshly spilt blood, and when he looks at Wren's arm, he sees the still bleeding cuts.

"It's nothing really. Just some research, and the bones are from the kitchen. They waste so much food around here, so Silje picked the scraps clean for me."

"Wren."

"All of the components are there. It should have worked, but I can't get it right. No matter what I change, the array is imbalanced."

"Wren."

"I think to make a counter-curse, you need something from the source of the curse. A part of the witch that cast it, but the witch was burned, so there's nothing left but ashes, but there has to be a way for another witch to reverse a curse. I just can't—"

As she carries on, her voice gradually becoming more and more manic, Kai makes his way around the table until he is right in front of her. She doesn't even seem to notice his approach. He puts his hands on her shoulders.

"Wren, you're bleeding."

She's crying, too. Not sobbing, just a single renegade tear trails down her cheek. He wipes it away and sits her back down in the chair to clean up her arm. Clearly, Wren was prepared to inflict harm on herself. There is a pile of bandages and disinfectant in her bag. She sits still and compliant as he works, cleaning and bandaging the cut. Thankfully, there is only one, shallow, made with the intent to draw a superficial amount of blood and not for

SONATA

a more concerning purpose. As though cutting isn't concerning all on its own.

"I know this looks bad, but I wasn't trying to hurt myself. I mean. At least, it's not a self-harm thing. I needed blood for the array. It only works with my own."

"Would not a needle have served you better?"

She shudders. "I can't stand needles."

"And what is this array for?"

Wren swallows, quiet for a long stretch of time, so long he wonders if she is even going to answer him. "I wanted to figure out if I could have cured your mother."

His eyes snap to hers. The blue in Wren's eyes is particularly vibrant today, nearly muting the green.

"The witch infected a lot of people with the same curse. Your mom, she fought it the longest. I didn't tell you because I didn't want you to have to think about it, and I didn't even know if I could figure it out, so I kept it to myself, and I... I can't help thinking if I'd been awake, I might have been able to help."

"How long have you been trying to figure out a counter-curse on your own?"

"A week."

He was afraid of that.

"Wren, my mother's death is not on your hands. She said herself her life was not a burden you should bear."

"She said that?"

Kaito nods.

"Right at the end. I begged her to hold on a little longer, hoping for—well, I don't know what I was hoping for. Regardless, whether or not you could have saved her is neither here nor there. The verdict has already come to pass."

Wren hangs her head down, staring at her lap.

"What's the point of being powerful if you can't save anyone you love?"

What's the point, indeed? A sentiment Kaito, too, has struggled with.

"Will you promise me something?"

THE HIGH PRIESTESS (REVERSED)

She looks at him curiously. "What?"

"Promise me you will stop practicing magic."

Her shoulders droop.

"Kai."

"Wren."

Wren's comm unit chimes, a sweet upbeat melody which has no place in this setting. Xipilli's name flashes across the screen.

"Sorry," she whispers, pulling the unit over and accepting the call.

"¿Mandé?"

Kaito can hear the tinny sound of Xipilli's voice over the line, but he can't make out the words. Quite possibly because the man is speaking in their home language. Wren frowns at whatever information she is being given and starts to say something in Derivan only to be cut off by her brother, and then the connection is severed.

Wren makes a frustrated sound. "Well, the council's adjourned. I don't know what stick crawled up his butt."

"Hikaru mentioned your envoy would be leaving tonight."

Wren nods.

"Xipilli dropped the bomb on me this morning. I figured I would work on this until the meetings were done for the day. Then I could find you before I had to leave later, but he now wants to leave in the next hour. He won't tell me why, but I guess later is now."

Now or never.

"What if you came to Murasaki with me?"

A hitch of breath, ocean eyes widening under damp lashes.

"Kai..."

"I can help you with your research, we can design a new tech system for you, and our doctors could perform your reintegration. You'll never have to use magic again."

Wren doesn't answer for a long, long time, so long his stomach coils in dread. Did he say something wrong?

"I can't just stop using magic, Kai, and I don't want to undergo reintegration."

And his stomach drops out. She doesn't want to undergo reintegration. Why would she not want to undergo reintegration? Why would she not want her tech back?

"Wren, you were in a coma for six days. You nearly died from the fever. If I hadn't been there to call you back, that magic would've destroyed you."

He would've lost her.

"I know."

"You know?"

She nods. "I know, and I understand you're afraid..."

Afraid? He isn't afraid. He's terrified.

"...and I don't know how to help you with that, but I can't just stop being what I am any more than you can stop being a technomancer."

"That's not what I'm saying."

"No, but it amounts to the same thing. It's just another weapon or tool like your saibāki. The only difference is I can use mine without tech assistance. That's really what frightens people so much about witches. We are what we are at all times, and they can't just flip a switch to turn us off."

That might be true, but...

"Our tech is designed to maintain a certain level of safety and control," he says. "There are redundancies in place, coded defenses, and mechanical repair systems. A fully operational augmentation will do what it is programmed to do %100 of the time barring any damage taken or cyberattack. It's trustworthy."

"So, you don't trust me?"

"I do trust you."

"But you don't trust my magic, and my magic is part of me."

Surely, it doesn't have to be.

"Wren, please. The war is over. Our doctors could perform your reintegration. You'll have time to heal and then you won't be defenseless. You don't have to suffer with this anymore."

"I'm not suffering from my magic, Kai."

She's not suffering? She's not suffering! He just found her with an open wound on her arm, beating herself up trying to

354

find a counter for a curse that already ran its course, and for what? Because she felt obligated to put her powers to use. And not even that...

"It nearly killed you."

The force of his voice startles even Kaito, and Wren's demeanor shifts entirely. The previous calm evaporating, replaced with defensive instinct.

"And no one ever died from overusing their augmentations? Weapons misfire all the time. Connections can short circuit and fry a neural net. When was the last time you had to use a maintenance stim to avoid tech atrophy? What would happen if you didn't have access to one?"

"It's not the same, and you know it. We know how to maintain our tech, and augmentations can be fixed when they take damage."

"And I can't be."

There's steel in her voice.

"That's not what I mean."

"But it is. You and Xipilli. You're exactly the same. You think you can fix me, but I'm not broken."

Wren unfolds herself as she rises to standing, her materials jumping off the table and into her arms. "I can't go to Murasaki, Kai. My brother needs me, and Deriva needs to be rebuilt."

She moves around him, neither angry nor sad. Upset, certainly, but there's a forlornness about her he's never witnessed before, worse even than those days when song stayed away. She drifts past him like a ghost, a shade that could disappear if he closed his eyes too long.

"Wren, wait."

He catches her elbow, not in a grip, never again will he grip her like that. It's just a hold, his fingers woven under her arm like a basket.

"What?" Wariness tinged in her voice.

"Do you remember my serial number?" He cards his fingers through hers.

"Yes."

Her answer is plain, simple but filled with trepidation. Despite that, relief floods through him. He still has hers as well. The numbers to Wren's technomancer augmentations, given to him the first time they made love. It's coded into his own system, the echoes of a synchronization long past. How often did he reach for her tech system when she was missing? How many times did he call to no response?

"It is yours to use."

Even if she never does.

"Wouldn't you rather I forget? After all, mine is of no use."

He shakes his head. "That matters not."

"Yes, it does."

"No, it doesn't. I didn't give you my serial number because you were a technomancer. I gave it to you because you're you."

"That girl doesn't exist anymore, Kaito."

Then who is this person before him? Who is the woman who held his hand during his mother's funeral? Who is this woman who has spent the last however many hours slaving over how she might have saved his mother's life? Who is this woman who walked alone into battle, knowing there was a chance she would never return?

If she isn't Wren, then who is she?

But his voice catches in his throat because in her distress, Wren flexes her aura, the triskele glowing bright as daylight and sending a pulse of viridian light cascading along the wild script framing her face.

His flinch is damning.

"Perhaps you should decide whether the person you want is really me or someone who doesn't exist anymore?"

"Wren…"

But his call goes unanswered as she leaves him behind. Left to curse his own inability to find the right words as her energy fades into the ether.

THE HIGH PRIESTESS (REVERSED)

Several moons later, close to midnight, Kaito's comm unit rings. He doesn't recognize the call number, but there aren't many people with his information who could contact him personally like this, so he answers.

"Miyazaki."

"Kai?"

It's Wren. He wasn't expecting her to call so soon. He wasn't expecting her to call at all, really, their last conversation ending the way it did, but she sounds shaky. Her voice quivers, her breathing heavier than normal

"Wren?"

"I had a nightmare."

Her words are small, fragile like he could fold them in his hand and break them with a twitch of his finger.

"Are you alright?"

"I—I know you're not exactly happy with me right now, but I... We got back to Cresta de Corail today, and I just..."

She chokes. She is in Cresta de Corail, her home with her family. The place where she lost everything.

"Wren—"

Kaito settles himself into a chair.

"You know what, never mind. You're probably busy, I shouldn't have bothered you—"

"Wren, it's okay. Talk to me. I'm here."

There's a hitch in her breath on the other side of the line. A tense moment passes where he doesn't know if she is going to close the connection or maintain the line, but eventually, Wren starts talking.

She talks about the weather and the water and the beach. She tells him about a new song she is composing. She talks about Xipilli's reconstruction plans, about how she thinks Irene and her brother might be becoming more than friends. She talks about everything and nothing. She doesn't tell him about her nightmare. She doesn't tell him what brought on her panic attack. She doesn't talk about what happened, and she doesn't have to.

He listens to the sound of her voice, musical even when she isn't singing. He listens as her words grow stronger, lose their uncharacteristic fragility, and become more sure. And when she tires of talking, he plays for her, the notes of the piano folding into near inconsequential soundwaves to travel through her comm thousands of miles away from him.

He is there despite the distance between them, and for just this moment, it has to be enough.

The next day as Kaito, his brother, aunt, and the rest of their envoy depart Seraphim, a broadcast airs of Wren executing the goblin king at the center of the coral throne room, and Kaito knows exactly why Wren called.

"O Shahrazad. You are the oasis in the desert of my dray old soul. Do not empty yourself into the King's hands. He will only spill you."

Quote taken from *A Thousand and One Nights*
An ancient text by Anonymous

23

THE QUEEN OF CUPS
(REVERSED)

Present – 11th Day in the Month of Falling, 1877 – Aureus'
Outskirts – 10:15AM

W REN DRAWS THE KNIFE FROM HER PACK.
A simple kitchen knife, it looks like the kind of tool
used to carve up a flank of meat with a simple black handle.
This is the knife she used to conduct the cleansing ritual on
the Miyazaki family's temple. It is also the one she used against
Summer just last night. Just a mundane knife, overused by
whatever chef decided it was their favorite.

Summer had laughed when Wren threatened to carve her
open with it, and Kaito hadn't given it a second glance when she'd
used it to cut open the bird's belly in the wendigo's basement,
and why should he? There's no magical residue, no vibration,
not even anything carved into the handle to make it look like
anything more than a common cooking utensil taken from a dust-
gathered knife block. Nothing interesting here.

But looks can be deceiving.

"Avstå från min klädsel."

Wren's voice drops into her lowest register. The octave rumbles in her chest as she sings the release weave, and the longer she repeats the refrain, the more the blade comes alive. Steel melts into bone, black as night and peppered with starlike speckles of ivory. The angle of the blade curves, a thick rib bone inset into the hilt and sharpening on both sides to a deadly point reminiscent of a raptor's claw. About halfway down the blade is a backward facing point designed to rend flesh on the pull out. The hilt shifts from plain plastic into corded black leather wound tight around the head of a femur with a loop around the base large enough for her to slip a finger through for easy single-handed manipulation.

Lacuna—The Soul Eater. Wren's athame.

Until now, she's kept it warded, locking its more sinister abilities away. The kitchen knife illusion is a side effect of the ward, but now she's dismantled it, Lacuna sparkles in all her magical splendor. Light reflects off the blade's obsidian edge to glance off the palm leaves over her head, searingly bright under the desert sun. If she looks long enough, she knows she'll be able to see the trapped souls within the blade: Llywelyn, Absko, a nameless corporal, Yggfret, and... this is the only one Wren regrets... Irene... the only person killed by Lacuna's blade who didn't deserve her fate. And the worst part of it, Wren doesn't even remember how it happened.

"Alright, Yggfret. Time to talk."

From the blade's depths, a swirl of red magic begins to unravel. It coalesces at her feet, building higher and higher like a sandcastle before once again the Goblin King, Yggfret Bloodfang, hovers before her, or rather, Yggfret's ghost if she wants to be precise.

"*Min dronning*," he offers with an incline of his head.

"Tell me who dropped you in the lake by Shinka Temple."

"I do not know."

"You don't know?"

"I thought it was you, *min dronning*. Your touch awoke me."

THE QUEEN OF CUPS (REVERSED)

Not possible. Wren fished Lacuna out of the lake after the wendigo matriarch was killed. She spent two days haunted by the ghosts of the temple trying to find a means to reverse the curse, while tending to a recovering Kaito and blatantly ignoring the pull in her stomach toward the lake. She finally gave in and went for a dive when the call kept her awake during a particularly rough gloomtide the third night.

"And how long ago was that?"

"Almost two years ago, *min dronning.*"

Yup, not possible. Two years ago, Wren was very much six feet under.

"How?"

Did someone mimic her energy signature?

"Your guess is as good as mine, *min dronning.*"

"So what—you just decided to float around doing nothing for two years until Kaito and I showed up?"

"It takes time to build up enough potential energy to exact change, and what sort of *villdød* would I be if I merely sat back and ignored your glorious return, *min dronning*?"

"Enough with the formal address!"

"My apologies."

The spectre cows, reclining in on itself in deference. Though to what, she isn't entirely sure. He's only at her command because she has him trapped in her athame. The constant mocking and calling her "my queen" is getting really old.

"Whatever. Why don't you make yourself useful and give me a scope of the city?"

"As you wish," he declares with a bow.

The *villdød* disappears in a gust of ghostly wind barreling towards the cityscape nestled on the horizon.

Aureus—the capital city of Sekhmeti—sparkles as bright and golden as the coin for which it is named. The skyline is truly something to behold and glimmers so Wren finds herself longing for a decent pair of sunglasses on approach. Towering metal giants, framed by arches and traffic lights, stand nestled within a circle of classical temples, walls, and towers built from clay and magic. A city carved in gold and adorned in jewels—why, simply looking upon it makes you feel rich. But at the heart of such wonder, the bleakest of portraits taints the visage.

A great statue of the goddess, Aset, rests neglected against the greater steel pyramids of the first reigning technomancers of Sekhmeti: the Pharaoh-Queen Nefertiti and the Raja Oman Iyer—like conquering warriors, professing to have beaten down a goddess of creation.

Well, the jokes on you, majesties. You died while she still lives on. In fact, she's been gardening.

Carved by the desert-dwelling witches, Aset's statue was handmade from the finest of marbles, a desert auric veined with pure gold. Time and neglect may have crumbled the edges, but out of the weathering, desert flowers grow: vibrant purples and pinks, the purest of whites, and happiest of yellows. They are the only living matter Wren can see from her little desert oasis. She wonders if the floras are left undisturbed out of respect or out of fear. Probably the latter.

Industrialization may kill godliness, but it can never actually kill a god or goddess.

On her shoulder, Silje gives an irritated "mmff!" The cat's pupils narrow to the thinnest of slits before she gives up her scrutiny and buries her whiskered face in Wren's hair. Not that it does much good. Atalia's dirty blond locks reflect back just as much light as what shines on them, and irritation rolls off her familiar. Silje never liked it when Wren decided to don a glamour in the past. Why on Deus should she start liking it now?

"Well, do you have a better idea on how to get into a central League city? Go on, I'm all ears."

She takes the annoyed mew she receives in response as an indignant "No."

"That's what I thought."

After Silje teleported them across the border, Wren found herself a decently priced c-4M3L for the desert trek to Aureus. About six hundred years ago, after the regime of Sekhmetian witches were taken down via atomic force, radiation in the area caused pretty significant alterations in the local wildlife: coyotes began using echolocation to hunt, fruit bats developed bioluminescent fur, local venomous snakes lost their potency, and the jackalope nearly went extinct entirely after the chupacabras stopped targeting goats and instead decided the antlered rabbits were a much tastier meal—they're still severely endangered, now considered more folk legend than actually historical creature.

Amidst all the mess, specialty programs were adopted by both hexen and human+ to solve the problem: radiation filters for newborn animals, cleansing spells erected over specific acres of desert. Both sides attempted to restore the potency to the snake population—the witches via spellwork which accidentally created the Àfe-alwaqif (The Upright Serpents, a hexen peoples with a human upper body and a serpentine lower half) and the +ies via gene splicing. The results made the snakes highly aggressive and far too toxic.

But the animals hit the hardest were the domesticated camels, the primary source of farming labor, milk, and—most importantly—transportation in the desert heat. They would be born without legs, lacking vital internal organs, sometimes even sporting two heads. Within a single generation after the technomancers rose to power, the population was decimated, and the new raja and pharaoh nearly lost their rule over it.

In order to save the camel (and their power), the posthumans began to augment the livestock. Several centuries on and the practice has become something hardly worth batting an eyelash at. In recent times, with the radiation levels finally dropping, fewer and fewer camels are born needing life-sustaining augmentations, but on occasion, a calf is born needing human+ aid to survive, and the animal will fetch their owner a pretty penny when sold to the local department of transportation for overhaul.

Personally, Wren finds the practice more than a little distasteful. Animals should be allowed to be animals, not cybernetically enhanced pets, but they are well taken care of, at least, and the penalties for the abuse of a hybridized creature is punished almost as strictly as witchcraft. Almost. You won't get burned at the stake for caning a camel, but you'll spend a good chunk of your life staring at a piss-stained prison wall for your troubles.

Wren's cyborgean steed is one part machine to two parts organic double-humped desert camel. Its head, neck, hind hump, and rump are all unaugmented, 100% pure-bred ungulate, the fur coarse and thick. The rest, however, has been installed with various mechanical augmentations to help the creature survive in the desert heat. A water filtration system, mechanical legs, skeletal enhancements along its cerebral vertebrae, and the ability to carry more than four times its weight.

Her c-4M3L, which she's named Lucy by the way, is presently grazing from her feed pouch in the shade of a palm tree. Exhaust puffs from the pipes along her barrel shaped torso, and her front hump has opened up to erect a large umbrella which Wren is quite thankful for considering the air around her must be in the triple digits. Ør may be a mild sun most of the time, but in the parts of the world where he reigns over all, he is just as brutal as his far-off cousin Sol. Not that she's planning on taking a cross-dimensional trip to Death Valley anytime soon. Is it even possible to return to Earth? Is it still there? Probably not. Surely, the humans blew themselves up by now. Is it worth looking into? Maybe as a fun side project.

Yggfret reappears, floating inside the river mist.

"The city is crawling with technomancers. They're like hornets, buzzing about making a general nuisance of themselves. Unfortunately, when technomancers sting, they don't die shortly thereafter."

"And Summer?"

"Right where you expect her to be. Licking the feet of her technomancer husband when she isn't being beaten by him."

Wren winces, recalling her broken ribs. "Thank you, Yggfret. You can go back."

With a dip of his head, the spectre dissolves, returning into Lacuna's heart. For a split second, the other witch's eyes stare out at her from the blade's reflection before sinking into its depths.

The viridian coating of Wren's magic quiets, and she offers the athame to her familiar.

"You sure you'll be okay out here? You're not exactly in top form."

Silje blinks at her, long and slow, before swiping the blade from her hand and jumping down to settle in a patch of grass next to the riverbank. Dropping Lacuna blade first into the mud, she kicks her hind legs in short brushes to bury the weapon. Wren won't be taking her athame into The Shard.

The building's security has always been tight with only certified technomancers and adepts permitted to carry weapons of any kind within, and when it comes to anti-magic technology, Sekhmeti has always boasted top-of-the-line systems: infrared technology, disillusionment scanners, dispel parameters, even fairy foggers that will kill any pixie unfortunate enough to inhale the fumes.

However, unlike most witches, Wren was raised a tinkerer of clockworks, comm units, and computers. She knows her way around such things. Undetectable spells and enchantments are easy enough to manufacture through potions and wearable jewelry. Disguising her weapon, however, would be something else entirely. Even if she were to reinstate the warding, the risk of its discovery is too high, and should someone find it on 'Atalia's' person, it would out her immediately as a witch if not outright name her for who she really is.

When she is done burying the blade, Silje dips a paw into the water, laps up the droplets, and then coils herself into a ball right there with her tail hanging half-heartedly in the stream. Nevermind Wren saw a few crocodiles floating like bits of wood a few meters back. The cat is entirely unconcerned.

"Okay, well, try not to get eaten while I'm gone. You're not exactly the apex predator around here when you're fun-sized."

The cat brrps at her, and the witch just shakes her head.

The netherbeast has never enjoyed entering large metropolises, especially not one like Aureus which is more metal and concrete than dirt and grass. They don't even have a public park to Wren's understanding, and why would they? The city is in the middle of the desert. (The question of how Silje would manage in more environmentally friendly cities like Tokiseishu, where every building is topped in soil and greenery, wanders through her head before she forcefully banishes the thought away. After all, she's already been banished from Murasaki by the emperor himself.)

Silje's aversion has something to do with the noise and the static interference the technolyzed-scape causes her, which Wren understands implicitly. Augmented humans have a way of interrupting the natural patterns of the world. It's why most fae, netherbeasts, and even some species of hexen avoid the inner city. It isn't so poignant for Wren. The frequency she is attuned to will shift a bit, and she'll have to find a different tether to the natural world. An easy if not annoying shift she needs to make lest she wants her own necrotic magics to leak all over the sidewalk like battery acid. Which, as fun as it sounds, is not a pleasant experience for her or anyone around her. It's happened to her a few times when entering a densely populated area. She's never had it happen to the point where she couldn't reorient herself and manage to channel an altered version of her magic, but it is tiresome to do so. Kind of like when a cell phone overheats from having to keep its WIFI hotspot on for too long.

Before she heads into the city, Wren draws an array into the damp sand a ways from the bank. Just a little something should she find herself needing a quick getaway. Hopefully, she doesn't. Teleporting herself anywhere is a huge tax on her power, and the distance she'll be going if she evokes this circle will be enough to knock her on her ass for a few days if she doesn't permanently lose her mind first. Thankfully, with Silje, the feline will sense her magic and help her make the jump if she tugs on the line. No telling how effective it will be in blocking the inevitable crash. She may find herself teleporting out of trouble just to land face first in a more dire situation.

As much as the city glitters in the sunlight, walking through the streets is an entirely different perspective. Oh, there are sparkling billboards and flashing lights, titanic screens and the roaring screams of stadium crowds. But between the sparkling streets, hidden in the shadows of the alleyways, is a secret world, kept silent by averted eyes and uncaring hearts reluctant to confront the horrors of the world seated in plain sight.

A pile of newspapers provides a makeshift sun shelter/ blanket for an old man sleeping on the steps of the library; she would worry he was dead were it not for the constant twitch of his bare right foot. A woman pushes a shopping cart full of ratty clothing, discarded bottles, and tin cans down the sidewalk; a sharply dressed businessman spits at her just for existing. A pair of children try to catch the attention of passersby by making their little dog jump through rings and balance balls on its nose; an empty hat sits to the side with a few ugly coins tossed in as an afterthought. As Wren passes, she tosses a handful of bills in, enough to feed them for at least a month. The little girl's face, crusted with dirt and grime, lights up with a smile, and for a moment she looks like an ordinary child rather than a street rat abandoned by the system. Her head is shaved—probably due to a lice infestation. She reaches for Wren, but her big brother tucks her into his side looking at 'Atalia' with the utmost distrust, so Wren ducks her head and carries on.

The homeless and impoverished, people left destitute in the wake of war and destruction. Some of them are victims of circumstance, others cast off by society which deemed them unnecessary, and others still the fallen family and friends of others once accused and slain for being a hexen. Never mind none of them were actually witches or lycans or vampyres.

She drops Lucy off with a c-4M3L caretaker outside L'Amor Lux's guild quarters, and the Madame greets her at the door and welcomes 'Atalia' inside to rest and prepare for the party she will be attending this evening.

"You must be travel weary, my dear. Replenish yourself for this evening."

Wren nods, gratefully, sighing with relief as cool air relieves the heat on her skin and dries the sweat beading at her brow. But there is no rest for the wicked. She has much to do if she is going to be ready to face Summer once again.

7:22 PM – Sekhmeti's World Trade Building – The Shard

Wren finds herself one of nine other Fireflies chauffeured into the grand ballroom of The Shard. Their task is to entertain, dazzle, and provide companionship for the aristocrats, technomancers, and royalty in attendance.

Atalia was originally from Ebele, so Wren dons the traditional garb of an Ebelean Firefly, the vibrantly colored kente cloth wound tight around her breasts and hips to cascade down to her feet. The pink, yellow, and orange patterned zigzags of color are not the most practical for subterfuge, but they complement Atalia's mocha skin beautifully, and next to the other Fireflies who wear equally bold colors, she fits in just fine. She prances her way into the ballroom, beaded bangles and necklaces jingling sweetly, her midriff showing, and her hair wrapped in cloth to match her attire. All the bells and whistles of an entertainer and a servant of love adorn her. Earrings dangle delicately from her once again pierced ears, a ring bouncing in her navel, also newly re-pierced. *Pluma negro!* The downside of having a beautifully remastered body means having to recreate all of the intentional markings she made there in her first life. She would say she's never been poked by so many needles in such a short amount of time, but that would be a lie.

Anyway...

Her mother had her ears pierced when she was an infant, and she'd chosen herself to have her navel pierced when she became a chrysalis and adept trainee as a way to honor her recently deceased mother. Freya had also had a belly button ring, and Wren used to love watching the gems dangle and sway whenever her mother danced for her father. She'd added other piercings over the years, mostly to her ears. She had a nose piercing for a while but took it out not long after getting it. It was too annoying to maintain and made her feel perpetually like she needed to blow her nose.

'Atalia Vaishi' is greeted with the other Fireflies at the entrance to the ballroom where, lo and behold, 'Chiamaka Nagi' stands to inspect them with her dear husband, Donarick J. Thames. The pair almost seem to float, regal and peerless, as they welcome each entertainer with warm smiles and barely concealed evaluations. 'Chiamaka' glitters in a jewel-toned sari accented with silver adornments: earrings, bracelets, and a half-sun/crescent moon pendant necklace.

Wren recognizes it immediately: the other half of Zenza's necklace from Xipilli and Atzi.

When it is Wren's turn to greet them, Thames takes her in, eyes roving her form slowly enough to make discomfort rear its ugly head in Wren's gut. She doesn't need empathy to know the look of lust on a man.

"Ah, Miss Vaishi, is it not?"

Wren offers a bow. "Yes, Primarch."

"I had the pleasure of reading through your credentials. Perhaps we can schedule a private session in the next day or so? I so look forward to seeing you perform."

Wren almost gags right then and there, but she maintains her façade. She doesn't plan on being here long enough to schedule any such session with anyone, least of all this man.

"Of course, sir," she says with a curtsy, looking up to chance a look toward 'Chiamaka' who, in direct contrast to her husband's cool interest, pales when she meets 'Atalia's' eye.

That's right, Summer, thinks Wren. *I'm here for you.*

"Let them eat cake."

Marie Antoinette (Allegedly)

24

ACE OF WANDS

11th Day in the Month of Falling – The Shard

"GLAMOROUS" DOESN'T EVEN BEGIN TO describe the extravagance that is The Shard's opulent ballroom. An overabundance of silk and gold filigree, fountains of wine and brandy, Fireflies dancing and flitting from patron to patron, banquet tables packed with food that'll be tossed into the trash later. If someone were looking for debauchery, this would be the place to be. Gluttony, lust, and sloth all celebrated like virtues owed the brave and powerful sons and daughters of technomancy for their gleeful slaughtering of "heathens."

To think she used to be one of them.

And if the visual display wasn't nauseating enough, amidst a crowd this size, the texture of so many mixed desires on her psyche makes her want to puke.

Imagine being at a buffet and smelling all of the different foods at once but having just recently recovered from a stomach bug. Disgusting, yes. Now imagine it isn't your nose smelling all of the foods but your innermost heartstrings trying to resonate with

SONATA

all the different tones and chords around you. It's disorienting at the least, downright disturbing at best.

It's enough to make her want to vomit, assuming, of course, she doesn't lose her mind first and go on a rampage because some old aristocrat is too busy lamenting his forgotten, ahem, disfunction treatment while ogling the boobs of one of the younger women to realize the girl is completely infatuated with a female Firefly dancing across the ballroom floor.

Not like it would be the first time she lost herself in her magical emotions...

If she remembers correctly, it was in this very room where the fool Farqaad boasted about bashing in the heads of lycan infants to a sea of applause. Wren only regrets that Kai stopped her before she could make him choke on his own electronic cigarette in front of the entire assembly. Not that it matters. He got what he was due in the end.

Donarick Thames takes the podium with all the grandeur of an overzealous penguin in a tailed tuxedo.

"Ladies and Gentlemen, on behalf of our most gracious host, I would like to welcome you to this evening's festivities. Jamar, you have truly spoiled us all this fine evening."

The pharaoh stands just behind Thames, dressed to the nines in a gilded gold and black suit. Thames lifts his hands to lead the room in a round of applause for the host of the party. Wren's eyes peruse the relatively small crowd of twenty to thirty people as Thames drones through the rest of his speech, and she reminds herself to be careful. There are faces she recognizes, others she doesn't—leaders from the smaller countries, and young technomancers just beginning to make their way through the ranks. A crowd of beautiful people, augmented works of human art, every person deadlier than they appear, and she represents everything they have worked tirelessly to snuff out.

"It has been a year of progress since last we convened like this. Another year of pushing back the hexen and reclaiming Deus for our righteous technologies, and we have many to thank for our victories. May we raise a toast to those lost over the years in this war against heathenism and magical tyranny."

A round of "here, here" goes up around the room, and Wren watches as the room raises a glass to their "glorious dead," downing the drinks in large gulps. Many of the Fireflies also take part, 'Atalia' going through the motions of taking a small sip from the champagne flute in her hand.

Thames smacks his lips together as he finishes drinking.

"I am so pleased to see some of our greatest League countries represented here today: Ebele, Deriva, Sekhmeti, of course, Aighneas, and our brothers and sisters from Pendleton, Indra, and Nezha. We regret of course the absence of our friends from Murasaki, though Emperor Hikaru assures me of his appearance eventually. Hexen trouble at the border it would seem, but we can all take it as assurance that they continue to fight the good fight with us for the sake of science and truth even if their methods seem a bit unorthodox."

A round of laughter courses through the crowd, and Wren can't help but feel a bit indignant on behalf of the Miyazaki family. What right do these fools have to laugh at the most powerful country in the league?

"Our greatest inventors have been working diligently to aid us in our endeavor to bring to light every last witch, vampyre, lycan, and other unholy magical abomination in this world still lurking in the dark. They hide among our people like vermin, feeding off and stealing away their livelihoods to further their own agendas. Well, I tell you, brothers and sisters, no longer."

An aide steps forward, a metal case in hand which she passes to Thames. Thames opens the case, carefully extracting the contents to showcase to the entire room. The mechanism in his hand is a wide ring of steel and glass. At the push of a button, a ring of lights flickers in a loud neon green.

"Ladies and gentlemen, it is my honor today to present to you the latest in wildmagic detection technology. A simple advancement from the magic suppressing cuffs widely used by our adepts, this device goes one step further. Rafka, if you will?"

A door opens toward the back of the room where, if Wren remembers correctly, there is a small antechamber. Into the ballroom steps a tallish technomancer, more cybernetic than organic, escorting another man, an organic by the looks of him, into the room. The organic, wan and malnourished, is garbed in the puke yellow jumpsuit of a prisoner. Thin and frail looking, the man is older, a long beard reaching nearly down to his knees and a balding head crowned in grey fuzz. He walks, hunched over and limping as Rafka pushes him along.

"This man was accused of witchcraft after a woman who visited his tea shop suffered a miscarriage. We suspect the miscarriage was caused by the tea concoction she ingested at this man's recommendation."

"She didn't tell me she was pregnant. I wouldn't've sold her that tea if I'd known she was pregnant. I ain't no witch! Just a humble herbalist!" the man shouts out to the crowd. Wren frowns. The man is telling the truth. He probably crafts the occasional tonic and potion with the intention of curing a headache or a fever, and working such materials would naturally expose him to wild magic. However, any magic in his system is null compared to a real witch. He might be a magnet, someone who naturally attracts wild magic but doesn't have a means by which to use it. Hardly the makings of a witch.

"Well, that remains to be seen."

Rafka wrangles the old man up the stairs and onto the dais. The captive falls to his knees as Thames raises the ring of metal into the air.

"My friends, a demonstration of this invention."

Thames leans down and hooks the device around the struggling man's throat. It clicks into place, and Wren holds her breath as it activates. The dials and lights on the collar flicker between yellow and green, yellow and red, yellow and green before finally settling on a poisonous red. There is a hissing sound like steam being released from an engine followed by a horrible whirring wail. Three small panels along the outside pop open and wired appendages, spidery and mechanical, unfold.

Arrow shaped heads point directly at the man's spinal column, and without further fanfare, a trio of lasers shoot out.

Wren inhales violently.

The man drops dead to the floor of the dais. It is quiet enough to hear a pin drop in the hall as the device powers down, tucking away its spiney weapons. The lights return to a clean green default, and Thames bends to unlock the device from the man's neck. When he raises the device back up, the technomancers in the room begin a steady buzz of incredulousness, some even applauding the display. Thames encourages this, offering a bow to them all, inspiring more clapping to join the initial hesitant applause as Rafka drags the now dead man's body away.

"The device detects the presence of wild magic. Should the threshold of power be met, the device enters an automatic killswitch protocol. Internal decapitation via three fine-pointed lasers. Clean and swift. Merciful and effective. A humane alternative to the witch burnings and hangings of old. No more must we play a guessing game with those who do not exert outright evil against us, for in my hand sits the future of witch-hunting in Deus. Ladies and gentlemen, I present to you, the new and improved Guillotine."

Wren pales as a round of applause goes up through the crowd.

So, a collar that works as a sensor, a negator, and an executioner when placed on the neck of a witch, or as she understands, any person linked to wild magic.

"I hope during this conference the League can come to a favorable opinion on this discovery. With your go-ahead, we can begin manufacturing more of these guillotine collars in order to..."

Wren stops listening and downs the rest of the champagne in her hand before snatching another flute off a wandering server's tray. She excuses herself to the ladies' room, weaving through rapt audience members as she chugs down the second glass.

Fumbling her way into the bathroom, she nearly trips over her own feet, high heels doing nothing to help her balance, and catches herself against the lip of the sink.

Sweat beads at her brow. The tap twists open, cool water splashing into the basin. Damping a few paper towels, she dabs the sweat off her face, breathing heavily. The pain of the slain man chars through her senses like an electrical burn. The white-hot burn of the laser shocked through her own senses as though she herself were the one submitted to the collar. A total stranger and in the timespan of blink, she'd known him better than anyone else the world ever could—a lifetime of emotions all condensed into one single moment, the big bang in reverse. His desperation, his despair, his love and loyalty, and most of all, his honesty. His death rattle hadn't even fully expelled by the time his body had dropped to the silk-lined stage. How quickly the device severed his spine!

Fuck the rag and any smears to her make-up! It's supposed to be waterproof anyway, and if it isn't, she's a goddamn witch. She can glamour make-up onto herself if she wants to.

She splashes water on her face, cold and grounding, downing the rest of the champagne she carried into the washroom with her. The bubbles dance on her tongue and ache down her throat as she swallows. The liquid hits her empty stomach like a bomb, making her even more nauseous, but she grits her teeth and gropes the lip of the sink, staring down at the water swirling down the drain. There is a small whirlpool forming in the shallow puddle at the base. Something must be clogged in the pipeline. Guess this place isn't as fancy as it markets itself to be.

That man was as innocent of witchcraft as Wren is guilty of it. A widower who lost his wife and twin daughters in the war during one of Seraphim's raids on Aureus and made his way forward in the world without the people he loved most. He'd been at work, tending to the gardens of some wealthy aristocrat on the outskirts of the city when the bombs came down right over his home. In the aftermath, he quit his job as a gardener and began tending his own gardens, growing herbs and teas and selling them to rich ladies needing a place to gossip and find their own place in the wake of a war which had nothing to do with them. A naturalist who made an honest mistake and gave a pregnant woman a mixture of herbs that would have been completely benign otherwise. Now he's dead, his execution no more than a demonstration for the newest and latest genocidal technology the League can conjure. A technology that doesn't discriminate on the basis of the wearer's wild magic level. It merely seeks to detect it. And what exactly are they going to do: go around clapping collars on everyone to see who dies?

The thought alone makes Wren sick to her stomach. How many adepts and technomancers themselves have traces of wild magic in their bodies? Wild magic exists everywhere, thus the definition of its name. You can't execute someone just because they've come into contact with it.

She opens her eyes after a long exhale and nearly bludgeons herself on the stall door behind her. Chiamaka's ghost glowers at her from the very door she nearly whacked her head against.

"Odin's beard!" she curses under her breath. First in a dream, then in broad daylight, next the kitchen of a diner, and now in a bathroom of all places. At least she wasn't on the toilet. The spirit looks at her blankly. "What?! Not going to strangle me? Oh, come, let's be three for three."

The ghost looks at her as if to say, "Don't tempt me." Mjolnir's mallet! She is not sober enough to deal with spooks right now.

"Alright, alright! I'm here! What more do you want from me?! Summer used my name to label our niece a bastard and used yours to have her banished. If I'd known I..."

She never would have let Summer survive the shamble horde. Damn the consequences!

For a moment, Wren wonders if the ghost is going to answer her, but instead the apparition just waves at her as though gesturing her into the stall. Wren's left eyebrow twitches. She is so not about to go into a bathroom stall with a ghost. For all she knows, the damned thing will try to drown her in the toilet. She's never been on the receiving end, or the giving end, of a swirlie, and she isn't planning on it anytime soon.

"Look, I don't know what your problem with me is, but I've got someone to kill, and I believe it's someone you also want dead, so if you don't mind—"

Wren turns to leave the ghost to her fuming, heading for the door, but Chiamaka flickers from her place under the stall to right in fucking front of her. To her left, the janitorial closet swings open, and she finds herself shoved inside.

The door slams shut on her nose, and Wren lands in a painful heap next to a cleaning bot. Bottles of disinfectant and spare rolls of toilet paper fall from the shelf onto her head, flooding the cramped space. *Emphasis on "cramped,"* she thinks, elbowing a now broken broom handle out of her thigh. *Koi! The thing nearly broke off somewhere it has no right to be.*

"Why you—"

Chiamaka shushes her with a chilly finger over her lips. The touch saps the warmth from Wren's cheeks. Then the door to the washroom opens and in steps the devil herself.

"Goddamn it, Witch! Get a hold of yourself!"

The living 'Chiamaka' curses in a voice that isn't remotely reminiscent of the Ebelean princess.

The ghost scowls, smoldering around the edges, as though giving her a begrudging "You're Welcome." Outside, she hears the faucet twist, and the sound of running water fills the bathroom.

Beside her, the cleaning bot's sensory light flicks on. The child-sized bot is old, dusty with disuse and looking quite sad with its arms angled haphazardly around its various cleaning accoutrements, but it clearly still works, making a beeping sound at Wren's proximity.

"Is someone there?"

Wren quickly twists one of the knobs on the backside of the robot, activating it fully, and tucks herself into the cramped corner, purposely wedging herself under the cleaning supplies. The robot turns on with a "beep beep" and flurry of mechanical limbs as it spins the broom into its tong-like hands. Its door slides open, and the bot wheels forward, sweeping furiously.

"Ah!"

ACE OF WANDS

A tense spattering of ozone, a clang of metal, and with a small explosion, the robot bursts into its individual parts.

"*Meinfretr!* Cursed androids!"

Summer spits and sputters in frustration. One of the pieces clatters against the closet door, making the smallest of cracks. Wren inches her way forward to see 'Chiamaka' hunched over the sink, crying. The woman is shaking violently, her dress twitching around her in response to her sputtering magic. The silver chain around her neck even levitates off her skin. Her form flickers, void spiraling around her in chaotic spirals. One moment she's Chiamaka, the next she's Summer, then Chiamaka again. She screams at her own reflection, fists pounding into her own head.

"Stop telling me what to do!"

She punches the mirror and the glass shatters. Shards fly all over the floor and countertop, cutting the woman's hand.

"*Ololufe?*"

A deeper voice calls from the door. It's Thames.

Summer looks up, her face settling on Chiamaka's visage, her hair limp with water around her face.

"Darling?"

"What's happened? Are you alright? Did someone attack you?"

"I—"

"Are you losing control again?" his voice hardens.

"No, darling. The cleaning bot just frightened me, is all. You know how jumpy I get whenever we're in a strange place, and the wards here are—"

"My love," he growls, the call more warning than endearment. "We've talked about what would happen if you were exposed here."

"There's no one here. I even locked the door."

Slap!

Skin on skin. The back of Thames' hand strikes Summer across the face.

"And I unlocked it as easily as flipping a light switch. Now, pull yourself together and drop that disgusting guise while I'm speaking to you."

"Yes, dear." The glamour falls away, leaving behind pale skin, red hair, and quivering freckles.

Thames smiles, reaching up to fix the necklace and stroking Summer's cheek.

"There. Much better. Now I can stand the sight of you even if you're still a disappointment. First, you failed to recover Faust from Miyazaki custody, then you failed your one assignment in Chairomura. I went through so much trouble to ensure Zenza Nagi saw fit to take that case. Countless hours of coding and ripping apart Deriva's firewalls just for you to fail at killing the little brat, too."

Thames wants to kill her niece.

"I told you it wasn't my fault. She wasn't alone the way she was supposed to be."

"Yes, a Firefly and two Murasaki trainees. Truly the stuff of nightmares for a witch like you. Explain to me exactly how meek, little Atalia was capable of obstructing your mission."

How curious? Does Thames not know who 'Atalia' really is? Did Summer not tell him about Wren's return?

"Tell me: did the little minx somehow develop a backbone in the sanatorium? Or did you lose your nerve the way you always do when it comes to following through? Or wait! Don't tell me. You fell for those pretty eyelashes and couldn't be bothered to remember your long-suffering husband who has done more for you than you could ever repay."

"No, that's not—I–I don't know what happened."

An unsettling ripple rolls over her synapse as Summer lies through her teeth, omitting the truth despite the wrath of her husband. But why? What does she gain from keeping Wren's identity a secret?

"Of course, you don't. Blessed is a man whose wife is such a failure at following orders." Thames prays to the ceiling, and before Wren can blink, winds both hands around Summer's throat. The woman chokes and gasps, clenching at the man's fingers to pry them off.

"Do you want to keep your power? Or do you want to make us both look like fools when Xipilli turns the tide in his niece's favor? Huh? Is that what you want? The both of us hung out to dry because of your stupid mistakes!"

As suddenly as he grabbed her, he releases her.

"No matter. We're lucky the man was foolish enough to bring his wayward niece with him to the conference. We'll have the opportunity to rectify your mistake here. Go to the kitchens and tell Cag'n the plan has changed. He now has a second objective to accomplish, and afterward, go to your room. I don't want you anywhere near the ballroom. Not while your..." He sneers. "...*ailment* is misbehaving so. Get yourself under control before I do it for you."

Summer sobs, fist clenched in her skirts.

"No, that's... that's not necessary. I can fix it."

"See that you do."

Her head bowed, pale drops of glistening water drip from her face to land on the floor amongst the mirror glass.

Thames tuts. "Oh, come now." He steps into Summer's space. Though she hunches in on herself, he cards his hands around her face, gentle as a lover. "There, there. You know I only do and say these things because I love you so. If anyone were to find out what you are, who you are, they would take you away from me. They would destroy you, destroy us, and there would be nothing I could do to protect you. You know this, don't you?"

Summer's head bobs.

"That's my girl. Now, give us a smile, won't you?"

From where she sits, Wren can't see the woman's face, but she can see her head lift. Wren closes her eyes, turning away as Thames leans down to the witch's face, and the pit of Wren's stomach drops out of her belly.

Before the League gained power over the continent, Fireflies were little more than household pets for wealthy Hexen aristocrats. As men and women who could not use the same scope of magic as their Hexen masters but who had a touch of the wild in them, Fireflies might be trained in love magics as a sort of mercy. To be given the honor of being a love mage to a wealthy lord or lady was seen as an honor.

Unfortunately, their lack of autonomy and civil rights often meant these Fireflies were victims of horrible treatment. Helen De Santos was one such Firefly, and while she may not have set out to change the world, her actions against her abuser would unequivocally alter the way the war between science and magic would unfold.

An Excerpt from *Love Bugs: Deus' Fireflies and their influence in World Politics*
By Madame Kali De Vrie, 1747 A.P.

25
FIVE OF WANDS

THERE ARE FEW THINGS WORSE THAN THE cruelties of men. Wren experienced it in another life: beaten, violated, and left for dead. The path she walked to find her vengeance had been arduous, staunched with sinister plots and paved with blood. She doesn't regret the things she did to become the person she is. When you've suffered atrocity, you have to claw your way out of the grave, breaking the skin, splintering wood, and choking on dirt if you ever want to see the light of day again. And Wren did it; she survived the worst kind of hell; she carved her way out of purgatory and dropped her tormentors there instead. If people want to name her a demon for doing so, let them.

Rolling over and allowing herself to be destroyed wasn't an option.

Thames leaves Summer to collect herself, and for the longest time, Summer doesn't move. The water runs at full blast and the destroyed bot give a few last spurts of electricity. Chiamaka's ghost hovers behind Wren, radiating a bloodlust colored something far more complex: pity.

Chiamaka feels pity for the woman who killed her, and that, in and of itself, is a complicated thing. How much of Summer's evil is due to her desire to please a man to whom she will never be enough? How long has his boot been pressed down on her neck? Since the execution? Since the war on Seraphim? Since Lorelei? Before?

She can't imagine living like that. Nothing could be worse than living with a person whose affection is measured by every bruise they imprint on your skin.

Wren wouldn't have called it abuse, but life after her mother's death had been very different under the firm hand of her stepmother. Elisabeta tried to tame her, but Wren was headstrong and stubborn, unflinching in the face of the woman's ire. Albeit, as much as her chore list expanded and her training regimen increased, Elisabeta never struck her. She can't even imagine what Tlanextli would have done had Elisabeta ever hit Wren outside of a sparring lesson.

Perhaps, Wren will be doing the woman a favor when she finishes this cat and mouse game they've been playing since the light rail, putting a lame horse out of its misery as it were. She could do it now. Touch Summer with her necrotic magic and rot her living, breathing husk from the outside in. Naturally, Chiamaka is anxious for her to end it.

Seriously, what is it with people bullying her into avenging them? First her resurrectionists and now a dead princess. It's completely unfair. No one's going around avenging her death. At least, she's pretty sure no one is. Eh! If they were, she'd tell them to stop, anyway. She'll manage her own compensational bloodshed, thank you very much.

The cut on her arm, bleeding again, wants just that, yet something holds her back. Maybe it's the curiosity to know Thames' plans. Maybe it's because she knows better than to kill somebody in the middle of a very public bathroom. Maybe it's because Summer looks so meek and meagre, it would feel like smashing the head of a newborn puppy against a rock.

Eventually, the water shuts off and the door opens, closing again with a click, Summer gone under the guise of an Orisha to fulfill her loving husband's wishes.

FIVE OF WANDS

Showtime.

Arranging and settling herself down in a forcibly cleared space, Wren opens her purse. Out of it, she summons a small vial of creamy viscous liquid.

She sets it down in front of her, then feels around with her empathy to make sure no one is close enough to hear her. It's no guarantee what with neural networks capable of evading her psionic abilities, but Summer and Thames have both left the bathroom. She's alone and if she happens to turn on all of the sinks for the extra white noise, who's there to think it odd?

Her song begins as barely more than a whisper in the hush of a dusty broom closet.

Spiderwebs on a corner chair
They glitter in the light
But on a darkened midnight fair
No trace of them in sight

A cat sets foot so quietly
Upon the weakened beams
Not a trace of it be spritely
Save in your darkest dreams

Of all the things unseen, I fear,
Mine most of all you'll face
With tender secret thoughts held dear
By sight you cannot trace.

The liquid in the vial shifts from the cream texture to something translucent. If Wren didn't know better, she would think the vial empty. A Tonic of Invisibility. One dose of this and no one will be any the wiser of her presence. She prepared it specifically for this task, being unseen a fairly desirable trait for snooping behind enemy lines.

She swallows the potion. It's like drinking air.

SONATA

The tingling starts in her toes and makes its way up to the top of her head. She closes her eyes and lets the sensations wash over her, cool as spring rain and warm as sunbaked lagoon water. When next she looks down at her hands, they are perfectly invisible to the eye. Thirty minutes is all the time she'll have with the amount of potion she drank. Her clothes of course are still visible, so she strips them off and tucks them inside the empty mop bucket.

Wren scans the hallway. There is no one around, and there is only one camera across the way from her, panning from side to side in slow circuits. There is no doubt in her mind it has a heat-tracking system, a natural counter to ghosts and invisibility magic, but if she isn't in its line of sight, it can't find her. Invisibility potion for the humans, good old fashioned evasive maneuvers for the technology: what a dream combination. By the time she exits the bathroom, 'Chiamaka's' emotional signature is nearly out of range, but if she focuses on the charcoal echo of the woman's lingering bitterness, there's no fear of losing her.

Wren follows it, trailing the wall, quiet as a ghost and entirely undetected by passersby.

Summer takes the side corridor, trailing down the hall toward the kitchens, fiddling with her comm the whole way there. She slinks up to the swinging door where the wait staff shuffle in and out with plates of varying hors d'oeuvres and glittering flutes of champagne. 'Chiamaka' smiles and nods as several waiters bow to her before carrying on with their duties, and as soon as the coast is clear, she ducks into the kitchens, and Wren scrambles to dive through the open door before it can shut on her.

It's hot in the kitchen, a sauna compared to the rest of the building. The desert heat bakes in through the windows, cooking the staff as easily as the ovens churn out fresh biscuits and tarts, and along with the heat, as these things are wont to do, absolute chaos reigns supreme.

The head chef tastes and commands and directs his underlings like an army general, a spatula in hand making a wonderful substitute for a baton or sword, and the men and women under his charge jump at the slightest glance of his eye. A pot bubbles over on the stovetop; a young sous chef fusses it back to a manageable boil. Steam hisses from a pan as someone flicks oil over a pile of vegetables and meat, flames licking the knuckles of the cook tending the stir fry. A stack of plates shatter on the ground as two servers collide, inciting the ire of the king of the kitchen. The man, round and red-faced, as is appropriate to his profession, sets the final touches of a lemongrass garnish over a slice of smoked salmon before cracking a rolling pin at his out-of-line soldiers.

"That's coming out of your paycheck, you idiots! Now, clean up this mess!"

"Yes, sir!"

Summer clears her throat, demurely. "Oh, chef?"

"What?!" yells the man, whirling around and startling the instant he spots 'Chiamaka,' and Chef immediately goes into a kowtow, his disposition taking a 180.

"Your Majesty, welcome to our humble kitchen. Are the appetizers in the ballroom unsatisfactory? Which of my staff should I have fired to rectify any offense?"

"Not at all, good sir. There's been no offense. I merely wish to take a tour of the wine cellar. Your pharaoh has recommended one of the old vineyards to me as a digestive following your succulent presentation this fine evening."

"Always a pleasure to service the most decorated names in the League." The man preens, blushing even redder.

"I believe you have an aide named Sungzou who is quite knowledgeable in such tastes."

"Of course, your majesty. Right this way. Sungzou, show her majesty to the wine cellar, and be sure to serve her our finest."

"Yes, sir!" A man, dark skinned and bald, steps forward from behind one of the kitchen racks. "This way, ma'am."

He bows as he gestures the mimic queen forward. There is a cellar door at the far side of the kitchen, and Wren moves forward to follow, barely squeezing past as the cellar door slams shut.

"How can I service the Orisha of Ebele?"

"Drop the act, Cag'n. You know very well why I'm here."

The man snickers. "More orders from the head cyborg himself, I take it."

"Yes, and you'll do well to follow them."

"Would I deign otherwise?"

"How close are you to your target?"

Target? Does she mean Zenza or someone else?

"Last I checked, I didn't answer to you, Helsdottir."

"Last I checked, you were rotting away in the stakes before my husband thought you useful enough to save, so answer my question, shifter."

Wren raises an eyebrow. Shifter? As in shapeshifter?

"I have the target in position. I'm simply waiting for the party to disperse before I make my move. Can't be too cautious with so many posties about."

"Good, see you take care of it, and when you're done, come find me on the terrace. We have another bit of business to manage."

"Oh?"

"Yes. I'll explain later. Just know that you and I are not the only hexen in this building."

The man's face darkens. "What?"

"And if things go the way I plan, we'll be making fools of the humans before long, so shut up, finish your task, and then come find me."

Behind Wren, the cellar door opens. "Sungzui, Chef wanted me to tell you about this particular vineyard for her majesty— Oh! Sorry, I didn't mean to interrupt."

Summer and 'Sungzui' turn to the new arrival so abruptly, the attention startles the young server—the same one who dropped a pile of plates earlier, and she drops the bottle of wine in her hand. It hits the floor and shatters at Wren's feet. The liquid creases into her toes and the puddle forms lopsided around her feet just long enough for 'Chiamaka's' eyes to dart down to her feet. She jumps away from the cold fluid. It's a mistake. The wine splashes from her feet onto the tiled floor, and the server freezes in wonder, having ducked to pick up the mess, as Wren's steps manifest in little outlines of wine on her way to the door.

She reaches forward, curious, and her hand meets Wren's calf before she can move farther out of the way. The apprentice freezes, hand held still in front of her face where she previously touched something warm and fleshy.

"Ghost in the kitchen!"

Wren darts for the exit, dodging past a waiter. She flips the tray in his hands, nailing the man in the face, and tips over the nearest bowl of iced punch. The fruity liquid sloshes along the tile, taking the feet out from under several staff members including Chef, who ends up on his backside on the floor with a bowl of freshly served soup on his face.

"Who is responsible for this!" is the last thing she hears as she disappears through the kitchen doors.

Wren hurries her way down the hall, dodging sentry drones and guards alike as the kitchen bursts into an uproar. It's a gamble whether or not any of the bots she passes have heat-sensors, and she sincerely hopes they don't because no amount of invisibility will mask her heat signature. And there's wine between her toes, sticky and sour smelling. Someone just had to drop an entire bottle of wine right at her feet! She wasn't exactly in the way either. Jumpy, clumsy, apprentices!

She isn't quite sure how she manages it, but she does indeed make her way back to her bathroom custodial closet to find her clothes still messily piled on the ground. She waits the few extra minutes needed for the invisibility potion to wear off then hastily redresses.

Sneaking back into the ballroom, Wren begins a slow circuit through the room, dancing between bodies, serving fine wine and eyelashes while listening to surrounding conversation. The ruckus from the kitchens does not appear to have made it into the ballroom, not yet at least, the staff handling it as is their duty while everyone else goes about the business as usual. If anyone notices the hiccup in the flow of food and wine, no one comments.

Rhiannon is chatting with Wang Yixing, the political leader of one of the smaller countries called Chongzu west of Murasaki and south of Sekhmeti. Art Lionheart talks amicably with Jamar and Selene. A part of her is gladdened to see her old classmates alive and well, another part saddened to see so many absent and never to return.

A dancing couple laughs as they move about the floor; they look young, probably around the same age as she and Kai when they were certified, and she smiles as she passes them, a word of blessing falling from her lips for young love. She is offering a glass of wine to an older kindly looking gentleman when she looks over to her left and nearly drops the glass in her hand.

"Ah, Emperor Hikaru, you missed a most impressive display. We were worried you wouldn't make it."

Hikaru converses with an older gentleman Wren doesn't recognize but is wearing Aighnean colors, his military blues impeccably pressed and ironed as to be expected of anyone under the Morrigan's firm hand, though, she guesses, President Morrigan Gewalt is long dead.

"Yes, President Ackram, I was worried as well." (Ah, so this must be Gewalt's successor.) "We were delayed by some rather unexpected mischief on the part of some of our trainees."

Beside Hikaru, dressed in working Murasaki leathers is Akari, looking sheepish and very tired, pale from lack of sleep and suppressing yawn after yawn after yawn in deference to Hikaru's calculating eye. Wren holds back a laugh as the girl teeters sideways before regaining her feet.

Did the poor girl get herself assigned royal guard duty for her infraction? Poor lamb. Wren wonders what punishment Renki is serving. Is it better or worse than sleeping in four-hour shifts, not being able to sit down for hours, and having to pass on the oodles of succulent food passing right under your nose?

"Teenagers," laughs Ackram. "They think they know everything just because they're old enough to participate in the trials. It won't be until they're somewhere between our ages that they realize just how little they truly know."

"Yes, while confidence is important, it must be tempered by humility."

Akari's face twitches, and Wren covers her mouth to chuckle. When she next looks up, Hikaru is looking right at her.

¡Mierde!

"Are you planning to stay the length of the conference or just for the planning meetings?"

"Excuse me, but there's someone I need to speak with."

Hikaru moves past Ackram and makes directly for Wren, expression hard even as the president calls "to doo loo" behind him.

This is no good...

She sets down the platter of wine goblets and hurries away.

"Ah, excuse me. Pardon me," she says, threading her way through the crowd to escape from Hikaru, but as you can imagine, while the crowd parts like the Red Sea for the emperor of Murasaki, it closes ranks against Wren until a hand wearing a gold signet ring identical to Kaito's save for its difference in coloration appears in front of her nose.

"Miss Vaishi, may I bother you for a dance?"

People are whispering. Dare she refuse the emperor of Murasaki in front of a room full of onlookers? Akari looks like she badly wishes she could disappear into the nearest wall.

"Your Excellency," she says, forcing a smile and allowing Kaito's brother to lead her to the dance floor.

Hikaru's hands are steady, if a little awkward, as he pulls her into a classical hold. "I see you made your way out of Murasaki."

"As you instructed."

"What do you think you're doing here?"

"Not entirely sure what you mean. I'm a Firefly; it's only natural I would gravitate to places where high society congregates."

"Don't play dumb with me," he hisses in her ear. "If you had any sense, you would have disappeared off the face of Deus, not chosen to parade yourself in front of the very people who would see you burned at the stake a second time."

Not all of us shove our problems in a skeleton closet, Emperor.

"I don't recall a stake, but I understand your concern."

The emperor distinctly looks like something foul nudged its way under his nose. He clears his throat and twists her through a quick rotation. "Where is Kaito? I need to speak with him."

Kaito? Why would Wren know where Kaito is? Hikaru himself kicked Wren out the moment she became more threat than help. Though, if she were being petty—and Wren has always had a natural talent for the art of pettiness—she highly suspects the sudden dismissal was more a reaction to her and Kaito's unplanned reconciliation. He'd been terribly unamused by the hickey on her neck. Wouldn't want the Songstress of Lorelei getting her tenterhooks back into his darling *didi* again, after all. Yet now he's asking *her* where *his* brother is?

"He's your brother. Shouldn't you know?"

Hikaru's eyes narrow as though she's said something purposefully scathing just to annoy him. Well, she was being purposefully scathing but not to be annoying.

"This is not a game, witch," he hisses.

And she isn't playing one. She has no idea where Kaito is. Surely, he's off on a case somewhere following his orders as is right and just, so shouldn't Hikaru of all people know where he is?

"Don't you have a link to his GPS system? Track him yourself. You've done it before."

Her question (or maybe her statement of fact) nails a tender button, apparently. The man recoils, his grip on her hand loosening, and for a full eight measures of music, he says nothing.

"Leave before you get yourself discovered. This is no place for hexen."

Oh, if only the man knew just how many hexen are wandering around this venue, and those are just the ones Wren knows about.

"Thanks for your concern, Excellency, but I'm afraid—"

Wren freezes. She stops following Hikaru's lead entirely, frozen in place as a flash of Derivan silks catch her eye.

Faen!

Wren has miscalculated. She has miscalculated badly. Xipilli Moctezumo's dark gaze finds hers from across the room. Xipilli, who may not know her identity, probably hasn't forgotten what happened on the light rail trip less than two weeks prior, and considering the man next to him, Quetzal, still wears the remains of an electrical burn across his right arm, the memory is quite fresh indeed.

"Thank you for the dance, Your Excellency, but I'm afraid one of my sisters is calling."

Wren turns, extracting herself from Hikaru's hold as Xipilli rises to standing, brushing off the Firefly currently attempting to sway him. Saying "fuck all" to propriety, Wren makes a break for it. A distasteful encounter with Kai's brother is one thing. A second with her own might very well result in bodily injury. She runs, holding a hand over her mouth and feigning sickness to get people to move out of her way. It's amazing how quickly people move at the threat of someone puking all over their custom-made finery.

As an extra precaution, she shoves past a young man casually serving himself a plate of food at the buffet table. "So sorry," she cries, exercising a bit of sleight of hand to run a finger over a half-eaten chicken's flank before stumbling away. As she disappears back into the crowd, the chicken hops up from the dish and begins hopping its way across the table to the screams of every man, woman, and child in the vicinity. It even jumps onto a woman's head, burying itself in the fine arrangement of feathers poking from the top of the lady's hair... probably trying to reclaim some plumage.

The spectacle inspires as much horror as it does laughter, and if Wren happens to catch Akari being scolded by Hikaru for laughing at the display, she only hopes the girl doesn't dig herself into an even deeper pit with her mentor.

In no time at all, she is rushing past the doors to the ballroom into the hallway where several staff members are hurrying to corral the now rampaging chicken, but by the time they get there, Wren's magic will have completely evaporated from the cooked corpse, leaving nothing but a stuffed chicken, a traumatized noblewoman, and flustered diners in its wake.

She turns back to check for him and sees nothing. *Whew!*

Congratulating herself on her successful evasive maneuvers, she leans against the nearest decorative statue, a marble effigy of the goddess Aphrodite, a single perfect breast exposed to the wind. No sooner does she catch her breath when a hand closes over her bicep.

"Trading one Miyazaki brother for the other?" Wren yelps as Xipilli tugs her roughly down the corridor. "Miss Vaishi, isn't it? A word if you don't mind."

Wren stumbles as her brother yanks her down the hall.

26
THE HANGED MAN (PART 1)

Fourteen Years Ago – 12th Day in the Month of Falling 1863 – The Shard, Sekhmeti – Four Months after the End of the War

KAI TAKES A DEEP BREATH AND KNOCKS.
Wren opens the door partway, sees him standing there, and huffs, anger already decorating her brow.

"What do you want, Kai?"

"May I come in?"

"I'm not exactly interested in company."

Wren turns to close the door on him, but he shoves his booted foot in the jamb.

"Wren, this is important."

He doesn't have time for her petulance right now. She doesn't know it, yet, but the council is set to demand recompense against her. She made them all look like fools, and worse, she put her power on display for everyone to see. War hero or not, the council would not suffer a witch so volatile to live freely, not if they could force her into a cage. Kai doubts they could ever tame Wren. Kai doubts they could ever break her, not after everything she's already survived, but that doesn't mean he wants to see her fight this.

She eyes him warily, searching his face for something he can only hope she finds.

"Please," he breathes.

Like a bound rope given slack, Wren slumps into herself, and the anger melts, replaced with exhaustion and pain. The bags under her eyes are darker than he originally thought, deep bruises under tender flesh.

"Okay…"

They find a place to themselves in one of the rooftop greenhouses. Wren settles herself in a low tree branch while he leans against the trunk, arms crossed, waiting for her to speak. Judging by the way she's studying the laces of her boots, that will be sooner rather than later.

"If you lecture me, I'm leaving."

It will never cease to amaze him how much of a brat she can be at times.

"Your sister sought me out. You haven't been eating. You're not sleeping either. She says you wake screaming from nightmares whenever you do. She came to ask if I knew any way to counter the effects."

"Oh, and what did you tell her?"

"Chaos breeds more chaos. Your natural powers damage your mind and your body. The only way to lessen your symptoms is for you to stop using magic. These entities you commune with, they are bringers of madness—"

"That was one time!"

"It doesn't matter. One time opens you to a second and then a third. No one can resist the call once they begin to descend, and the average person would destroy themselves upon acquiring even a fraction of what you have."

"It's a good thing I'm not the average person then, isn't it?" she says with a cocked grin on her face. She clicks her heels together and does a stupid, bouncing dance like she's just cracked a hilarious joke.

A lesser person would have shouted at her for the arrogant banter, but Kai shakes his head and rolls his eyes at her attempts to derail the conversation. "Wren, please. Be reasonable. No hexen in history has ever resisted the call."

"What would you have me do? Give up my power? Be a normal person? Find myself a boring lord to marry, settle down like a good little housewife, and worry more about what to cook for dinner than anything actually important? Che! Don't make me laugh."

"Must you always twist my words?"

"Then speak plainly."

"Stop practicing magic. You don't need to fight anymore. With enough time, I'm sure the effects will diminish. You are a brilliant inventor and a learned scholar. You would be an amazing teacher and an asset to any council."

"Now you sound like Xipilli." She huffs, rolls her eyes, and jumps down from the tree branch. "Kai, this is who I am. Stop trying to fix me when there is nothing to fix."

"I cannot sit back and watch you destroy yourself."

"Well, I would rather destroy myself than be destroyed by somebody else!"

He balks, taken aback at the ferocity of her sentence. She fumes at him, her lighthearted mask burned to ashes, the color rising in her cheeks and in her eyes. She twists away and wipes at her face. Her breathing is heavy, and he takes a step toward her, carefully, as though approaching a wounded predator.

She's always preferred to hold dominion over her own fate, but now, stripped of her titles, she has lost every scrap she has fought for her whole life.

"Tell me what happened in the hall then. Is this how you plan to destroy yourself, by marking yourself a threat to the League?"

"What does it matter? What's done is done."

"It does matter. Wren, you cannot attack people with your abilities. It's bad enough they have already stripped you of your technomancer status. How much more do you think you can push them before they call for your arrest?"

"I'm not scared of the council."

"How petulant of you."

"I can move things with my mind, Kai. I think I can take care of myself just fine."

"Witchcraft, Wren. Wild and necrotic magic. You know what the long-term effects will be."

She's angry with him as expected, and he is fully prepared for the argument about to ensue. This is not the first time they've had this argument, and it probably won't be the last. But true to form, Wren surprises him. Where he expects yelled accusations or defensive excuses, he gets only calm, her eyes hardened emeralds as she looks at him sadly.

"I'm a witch, Kai. My magic is as much a part of me as my hair color. It's not an augmentation. It's in my blood. A witch without magic is a dead witch, and if you can't accept that then… I don't know. What will be, will be, I guess."

Something about the way she speaks doesn't sit right. Something inside of her words doesn't compute. Something ominous and dark.

"Wren," he starts cautiously. "You know I would never hurt you."

"I don't think you can make that promise, *mon rivage*."

The sadness in her voice is so much worse than any anger he was expecting, and his adrenal system goes into shock at the sudden shutdown when he was expecting the fight or flight response. He closes his eyes.

"Do you think me evil, Kaito?"

"No."

He answers easily and truthfully. It's not even a question.

"So, if I'm not evil, doesn't that mean my magic isn't evil either?"

"It's not that simple."

"Answer the question. Yes or no? Is my magic evil?"

He hesitates. He hesitates, and Wren turns on her heel to leave, and the panic that overtakes him in that moment… It's suffocating. Because he knows! He knows implicitly. If he doesn't answer, if he answers wrong, if lets her disappear, he will never see her again.

"No!"

She stops, and the air returns to his lungs.

"No. Wren. I don't think your magic is evil."

She turns around. A slow, eternal turn that takes eons, but he waits. He waits for emerald eyes and a glowing triskele. He waits for wild script and untamed magic. He waits for Wren to look at him, and after an age, his waiting ends, and Wren greets him with a watery but hopeful smile.

"Go on, then..." she provides, and her eyes urge him to continue quietly, and he aches at the hollowness in her cheeks, the pallor of her skin, and the weary look in her eyes as though she has lived a thousand lifetimes already and each one has ended in disaster. "If I'm not evil, if my magic isn't evil, then what is it?"

"I want you to be safe, Wren. The backlash of a misfired spell could kill you. Never mind the strain this is placing on your system. I am not looking to turn back time or force you to be someone you are not. I want to know you are alive and well and whole, not fighting for your own sanity against a force I can't even begin to understand."

She doesn't say anything for a long time, so long he wonders if he's fucked it, after all. Said the wrong thing and alienated himself from her irreparably.

"Wren—"

"You want to know what the worst thing about being a prisoner was?"

"Tell me."

"It wasn't the beatings or the broken bones. It wasn't even being deactivated and violated. It was being helpless. Alone in the dark with none but pain as a friend."

His hand rises wordlessly, but he does not touch her, even though every fiber of his being wants to. He may not be an empath like her, but he feels her pain like a stab into his very core. He's hurt her with this conversation. This point of tension keeps circling and circling around them, tightening like a noose around both of their necks. Some days he wonders which of them will kick the chair out from under them first.

"I never want to feel that way again, will never allow that to happen to me again, and if your answer is for me to give up my power—"

"That's not what I want." She goes very still. He can hear her choking back tears. "What I want is to help you, Wren."

"I don't need a white knight, Kai."

"You're right, you don't. You can protect yourself better than anyone else I know. I am not trying to be your rescuer." He holds his hand out. An offering. "I want you to be able to live your life the way you want to. I am not trying to impede that or turn back the clock to a time before the war. I do not seek to change or fix you. I'm worried for you."

He braces for a storm, but it never comes. She's listening.

"I am not trying to be your rescuer, Wren. But if you would let me, I would like to be your partner."

She looks slowly from his hand to his face, a haunted look in her eye. Her hand lifts. She waffles, halfway to taking his hand before she changes direction and clenches the fabric of her skirts instead.

"I don't want to hurt you."

And her words bring a whole new light to their conversation.

During her confrontation with Farqaad, she telekinetically forced an electronic cigarette down the man's throat. She would have kept it there, too, had he not interfered, responding only to him despite the calls of her brother and the other council members. The man would have asphyxiated on his own arrogance. Had she chosen to attack him in any way other than her magic, he would have wholeheartedly agreed the man deserved his fate for the poison he had been spitting. But ... a punch, a stab wound, a bullet to the brain, anything would have been better than magic.

"You were not in control."

"I was. I am... Mostly. I think I am. It's just..."

"It's just what?"

The Hanged Man (part 1)

She bites her lip, shuffling on her feet and staring at the ground.

"I've been losing time. Sometimes I'll wake up, get dressed, and the next thing I know, the whole day is gone, like a book with whole chapters torn from it. I'll go to sleep and find myself waking up with mud all over my night dress and my boots back on my feet, like I've been sleepwalking, but who puts their boots on while they're sleepwalking? And today... One minute the asshat was talking, and the next, you were telling me to get the damn thing out of his airway... And the headaches... Gods, my head hurts all the time."

"How long has this been going on?"

"I'm not sure. Since the war ended, I guess, but it's gotten worse."

He steps into her space carefully, relieved when she doesn't tense up at his closeness, and when he raises a hand to hover by her face, she leans into him, a soft sigh falling from her lips. She is so, so tired. She radiates it in bounds. He has never seen her like this.

"I'm afraid."

The tightness in his chest uncoils as she softens beneath his touch. Her armor is completely dismantled, her trust in him suffocating and life-giving all at once as he ushers her into his embrace. Her hand and forearm rest on his chest, and she tucks her head under his chin.

"Come back to Shinka with me." He feels her tense up, prepared to fight him on this again, but he cuts her off. "Not for anything other than to get to the bottom of your lost time. We need to know what is causing your lapses. We can find the answer and deal with it together. You don't have to do this alone, Wren."

He tilts her chin up to him. Her green eyes are tired and sad. He hopes his own silver can convey the strength of his resolve, his determination to stand by her as long as she will allow him to.

"Okay," she says, barely a whisper.

For a moment, he believes his ears are playing tricks on him. "Really?"

"Yes. Okay," she says it again, surer this time. "I'll go with you."

And the unabashed joy Kai's relief inspires spills through as he beams down at her. Her cheeks color in embarrassment. She tries to avert her gaze, but he calls her attention back to him. The distance between them closes, and the warmth of her lips hovers barely a breath away from his own.

"Kai, listen. There's something I haven't told you yet—"

"Ahem..."

Wren backs out of his embrace. Kaito looks up to find Donarick Thames shuffling awkwardly at the top of the courtyard. He bows, looking rather abashed.

"So sorry to intrude, Kaito–san, but I have just received word on some rather unexpected happenings downtown. I was thinking your skills would be quite valuable if I could request your assistance."

Kai's eyes narrow, but Wren voices his disdain. "Are not Rameses' people qualified to handle cases in their own capital?"

"Ah, yes, Lady Wren, that would normally be the case; however, it would seem this involves a cyber ghoul, and we know the Miyazaki specialize in such fiends. It would be an honor if you would look into it for us, Prince Kaito."

His teeth grit, but Wren's hand on his chest brings him back to himself.

"It's alright, Kai. We can speak more in the morning." She smiles at him, eyes closed, and the brilliance of it chases the darkest shadows from the entire courtyard. He takes her hand in his and presses his lips to her knuckles.

"Then sleep. I will see you tomorrow."

She nods.

"Tomorrow."

She gives a small bow of her head to Thames in deference before leaving in the direction of the guest quarters she has been assigned. Once she is out of sight, Kai turns back to Thames. "What is the case?"

Don Thames bows deeply and leads him to the foyer.

27

THE HANGED MAN (PART 2)

K AI DOES NOT RETURN TO THE PAVILION
until around six in the morning which is around the time
breakfast is to be served before the day's conference. He is tired
and frustrated by how long the case lasted but used to staying
up through the night when working a case. He'll handle the
missed night's sleep with just a few hours rest after breakfast and
the morning's meeting. He freshens up his appearance before
making his way to the dining hall.

His brother is seated already, and while he looks well for the
most part, there is a pained look on his face.

"Are you well, *Nii–san*?"

"*Ohayo*, Kaito. Yes, I am well. I just seem to have an odd
headache. I am not accustomed to consuming wine, so this must
be the side effect."

Kai hums in acknowledgement before taking a seat
beside him.

Several more attendees enter the hall including Xipilli, Chike,
Jamar, and Atzi. All those who enter also appear to have a look of
discomfort about them, ranging from hands rubbing briskly at
temples to red eyes and outright nausea. This is especially odd

on Xipilli and Chike. These two should be well acquainted with the consumption of alcohol.

"Were you able to speak to Lady Wren?"

"We spoke."

"And?"

Despite his headache, Hikaru's eyes sparkle over the rim of his teacup. Kai himself softens at the fondness there. He focuses on pouring his own tea—a clear jasmine tea to help chase away the drowsiness.

"She has agreed to return with us to Shinka."

Hikaru's smile is soft but glowing. His hand comes up to rest on Kai's shoulder.

"I am glad for you, *Otōto*."

None but his brother, or Wren herself, would recognize the small quirk of his lips as a smile.

The hour arrives for the conference to begin, but there is a hold-up. The minutes continue to tick by, and the meeting start is pushed further and further as the primarch is still missing. Pharaoh Rameses, normally a meticulous man, is uncharacteristically late. At ten minutes past the hour, Jamar sends servants to look for him. He overhears Irene inquiring about Wren and notices she too has not arrived.

"Xipilli, did Wren decide to forgo breakfast? She is unwell?"

Xipilli rolls his eyes before dismissing any worry she may have with a gruff wave of his hand. "She's probably just slept in. My sister is as lazy as she is talented. She probably spent half the night devising some convoluted new theory."

Atzi laughs into her hand as an aide runs in to report to Jamar.

"Your highness, your father was not in his quarters, but we are searching the premises. While we have not yet found Pharaoh Rameses, there are traces of blood throughout the compound."

Immediately, every person in the hall is wide awake and looking around in hushed whispers. Xipilli and Chike share a look, and Xipilli pulls out his comm and begins typing a message. Atzi looks up, concerned, at her husband and brother. In her arms, Zenza begins to fuss at her father's sudden aura of unease.

The Hanged Man (part 2)

Jamar rises to his feet.

"Play the security cameras. Now! Find where my father was last."

"Yes, my liege."

A security droid floats in from outside. It revs itself up before its projector lights up to throw its images on the hall screen. Kai and his brother rise as does Xipilli and a few other technomancers and adepts. The screen follows Rameses as he exits one of the billiard rooms after smoking cigars with a few others the evening before. The primarch bids farewell to several other technomancers before making his way to his rooms. The doors close and the recording fast forwards as several disciples and droids pass over the course of several hours in which no one enters the room. The scene stays much the same until the time stamp on the cam reads about 3AM, late enough most everyone in the compound should have been asleep.

The door to pharaoh's quarters opens and Rameses steps out. He stalls for a moment as though calculating a decision before turning and making his way down the hall. The cameras flip through his tracks as he goes until he comes to a door in the wing the guests from Deriva were assigned for their stay. He begins to punch in the room's unlock code.

"What the hell?"

"Isn't that Wren's room?"

"It is," says Kai, his brow furrowed as the man lets himself in.

Xipilli grabs Jamar by the tunic. "What the hell was your father doing sneaking into my sister's room!"

"That can't be right. My father hasn't any reason to visit a lady's chambers after dark. This is a mistake."

"My liege, those are indeed the rooms assigned to Lady Wren Nocturne," says Thames, who looks as though he is about to be ill. Horror clouds Jamar's expression. Atzi's hand comes to her mouth in a quiet gasp.

"But why?"

"That lecherous bastard!"

"Xipilli, please." Atzi's voice is gentle but distressed. She too is looking at the screen as the bot fast forwards. The time marker ticks forward by an hour, two hours, a half hour more before anything new happens.

There is a collective gasp around the room when Wren stumbles out of the door and promptly vomits on the carpet. She wears nothing but a torn nightgown and she is covered in blood. She grips at her head and rocks herself, body shuddering in utter agony. Her eyes rapidly shift from the bright green glow of her magics to pitch black and back as though an alarm were sounding in her head. When the fit passes, a look of pure panic crosses her features, and she dives back into the room. Moments later, her travel cloak wrapped around her and her satchel over her shoulder, she reappears. She takes just one moment to acknowledge the security cam before she opens up a cut on her hand and draws a sigil. Her image blurs and then disappears from the camera view, though they can see where the tapestry moves as she runs down the hallway.

"Have the guards check those rooms, now."

They shuffle away while Jamar collects his sword and summons another droid. Chike picks up Agni and follows. Atzi tries to follow, but he asks her to remain in the hall before heading straight for the guest wing. Xipilli yells for Irene to get a hold of Wren via her comm as he storms from the room.

Hikaru and Kai share a look before following.

When they arrive, one of the guards is puking into a trash bin and the others looks just as green around the gills. Jamar steps into the room, and all the blood drains from his face. Xipilli has much the same reaction as does Kai's brother but less so. Kai steps in behind him.

The scene is a gorefest. Rameses lies dead on his back, hardly recognizable were it not for his askew robes and the signet ring on his finger. His throat has been ripped out and his insides torn asunder. The sight of the corpse, completely lacking in proper coverage on his lower region, leaves no question as to what occurred or rather what the man attempted to do prior to his death.

Fury rips through Kai.

Jamar is the first to turn away from the bloody scene.

"My Liege, there is no sign of Lady Nocturne anywhere in the building. It is believed she left on foot."

"On foot?"

"Of course, the witch left on foot. Where she's going no machine can take her."

Farqaad steps forward. His face is red, and he looks thirsty for blood.

"It would seem Sekhmeti has landed the case of a lifetime. It's been so long since we've seen a proper witch hunt. Shall we hunt the murderess down?"

Xipilli rounds on the man. "Murderess? Clearly, this was self-defense."

"Self-defense! Does that look like self-defense to you? She tore him to pieces."

"It looks to me like a lecherous fool paid dearly for his whiles."

"How dare you!"

"How dare you! Wren is my sister, a member of the Moctezumo royal family, and an honored war hero. Your distinguished pharaoh overstepped the moment he entered this room without invitation."

"And how do you know he did not have an invitation?"

"Excuse me!"

"Your younger sister's reputation precedes her, Your Majesty. I hear she takes well after her mother. Is it not said that she openly shares her bed? You can hardly expect our primarch to refuse an offer from willing whor—"

The man finds himself cut off as Kai's katana rests against his throat. Kai's sights whirl agitated and dearly wishing to record himself killing this whelp.

"Finish that statement and it will be the last you ever speak."

Hikaru's hand closes on his bicep.

"Kaito."

Kai turns to look at his brother. Hikaru's sights are active as well. He can tell he is already establishing a virtual parameter.

"Go with caution."

He does not need to be told twice. Wren is running, and she's had an hour's head start. He only prays Wren has her comm unit, and if she does, he hopes she is in a frame of mind to answer.

He gets on his lightcycle, revs it up, and drives.

"Call Wren now," he instructs his A.I.

"Dialing…"

The call tone begins to chirp in his ear. It goes and goes and goes, but she doesn't pick up.

"Call again!"

"Dialing…"

There is no answer on the second or third attempt, but the fourth time. The fourth time she answers. Relief floods his system, but it stales quickly.

"Kai?" Her voice is choked, coated with exhaustion and breathy. He doesn't hear the cityscape around her, so he turns his cycle toward the nearest speedway.

"Wren, where are you?"

"I… I don't know. Sobek's teeth! My head hurts."

"Wren, I need you to stop wherever you are so I can get to you. Just stop running. I'm coming to get you."

"No. Don't come after me!"

She is hyperventilating.

"Wren—"

"This will cause another war."

"Wren, stop. Think."

"I can't think right now!" She is in full blown hysterics.

"Stop, Wren! I can trace you through the comm. Wait for me."

"Kaito…"

"Please, Wren."

"Okay…"

"I'll be there soon."

She doesn't speak anymore after that, but she stays on the line. His trace finds her approximately 30 KM outside of the city limits. On his cycle, it will take him an hour to get there, but he doesn't have that kind of time. He floors the pedal and hacks his way into as many systems as he can to insure nothing impedes his route. Her breathing is stuttered and quick, and every few minutes, she goes into a coughing fit. He coaches her through a breath pattern. After about twenty minutes, her breathing is some semblance of normal.

"Talk to me."

"I—I don't know what happened. I went to bed, and when I woke up... I woke up to blood."

"You don't remember anything."

"No..." Her voice is barely a whisper. The silence stretches between them until the scream of an explosion echoes in his comm. Wren cries out.

"Wren, what's happening?"

"Attack drones!"

More blasts are unleashed. He hears her whistle, but then the line goes dead. He bears down on the accelerator. The distance will take thirty more minutes to cover.

He cuts it down to ten.

The scene looks like a warzone. Trashed robotics litter the ground, and the remains of a few of Wren's poppets lie scattered to bits around them. Three more bots fly by over his head, and he goes off road to follow them into the dunes. He can't identify the tech flying around. There are no ID markers, and they don't bear the marks of any nations, but if they're here, their human interfaces won't be far behind.

The desert sand is harsh and unwieldy behind the wheels of his cycle, the smell of heated rubber meeting his nose, the temperature rising even this early in the morning. He can barely keep up with the droids, but it doesn't take long before the sounds of explosions meet his ear, and the feel of Wren's dark energy on the air makes his skin crawl. She flits around the riverbank in a small brush of trees, dodging blast after blast before a wave of her hand directs one of the droids into its neighbor. There is a shower of steel, and Kai leaps from his lightcycle to slice down another one.

He buries Tsukuyomi's blade into the sand and sets his territory with a pulse of saibāki. Out of the corner of his eye, Wren goes down, a shot burning straight through her shoulder. Her fighting aura dissipates. He concentrates, hacking into each bot within his radius and deactivating them. They drop like flies one after the other while he slashes with Amatsu at the ones he has yet to gain control over.

A few moments later, his field of control is clear of enemy tech.

Wren crouches on the ground, holding her shoulder. Dark energy pulses green from her right hand as she pushes magic into the wound.

She didn't change before racing out of the compound. She still wears a tattered nightgown, covered in blood which he knows is not all hers. It's jarring seeing her in so little dress, without the protective layers of her corset and skirts and layered dresses, her hair askew and stuck through with foliage.

But her eyes... Her eyes are wild, pulsing with electric green power.

"Wren," he calls her name.

No response... It's almost as if she doesn't see him. He moves forward, but she flinches backward so violently, he immediately ceases all motion.

"It's just me, Wren."

She holds her handless forearm out in a halting gesture. "Stay back... I don't want to hurt you."

"You aren't going to hurt me."

"You don't know that."

"Yes, I do."

"Well, I don't!"

He is floored by the sheer force of emotion in her voice. Pain cut through with sorrow and intense self-hatred. Tendrils of power shimmer around her. They lick at the grass, the trees. The grass withers, dies, then regrows as black weedy strings. Gouges appear in the tree bark before the wound heals over with grotesque thorns and thrashing vines. He realizes belatedly that she isn't singing, is not channeling her magic through her voice as she normally does.

"Sing, Wren. You have to sing."

She shakes her head violently, both hands coming to either side. "I can't! My head!"

"Then hum."

She swallows and does as he says. It isn't a melody per se. It isn't even really a song, just a jumble of disjointed notes, whichever she can latch onto and piece together. Many of the textures fall sharp from the damage to her throat, but under his encouragement, she keeps going and slowly the darkness recedes, and the world around her clears.

As soon as it does, she collapses, heavy to the ground, so fast he barely catches her. He digs into his qi and feeds calming wavelengths into her neurons. The effect is immediate; the tension in her body drains as her eyes flutter open. Even now, he finds her beautiful. She looks up at him and smiles the way she only ever smiles at him. The moment is drawn, colored, and then erased as easily as pressing Ctrl-D.

"They're coming..."

Yes, his neural net confirms, there are indeed several technomancers making their way toward them.

"Miyazaki–sama, it is good that you've found her. Arrest her before she can get away!" The shout comes from General Farquaad as the group makes their way through the dunes.

Kai looks at Wren. Wren looks back at him.

"You should back away." Her eyes are sad as she says it. When he doesn't move, she bares her teeth and hisses, "Move, Kai!"

A pulse of telekinetic power hits him right in the chest and sends him skidding backward across the sand. Wren hits the ground hard without his support, though he doesn't think the shine in her eyes has anything to do with physical pain or magic. She swallows it down as she finishes pushing him away and stands. He is back on his feet in a split second, reaching to grab her arm even as she moves away.

"I'm sorry," she says, pulling back even farther.

She whistles, and a dark tendril lashes at him as Xipilli, Thames, Jamar, and Farqaad crest the nearest dune. Behind them, follow several adepts, robots, and drones.

"Nocturne!" calls out Farqaad. "You are under arrest for the murder of Primarch Rameses Sahra."

She laughs, a low chuckle in the early morning air. "Oh? Is slaughtering pigs a crime now?"

"Wren, this isn't the time for jokes," shouts Xipilli. "Come back, so we can figure this out."

"No, Xipilli." Her brother's name falls from her lips, slow and methodically. "You and I both know that isn't possible."

Her hand lifts. The gathered forces stiffen. Kai pulls himself off the ground.

"Songstress," starts Thames. "Did you plot to kill the primarch in cold blood?"

"It doesn't really matter how I answer, does it?" She pantomimes a curtsy to Jamar. "Long live the Pharaoh."

"Wren, stop! This is not the way to handle this," shouts Kai.

She ignores him. "Consider this my defection, Vulcan Moctezumo. My loyalties are no longer with Deriva."

Xipilli marches forward, incensed by his sister's antics.

"Wren, this is not a game!"

"Isn't it, though?" she asks and a high-pitched trill falls from her lips. Xipilli goes flying into Jamar. Both men are thrown to the ground. Two factions form at this point—Xipilli, Kaito, and the Derivan adepts against the Sekhmetian forces craving blood for blood. And Wren, stuck in between, uses the chaos to her advantage. Energy swirls and bonds together to make a green vortex. She runs for it as energy blasts begin to rain down on her. One hits her thigh, and she falls.

General Farqaad is on her in the next moment. His war hammer gleams in the morning light. Before it comes down on Wren's head, a set of massive jaws close around his torso, and he is flung like a ragdoll against a nearby tree. A series of cracks sound as his meat husk hits the bark and topples to the sand dead, spine broken.

Several adepts move forward, but their path is immediately blocked by the gigantic form of a monstrous cat-like creature. It roars at them and slashes.

Its sudden appearance is as telling as the misty tips of its fur: a displacer beast.

"A witch's familiar..." Donarick whispers in awe.

Wren makes her way back to standing and limps for the portal. The beast follows her, the eerie green glow of its black fur darkening the world around it. The bots open fire on it. The bullets do nothing to deter the animal even as it bleeds black blood over the ground. Savage claws shred metal and flesh as it defends its master.

"Don't let her get away!"

A shrill note falls from Wren's lips, and Farqaad's corpse rises at her command. Explosions go off at Jamar's command. Farqaad's poppet flickers in the way, catching Jamar around the neck. Kai and Xipilli move forward to intercept the blasts, but another shot cuts through Wren's shoulder. This time she does not fall. Wren rushes to the panther and pulls herself onto its back. In one bounding leap, the giant cat dives into the portal she erected, and immediately it closes around them.

"Wren!"

She turns back to look at him. Tears streak through the tracks of blood and sand on her cheeks.

I'm sorry, mon rivage. I really did want to go with you.

The words echo, not in his head but in his heart, and the portal seals, Wren disappearing into thin air, and Kai is left behind once again.

Two stars pulled out of orbit.

There is a reason the monarch of Deriva is called the Vulcan, and it isn't simply for the volcanoes that comprise Deriva's isles. Volcanoes are furious and ruthless, their eruptions relentless and uncompromising. Their fury can demolish towns, destroy forests, and evaporate rivers, but out of the ashes of their rage, new life blooms. The lava makes room for creation, and the nutrients enrich the soil for green things to grow.

All life began in a primordial fire. This is how the isles of Deriva came to be.

Excerpt from *Oceania and the Seas of the Pacificum*
By Naomi Hart 1827 A.P.

28
STRENGTH (REVERSED)

Present Day – 11th Day in the Month of Falling – The Shard – 10:11 PM

XIPILLI HAS ALWAYS UNDERSTOOD ONLY PART of what it means to be a Vulcan. He wears his fiery rage as easily as a necktie and pairs it with the brimstone jacket of impatience and bullheadedness.

Wren finds herself tugged down the corridor and into the elevator. She winces as Xipilli's on-brand irritation floods through her via his grip on her forearm. He is all sharp anger and grim determination; it's the same kind of focus and toxic energy she would expect from an overzealous video gamer: too competitive and too ready to take any slight as a personal offense. She became well accustomed to the taste and texture of Xipilli's temper tantrums and mood swings in the short time she remained in Deriva after her miraculous return, some of them aimed at her, most of them not, but this is just the first sputtering burps of an eruption Xipilli has been carefully and meticulously building up over the long years of her absence.

It's too much all at once, so she twists and pulls and attempts to break out of the man's hold even as the mechanical gauntlets around his wrists guarantee him absolute control over her movements right up until the elevator opens and Xipilli shoves her, quite unceremoniously, into the nearest guest room face first with such force that she goes careening to the floor.

"Really! I have never suffered such treatment, and here I thought everyone in attendance here would be at least mildly mannered."

"Hush, witch!"

"I am not a w—!" Wren quiets as Opochtli is thrust into her face. The trident crackles. "Now, now. No need to get violent," she says, raising her hands.

"What are you doing in Sekhmeti? The last I remember, the Miyazaki clan was taking you into custody."

"And in their custody I was for a while. His Excellency saw me back onto my feet himself. Even gave me some nice meds for the concussion you gave me."

Xipilli frowns. "Hikaru?"

"Yes, I have the credentials to prove it."

Wren wrangles her ID cards out of the pouch at her hip and thrusts them under the king's nose in retaliation for the weapon being brandished in her direction. Xipilli's eyes roll to scan the IDs before returning to 'Atalia's' face.

"And I suppose you expect me to believe you are not a follower of the Songstress of Lorelei despite that glittering display on the light rail? My man still bears the marks of that lightning strike."

She starts a backwards chant in her head in case Xipilli decides to hit her with a dispel casting, though he would need to stab her with the triton to do so, and it would be rather unbecoming for a vulcan to attack a certified Firefly at a League sanctioned party. Thank goodness she had the good sense to make a protection amulet before entering the palace.

"Vulcan Moctezumo, I have never been nor will I ever be a follower of that witch."

And she has never spoken truer words in either of her two lives to date. It's laughable really. Especially since he doesn't believe her in the slightest.

Her brother is starting to go grey around the temples, a little salt and pepper in his sideburns and his goatee. He should really look into an augmentation for that, or at least take up mediation, lest he go totally grey by the time he is forty. And what's with the goatee, anyway? It only serves to make his already pointed chin even more severe in angle. (She would know. She once cut her knuckles on that chin.)

"So, a liar as well, just like your mistress. Mark my words, Miss Vaishi, you'll regret ever having dabbled in the dark arts just the same way your proprietor came to regret her choices in the end."

Wren chuckles, dark and ironic. "Do you have regrets?" Opochtli falters in Xipilli's hand. "She was your sister after all."

Xipilli reels backward as though slapped. A spark of anguish traces across her awareness as an echo of his emotional turmoil, telling even as white-hot fury replaces it.

"How dare you—"

"*Tio!* The pharaoh is looking for you! Someone thinks they saw a fairy in the kitchens!"

Through the door bursts an excited Zenza. The girl practically dances into the room, the glitter in her braided hair dusting onto the floor, her cutesy evening gown floating around her in bubbly ruffles and ribbons. The half-sun/crescent moon necklaces bounces happily on display at her throat.

"May I go see what they found—" The teenager halts with a jolt at the sight of 'Atalia,' Xipilli's triton still pointed at her face. "You!"

Wren puts on a dramatic sigh, lifting a hand in a dainty half shrug. "Yes, me. Hello, darling. Long time no see."

"What are you doing here, you lunatic!"

Ah, teenage girls are such charming creatures.

"Zenza," snips her brother. "¡*Calmaté! Dime,* what's so important that you barreled in here screaming your head off?"

The girl jolts to attention at her uncle's bark. "Umm, one of the chefs said they saw a nymph or a dryad or something in the kitchens. Pharaoh Sahra was asking if you wouldn't mind bringing Opochtli down since it can shock out any hidden Fae."

"Did he?"

"Si, Tio!"

Xipilli glances over at 'Atalia,' suspiciously. Wren merely shakes her head and shrugs, giving the man an innocent, pouty look. Xipilli pulls his comm out of his pocket, types in a quick command, and before she can properly react, a 5Ki SErP4nt throttles through the air from the man's luggage. The mechanical snake winds its way around her right wrist, spins her around, captures her left wrist, and bites down on its own tail, effectively making itself a fancy set of handcuffs. It winds itself so tightly her fingertips go numb. She grinds her teeth, a heavy pressure forming in her head, but her glamour holds strong, the protection amulet doing its work. *Sheesh!* At least this thing won't dampen her magic.

"Zenza," calls Xipilli. He does not look away from Wren for even a moment. "Stay here and keep an eye on this wretch. I'll be back once I find out what's happened in the kitchens."

Now, Wren knows her brother is no fool. He probably very much suspects something is amiss with her, not the least of which is believing her (Ahem... Knows!) her to be a witch. He spares her one last glance and then storms his way out of the room, a tsunami hurtling toward its destination. Thankfully that destination is on the opposite side of the building from Wren.

"But Tio!" protests Zenza.

"You think you're old enough to take a case on your own without telling me, then you are old enough to babysit a hostage."

"You're leaving me alone with—" The door slides shut with a hiss behind Xipilli. "—a witch..." The teen huffs and crosses her arms, grumbling. "And you ranted and raved about me being a lunatic for going off on my own. Who's the lunatic now? *Que loco...*"

Wren, leaning back against the couch cushions with a sigh, looks over at the girl with a trademark shit-eating grin. "You know they used to think lunacy was purely for women. Something about our cycles being linked to the moon, but we've long since proved that men are by far the more volatile gender. Ever prone to cravings for war and violence. Ever under threat of their egos being torn to ribbons. You know in the olden days, men used to march whole crusades against so-called witches just because the women in their village were getting too uppity?"

Zenza rolls her eyes at Wren's lecture.

"Who let you into this conference, anyway? I thought they vetted all of the Fireflies."

"They do," affirms Wren. "I was admitted into this event's entertainment retinue quite legally, so if you wouldn't mind being the sensible one of the two of you, I would really like to be on my way."

"Hn!" scoffs the girl, shaking her braids out. "Not a chance. I'm already grounded because of you, and I'm not about to get myself into even more trouble for not following to directions."

"It isn't my fault you snuck away from home."

"You got me caught!"

Agni, resting nozzle down in a little weapon's rack by the door, activates. The weapon unfurls a pair of legs toward its nose and swivels itself around until it's pointed at Wren. Wren scoots backward, hands up.

"Whoa now! No need to start aiming weapons at unarmed hostages."

"Payback's a bitch. Consider this recompense for leaving me tied up with Renki and Akari."

"Yes, because the better option would have been to allow three unruly teenagers to keep mucking about by themselves. You should be thanking me for keeping you alive."

"Just sit still and be quiet. You even think about doing anything, and Agni will incinerate you so fast, your head will spin."

Zenza strides across the room to what is no doubt her half of the en suite, and disappears, leaving Wren with an aggressively glowing rifle. She wonders idly if the weapon recognizes her, if it knows it's aiming at the person who killed its maker.

She hopes not.

Zenza returns a few moments later, changed out of the evening gown in favor of a comfortable pantsuit. She finishes pulling pins out of her styled braids and fluffs them out with a sigh of relief. She then begins to wind them all together into a large coil at the base of her neck, tying it off with a ribbon. The movement causes the clasp of her necklace to swing to the front. She fixes it with a frustrated tut and tucks it away.

"Planning on disarming that rifle?" asks Wren.

"No. Why? You nervous he's going to shoot you?"

Zenza raises an eyebrow at Wren as she grabs a tool kit from her uncle's supplies and traipses her way over to a nearby desk. She seems to have commandeered it as a workbench. She sets the kit down with a grunt and a bang, glaring at Wren as though daring her to say anything about her upper body strength.

"Not at all, princess."

Zenza snorts, in a rather un-ladylike manner. It's endearing. Atzi would have probably laughed about it, too. Xipilli would find it appalling.

"Whatever, since I'm stuck here, I can at least get some work done on this automaton. Tio says I can't go on another case until I manage to get it working again. I'm pretty sure it's a ploy to keep me in the house forever because this piece of junk is wrecked."

Wren's interest piqued, she watches Zenza to pull out various wheels and cogs from a bag on the floor and sits quietly as her niece begins to tinker. So Xipilli allows their niece to experiment with her own inventions. Good. Innovation and creativity are important skills to possess in this line of work. A technomancer can never count on just being handed a piece of equipment, especially if they work with anything above even the most modicum of difficulty levels. Her niece immerses herself in her work, and a small smile teases the edge of Wren's mouth.

When Zenza was just an infant, she used to scream and cry for no reason other than she wanted someone to hold her—that someone usually being her mother or father. Wren still remembers the day she got to meet Zenza as a babe. Not a day

Strength (reversed)

after Wren's triumphant revenge over Llywelyn, Xipilli brought Wren back to League headquarters and immediately corralled her to their big sister. Imagine Wren's surprise to find Atzi nursing a colicky baby. Atzi had been glowing, her cheeks still fuller from the pregnancy weight, full of life and joy, healthy and happy in the arms of her proud husband if not a bit tired and frustrated from the fussy baby in her arms, barely more than a few weeks old and already a spitfire of energy.

At the sight of Wren, Atzi leapt up so fast from her recline, Chike and Xipilli nearly tripped over themselves to make sure she didn't strain herself, but Atzi shrugged them off to pull Wren into a wet, tear-filled hug. Immediately after, Atzi offered Zenza for Wren to hold, and to be quite honest, Wren hadn't exactly known what to do at the time, staring down blankly at the angry, purple-faced infant with too-long dark lashes and a head of fuzzy brown hair. Fae was never so fussy, but Zenza quieted the moment Atzi placed her in Wren's arms, and Wren allowed herself to enjoy holding her niece for the first time. Then Zenza, quiet as a mouse and just as innocent, latched onto her psyche with all of the power of a non-verbal infant recognizing she was now being held by somebody who could feel her every want and desire.

Seriously, if anybody ever wants to drop an empath, shove a baby they've never met at them, because Wren just about fainted with Zenza cradled to her chest. The little rodent latched her little pudgy fingers into Wren's psyche hard enough to bruise, and she didn't let go for hours, even after Wren handed her back to her mother with a simple statement that Zenza was still hungry. After the initial meeting, it gets easier to filter the foreign emotions out, and she actually became rather fond of sitting up with Zenza in her parents' stead.

Bang!

"Ow!"

Wren's attention leaves the past and returns to the teenage version of the baby she was just reminiscing about. Another clatter sounds, and Wren finds Zenza waving her hand wildly in the air.

"Need some help?"

Zenza looks up from her work, thumb still tucked into her mouth from smashing it with the hammer. "Hn! What would you know about mechanics?"

Wren smiles at the teenager. "Don't be so judgemental, young lady. I may not be a technomancer like your uncle, but I know my way around a screwdriver. Come on, let me out of this little ouroboros bot, and I bet I can help you get your droid working in no time."

Zenza looks from Wren to Agnithen back again. "You know, my uncle doesn't think you're just any witch."

"Oh?"

"He ranted all the way back to Deriva about how he was certain you were my dead aunt."

Wren winces. "Did he now?"

"Yup. He does that every couple of months. Mistakes some poor woman for channeling her spirit and makes sure they end up in the middle of a funeral pyre."

"That's Xipilli. Always prone to overreacting," Wren mutters under her breath before asking Zenza, "Well, you've spent more time with me than he has. Do you ever think he's right?"

Zenza shrugs. "No. From what I hear my aunt was a lot smarter than you." *Why this little—!* "Besides, he's kind of paranoid. She's dead. Kind of a finality, don't you think? Necromancer this, Necromancer that... Hah! Even if she could come back, she would be well advised to stay that way for what she did to our family. I'd shoot her myself if I ever got the chance."

The fourteen-year-old's dark gaze settles on Wren, heavy and meaningful, and Wren knows implicitly the girl means it to the very fiber of her being. Wren glances warily at Agni, still trained on her. She knows what it feels like to be shot by Agni and would really rather not experience it again.

"Besides, why would the Songstress of Lorelei slum it with a bunch of teenagers in a border town trying to keep from being eaten by a lightning bird? Not to mention, since you are a witch, you are either completely insane or really stupid to wander into a technomancer conference, so the way I see it you can't be much of a threat either way."

"Can't argue with that logic."

"So, which is it? Stupidity or insanity?"

Wren purses her lips, feigning deep thought. "Perhaps a bit of both. Genius is commonly mistaken for insanity, and stupidity is relative to the subject and situation."

Zenza studies her for a moment longer before getting up from her chair with a tut. She deactivates Agni. The rifle powers down with a hiss of exhaust before tucking away its legs and returning to rest nozzle down in the rack. Then Zenza ambles her way over to Wren, shuffling her feet as though she couldn't care one way or the other how she came off to other people. The girl leans down, and Wren hears a click as the girl presses the SErP4nT's eye. The automata unravels itself from around her wrists then hovers away to curl up in the same basket Xipilli summoned it from.

"Thank you!" she whines, pulling her wrists up to rub them.

"Yeah, whatever...Ack!" Zenza wheezes as Wren glomps her around the shoulders in a tight hug.

"My savior. My heroine. The most esteemed of monarchs in Deus. How can I ever repay the kindness of such a merciful ruler?"

"Get off of me, you lunatic!"

Wren relishes in just a few more seconds of holding onto her niece until, giggling, she releases the teen. "Alright, what are we working with here—?"

The words die on Wren's lips as Mano comes into view on the workbench. Her old prosthetic, her left hand once upon a time. Mano had been with her since she was ten years old until, seven years later, it was forcibly ripped from her arm. She still remembers how it felt to have the nerves in her wrist severed at the attachment point, the phantom pain of it surging up her arm.

"I am trying to fix this piece of junk back into working condition. I thought I would try and take out the mainframe completely and just start from scratch, but then I would lose all of the data storage. Maybe give it a new exo-skeleton since I don't need a prosthetic hand. Maybe something cool like a spider."

"You realize this was once somebody's prosthetic, right?"

"Yeah, so. It's not theirs anymore, is it?"

Fair enough but also not quite right.

"Your uncle gave you this to fix."

Zenza sighs. "Yeah. He got all high and mighty about it." The girl puffs up her chest and strokes an invisible beard. "'You want to go exploring on your own, young lady, well prove you can take care of yourself and build yourself a companion out of this garbage.' Pretty sure he thinks it's unfixable. He's such a stiff."

Wren chuckles at her niece's, frankly, good imitation of her brother. He is such a grouchy bear sometimes. Zenza crosses her arms over her chest and scowls at 'Atalia.'

"Why? Do you know something about it?

Wren shakes her head. "No, I was just surprised to see you working on something so trashed up. This thing must be at least twenty years old."

Zenza shrugs her shoulders, picking the screwdriver back up.

"Eh, old and new are pretty relative when it comes to technomancer technology. The parts may be ancient, but whoever its previous owner was, they made some pretty sick enhancements. This thing has a pocket storage dimension glyph drawn into it, inlaid data analysis tools, and the kind of exoskeleton I would expect to find in an automaton rather than a prosthetic. Now if only I could get it to turn on, so I could see if the stuff actually works or if the owner was just a regular run of the mill nutcase, but I don't think my uncle would keep an idiot's failed project in our vaults, do you?"

"N—No. I suppose he wouldn't, would he?"

Why had Xipill kept it, though? How had it even been returned to Deriva? Xipilli never mentioned it being there after her return to civilization.

"Whelp, why don't you hand me a screwdriver, and we can take it apart together?"

STRENGTH (REVERSED)

Zenza makes a face at Wren, and the witch can feel the disdain rolling off her in waves. Oodles and oodles of teenage angst... but she hands her the screwdriver. Wren pulls over remains of her old prosthetic and sets to work, guiding Zenza's hand as she helps her find and replace the various nuts and bolts of the little automata, and if she starts to hum halfway through replacing the exoskeleton, Zenza doesn't notice until she has already laid her head down on the desk and fallen right to sleep.

The old lullaby always worked when Zenza was a baby, too.

Hush, my wildling, why fight your sleep?
When rainbows dance and raindrops sing,
Hush, my heathen child, don't cry,
My heart and yours are one tonight.
And though the sky-king rumbles and screams,
You're safe inside my arms and wings.
Hush, my baby girl, and fly
For magic lives eternal in dreams.
She gifts her bounty on your head,
For none to keep but thine in my stead.

"Hush, My Wilding"
A lullaby from Freya Nocturne to her daughter

29
TWO OF SWORDS
(REVERSED)

12th Day in the Month of Falling - The Shard – 12:00AM

THE MANTLE CLOCK CHIMES MIDNIGHT AS Wren applies the finishing touches to the new and improved Mano. Though "Mano" won't be its name for much longer. She'll let Zenza rename it.

Xipilli has not yet returned, which is a bit disconcerting. It's almost midnight; surely he wouldn't leave Zenza alone so late at night, though she guesses the girl isn't alone, not that Xipilli trusts 'Atalia' further than he can throw her, but Wren... Nah! If Xipilli really thought 'Atalia' was his younger sister, he would have tossed her out on her ass the moment he got ahold of her. Regardless of whatever has kept him occupied, she won't look a gift horse in the mouth. Zenza, now curled up and fast asleep on the sofa, lets out a soft sniffle and buries her face farther into the cushions.

If only she had a camera.

The witch picks up the little robot and holds it in front of her face. She twists the wind-up key at the top five times.

"Mano?"

The little bot lights up as easily as last she used it to rescue her brother that fateful day in Cresta de Corail. Its nodules glow a soft blue, and it hops from digit to digit, excited by the sound of Wren's voice.

"Hello, old friend. Have you been sleeping all this time, too?"

Mano waggles in her hand, spinning about on its fingertips before settling back to lean against her thumb. The wrist joint tilts from one side to the other as though asking a question. Wren raises her left hand to the bot.

"Yeah, it's been a long while. Things have changed a bit. I can't really explain it to you though, but I'm still me, mostly."

Wren angles the mechanical hand, so Zenza is in front of Mano's scanners.

"That's my niece, over there. Zenza Nagi. Atzi's daughter. Almost all grown up. Can you believe it?"

The automaton scans Zenza's features, making little notes in its servers: tiny beeping sounds which Wren recognizes as the creation of new data files in Mano's limited artificial intelligence.

"I'm going to transfer ownership over you to her, okay? I think she could use a helping hand from time to time."

Mano rises up onto its index, middle, and ring finger, curling its pinkie and thumb in an imitation of a human setting their hands on their hips in anger.

Her old prosthetic may not be the biggest bot around, but she's nothing to shake a finger at. Mano got her out of some tough situations when she was a teenager. The hand is set up with shielding tech and alert systems, so with someone out for her young niece's blood, the prosthetic is perfectly equipped to protect her.

Wren giggles at the bot's antics.

"¡Hay! ¡Lo *siento!* Bad joke, bad joke. Do you understand what I'm asking?"

Mano flips itself up, index finger extended to the sky, and quirks the finger twice in affirmative.

"Thank you, Mano."

Two Of Swords (reversed)

The bot stutter-stops through a flourished bow, and without her prompting, it spits out the data chip containing all of the data from while it was Wren's prosthetic. She tucks it away into her bodice while Mano jumps out of her hand and crawls her way over to Zenza. The mechanical hand leaps up onto the couch and curls up like a five-legged cat on the girl's stomach.

It would be a sweet sight were it not for the burning ghost hovering about the sofa.

Changed into clothing more appropriate for assassinations, Wren treks her way down the hall, barefoot in a pair of black wrap pants under a floor-length skirt, a long-sleeve top, and cropped wrap vest. The majority of the tower is quiet. The number of servants running about has diminished—she only sees two on her way to the rooftop terrace, and most of the Fireflies have turned in either to their personal quarters or with their chosen patrons for the evening.

When she passed by the main hall earlier, there was no one around, the ballroom emptied out. One of the straggling servants informs her that the majority of the technomancers either retired to their rooms or moved to the sky lounge on the topmost floor of the skyscraper to play pool and cards and gambling their wealth away while smoking fancy cigars. If it weren't for the fact they tote their incredibly dangerous weapons around like fashion accessories, you'd never think these people hunted monsters for a living.

It's no guessing game to find the person she is looking for. Bloodthirsty ghosts hounding your footsteps have a tendency to make sure you go the correct direction. Hel, at some point Chiamaka decided she wasn't moving quick enough and flew straight through her on the stairwell, so she moves like a woman possessed to stop the ghost from clawing into her synapses and ripping her mentalscape to shreds. By the time she reaches the terrace, she isn't quite sure whether the itching fury she feels is actually hers or Chiamaka's. Perhaps a bit of both.

A small flex of telekinesis, and the door opens for Wren as easily as a music box.

There is no one else around, the terrace dark save for the moonlight drifting through the skylight. It's changed since she was last here. It's enclosed now, greenhouse windows surrounding most of the area braced with tiled steel plating for extra support. Additionally, the garden has been made into a strange mix of a botanical walkthrough and a museum of sorts. There are weapons on display, paintings baked into the pavement, and colored in-sets in the glass in the shape of insects and animals, finely decorated vases, carved statues, a central fountain, and even a sundial erected in a clear patch of grass. The tree where Kaito asked her to return with him to Murasaki has grown taller, its branches cut in such a way that climbing them would be difficult for even the most skilled tree-climber.

She'd agreed that night, accepted Kai's offer and gone to bed easy for the first time in a while, knowing the next morning she wouldn't have to be alone anymore. She could tell Kai about Fae and maybe even have a life that wasn't characterized by bloodshed and war, but then Rameses—that bastard! He hadn't managed anything, she knows, she'd checked herself over once she had her head back on her shoulders and the hounds were far enough back in her rearview mirror, but oh, how she wishes she could remember how she killed him. Part of her hopes she drew it out, recompense for any other women that animal defiled.

There are more flowers on the terrace than she remembers and a memorial for the bastard who tried to sneak into her bed fourteen years ago. His ugly mug, carved in stone and encased in gold just like every other gilded thing in this place. It's an extraordinary likeness; they even captured the hedonistic glimmer in his eyes with a lovingly carved memoriam engraved in the base of the bust:

A ruler, a husband, and a father,

TWO OF SWORDS (REVERSED)

Here lies Pharaoh Rameses Sahra

A man taken too soon by unspeakable evil.

She laughs. That's right. "Unspeakable evil." That's what she is. Rameses was her first victim. His death truly named her a witch. His murder awarded her the moniker: The Songstress of Lorelei. "Hope you're enjoying Hel, Sahra. You know what they do to rapists there." She kicks dirt onto the bust, spits a curse into the ground for any who might worship at the grave, and moves on.

The view of the city from here is breathtaking. Thousands of flashing lights and swooping vehicles, a sleepless city, as most metropolises are, despite the coming witching hour. It's unreasonably amusing that humans love to celebrate in the darkest parts of the night, comforted by the synthetic glow of neon lights and the pounding of a club's bass. The city has nightlife, but it's hardly a true night when man-made stars blaze out of the windows of every home, bar, and dancehall.

Historically, in the time before electricity and the Edison bulb, when superstition ruled most households, people wouldn't dream of leaving their homes after sundown—too many monsters go bump in the night, and there's not enough garlic or holy water to fend them all off. But when the factories began replacing people with machines and the gaslights became notches on an electrical grid, people stopped being afraid of the dark because it no longer seemed like a threat. Darkness became nothing more than a starving rat which could be frightened away with the mere flick of a light switch. Long gone are the days when only hexen thrive in the darkness.

Monsters aren't so scary when you can shine a flashlight on them.

'Chiamaka' stands at the edge of the enclosed terrace in a simple nightgown, a shawl drawn tight around her head and shoulders as she looks out at the skyline. Wren stops a few feet from the woman, watching her watching the city, and knows: Summer knows she is being hunted.

"I was hoping I'd blown you to bits. How did you survive?"

"Funny," says Wren, crossing her arms over her chest. "Here, I was hoping you'd blown yourself to bits as well."

"Tell me. Why Atalia? Glad to see you've found a use for her in death. The girl was useless in life."

"You speak so basely of a child you helped destroy? She was fourteen when your husband attacked her."

"Me? Destroy such a meek little lamb? Please," scoffs Summer. "My dear husband helped himself to that little minx."

"Your husband raped Atalia, and you banished her. You condemned her for a crime committed against her. That makes you just as responsible for her suicide as him. Why? Because you were jealous?"

"Jealous. Me! Thames is my pet."

"Do you often let your pets beat you senseless?"

"Every animal becomes destructive when it isn't stimulated."

"So, you were subverting his attention from you to someone with even less means to protect herself."

"He needed a new toy to play with. Atalia was a convenient scapegoat. That still doesn't explain why you care so much about the little opheliac of a debutante?"

Atalia wasn't suicidal. She was desperate.

"Everyone deserves their vengeance." Chiamaka's ghost hovers motionless by one of the statues. "Especially those who can't take it for themselves."

"Oh! Enough with your fucking hero-complex! Stop acting like you're a better person than I am. We're the same."

"I'm nothing like you, Helsdottir."

"We're both witches, Nocturne. We're both killers..."

You are not a killer, Wren. Kai's voice echoes, a distant memory in the depths of Wren's heart.

"...We're both evil..."

I do not think your magic is evil. A conversation from before she was damned.

"...The League sees no difference between us. We're both monsters!"

— 434 —

Wren, you are no monster. What kind of monster is capable of love? Conversations had in the intimate dark while Fae slept in the next room.

"The only difference between us is you've died once already, and you know what they say: 'Something that can be done once, can be done twice.'"

Summer whirls on her, her nightgown flaring around her legs as a whip of black magic slices through the air, aimed for Wren's face. Wren dodges backward, her own magic sparking as a vase flies toward Summer, shattering against the woman's side. Viridian tendrils weave around her fingers, and when Summer's void whip reaches for Wren a second time, green necrotic magic tangles with the lash, stalling it in thin air.

"You're wrong, Summer. I may be a witch. I may be a killer. I may even be a monster, but you and I are nothing alike."

"Aren't we?"

"No, because after everything is over, after the blood has been spilt and the world burned to a crisp, you would crown yourself queen."

"Spoken like someone born to power and privilege. You abandoned us," Summer hisses. "You left us alone and at the mercy of machines! I did what I needed to survive, and I will keep doing it for as long as I have to!"

"And after you kill me, what then? Will your technomancer treat you to roses and chocolate? No, he'll praise you today, and by tomorrow morning, he'll be looking for his beautiful punching bag."

"Shut up!" Summer screams, yanking the whip out of Wren's hold. It coils like a snake at her feet with a hiss.

The whip fattens, mist solidifying into silky smooth scales, and a forked tongue flares as a great two-headed serpent glares in Wren's direction. While one head sports great fangs, dripping with venom, the other stares with unblinking eyes which glow a paralyzing yellow. Wren avoids meeting its gaze. To meet the evil eye of a basilisk is to never see another sight again.

¡Mierde! Her telekinesis only works properly when she has line of sight on something.

"Meet my Jormy, Songstress."

The snake strikes with its fanged head. The nearest statue flies forward, blocking those jaws from closing on Wren. Catching the stone, it winds tight, shattering it in the blink of an eye. Pieces scatter as she ducks behind another and nearly comes eye to eye with the other head. Slapping her hands over her face, she flings a hand out blindly. There's a fleshy thwack, the crumbling of stone, and a thick muscular tail, wide as her thigh, crashes into her stomach.

Her feet leave the ground, and the wind whistles through her ears.

"Argh!"

Her back meets the greenhouse glass with a crunch, spiderwebs cracking along the pane. The world spins as she opens her eyes, and another wave of dizziness washes over her when she sees the long plummet to the ground level

"You should have stayed dead, Nocturne."

A ghostly touch on her head and she senses the tail coming. The interruption of air is followed by the sharp cacophonous chime of shattering glass. In the cracked glass by her head, she catches a reflection of the basilisk, and she moves, rolling out of the way, looking for Summer and her pet snake in the reflection of the shattered glass at her feet as she begins a new aria.

J'ai vu ta verdad
Je tu mensonge

Into the words, she folds the faded recollections of her death waters: the drifting river, the stagnant ocean, the breathless elegy. Weightless and eternal. That's what her death felt like, at least the extent of what she remembers. She doesn't remember if there was a light. She doesn't remember if there were pearly gates or a grand warriors' hall or an eternal garden paradise. She doesn't remember if her soul was weighed or if anyone greeted her. She doesn't remember a ferryman or hellish circles or an in-between.

All she remembers is the feeling of warm weightlessness, of drifting and being and existing in this place of non-existence.

Desplegar
Se dérouler
Desplegar
Se dérouler

The language of her home rolls off her tongue like a memory film off a spinning reel. She digs her hands into the earth. Searching, calling, awakening. Where there is life, there is death, and through the very ground, she can call upon it: corpses of insects and plants and mushrooms, things that die every day without anyone caring at all. She tugs their energy to her aid to guide her senses.

The serpent's fanged head hisses at her, venom spraying over her hands. It burns her skin. She yanks her hands out of the ground, pulling with them, as though tied to her fingers via invisible strings, the roots of a baobab tree. A newly dead baobab tree already rotting from the inside out. The desert adansonia topples over on top of the serpent, pinning it in place before it can reach Wren, and she races for the nearest water fountain only to be cut off by Summer, who grabs her by the hair and tugs.

"Dinner's served, Jormy."

The snake changes direction, its paralytic stare alighting on Wren, who screws her eyes shut and keeps singing.

Mnemosyne no olvides
Je me souviens Melinoe

She twists in Summer's hold, feels the hair rip from her scalp, and thrusts her venom-soaked fingers into Summer's eyes. The woman screams, Wren holding firm as the other witch seizes in pain.

"Let go of me, you bitch!"

Chiamaka's ghost touches her again, and through the spirit's eyes, she sees the basilisk clear as day, barreling toward them, unmindful its master is also in its path, and Wren throws herself into the fountain, Summer along for the ride.

Desplegar
Se dérouler
Desplegar
Se dérouler

Wren lands in the water, the wash bringing an instant relief to the burn of the venom. Summer sputters and chokes, coming up for air. Zenza's necklace dangles violently around the other witch's neck, and Wren reaches for it.

"This doesn't belong to you!"

With a snap of metal, Summer's necklace breaks into Wren's fist. Summer makes an outraged noise, and Wren grabs her by the back of the neck.

"Let go of me—"

Desplegar
Se dérouler
Desplegar
Se dérouler

Rot seeps from the ground. Wren's magic curls out of carefully tended compost, out of the decay that provides the nutrients for life, and ghostly tendrils spiral around the great serpent. Its scales peel from its body, blisters opening as necrosis forces it to shed its skin. It writhes in agony as Wren's song overtakes it, flailing so hard it flings itself into the glass of the greenhouse.

The massive tail strikes twice, and on the third impact, the glass shatters, and the serpent slithers over the edge to plummet to its death.

"Din hora!!"

Two Of Swords (reversed)

Summer throws her head into Wren's cheekbone, twisting to get her hands around Wren's throat, but Wren shoves her back down. Drowning is a better death than the witch could ever deserve. Summer splashes, fighting for air, but Wren holds tight.

The woman's struggles diminish, and Wren shuts her eyes.

"I'm so sorry."

Just as Summer's body grows heavy, a bag comes down on Wren's head, and she's viciously pulled backward.

Alarms blare in the background.

Her knees hit the floor as she is shoved forward. And (*Ouch! That's going to hurt later.*) the heels of her hands catch her before she could slam face first into a stone pillar.

People are yelling and shouting. She can hear Summer sputtering and choking, getting the air back in her lungs as people rally around her.

"That wretch tried to kill me!"

When she pulls the hood off her head, she meets the glowing mechanical eye of a technomancer. Thames glowers down at her, and behind him Rafka holds a spear to her throat.

30

EIGHT OF SWORDS

A CROWD FULL OF FACES SHE ONCE KNEW: Lionheart with his sword at the ready. Selene, a plasma arrow cocked on her mechanical bow. Jamar standing with his laser tipped spear at the ready. Xipilli, her brother, who now looks upon her like a stranger. Well, she is a stranger, isn't she? She wears Atalia's face, the face of a girl twice their junior. In a past long gone, she stood beside them on a graduation stage, accepting their technomancer medallions. She went on missions with them, fought beside them, and, toward the end, waged war against them. All of them have aged twelve years while she remained unchanged in the eternal frost of death. They don't even know the name of the person they are looking at.

Among her former classmates are Zenza, Akari, Quetzal, Lockecraft, Rafka, and Hikaru. Hikaru, stiff and disapproving, looks like he's about one sneeze away from a meltdown. And at the center of them all is Thames, looking exceptionally self-important as he angles to take control of the situation.

"Explain yourself."

Thames' demand is met by a chorus of outraged agreement. Enraged faces staring down at 'Atalia,' caught red-handed trying to drown the faux queen. Chiamaka's ghost appears behind the woman, eyes glowing with angry deadlights. Wren breaks through the noise of the uproar.

"That isn't Chiamaka Nagi. She's a witch! She's been impersonating the Orisha for who knows how long!"

"Liar!" shouts 'Chiamaka.' "Donarick, honey, you can't put up with this. I demand she be executed right this—" The woman cuts herself off as the ghost barrels straight through her, no doubt chilling her to the bone. A sweat breaks out on her brow, and Wren is absolutely sure that, were it not for the glamour, the witch would have gone notably paler. The impersonator's eyes go wide as she looks for the source of the sensation, but upon finding nothing, she stares at Wren in abject horror. There is only one witch in this room capable of communicating with the dead, and Summer is no medium, nor is she attuned to the realm of the dead.

"Earlier this evening," Wren continues, "I caught her and Thames plotting to murder the rightful Orisha of Ebele, Zenza Nagi. If you don't believe me, there was a cleaning bot in the room with them. Check its databanks."

Thames laughs.

"You want us to use a cleaning bot's records as evidence for witchcraft and conspiracy to commit murder. That's absurd! Besides, what gain would a bastard child's death give us? Really, Hikaru, these are the kind of Fireflies you graduate in Murasaki."

"This woman is no citizen of mine."

Hikaru's voice is unyielding. Beside him, Akari pales. Wren resists the urge to roll her eyes. She doesn't expect aid from him; why would she when he kicked her out of Snowfall?

Xipilli inserts himself into the conversation.

"Ebele is no friend of Deriva's, and I have no reason to believe the words of a known liar. If a plot to kill my niece is at hand, I want a thorough investigation held."

Jamar steps forward to 'Chiamaka's' defense.

"Xipilli, be reasonable. Ebele and Deriva suffer their differences, but this woman just tried to kill Chiamaka. Attempted murder is attempted murder."

"If what the Firefly says is true, and this woman is indeed a witch out for my niece's blood, then it is not attempted murder, is it?" he challenges, and for perhaps the first time in a long time, Wren is grateful for her brother's ability to hold a grudge.

"He's right, Thames," Art Lionheart seconds. "Take the Firefly's account,"

Thames sighs. "I really don't believe that necessary."

"I care little for what you believe is necessary, Thames. Jamar, draw up the record."

Jamar's eyebrow quirks up at being addressed as such by Xipilli.

"I, too, am quite interested in confirming what the Firefly claims," Finnick Lockecraft inserts. The wizened technomancer, as frail and rickety as he looks in his cybernetic chair, speaks with the authority of a man long battle-hardened and respected.

Upon another council member coming to support Deriva's Vulcan, Jamar nods to one of his men. The hub at the center of the veranda revs to life, and the attention turns from Wren to the holoscreen.

Heaving a small sigh of relief, Wren takes in her surroundings. She is close to the edge of the terrace. Almost too close for comfort, and beside her in a glass display and warded against theft is a weapon's rack. Technomancer blades, witch's athames, an oddly shaped bow, and a hilt that glints bronze in the moonlight. A very familiar hilt, one Wren hasn't seen since it was taken from her years ago.

Jamar's man speaks up.

"The cleaning bot she is referring to appears to have had its mainframe wiped due to a malfunction earlier this evening."

"Ah, what an unfortunate oversight."

Malfunction, her ass! Summer blew the damn thing up earlier. Thames must have wiped the data disk afterward.

"See! Proof she is lying," shouts 'Chiamaka.'

"All that proves is your housebots are as lacking as the rest of your tech," spits Xipilli before turning to Atalia. "Present another angle of your case or yield, Firefly. Or perhaps you'd like to confess to the accusations against you?"

Wren takes a step back at Xipilli's tone, but she squares her shoulders and responds calmly.

"I told you, she summoned a snake. That's how the window was broken. Check the street-level. It's probably flattened itself on the pavement."

"There are no snakes, nether or otherwise, dead in the road, Miss Vaishi, and you have no other proof to this so-called fact," adds Thames. "It would also seem as though you haven't any neural augmentations, so how can we possibly expect you to corroborate your story?"

"Do you or do you not have any type of lie detector in all that tech of yours, Primarch?" snips Wren.

The man offers her a lopsided grin. Creepy and self-indulgent, it makes her skin crawl. "Miss Vaishi, such augmentations are terribly unreliable."

The radical of Thames' mechanical eye spins, and Wren knows without a doubt he has the tech necessary to distinguish a liar from a truth-teller. Of course, that also means there's a good chance he has other augmentations wired into his skull, and the scope of those, she can only guess.

"But," he continues, "we could test your legitimacy in another way."

As though summoned, a guillotine collar appears in his hand. The device looks innocent enough, inactive in his palm, but Wren has seen its capabilities. If it'll respond to the latent magic in normal man, it'll end her second life before she can so much as blink.

"You are not putting that thing around my neck."

"But, Miss Vaishi, it really is the best way to confirm you are indeed not a wild magic user."

"I am not a witch. She is!" Wren points at Summer, where she stands tense and furious, before redirecting the gesture to Thames. "And you're her handler just like your father before you."

Thames goes stiff as a board. Absolute silence reigns through the room, pregnant with tension.

"That," begins Thames, dead-serious, "is a serious accusation you are making, Miss Vaishi."

"Not so serious as plotting to kill the heir to Deriva," Wren fires back.

"Oh, why are we still discussing this? She tried to kill me!" Summer shouts. "Put a guillotine around her neck and be done with it."

Thames, device in hand, approaches Wren, and she backs up.

"Since when does Ebele seek to so readily silence those who would challenge it? Is your reign in such peril, Nagi?" asks Xipilli, but it is not Summer or Thames he is looking at.

Xipilli's eyes are deadlocked on her, calculating in a way she isn't accustomed to seeing in her brother who is normally a loose cannon. At least, that's how he was a lifetime ago. Right now, he waits, holding his action until further information can be gathered. He stares her down, not unlike he did when they were children playing a game of chess, daring her to make a move. A look she usually responded to by making a move which under any other circumstance would have felled her king but almost always worked in her favor against her brother.

"Vulcan Xipilli, please. Surely, Deriva would see the end of any witch as a small victory. The guillotine is a perfect judge and jury for these things. You saw as much during our demonstration."

"What we saw was an old man executed without a proper trial because he met the parameters of a barely tested technology," inserts Lockecraft, the old cyborg so quiet up until now, everyone stalls to consider his words.

While Thames is left side-armed by Lockecraft's dissent, Wren pushes her case further.

"Put the device around her neck," shouts Wren, pointing at Summer. "She's the imposter, a witch who's stolen Chiamaka's appearance."

"Is she now?"

"Yes, and I can prove it."

"Can you?"

"I can." It's a bold-faced lie. She is stalling, for what, she doesn't know, and Thames knows she's stalling. She can tell by the cocky sweep of smugness currently wriggling its way into her head.

"Then present your so-called proof."

She doesn't have any, not with her. She has no physical proof of Summer's magic other than the testimony of two teenage girls who never actually saw the woman's face. Her eyes shift around the room, looking for an answer or an escape route—she doesn't know. Chiamaka's ghost hovers at the edge of the ceiling, Chiamaka's ghost who is currently fuming down at Wren like a bat out of hell, gesticulating wildly from the necklace around Zenza neck to the necklace in Wren's hand. Chiamaka's necklace! The one gifted to her by her brother at Zenza's hundred days ceremony, a blessing and a token that Chiamaka would act as Zenza's guiding light as proxima-mother. A truth Xipilli can corroborate, having been present along with Wren, Atzi, and Chike himself.

"I have but one question for Her Majesty. If she is able to answer my question correctly, I will concede defeat."

The imposter scoffs.

"As if any question you ask can prove me guilty of a crime I did not commit."

"Who gave you this necklace?" asks Wren, holding up the charm in her still tangled in her fingers, gleaming silver under the harsh electric lights of the city.

Summer whirls back as though struck. Her hand flies up to her throat where the pendant once sat. "What! That old thing? I've had it for years. I can hardly remember who gave it to me."

The ghost in the rafters ducks into an alcove, and Xipilli's eyes flash. "You don't remember?"

'Chiamaka,' still dripping fountain water, looks at him in surprise.

"What does it matter to Deriva whether I remember who gave me a good luck charm? If you aren't going contribute anything of meaning, I suggest you leave, and take your bastard niece with you."

Xipilli's fists clench. "Chike gave Chiamaka that necklace on Zenza's hundred-day celebration—the day you and I swore to protect Zenza as our own should anything ever happen to her parents. I was given the counterpart. Those 'good-luck charms' were given to us for safe-keeping until Zenza reached her age of majority. I expected you to deny her this birthright, considering you renounced her. I didn't expect you to have the audacity to wear the pendant, yet you've worn it every day since. I figured you kept it because your brother gave it to you, but now, you say you don't remember who gave it to you?!"

"Well, I—I..." 'Chiamaka's' eyes go wide as saucers, caught in her own lie. "Why would I want to reveal something so personal to a room full of strangers?"

"¡Mentirosa!" shouts Xipilli.

"So, you would rather lie to a room of people when you are already being accused of being a liar," adds Wren.

"No, that's not what I—"

The woman never finishes her sentence because Thames snaps the collar around her throat. It activates instantly, radiating with red light as it whirs to life. The sound of it a howl on the wind until Summer's screams overtake the noise. 'Chiamaka's' eyes shine with shocked betrayal at Thames who backs up as those irises turn from dark mahogany to the palest of blues, and the witch's glamour melts from her visage.

Summer Helsdottir stands before the technomancer council, alive and well and dispelled of the facade she has been wearing for years. Witchcraft-darkened fingernails claw at the collar; tears of desperation fall from the summoner's cheeks. The collar opens up, wires exposed and winding up to aim sharp pointed arrows directly at Summer's spinal cord. There is a flash of light, and Summer topples over dead, internally decapitated by a pair of hyper focused lasers.

Wren looks down in horror as Summer's unseeing dead gaze lands on her, looking away as the laser beams burn the body from the inside out. Red flames rise from the corpse until nothing is left but ash. A shock of magic washes through Wren's body as Summer's echo escapes her disintegrated meridians, dispersing into the ozone.

The collar, job done, goes quiet. The red lights dull to yellow and then a cool green, blinking until Thames bends to pick up the device from the pile of Summer's remains.

"Summer Helsdottir... But how?"

"But what of Chiamaka? Did Helsdottir kill her and take her place? How long has she been pulling the strings of Ebele?"

"What of Princess Zenza?"

"Did Summer fabricate the renouncement?"

"The coup d'état against the princess must have been a ploy to seize the Ebelean throne for the Hexen."

The whispers continue around the room as people speculate the how, when, and why of Summer's impersonation of Chiamaka. In the corner of Wren's eye, Chiamaka's ghost, no longer alight with spectral flames, bows and fades to nothing. Wren closes her eyes and wills Chiamaka's soul to finally rest with her family, her death avenged and her impersonator brought to justice, even if Wren doesn't agree with this particular brand of execution. As the spirit drifts into the veil, a tingling sensation dances up Wren's forearm, like a wound rapidly healing.

"How did you know she wouldn't know the answer?" Xipilli's voice breaks the cacophony of hushed whispers fallen over the room. He glares daggers at Wren. He steps forward when Wren doesn't answer. "Better yet, how did you know the answer? I am the only living person who knows the importance of Chiamaka's necklace, and I most certainly did not give you any such information."

Aww, so the ruler of the isles allows the tempest to unfurl. Zenza's eyes widen as she looks from her uncle to 'Atalia's' face.

"I never said I knew the answer."

"But surely you had an idea what the answer would be. Didn't you, Miss Vaishi?" inserts Thames. "An answer you could only have gotten from the dead."

Wren backs away as Thames crowds closer to her. Her back meets one of the shelves, the weapons and trophies from wars long ago fought clatter as she muses them. "Princess Zenza wears a matching necklace, so I made a lucky guess."

Xipilli's hand clenches. He takes a step in front of Zenza. A protest forms in the muscles of his jaw, but Thames continues as though she hadn't even spoken.

"Necromancy is considered the highest of forbidden magics. Ever since the Songstress of Lorelei nearly tore the world apart with her powers, known practitioners have answered for their crimes with blood and fire."

A hush falls over the room at the mention of Wren's title.

"Xipilli, weren't you telling me the other day of a woman matching Atalia Vaishi's description conducting spells on the light rail? How she apparently rebounded Opochtli's lightning with the flick of a finger? I also received a mission summary from Murasaki no Yama about a corpse poppet being resurrected at Stonehearst Asylum, the very same asylum Miss Vaishi was rumored to have been housed mere weeks ago. Isn't that right, Hikaru? What a skill for a former sanatorium patient to exhibit, wouldn't you say?"

Several of the technomancers in the room draw their weapons, aiming them in her direction. Apparently, they've forgotten she just accused Thames of consorting with Summer knowingly.

Dei! He put the collar around her neck himself. That rat bastard!

Wren could fend off one or two technomancers but ten, no. Not here. Not by herself. Not while the wards around the facility stand. She needs to get out of the compound. Out of the concrete prison and into the wilds where she can commune with nature, but there are five bodies between her and the nearest exit, the only possible means of escape is the window at her back, followed by a sixty-story drop.

Thames reactivates the collar.

"If you are innocent, we can just slip this around your neck. It will beep three times and then turn green, and we'll have cleared up this whole misunderstanding."

He takes two steps toward her, and Wren reaches blindly for the nearest weapon she can touch. A hilt finds its way into her hands. She spins it into a battle stance and activates it with a press of both thumbs. Xipilli's eyes widen to saucers and gasps of astonishment sound through the room as twin beams of green pulsing energy scream to life.

"You're not putting that thing around my neck."

Thames backs up as the beam crackles too close for his comfort. Despite the weapon flashing in his face, the man's face splits in an eerie grin.

"Oh my!"

("It's her!" "It can't be her." "Who else could possibly activate that weapon?")

"Wren?" calls Xipilli, shell-shocked.

Wren looks down at the weapon in her hand. A double-sided hilt, one side brass/the other copper, the metals twining about each other like an oceanic yin yang and inlaid with the finest of sea glass. And out of each opening, twin beams of emerald light extend to form a pair of crooked blades, like a pair of kalis, deadlier than a laser and made purely from Wren's lifeforce. Once upon a time, the ætherkalis' blades had shone a pristine golden. She picked up her old technomancer weapon and didn't even realize it.

Mångata hums, sparkling with excitement at being held by its maker once again after so many years.

"It's true..."

Behind Xipilli, Zenza looks at her in abject horror. This is the Firefly who helped her rebuild an old prosthetic just a few hours ago.

"A witch among witches. The Songstress of Lorelei, Wren Nocturne."

Thames's eyes glint with malice as he looks at her.

"But that's not possible," says her niece. "Wren Nocturne is dead. It can't be her. Right, Tio?"

"Mångata only responds to its maker, princess," answers Jamar. "The Songstress of Lorelei was the mistress of death. A talented necromancer and witch. There is no telling what kind of dark rituals the witch may have forged before her destruction."

"This is turning out to be a most interesting conference."

Quetzal and Lionheart brandish their weapons toward her. 'Atalia' spins Mångata in hand and deflects their blows, falling back as she kicks Lionheart in the chest. She drives one of Mångata's beams into the wrought iron casting bracing the glass, and sparks fly as the grating falls to the ground with a clatter. She waves a hand, and the grate goes flying across the room into another set of technomancers looking to close in on her. A gunshot fires, and the bullet grazes Wren's shoulder.

"Miss Nocturne," everyone stills at Thames's voice. "You don't honestly expect us to believe a useless Firefly managed to activate a weapon the most talented of technomancers have failed to even coax a spark from. Surely, there's no point in keeping this glamour of yours up."

She sighs from where she stands in a defensive position. Xipilli's eyes burn into the side of her face, hands fisted at his sides. Behind Xipilli, Zenza stands wide-eyed with Agni fired up and aiming directly at the woman she knew to be Atalia Vaishi, someone who she may have come to trust over time, but who now stood accused of being Wren Nocturne, her estranged aunt, the murderer of her father and little brother.

"I'm sorry, Zenza. I really, truly am."

Various weapons aim in her direction. A few electric sabers, sonic blades, and a stray pulse cannon or two. She eyes them all carefully as her left arm lifts. A green simmer passes over her form, and Atalia's face disappears. Blonde hair turns to the deepest blue black. Her skin pales, and her eyes change from dark brown to a watery blue green. The sigils under her skin spark and glow, and at last, the Songstress of Lorelai stands, for all the world to see, alive after more than a decade in death's embrace.

There is a collective intake of breath as the adepts nearest her take a noticeable step back. Xipilli's gaze hardens, Hikaru's eyes close, Akari gasps, and Zenza flinches. Thames's expression turns manic.

SONATA

Thames claps his hands together as he takes a step forward.

"Well, I'll be damned. The Songstress of Lorelei back in the flesh after all these years. Forgive me for not welcoming you properly, Lady Nocturne. Had I known it was you, I would have ensured a better reception for your arrival. "

Wren's brow furrows. The man's eyes flicker to the pile of ashes that were once his darling wife—a wife who in the eleventh hour betrayed him. Summer didn't tell him about Wren's identity, and for her secrecy, she paid the ultimate price. Death by the man she gave her heart to.

"Tell me, Songstress, what have you done with my true wife?"

"What?" asks Wren.

"What have you done with my wife?"

"Don't you mean the witch you married as a thank you for killing off one of your opposers?"

"Chiamaka Nagi was my wife."

Is Thames trying to turn Summer's subterfuge back on her? He was in cahoots with her!

"Chiamaka has been dead for six years."

"According to the weaver of lies," he shouts over her. "You've set yourself up well, Lady Nocturne. Even bringing to heel one of your own followers to maintain your cover."

"One of my followers!"

This cad!

Wren moves at the same time as Thames, a pulse of power pushing anyone within five feet of her backward. Thames flicks his hand out, the electric surge of his energy whip striking the floor in front of her. Wren pushes herself back before the collar can touch her, but it's the shot fired from Agni's barrel that hits Wren square in the stomach. Xipilli knocks the weapon out of Zenza's hold, and Wren shouts in pain, closing her eyes as she is flung through the window. Zenza looks on in horror, having fired the shot that could potentially kill the Songstress a second time.

The glass shatters at the force of her body going through it, and she falls.

Eight Of Swords

It's a strange sensation, freefall. You'd think you'd be hyper aware of your last moments before death, especially the second time around, but there isn't anything, really. Nothing tickles her awareness other than the throbbing pain in her side and the twitch of anticipation of the pain hurtling rapidly toward her when she impacts the pavement. She inhales once, exhales, and surrenders to gravity. So that's it then. It's over. Second chance blown to smithereens.

She wonders if non-existence will be worse than the afterlife or if having her soul ripped apart will hurt worse than being burned alive when a pair of strong arms wind around her torso. Wine red fabric obstructs her vision, her descent ceases with a jolt, and a loud crash later, she finds herself back on solid floor in someone's lap. A hand applies pressure to the wound in her abdomen. Violet light floods through her eyelids and she grits her teeth as violet lifeforce is shoved into her, followed by the sharp prick of a needle.

A medi stim!

The familiar healing fire of the tech bots floods her system, and she cries out as the wound stitches itself back together. When the fit passes, she breathes heavily through her nose and opens her eyes.

When she looks up through her lashes, Kaito's silver gaze greets her.

And when the masquerade comes to an end, all that will be left is the bare-faced truth.

31

TWO OF CUPS

KAI WINDS AMATSU BACK IN FROM WHERE he'd stuck her into the side of the building in his mad dive for Wren.

"What are you doing here?" she rasps through clenched teeth.

Kai's eyes flit down to see Mångata gripped in her hands, her glamour no longer in place, and he understands. Somehow, this had been a set up. Wren's cover blown, her false identity in shambles. Their opponent two steps ahead in a game of chess Wren didn't even know she was playing.

Wren appears manic, eyes bloodshot and unfocused, shaken to her very core even as Kai folds his hands around her shoulders, pulling her in close. Silver eyes scan her for injuries. There are plenty to be found. Blood drips from her arms from fresh gashes, bruises around her temple, and a split lip, but it's the bullet hole in her stomach that concerns him most. He recognizes Agni's work on sight, an injury made by a bullet heated to white-hot temperatures cauterizing on impact even as it destroys everything in its path. At least none of her vitals have been hit.

"You shouldn't be here!"

"Regardless, I am."

The alarms begin to sound.

Two sentry units whir to life at the end of the hall. Kai pulls her tight to his side, and before the sentry-bots can fully register their presence, he cuts through them with a wave of saibāki from his tanto.

"Come on."

Kaito grits his teeth and tugs her forward. He runs, Wren keeping pace alongside him, through The Shard's hallways. His hand keeps a firm grip on her waist as he shoulders his way through several doors and into a stairway. Already, he can hear voices echoing down the top of the stairwell and the banging of doors opening and closing at the bottom.

Wren twists the railing to block off the descent of several operatives.

Kai releases Amatsu once more to embed the sword into the cement wall. He secures his hold on Wren and jumps. Twenty-three is nothing compared to the near fifty he just dove from, and upon landing, he kicks his way through a guard just entering the well.

Wren shoves her power outward, tripping several others.

"Kaito Miyazaki, whatever you are doing, you need to stop right this second," she shouts as he calls back his sword.

In answer, Kai kicks through the door, grabs her by the arm, and races forward into the Shard's main lobby.

Halfway to the exit, Sekhmetian adepts surround them, several bots uncloaking themselves. Their tech sigils glow orange as they aim their weapons at him and Wren. Wild magic lashes out from Wren's center, tossing away several machines. In this same breath, she pushes him away. Green tendrils of power wind around his right arm and raise his katana until it points directly at her throat as Thames, Xipilli, Hikaru, and the other technomancers step out of the elevator. From the point of view of an outside observer, it would appear he cornered her himself.

"Wren!"

"You can't come with me."

Kai's eyes narrow even as he spies Wren's fingertips tracing sigils into the air. The ground at her feet darkens as power pools below her. Thames' mechanical eye glows and the flesh side of his face pulls into a smirk at the sight of Kaito, swords drawn staring at Wren in thinly veiled frustration.

"Prince Kaito, what a surprise to see you. I had no idea you would be coming to the conference, or did you realize as well that the Songstress had resurrected? How fortunate you've cornered her for us. You always were the best of us at dealing with Wren Nocturne."

Opochtli crackles in Xipilli's hand, and Wren shifts her attention to her brother and Thames.

"What are you waiting for? Arrest her."

Kaito's sights whirl, and he breaks the telekinetic hold she has on him. Wren snaps her head to the side as he steps in front of her. She tries to reign him back under her control, but with the magic inhibitors surrounding the compound, it's fruitless. His repellents are too strong.

"I will do no such thing."

"Kai, don't!"

Her eyes are pleading in the electrical light of the overhead chandeliers. She shakes her head at him. His eyes flash from her face to the Primarch as he takes her by the arm and shoves her behind him. Both of his blades drawn, he glares down at nearly the entirety of the technomancer council: Donarick Thames, Art Lionheart, Jamar Sahra, and Finnick Lockecraft. The only one absent: Rhiannon Gewalt. Beside them, Hikaru, his brother watches in horror as Kaito throws aside everything he has ever fought for, or at least, what his brother believes he has fought for his entire life.

"Anyone who seeks to kill this witch will have to go through me first," he tells them, defiance in his eyes and a dare in his stance.

"Really, Kaito–sama? I doubt Murasaki no Yama would stand between the League and the Songstress of Lorelei, or have you perhaps been bewitched?"

"Yes!" shouts Wren. "That's the way of it. He's under my spell, so back off before I sic him on you."

Kaito's eyes narrow at Wren's meager attempt to absolve him of responsibility for his actions.

"No," he announces, loud and clear so there can be no misunderstanding.

When he turns to her, Wren's face is in a panicked mess, cheeks pale and lips trembling, her hair sticking out at odd angles and tangled with ornaments. Dressed in torn, bloodied silks, she looks wild and untethered. He stands near enough her tendrils of power caress his arms and legs. The triskelion on her forehead shimmers through the heavy fluorescent lights even while her wild script is quiet, dormant beneath her skin. Hn, she seems to have lost an earring at some point.

"My mind is my own."

Wren shakes her head at him about to say something when Thames cuts her off.

"Very well. If it is as you say, highness... Kill them both!"

Kai swings around, both weapons in hand, as the first adept lunges forward. Mångata screams to life as he parries the blow with Tsukuyomi. Wren's back meets his as she twists out of the way of an oncoming bullet, and something slots back into place that has been missing for a very long time.

Wren and Kai dance. Their weapons clash and sing against steel and plasma. Two bodies connected by space, time, and kinetic energy. Synchronization comes easily, resonance just one step beyond, and the alignment of yin and yang vibrates through their very souls.

Mångata rips through a hover drone. Wren ducks under Kai's katana as he swipes backward, the blade whistling through the air before meeting the soft flesh of an attacking adept's belly. From where she squats down, she swipes the legs out from under another and Kai drives Amatsu into the adept's chest and leaves it, setting a virtual parameter just in time to catch several remote hackers trying to nullify his tech. He rewinds the coding and turns it back on them, shutting down their virtual readers while Wren channels her magic outward.

He can hear it.

Two Of Cups

The wild magic in Wren's blood sings, and the beauty of it, the wildsong, flows in and around him. At his feet, Wren's magic pools, weaving in and out of the fabric of reality until Kai finds himself sinking down into a newly manufactured array.

"Wren, what are you doing?"

Wren sings in a tongue he never thought he would one day describe as beautiful, hexenspeak. It is not a siren's song or a spellweave. Nor is it a soothsaying. These dulcet tones land bittersweet and somber at Kai's feet, a requiem for the souls of the fallen. A blanket of fog swirls around them. The ground shakes and the lights blink out.

"I can't see."

"Where are they?"

"What's happening?"

A scream sounds to his right as an adept goes down, attacked by something in the dark. One of Wren's ghouls?

Kai activates not just his night-vision but his dead-readers as well.

Shrieking undead flit around them, teeth gnashing for living souls. Several adepts quake in fear at the sight of them, one even graying around the temples as a pale spectre attempts to wind its transparent hands around his neck.

Mångata deactivates, and Wren's song shifts. The array at her feet shudders and opens into a portal.

"Kai!"

Under Wren's call of his name, Kai hears the sound of a weapon charging, something big like a blast cannon, and reaches for Wren as she jumps into the portal.

His fingers lace around hers, and the world divides.

The green shimmer space collapses in on them, and Kai's stomach is pulled into his throat as they hurtle through space/time. He swallows down the bile to keep from heaving and maintains a firm hold on Wren's hand. He lands hard on his feet, dizzy and discombobulated. The coolness of Wren's body keeps him from being set on fire, but the shout of his name and the alarm in her voice wretches him back from any comfort he might have taken in the knowledge he is still anchored to her.

Reality soaks back in as Wren's hands trail over him, checking to make sure all of his parts made it through. Rain falls cold onto his face, and he hears a cat yowling nearby. It is then he realizes they are outside, rain pouring down over them and the cityscape but a skyline on the horizon.

Desert rain...

Thud! *Itai!*

Apparently, she deems him intact enough to abuse because she punches him in the chest. It hurts but lacks any actual malice.

"What are you thinking? Go back before it's too late! Tell them I cursed you. I'm sure Hikaru will gladly corroborate."

She continues to shove at his chest, building strength as she goes, but he stands and takes it. Her fury, her fear, her tears. So long as it's her, he can take anything. She is a swirling tempest, the desert rain coming down on them a pale reflection of her all-consuming storm. He takes all of it without complaint, without even a wince or a stagger back. This does not hurt. This is nothing.

He allows her to rage until she tires, her energies too drained to continue her assault on his person. He tracks the bullet wound on her abdomen, monitors the damage done, and notes it isn't healing as fast as it should be, one of Agni's specialty traits. It will be days before it heals completely even with stims and Wren's own magical healing ability. When she wilts, he enfolds her in his arms, supporting her under her elbows and forearms.

"Leave," she whispers.

"I will not."

"Why not?"

"I am doing what I should have done fourteen years ago."

She sobs. "Don't do this, Kai. Your family..."

"This is my decision to make and mine alone."

"You can't throw your life away! Not for me!"

The last time he left her well enough alone because she asked him to, a promise made at her bequest. Wren, who takes everything onto her own shoulders regardless of whether or not the weight could crush her. Wren, who is damn near self-destructive when it comes to protecting the people she cares about. Wren, who begged him to stay away when he offered to help her. No, he's not doing this for Wren. He is doing this for himself because...

"My life was yours a long time ago, Wren."

"But they'll hunt you down, too!"

"So, I should allow them to hunt you down instead? I refuse. You turned me away once, and I was fool enough to listen back then. I know better now. You cannot change my mind."

"But I love you, dammit!"

The fight goes out of her then. She gives up, wincing as she collapses finally to the ground, damp desert sand mixing with the blood still dripping down her arm. She shivers in the chill as she chokes on her own sobs.

"I don't want to see you killed, too," she says at last.

Kai kneels in front of her in the sand, water seeping into the fabric of his pants where his knees sink into the damp earth.

"That nightmare already came true for me." Wren's attention snaps to him. He brings his hands to either side of her face and tilts her head back so he can look into her eyes, glittering with tears. "I will not allow it to happen again."

She scoffs, disdainful and piteous, eyes drifting away from his face. "You should have found someone else."

How many times has he been told the same? By his aunt who only ever wanted the best for him. By his brother who so desperately wanted some substantial means by which to measure how Kaito wasn't going to live out the rest of his days alone. By Renki, who, a child at the time, had only wondered aloud because he wanted his *tousan* to be happy. How many times, even, had he wanted to claw out the very root of his affection for a long-dead lover just so he could be at peace with himself? But companionship with another was the least of his wants even if it would make the nights shorter, warmer, less dark and dismal.

Now, Wren has the audacity to say the same to him. And if that isn't the most ridiculous thing to have ever come out of her mouth, he'll eat his own comm unit. It's laughable. Really truly laughable.

So hysterical, he laughs. Not aloud. There's too much bitterness surrounding the situation, but it is low and bassy in his chest, and when he catches a glimpse of Wren's expression, now confused and more than a little disbelieving at his apparent amusement, he only continues harder, his mouth quirking up at the sides, his eyes closing to crescents in the face of it.

"You think this is funny!"

He does not respond for a long time, choosing instead to fold her tighter to him, his arms winding around her shoulders as he finishes relishing in his amusement. They are in the middle of the desert, rain falls gently around them, dimmer now she is not unleashing a torrent on him. (Is she causing this? Would she even know the answer were he to ask?)

"Wren, look at me."

She refuses at first. So reluctant she is to look up at him, he has to curve a hand under her chin and physically coax her up.

"Wren, please, look at me."

Aquamarine eyes lift slowly to find his face. He studies her for a moment, then casts his eyes down. He busies himself with unraveling the bandage around her left arm, a show of mercy really so that she is not forced to meet his eyes, not yet anyway. The fabric falls away in bloodstained ringlets, pooling on the ground. The formerly bleeding cut is now closed, healed over with only the faintest outline of a scar left in its wake. That too will vanish with time. There are still two open slashes across her arm. They don't bleed at the moment, but the shine of bright red blood lingers in their pockets as yet unshed.

Kai's fingertips trace over these two markings pensively.

"Do you remember the night we danced in Shinka?"

She smiles sadly but nods. "How could I forget?"

Of course. How could she ever forget that night so, so, so long ago when he can't forget it either?

"Do you remember what you told me about Koi and Dei?"

"Some poetic nonsense about destiny and the double moon eclipse. I believe you said something along likes of 'Only hexen hold such superstitions.'"

The quote is wrong but the deeper tone she takes to mimic his teenage self is almost spot on. Kai resists the urge to sigh. She's not listening.

"The night you came back, the first time I saw you again, it was also a double moon eclipse."

"Was it? I don't remember," she says airily. He doesn't believe her for a second. It was only two weeks ago, yet she talks like she's lived three lifetimes since. He's lived them right along with her.

"You died." Wren flinches. "You died and I lost you. I have lived the last twelve years of my life feeling like part of my soul was torn from me."

"I'm—"

He shushes her before the apology can fall from her lips. "The Stonehurst case should have been a routine haunting and exorcism, and it was anything but. Someone pulled a lot of strings to bring you back under the perfect circumstances. Their motivation to incite your resurrection, to make sure I was there when you returned. There are greater things than either of us can know. Some cosmic machination I can't even begin to fathom is at play, and you know what? I don't care about any of it."

"Kaito, that isn't—"

"*Koi no Yokan,*" he says, cutting her off.

"What?"

"*Koi no Yokan...* There is no common translation for the phrase. No singular set of words capable of describing what it means, but the closest is 'the feeling one experiences upon meeting the person they will inevitably fall in love with.' I hadn't realized it at the time, but *koi no yokan* is what I felt the night we first met."

"You mean the night you pushed me into the lake."

Well, she pushed him, but that's beyond the point.

"Wren, when I found you in that asylum and it was like breathing again."

Tears glitter in her lashes. His hand comes to her face, and he angles her head back so their eyes meet.

"I don't want to drag you into the dark with me."

He looks at her, eyes soft.

"I would rather stand in the dark with you than live in a synthetic light." A choked sob sounds in the back of Wren's throat. "There is no one else, Wren. There can never be anyone else. You are my destiny. Do not ask me to walk away. Not again."

Her eyes avert down. The stillness with which she takes in his words is enough to cause him physical pain. He nearly bursts with it until she speaks.

"I know." She swallows thickly, and he feels the way her muscles push against his hands at the movement. Then she looks him square in the eye. "I know because I only see you, too. *Véxote.*"

The hexen term is not lost to him. Her face screws up as more tears escape her eyes. She hides her face from him. Kai's arms wrap around her. She holds him around the neck, burying her face in his shoulder. She is warm in his arms, despite the tremor racking her form, flesh and blood and bone and bright, bright lifeforce.

"Together, then?"

"Together," she agrees, a frightened whisper.

Fourteen years ago, she disappeared from the light in a whirl of necrotic energy and an apology on her lips, and not long after, she disappeared from the world entirely, burned to ash and dust by the bitter flames of hate and desperation. Taken by death. Alone and afraid and isolated from everything and everyone she ever loved.

Never again. Not so long as he draws breath.

He reaches around to his right hand, where his signet ring sits on his ring finger. A simple band of silver and gold inlaid with his family's crest, a crystal-clear shard of amethyst smoothed over the howling engraving of the okami. He slips it from his finger, reaching for Wren's left hand. No one would ever describe Wren as being dainty, but her hands are quite a bit smaller than his own. Naturally, it doesn't fit on her heartline finger the way it fits on his, so Kaito's hands, long fingered and slim from playing piano, gently slide the ring onto Wren's index finger where it fits, not too snug but not too loose.

She follows his actions, the gesture's meaning not lost to her, before looking back into his eyes. Her tears are drying, the smallest of smiles tugging at her mouth as she gives a breathy chuckle.

"So that's it then? We're going to steal away into the night? A vagabond prince and a wicked witch, saying 'fuck you' to the rest of the world."

He bridges the gap between them, his hands rising to find her own. Their fingers interlaced, she brings her forehead to his, and he just breathes long enough for it to sink in. This is Wren. This is him. This is them. *Is this what peace is?*

"For every day that Ør shines bright..."

The start to an old Deus devotional, written by their ancestors and preserved through war and famine, pestilence and death, and used by both human+ and hexen. Wren swallows, nodding, looking into his eyes as she recites the next part of the vow.

"...And every night the moons shed light."

Magic seeps into her words, and as Kaito takes the next verse, his own energy unfolds.

"Until the stars may die..."

"...beyond the time our hearts, in stillness, lie."

Wild ringlets of viridian coil around steady frequencies of violet.

"I give my life to you..."

"...Within my palm, I hold it true."

"In turn, your life I guard as mine..."

"...With you I trust my most divine."

The last verse they say together, green and purple encircling their joined hands.

"With you, my everything I twine and hold back nothing for all of time."

Wren tilts her head up, and he draws her closer, angling himself until she is pressed securely into his side. When their lips meet, the oath unfolds between them like a dove taking flight—a chaste kiss that lasts no more than a heartbeat but seems so much longer. As Wren presses her forehead to his, the triskele glimmers emerald in the dark.

"I don't have anything to give you."

He lifts her fingers to card through the woven necklace at his throat. "You gave me a token of your heart a long time ago, Wren."

"I can't believe you still have that old thing."

Seashells and malachite beads on a hand braided leather cord. He'd taken great pains to keep it whole these last twelve years, but he'd found no such effort was required of him. The leather never frayed, the beads never tarnished, and the shells never broke. Almost as though a piece of Wren had survived inside.

"Why should I part with the first bit of magic you ever wove for me?"

Magic that lived in her before even she knew of it.

"You ridiculous man."

He takes her barb easily, content to find her tears have ceased as he lifts her into his arms.

Kaito Miyazaki walks forward into the desert with a black cat shadowing his footsteps, Tsukuyomi, Amatsu, and Mångata secured to his back, and the Songstress of Lorelei, his soulmate, cradled in his arms while a storm brews at his back.

FIN.

Wren and Kaito's song will continue in
book 3 of the Nocturne Symphony
Scherzo

GLOSSARY OF CHARACTERS BY FACTION

Deriva:

- Tlanextli Moctezumo – Vulcan of Deriva – Father of Atzi and Xipilli Moctezumo with his first wife, Elisabeta De Claré and Wren Nocturne with his second wife, Freya Nocturne.
- Elisabeta De Claré – Vulcana of Deriva – Mother of Atzi and Xipilli Moctezumo. Stepmother to Wren Nocturne.
- Freya Nocturne – Second Wife of Tlanextli Moctezumo – Firefly and Mother of Wren Nocturne.
- Atzi Moctezumo – Princess of Deriva – Eldest daughter of Tlanextli and wife of Chike Nagi. Mother of Zenza Nagi.
- Xipilli Moctezumo – Current Vulcan of Deriva – 247th Trials Graduate – Wren's older half-brother.
- Wren Nocturne – The youngest child of Tlanextli Moctezumo – 247th Trials Graduate – Known Alias: The Songstress of Lorelei.
- Quetzal – Captain of Xipilli's Guard and technomancer of Deriva
- Zenza Nagi – Princess of Deriva – Wren and Xipilli's niece via their elder sister.
- Irene – A Landless technomancer who graduated with Wren and Xipilli. Declared loyalty to Deriva.

Murasaki no Yama:

- Mirai Miyazaki – Empress of Murasaki no Yama – Mother of Hikaru and Kaito Miyazaki
- Fumiko Miyazaki – Grandmaster of Shinka Temple's Adept Training Program – Twin sister of Mirai and aunt to Hikaru and Kaito
- Hikaru Miyazaki – Current Emperor of Murasaki no Yama – Elder brother of Kaito
- Kaito Miyazaki – Crown Prince of Murasaki no Yama – 247th Trials Graduate – Younger son of Mirai Miyazaki.
- Akari – Miyazaki trainee under Kaito's tutelage.
- Renki – Miyazaki trainee under Kaito's tutelage.
- Tanaka - Technomancer formerly under the Miyazaki family. Took part in a hexen-led attack to rescue Dr. Faust from Snowfall Palace.

Ebele:

- Absko Nagi – Orisha of Ebele – Father of Chike and Chiamaka Nagi
- Chike Nagi – Crown Prince of Ebele – 247th Trials Graduate – Husband of Atzi Moctezumo and Father to Zenza Nagi
- Chiamaka Nagi – Princess of Ebele – Younger sister to Chike Nagi and Zenza's paternal aunt.

Sekhmeti:

- Rameses Sahra – Pharaoh of Sekhmeti – Father of Jamar Sahra
- Jamar Sahra – Crown Prince of Sekhmeti – 247th Trials Graduate

Seraphim:

- Howard P. Thames – Pontiflex Catalan of Seraphim – Religious leader of Seraphim and father to Donarick Thames.

Glossary Of Characters By Faction

- Donarick J. Thames – Son of the former pontiflex. Present Primarch of The League.

Aighneas:
- Morrigan "The Morrigan" Gewalt – President of Aighneas. Killed by Summer Helsdottir.
- Rihannon Gewalt – Younger sister to The Morrigan.
- Arturo Lionheart – 247th Trials Graduate – Student of The Morrigan

Hexen:
- Yggfret Bloodfang – The Goblin King
- Summer Helsdottir – Witch
- Xena – Vampyre
- Zero – Shifter
- Jessabelle – Witch
- Mishka - Witch and Firefly of L'Amor Lux. Atalia's former mentor.

Stonehearst Asylum:
- Dr. Johannes Faust – Head Doctor
- Atalia Vaishi – Asylum inmate who led a group of patients to summon Wren back from the dead.

Notable Weapons of Deus:
- Mångata – Wren's Ætherkalis
- Lacuna – Wren's Soul-Eating Athame
- Tsukuyomi – Kaito's Katana
- Amatsu – Kaito's Tanto
- Opochtli – Xipilli's Trident
- Agni – Chike's Blast Rifle – Currently in use by Zenza

MORE BOOKS FROM 4 HORSEMEN PUBLICATIONS

ROMANCE

ANN SHEPPHIRD

The War Council

EMILY BUNNEY

All or Nothing
All the Way
All Night Long: Novella
All She Needs
Having it All
All at Once
All Together
All for Her

KT BOND

Back to Life
Back to Love
Back at Last

LYNN CHANTALE

The Baker's Touch
Blind Secrets
Broken Lens

MANDY FATE

Love Me, Goaltender
Captain of My Heart

MIMI FRANCIS

Private Lives
Private Protection
Run Away Home
The Professor

FANTASY, SCIFI, & PARANORMAL ROMANCE

BEAU LAKE

The Beast Beside Me
The Beast Within Me
Taming the Beast: Novella
The Beast After Me
Charming the Beast: Novella
The Beast Like Me
An Eye for Emeralds
Swimming in Sapphires
Pining for Pearls

D. LAMBERT

To Walk into the Sands
Rydan
Celebrant
Northlander
Esparan
King
Traitor
His Last Name

Horror, Thriller, & Suspense

Alan Berkshire

Jungle
Hell's Road

Erika Lance

Jimmy
Illusions of Happiness
No Place for Happiness
I Hunt You

Maria DeVivo

Witch of the Black Circle
Witch of the Red Thorn
Witch of the Silver Locust

Mark Tarrant

The Mighty Hook
The Death Riders
Howl of the Windigo
Guts and Garter Belts

Steve Altier

The Ghost Hunter

Young Adult Fantasy

Blaise Ramsay

Through The Black Mirror
The City of Nightmares
The Astral Tower
The Lost Book of the Old Blood
Shadow of the Dark Witch
Chamber of the Dead God

C.R. Rice

Denial
Anger
Bargaining
Depression
Acceptance
Broken Beginnings: Story of Thane
Shattered Start: Story of Sera
Sins of The Father: Story of Silas

Honorable Darkness: Story of
Hex and Snip
A Love Lost: Story of Radnar

Joe Davison

Cold Front

Valerie Willis

Rebirth
Judgment
Death
Mind Over Tennis: Mastering the
Mental Game

VALERIE WILLIS

Writer's Bane: Research
Writer's Bane: Formatting 101
Writer's Bane: Plot &
Foreshadowing

Writer's Bane: Revisions & Edition
(w/ JM Paquette)
Writer's Bane: Character
Development

DISCOVER MORE AT 4HORSEMENPUBLICATIONS.COM

www.ingramcontent.com/pod-product-compliance
Lightning Source LLC
Chambersburg PA
CBHW020516110726
47899CB00004B/1129